CW01502201

Out of Time

David Sykes

To Nicola,

from

David Sykes

For Jo, who encouraged me.

Acknowledgements.

My thanks go to Merril who read and re-read each chapter, Paul my race passenger who offered advice on military matters and especially to Lindy who proof read assiduously and gave constant support.

Prologue

16th July 1934, the Ardennes region of Belgium. The Englishman was afraid; despite the warmth of the day cold sweat trickled down his back. His companions, both French, unnerved him. He wished he had never let his sharp-tongued shrew of a wife talk him into this; if his duplicity was ever unmasked he would spend a long time behind bars. The three men put their shoulders to the back of the works van he had driven from England and heaved. The van moved slowly at first then gathered pace as it left the road and crashed down the hillside until it overturned at the bottom when it hit one of the many trees. The smaller Frenchman picked up a petrol can and cautiously made his way down the slope to the stricken vehicle. Glancing furtively about him he opened the passenger door and began emptying the can inside. Satisfied, he looked around once more. Seeing no-one, he threw a match on the seat and the petrol ignited with a dull whoof. The men on the road watched him as he picked up the can and climbed back up to the road where he placed it in an old Renault touring car. The flames took hold as the petrol in the fuel tanks ignited and the Englishman saw the famous logo on the van side become illegible as oil and rubber threw plumes of black smoke into the still air.

He never saw the blow coming; dazed he fell to the unmade gravel road where his legs were grabbed then he was dragged several yards, scratching his hands and face.

The Frenchmen hauled him to his feet where the taller man examined his injuries with genuine regret. He spoke in heavily accented English, "I am sorry my friend, but it was necessary to make zis look like a genuine accident. We will take you to a hospital and zis," he waved an arm airily at the burned out van with a wheel protruding from the rear doors, "zis will be buried deep in a Belgian scrap yard with only a very blurred photograph to show your employers what 'appened." He put his hand into his coat pocket then gave the Englishman a thick bundle of large white bank notes. "Ecoutez, buy zat 'ouse and keep your wife 'appy, whilst I can visit my private museum and admire the jewels you have given me."

Chapter 1 Iraq 200?

"Sergeant Green! Sergeant Green!" The shouted summons broke into the daydream of Parachute Regiment Sergeant Michael Green as he strolled across the dusty parade ground of his unit's headquarters in Iraq. The image of a cold beer faded from his mind as he turned to face the owner of the voice. "Boss wants to see you, pronto."

Green looked with disfavour at the messenger, Sergeant Mallow the company clerk and then followed his retreating figure. "Come on, Marshy, what's the flap?"

"Dunno, Mikey, but he's just got off the blower to that Yank outfit up the road."

Green paused mid-stride, his tanned and battered face creased with a frown. "Marines" he muttered to himself.

"Eh, what?"

"I said Marines, Marshy, and a few tanks if I remember rightly".

"Got no idea, Mikey, get a move on or he'll have my balls on toast."

Green chuckled at the rich Lancastrian accent. "How did your lot win the War of The Roses relying on porkers like you?" A reference to Mallow's thickening waistline which Green knew the sergeant was very touchy about. The sergeant's angry retort was cut short by their arrival at the CO's office.

Green strode into the ante room, quickly checked his appearance and rapped on the door marked Major Smythe.

"Come in." Green entered, came to attention and saluted smartly. "At ease, Sergeant." Major Jeremy Smythe, a squat, powerful man regarded as a hard nut even amongst Paras sat back in his chair and gazed at Green in frank appraisal. "It has come to my attention that you have been spreading gloom and despondency amongst your colleagues

7

contrary to Queen's regulations by grumbling about the state of our venerable Land Rovers and wishing that Santa would bring you an American armoured vehicle, to whit a Humvee, come the festive season".

Green looked at the raised eyebrows of his superior officer and quickly came to the conclusion that an answer was expected. "Sir." Least said soonest mended and ambiguous enough to buy him some thinking time.

"Well, Sergeant," declared Smythe "your wish seems to be coming true." He pointed at the window where two hundred yards away a pair of monstrous twin rotor Chinook helicopters each with a Humvee slung under its belly were descending. Green's jaw dropped open. "You, my lad, are going to pay for those vehicles and the other useful items contained within those helicopters."

Green's panicked expression softened the Major's habitually grim visage. He liked Mikey Green; he led by example, had been mentioned several times with regard to his courage and quick thinking under fire plus he invariably brought his platoon back mostly unharmed due to good soldiering. His acerbic wit had also brought him a few enemies within and without the Regiment. "Not with your sergeant's pay you will be glad to hear, but with your expertise," adding with a mysterious smile, "and not the expertise that the army has taught you."

Green remained silent, his talent was in demolition and whilst he was proud of his encyclopaedic knowledge of fuses and explosives he knew that the United States Marine Corps had never ever needed any help blowing things up.

Smythe stood up with a grunt. "Major General Briscoe Le May rang me this morning, do you know the man?" Green shook his head vigorously. "Well he knows of you, he asked for you by name and he is going to get you for a few days starting now."

Green's brow darkened. "But I'm taking my platoon to the village ten klicks North West of here tomorrow, Sir, and I've got three new lads to baby . . . err break in."

Smythe airily waved away his concerns. "They will have Sergeant Griffiths looking after them whilst you are with our gallant allies."

"But he's Welsh, Sir!" blurted Green, realising a millisecond later that he had pushed his luck too far with his notoriously short-tempered CO.

Major Smythe took a menacing pace forward, it was only Green's training and discipline that made him stand still, for his overwhelming desire was to retreat. "Your lads will have to cross that particular language barrier, won't they?" he growled, as he emphasised every other syllable by prodding Green's chest with a stubby forefinger. "Now! Ears open and mouth shut; your mission will be explained to you by that man there." Green stared out of the window at a tall, lean lieutenant in the uniform of the U S Marine corps, who had just climbed out of one of the Chinooks, clasping his M16 assault rifle and, after a brief conversation with a passing squaddie was covering the ground towards them at an easy lope. "You will do everything in your power to assist our gallant ally and make his mission a success. Dismiss!" Green came to attention, saluted and turned to go; Smythe strode across the room and held the door firmly closed as Green's hand reached the handle. "Do not speak to our embedded press chappie about this . . . err . . . operation, oh, and Sergeant, definitely do not mock the Lieutenant's name. He is very sensitive apparently."

Seething with anger and not a little puzzled, Green left the office and closed the door. Without looking, he spun on his heel and cannoned into a large body which staggered backwards and cracked its head on the support beam of the veranda. Green looked down. The man was fully five inches taller than him but not at the moment, sprawled as he was at the Para's feet. Green, appalled noticed a red smear on the white post and looked again at the man slowly getting to his feet.

"Correct me if I'm wrong, Sergeant, but aren't we supposed to be on the same side?" For the second time that morning Green's jaw dropped open as the distinctly transatlantic drawl and the officer's shoulder pips identified his victim as a Lieutenant in United States Marine Corps battledress. "Lieutenant Cagney, US Marine Corps, and I guess you must be Sergeant Green?" The Marine gingerly touched the back of his head, grimaced at the resulting pain and scowled again as he saw blood dripping from his fingers. He wiped his hand on his tunic then, frowning slightly, he held it out to the worried paratrooper. "Looking on the bright side, there may be a medal in this for me."

Green shook the proffered hand, the relief at the American shrugging off the incident outweighing his anger at being separated from his platoon – for the moment.

"We need to talk, Sergeant, somewhere quiet. If the press get hold of this we are both up shit creek."

Green pointed to the mess hall. "No one there 'til midday."

"Fine," responded the Marine. "But first I need to get the err . . . mission documents from that Chinook."

"I'll fetch them, Sir," offered Green, "you might be better going across to the medics' tent to get a couple of stitches in that cut."

"Good thinking, Sergeant, thanks. I'll see you there when your guys have sorted my war wound."

Thinking hard, Mikey Green ambled towards the stationary helicopters two hundred yards away, his surly mood returning as he realised he had wriggled out of any kind of retribution for his unconventional meeting with the Yank officer. His sense of injustice still ate at him; his platoon needed his steadying influence and leadership. He could manage without wasting time at an American base and he could manage very well without Americans full stop. He avoided the scrum of squaddies milling round the newly delivered Humvees and headed for the nearest helicopter. Although it was only nine thirty a.m. he could feel the sweat trickling down between his shoulder blades and leaking through his eyebrows stinging his eyes until he cuffed the liquid away with his sleeve.

Approaching the first Chinook, he was intercepted by the Quartermaster Sergeant who gestured at the contents of the aircraft's capacious hold. "Keep your thieving Yorkshire hands off this gear and fuck off back to where you came from."

Green meekly explained his errand and was overheard by the pilot who at that moment was climbing down from the cockpit.

"The loot's gear is in that bird," he yawned, gesturing with his thumb at the second Chinook.

Green put on his best 1950s BBC accent, "Why thank you, driver . . . err . . . do take the rest of the day off my good chap."

The thumb transformed into a middle finger pointing to twelve-o'clock. "Asshole."

Grinning, the Para hastened towards the second chopper. Its pilot was still in the cockpit swigging bottled water whilst an enlisted man sat on the edge of the hold his arm resting on the magazine of the .50 Browning machine gun provided as defensive armament for the giant transport helicopter. Green nodded amiably to the man sweltering in his body armour, helmet and obligatory mirror shades and asked him for Lieutenant Cagney's gear. Before the gunner could reply Green called over a young Para strolling by holding two large bottles of cold water and told him to give one to the helicopter gunner. The grateful gunner, bent almost double from the weight of his body armour trudged heavily to the young Para, nodding his thanks to Green as he passed. Green hopped up into the hold and leant through to the cockpit and with the assent of the pilot grabbed Cagney's bag. Jumping out of the helicopter he set off to the mess hall.

"Sarge!" The young Para, now with only one bottle of water, kept pace with Green. "Whatever you nicked from that Yank chopper has got to be worth a beer each to C platoon don't you think, Sarge?"

"Done," scowled Green, "Just keep your gob shut." Green felt the outline of the brand new night vision goggles he'd stolen safely stowed under his battledress blouse, the bulge concealed by Cagney's pack. "Must be losing my touch," he grumbled under his breath.

The mess hall was empty so Green strolled slowly to the medics' tent and was just about to ask the orderly for Lieutenant Cagney's whereabouts when "Jesus, Honey!" erupted through the canvas wall.

Green smiled happily then, pulling the heavy flap to one side, he walked through. Sitting on a plastic chair his face a mixture of pain and annoyance was the tall Marine. Standing behind him, a curved needle and thread in her small hand, was Captain Elizabeth Harding. She gave Green a cheerful smile. "The Lieutenant here has been singing your praises, Mikey." Green blushed as he always did when she used his first name. Harding was a couple of years younger than Green at twenty six, she was very pretty and even sexier. Green fancied her to bits, she knew it and he knew that she knew. She winked at Green and chuckled, "This patient has just compared me – unfavourably I might add – to Doctor Crippen, so, would you like to put the last stitch in, Mikey?" Cagney's glare spoke volumes and Green shook his head mutely. Harding's face creased with a mischievous smile as she prepared to insert the final suture. "I put a few stitches in Sergeant Green himself a few months ago Lieutenant and thanks to the morphine he did tell me a couple of teensy weensy little secrets."

She giggled and Green looked beseechingly at her, silently begging her to be quiet. She glanced up, amused by his discomfiture. "Apparently . . . " He groaned. " . . . Sergeant Green joined the army because the married women in his town wanted him and their husbands wanted his blood.....and do you know…" The rest of the sentence was whispered in Cagney's ear which made him grin for the first time in a while. She tied the final knot and snipped off the surplus. "All done," she trilled. "Off you both go to topple tyrants and end world poverty or whatever it is you rough boys do." Cagney picked up his M16, snatched his pack from Green's clutches and stomped out of the tent. Blushing furiously, Green risked a sideways glance at the smiling Harding and was rewarded with a blown kiss. He scuttled out and caught up with the American.

"Next time you let me bleed to death, you murderous Limey bastard,"
growled Cagney with some feeling.

The pair trudged silently to the mess hall where the tall Marine chose a table in the furthest corner of the largely deserted room. Whilst walking over the young Paratrooper had found his natural dislike of the man beginning to wane. Most Paras would reckon being called a murderous Limey bastard the next best thing to a compliment and Green's inherent good humour equipped him well for spiky encounters. He wasn't sure he liked Elizabeth Harding whispering sweet nothings in the ear of a Yank she had only just met though.

They sat and Cagney removed an A4 photograph from his pack and laid it on the table in front of Green. Green stared, his interest quickened.

"Well, Sergeant, what is it?"

Green looked intently at the image. It was a scene frozen in time with which he was intimately familiar; he had seen it many thousands of times when he had entered his father's workshop, for a copy was pinned to the wall above the bench. "That's Wal Handley at the Belgian motorcycle Grand Prix at Francorchamps in 1934. Jimmy Simpson had just won the 500cc race on the "works" Norton he is sitting on. The bloke behind is James Arbuthnot his mechanic. The bike was destroyed together with the 350cc version when the van they were in overturned and caught fire on the way home after the race. Arbuthnot was the driver."

"Maybe not," responded the American and placed another photograph in front of Green. Green lowered his eyes; this picture was much more recent and showed what looked to be the same bike leaning against a stone wall in a small yard. "Is it the same bike?"

Green felt the American's eyes boring into him trying to gauge his reaction.

"If it's not it's a very good fake."

The American stood, his shadow falling over the two photographs.   "What makes you so sure?"

Without hesitation Green pointed to the top of the engine in both pictures. "The cam box. This was a prototype and that casting will fit only that particular bike."

Cagney breathed a sigh of relief. "OK, Sergeant, you've sold me, get your gear. We're gonna buy a motor cycle. I'll explain as we fly."

Five minutes later Green was throwing his pack in to the Chinook, climbing in afterwards with his personal weapon, an SA80 assault rifle.

The pilot walked slowly round the aircraft, peering carefully at the rotors and scrutinising the underside of the fuselage. He emerged from below the helicopter and recognised Green.

"Lucky for you I didn't take the rest of the day off, buddy boy," he said without rancour. Green grinned sheepishly and studiously avoided Cagney's questioning look. The pilot hauled himself into the cockpit, went through his checklist and with a laconic "hang on" fired the engines. The big machine soared upwards in a maelstrom of noise and blinding dust.

Cagney reached up to where two pairs of headphones were hanging, threw one set to Green and placed the other upon his own head.

"I suppose you're wondering what the hell this is all about." Green nodded his mute assent; the American's voice competed with and just about beat the whine of the turbines and swish of the rotors. "It's pretty simple really; a very rich man who happens to be in the armaments industry and a real good friend to the Marine Corps is a vintage bike and car nut. He bought a Norton engine from the daughter of the late James Arbuthnot together with some memorabilia. There was a diary amongst his effects with an

14

entry saying Jacques wanted some information on the 34 twin cam setup and that he was going over. This rang alarm bells with our latter day Hiram Maxim because he knew that particular bike had been destroyed when it was being brought back to the Works in England after the race in Belgium, so he travelled to England to speak to Arbuthnot's daughter, who, in exchange for a generous retirement gratuity, gave him the whereabouts of the bike in France. The bike, however, wasn't in France, it had been sold on in the seventies to an investor who lives guess where?" Green, listening intently, shrugged. "In Iraq. I was tasked to buy it and you got roped in because we were advised by a Norton expert that although he himself was too old to be fooling around in a war zone, he did however know an expert who wasn't. . . his son!" Green's eyes saucered. "And, hey! You were only a few klicks away and the Marine Corps could afford a couple of Humvees and some goodies to buy your expertise in identifying the bike as genuine."

Green suddenly stiffened, his eyes tracking a vehicle speeding along the road several hundred feet below. He reached into his pack carefully moving his stolen night vision goggles under his spare socks and pulled out a battered pair of binoculars. Quickly he focussed on the vehicle, a pick-up. "Ask the pilot to go round, I want a closer look at that motor . . . not too near though" Cagney relayed the request and the huge transport helicopter swung round. "Hell's teeth, not that bloody close!" Green bellowed as the over enthusiastic pilot misjudged his approach and came within a hundred feet. The three occupants in the back of the pick up grabbed an AK47 apiece from under a tarpaulin and opened a sustained and accurate fire on the Chinook, penetrating the alloy skin with ease. The pilot heaved on the collective and the huge machine reluctantly yawed out of range but not before a 7.62 millimetre round blasted through the floor of the helicopter, hitting the breech of the Para's SA80 assault rifle and then bursting into fragments, one of which sliced open Green's cheek to the bone. He grunted in pain then was thrown headlong as the helicopter lurched. Tearing off his headphones, Green hauled himself into the cockpit where the pilot was calmly checking his instruments for possible damage that might affect the flying qualities of the aircraft. "How are we doing?" shouted Green. The pilot raised his gloved hand the thumb and forefinger forming a circle, a sudden grin emphasising his confidence, then pointing to the unused co-pilot's headset as he saw Green about to open his mouth. The headset on, Green motioned to the fleeing pickup a mile away creating its own dust cloud.

"Fly parallel to him and out of his range, I'll do him with the fifty before they reach that village and change into peaceful, innocent farmers." Green pointed to a cluster of buildings just visible in the distance, then tore off the headset and crawled carefully to the port-mounted machine gun.

Green swivelled his head to look at Cagney, mimed speaking with a hand gesture, pointed to the pilot and then to Cagney's headset. Thinking quickly, the American lifted them from his own head and slipped them on to Green's, looking closely at Green's head wound as he did so. The Paratrooper checked the ammunition box on the big machine gun. Satisfied, he cocked it and began firing short bursts at the fleeing vehicle. The pickup turned sharply off the road and on to a dirt track leading to the village. Green clicked his headset. "Get me in front of it – not too close, I'll kill the driver first." Cagney, listening in on a spare set was fascinated and appalled in turn by Green's professionalism and by his sheer cold-blooded ruthlessness. The pilot obediently swung the big machine ahead of the bouncing truck. The pickup bucked fiercely over a rut, ejecting one of the shooters. Ignoring him, Green fired two short bursts into the truck tearing apart steel and flesh alike. The truck skidded and landed on its roof. "Can you put us down nearby?" Green requested tersely.

"Sure thing," was the pilot's laconic response. "Nice shooting." The Chinook flared and came to rest amid clouds of sand and flying vegetation.

Green looked at the smashed breech of his rifle and caught Cagney's eye. "You got a spare weapon?" Cagney wordlessly removed his pistol from its holster and handed it to Green who cocked it, "Let's have a look-see."

They trotted over to the overturned vehicle, the surrounding area littered with motionless Iraqi bodies. The Para knelt and levered a body to one side. Underneath was an AK47 assault rifle which he picked up and checked, then handed back the lieutenant his pistol.

"Hey, Sergeant, we got a live one!"

They walked the thirty yards back to the prone figure that had fallen from the pickup before Green had savaged it. The figure, a youth of about thirteen years, lay still, his leg at an awkward angle, clearly broken. His brown eyes were glazed with fear and pain as he stared at the two uniformed men.

Green cocked his newly acquired rifle and pointed it at the boy. "This little bastard and his dead pals ambushed a platoon of Paras last week and killed a friend of mine; they legged it in that" -indicating the wrecked vehicle with the barrel of his AK. "I recognise the motor from intel reports, so for the sake of my mates I'm going to fill him full of holes and watch his life piss away." Green blinked, his vision starting to blur, he swayed drunkenly, feeling his legs buckle and the AK dropped from his nerveless fingers to the ground. Cagney suddenly realised the Paratrooper was suffering from blood loss and put his arm round the shorter man. Retrieving the fallen Russian assault rifle with some difficulty, he half carried and half dragged Green to the waiting helicopter. The pilot must have had his finger on the starter, for fifteen seconds later they were airborne. Watching the helicopter clatter into the distance, the injured Iraqi boy sensed he'd had a lucky escape.

Chapter 2

Sergeant Mikey Green emerged from a wonderful erotic dream where he and Captain Elizabeth Harding were sharing a bath. "I've always fancied you," he murmured fervently.

"I sure as hell hope you ain't talking to me, soldier." That voice, harsh, nasal and American definitely did not belong to Green's dream girl. Green's eyes jerked open; he was lying on a camp bed with a drip in his arm, dressed only in his shorts. An amused Marine private seemed to be enjoying the Para's confusion. "The lieutenant brought you in on the big bird yesterday; you was bleedin' like a stuck pig. He stitched you up good and put the drip up." He added as an afterthought, "Jeez, you snore some!"

Sitting up, Green observed Cagney walking towards him with a pair of aqualung tanks slung over one shoulder. He passed them across to Green's erstwhile nurse with a brief, "Get them filled." Cagney's other arm had a Paratrooper's uniform draped over it. He carelessly dropped it on Green then gently eased the drip from the Para's arm. "I paid a woman from the village to wash and iron these for you," adding unkindly, "I suppose you could always shoot her if the creases aren't up to scratch."

Green, feeling uncomfortable at the barbed comment, dressed quickly and pulled his jump boots on. He ran his hand over his face pausing at the unfamiliar contours of his stitched cheekbone. "This your handiwork?"

The American nodded. "I went most way through med school back home in New York and then thought what the hell and joined the Marines as a diver".

"Thanks, and call me Mikey".

"Maybe, so long as you don't call me Jimmy."

A trio of nearby Marines engaged in cleaning and maintaining diving gear looked away quickly in case their Lieutenant saw them smiling – not quickly enough as the Marine officer had been alerted by a chuckle. Cagney glared at them whereupon their restraint collapsed. Gathering their equipment up, they ran away laughing hysterically. Cagney swung round to see the Paratrooper with his fist jammed in his mouth trying to stem the gales of laughter within. Tears rolled down Green's face.

"Are you really called Jimmy?"

"James," said Cagney sadly, "I was Christened James, yet all my life I've had to endure this gangster bullshit – and now I get it from a little Limey bastard."

Green, recovering somewhat, corrected him. "That'd be murderous Limey bastard if I recall?" Green looked speculatively at the man putatively his superior officer and made a decision. Swallowing hard he said defiantly "OK, I'll lay off the you-dirty-rat stuff if you tell me what Captain Harding whispered to you."

A sly smile spread across Cagney's face, he tapped the side of his nose with a forefinger and lowered his voice to a conspiratorial whisper. "Classified information, buddy boy." Cagney jabbed his thumb over his shoulder at a large tent. "Get yourself some chow in there; we ship out in thirty minutes."

Green sat alone in an empty mess tent with three plates of food on the table before him. The cook had looked askance at Green's relative lack of height and decided he needed feeding up. He need not have worried; at five feet eight Green was not considered small in the regiment whose average height tended to be lower than "ground pounders". Swiftly three plates of food became two and then one as the hungry Para enjoyed his breakfast. Just as he was thinking that his eyes might be greedier than his belly, a burly Marine NCO carrying a heavy canvas holdall planted himself down opposite the Para. Secretly pleased at the interruption, for his appetite was more than satisfied, Green pushed his plate away and waited for the big Marine to speak.

"This is for you." The deep southern drawl stretched the four words a long, long, way as he pushed a small sheet of paper at Green. Intrigued, Green inspected it. "It says that the United States Marine Corps has deemed your personal weapon to be damaged beyond repair and this liddle ol'" Green smiled, "piece of paper says it was due to enemy action so you ain't gonna have to pay for it." The Marine rested his elbows on the table and sat his chin on his hands. "Now I know you gonna be with our lieutenant chasin' that ol' motorcycle," Green started and thought *is nothing secret?* The Marine saw his surprise and interpreted it correctly.

"Not too much the boys don't know around here," he chuckled. "We like our Loot; he's a real good diver. He may be an uptight son of a bitch who ain't learned to laugh but he looks after his guys pretty good, trouble is he ain't been shot at much and the guys want you . . . y'know, to sorta keep an eye on his welfare." Green sensed that this was a long speech from a man who didn't look as if he ever needed to raise his voice. "Trouble is" he paused and looked around carefully bringing his head closed to Green's, "Our Colonel, he ain't much of a soldier. I served with him in the first Gulf War and I still have some metal in me thanks to him being a useless goddam' asshole." Green gave an attentive nod. "He has a big black mark against him in the Pentagon 'cause a General the name of Cagney told it like it was in his report." The Marine looked Green in the eye, "Yep you heard the name alright; General Cagney is our Loot's paw – he's retired now back on the farm or whatever retired Generals do." The Marine spoke softly, "Jimmy boy joined the Corps 'cause it's a family tradition, not because he wanted to. He wouldn't thank me for saying this but it was a dumb thing to do. He was a happy doctorin' but no -! family had to come first and you and me know, Mr Paratrooper, if you're gonna join the Marines you have to WANT to."

Green inclined his head in agreement.

"Is your Colonel making Jimmy boy's life a misery?"

"You got it, Buddy; if boots need counting or latrines need digging he assigns our boy. He wants to break the guy – make him resign his commission to creep back to daddy with his tail between his legs."

"How's he holding up?" queried Green.

The Marine frowned. "He's doing pretty good so far but this assignment is a real biggie . . ." he paused for breath, exasperation writ large on his face. " . . . the guy has zilch experience of convoys, has a boatload of new guys straight from training and the Colonel has stuck that bust up Abrams with the convoy on a dirt road I wouldn't send a donkey cart down." He placed a meaty hand on the Para's arm. "Colonel Shithead wants Jimmy to fail; he hopes he'll get that Abrams stuck down the track and fall flat on his face like goddam' rookie." The hand squeezed tightly. "Do the good guys a favour and help him out – a medal or two would help," he added seriously.

Reaching down to the dirt floor the Marine hoisted the canvas holdall onto the table; it gave a satisfying clunk to Green's ears. Green stood, intrigued. The big Marine unzipped the bag and reached inside. The meaty fist emerged holding a weapon. "We intercepted a shipment of these last month, brand new and still in their grease. If you're gonna keep on letting the daylight into bad guys you're gonna need this" The Marine handed over a newly cleaned, dully gleaming, folding stock AK47; at the same time Green noticed the bag held enough spare magazines for a small war.

Green smiled his thanks as Marine Shultz – Green had clocked his name tag on his battle dress tunic – half turned as he walked away laughing. "Hey, Sergeant, you know what Jimmy," Green smiled at the irreverence, "called you? . . . a mur . . ."

"I know," interrupted Green, slightly irked. The big Marine shook his hand warmly and left.

Green, absurdly pleased by the generosity of Shultz and his mates turned his attention to the AK. He checked the action, folded the stock out and back again then slapped a magazine in. As an afterthought he stroked his thumb along the under-slung bayonet and grunted as a small cut appeared. Hefting the holdall and slinging the assault rifle over his shoulder he emerged from the tent as a Humvee pulled up alongside him.

A helmeted Cagney peered at him from the driver's seat looking tired and strained. "Get aboard; the Colonel wants to see us."

Green climbed in and they drove several hundred yards to an office complex. The American led Green to a door labelled C.O. where they were met by a harassed-looking Sergeant clerk who knocked at an internal door and showed them in. Both men came to attention and saluted. Green lowered his eyes and managed to resist smiling. The officer behind the desk resembled an immaculate Homer Simpson look-alike; Green wondered if he slept to attention and ironed creases in his wife to keep her smart. His name tag read Colonel Cyrus Guttenberg.

Guttenberg ceased his ostentatious paper shuffling then looked up simulating a badly acted surprise at their presence. "Waal looky here at what the cat dragged in; we got Lootenant purty boy and a gen yew wine war hero. Waal, isn't my life complete!" Green looked behind him for the war hero. "Yew, soldier boy, yew," ground Guttenberg. He slapped a sheet of paper on the desk along with a pen and lifting his bulk from the chair moved to the front of it. "Now, Sergeant war hero," the sweating, sneering officer stared contemptuously at the Paratrooper. "Write down here everything the Lieutenant needs to know about this Limey motorsickle and the big bird will take you back to your unit where you can drink tea with the rest of your pissant army and talk about Big Ben!"

"With respect, Sir . . ."

"Shut your goddam' mouth, Lootenant purty boy!"

Green saw spittle fly from the irate officer's lips and grimaced. Guttenberg glared at him but the Para was unmoved. *You're setting up Jimmy Boy for a fall you fat bastard* he thought sourly; *without my help he could buy any old tat and end up a laughing stock.*

"Can't be done," grunted Green screwing up the sheet and throwing the pen over his shoulder. *What you going to do now, bacon bum?*

The Colonel screwed up his piggy eyes in rage and bellowed "Do as you are ordered, son, or you are on a charge"

"My arse. You need my help; I'm the only expert within a thousand miles who can identify that bike."

The suddenly deflated Guttenberg growled, "Tell me something I don't know."

Green looked meaningfully at the officer's pronounced paunch. "Salad tastes nice."

White with anger Guttenberg threw two bags of dollar bills at Cagney. "Get this Limey jerk outa my sight and. . ." he added spitefully ". . . make sure you get a receipt for this money."

The two men hastily saluted and left climbing into the Humvee. Fifty yards later Cagney spoke. "Salad tastes nice?" The strain dropped away from his face as he laughed. Thinking about the likely repercussions from his own boss, Green smiled weakly and wondered if he had overplayed his hand.

Cagney halted the Humvee near the row of vehicles that were his convoy; still smiling he said "I'll brief you on today." Looking like a man who had just had a weight taken from his shoulders, he put a finger on a point on the large scale map. "This is where we are, we are heading down this track to link up with the coast road not far from the Iranian border – which accounts for our heavy presence here. After we hit the coast road Quom is two hours away and that's where we're headed today. We are suspending our other salvage operations for a few days for some as yet unspecified diving work at Quom. This baby," he slapped the dashboard of the Humvee, "is going as tail end Charlie to that convoy." The American pointed a finger at the twenty vehicle column, trucks, Humvees and one tank transporter, its low loader straining under the seventy tons of an Abrams main battle tank.

Green opened his mouth but Cagney forestalled him. "Our little mission is go thirty klicks from Quom. The convoy will halt here." His finger rested on a small town on the map. "We dash in, meet the man, give him a substantial amount of US dollars and load the motorcycle into the back of this vehicle – after you have verified its authenticity of course. Any questions?"

Green looked closely at the map his finger tracing their route." For a coast road it meanders well into the hinterland," he observed.

"You're right," agreed the Marine. "I asked one of the locals and he said the road followed the coast closely hundreds of years ago but the bays silted up"

"Another point," Green added looking thoughtful. "When matey boy's neighbours see us tapping politely on his door then leaving with his prize motorcycle, they'll like as not string him up as a collaborator. It's better if we smash his door down, knock him about a bit, shoot next door's dog and then take the bike. It'll be just another visit from the rabid hounds of the Great Satan – I think that's what Saddam calls you," he chuckled.

Green noticed movement over Cagney's shoulder. "You expecting company?"

The lead Humvee in the column was heading slowly towards them; it halted five yards from the men. A sweating, tired looking Sergeant emerged. "We're good to go, Sir"

Green nudged the officer and surreptitiously pointed at the map where he had written *check water, ammo, and extra fuel.*

"Thank you, Muller" said Cagney. "In ten minutes I will check each vehicle and they better have five magazines each for personal weapons, two gallons of water for every man and three full jerry cans of diesel"

The Sergeant started, he had delegated those checks to a corporal whose reliability was not the stuff of legend so he himself wasn't sure if every vehicle had the fuel, ammo and water loaded as the Lieutenant wanted. "I'll double check, Sir," stammered Muller and hurried off.

"Good move that, giving him ten minutes. He doesn't lose face now when you check and everything is as it should be."

Cagney sighed wearily. "Thanks for the heads up on the fuel and stuff, I never thought to ask."

"How many convoys have you organised?" asked Green "I bet this is your first one, I must have prepared forty, it's a learned skill. Don't beat yourself up. Oh and make sure all the fifties," he waved an arm at the half inch calibre machine gun above him, "have at least two boxes each"

Twenty minutes later the air was full of diesel smoke and noise as the convoy started up and revved their engines. Cagney had praised Muller for the standard of readiness of the men and vehicles. Muller had been pleased but felt a sneaking suspicion that the Lieutenant had put one over him. The American officer and the British non-com watched as the convoy lurched forward, then as the Tank Transporter cradling its wounded giant passed them, Cagney swung the wheel and they followed in its dusty wake.

Chapter 3

The Humvee bounced along the rutted track that constituted what on the map was described as a good road. A companionable silence existed between the men broken only by the occasional grunt as they struck a deeper than usual pothole. Cagney had dropped back behind the tank carrier to around fifty yards to avoid the diesel fumes and the dust it threw up. The Marine glanced at the Paratrooper sitting on his right, his AK47 resting on his lap like a favourite child. His head was swivelling constantly seeking possible threats. Reluctantly Cagney had come to the conclusion that he would never be as professional a soldier as Green and the realisation depressed him.

Barely twenty minutes into the trip, the lead vehicle reported a possible problem; a truck parked two hundred yards ahead at the roadside. The truck had two children in the back and no sign of the driver. The column halted and Green climbed on to the chained down Abrams tank in front of them. He quickly focussed on the truck with his binoculars then checked out the surrounding countryside.

Green returned to Cagney and said flatly, "It's an IED, the youngsters in the back have their feet roped to the truck – they can't get off. The bloke with the trigger is, I think, somewhere near that large rock" He nodded to an outcrop three hundred yards inland. "I reckon he's using a line of sight trigger so he can't hide behind it."

Cagney knew he had to take action, for the first time in his military career he needed to make a decision the consequence of which might be someone's death. He hesitated.

Green sensed that the Marine was in what was for him uncharted territory and might need a helpful nudge. "You have two options, Boss, you blow up the truck either with machine gunfire, maybe a cleaner job with the Abram's cannon or we find the trigger man and kill him"

Cagney pursed his lips, thinking hard.

"Personally," Green said, matter-of-factly. "I'd use the Abrams; your men won't like using the fifties on those kids."

"We'll hit the trigger man," growled Cagney.

"Good," chuckled Green, "I was hoping you'd say that, give me four of your fittest lads. You put suppressing fire on that rocky slope," he pointed, "for ten minutes, short bursts to keep his head down and cover the noise we make working our way around him"

Green disappeared with the troops Cagney had selected whilst Cagney drove up alongside the lead vehicle in the convoy. He ordered another Humvee next to it then the gunners from both vehicles fired short bursts alternating with each other at the target area their officer specified. They ceased fire at a gesture from Cagney when ten minutes had expired. A tense fifteen minute wait followed until the four young Marines and the Paratrooper swaggered into sight at the rear of the column. They were pushing an Iraqi in his thirties who was bleeding profusely from a head wound. Green marched up to Cagney, stamped and saluted as smartly as ever he had done on a parade ground. "One prisoner, Sir, just where you said we'd find him – a well planned operation if I may say so, Sir"

Cagney looked at the grinning Marines and knew his stock had gone up immensely with his men. "Carry on, Sergeant," he said crisply, accepting the proffered bomb trigger mechanism from the British Paratrooper.

"Sir!" bellowed Green, who then grabbed the thoroughly cowed Iraqi. He prodded the man in the chest. "You" he shouted, and then mimed walking with his fingers, pointing at the truck with his other hand. The prisoner looked away so Green punched him in the mouth knocking him to the ground. Two Marines hauled him to a standing position and Green repeated his instructions. The bomber nodded. Green then held up two fingers, mimed the height of the children and a walking motion. Sullenly the man again nodded. The Briton then showed him the truck ignition key which had been taken from the Iraqi when he had been searched. The Para pressed it into his hand, pointed to the truck and then to the coast. The beaten man inclined his head briefly. Green mimed running and shook his head vigorously, emphasising his meaning by gesturing at the alert young Marine manning a Browning.

With a resigned look the thwarted bomber walked slowly towards the truck, spitting broken teeth as he did so. Five minutes later the children had been freed and the truck was bouncing across the sand and dirt to a safe distance from the convoy. When he was sure all American eyes were glued to the truck Green surreptitiously reached across and flicked the switch of the trigger device in Cagney's hand. The truck erupted into a ball of fire spattering the desert sand with shards of metal and body parts. As the explosion died every soldier bar Cagney whooped and cheered; Sergeant Muller solemnly shook Cagney's hand before climbing aboard the lead Humvee.

The convoy rolled forward again, rumbling past the stationary Humvee with Green inside and the Marine Lieutenant standing on the sand. The convoy's crews, without exception, flushed with their small victory, noisily voiced their appreciation of their officer's actions as they ground past in a flurry of noise and dust. Cagney clambered into the driving seat and followed the column. He had never before known or felt such confusion; his head was spinning with conflicting emotions. The men – his men, were treating him with a genuine respect for his role in directing the small but successful action and they applauded his ruthlessness in killing the bomber. Cagney passed a hand over his weary brow, an act which did not pass unnoticed by Green. His lips thin and brow furrowed, the Marine felt wracked by guilt for enjoying his troops' goodwill yet so strongly feeling – no, knowing he did not deserve it. Cagney's hands tensed upon the wheel, his knuckles white.

"You did well then, Boss"

The Marine glanced uncertainly at the Paratrooper. "I'm a fraud, Mikey; you of all people know that."

"Not so, mate, and the more modest you are, the louder your guys will shout about THEIR fine officer. And . . ." he inclined his head towards the rear of the Humvee, ". . . this pair is certainly grateful for your leadership and compassion." Startled, Cagney looked over his shoulder to see the two Iraqi children wolfing his chocolate. He laughed, somewhat mollified. Adjusting the mirror he saw the little girl give the boy – her younger brother he surmised – the last piece of chocolate. Green continued "You led your men today, true you got help and advice from me but that's what NCOs are all about and," he went on earnestly, "there will be more opportunities to demonstrate what you showed today – and you will be up to scratch. Tell yourself . . . believe . . . today wasn't a one off."

Green reached behind the seats for his pack, he fumbled inside pushing past his iPod and newly acquired night vision goggles groping for the chocolate he knew was there. As his fingers closed on the chocolate, the Humvee hit a pothole, and the pack disgorged its contents into the footwell Cagney grunted his apologies and raised his foot from the accelerator pedal. He bent to retrieve the small book that had fallen beneath it. He glanced curiously at the title *An Anthology of First World War Poetry*

"You sure are full of surprises Sergeant; I was expecting one hundred and one ways of killing the King's enemies." Cagney opened the book and read the inscription on the flyleaf. *Dulce et Decorum est Pro Patria Mori, the old lie.* Underneath in the same hand was *don't forget this, Mum,* the date beneath was ten years ago.

"She gave it to me when I joined up," said Green quietly. "She was telling me not to do anything stupid and get myself killed." He went on.
"I'm leaving the army next year and I'm going to do what mum always wanted me to do." Cagney's eyebrows asked

the question. "Teach; teach English to teenagers. I may look like a bloke you wouldn't let in your house," Cagney's glance took in the badly broken nose, old scars and his own handiwork which would certainly leave a scar on Green's cheekbone. "But through mum I found I cared about the English language and I want to show young people how to become articulate, to feel good about expressing themselves...and with a bit of luck nobody will be shooting at me in school."

"You could have taught rather than joining up," Cagney remarked shrewdly. Green said nothing. "Unless of course the young and lovely Captain Harding got it right, and you were on the run from vengeful husbands"

Green pulled a wry face, the casual use of Elizabeth Harding's name as always made his innards churn around. "Just one husband actually. I needed to get out of town quickly, he was a big bloke, an ex-boxer, so I signed up for five years. Two months later he was killed in a car crash."

"But you stayed in?"

"True, I liked the army and the army seemed to like me." He paused as a small hand reached over for the chocolate he still held. Two pairs of anxious liquid brown eyes focussed alternately on Green and the chocolate in his hand. He poked a finger at his chest and said loudly, "Mikey." Green repeated the process with Cagney, earning a sour look when he said "Jimmy." Green shared the chocolate between the children noticing as he did so that the treat was so precious and unusual that no sticky residue was left on face or hands.

"Coast coming up," murmured Cagney, as he caught his first glimpse of the placid waters of the Persian Gulf. "We'll be hitting tarmac in about a mile"

And so it proved ten minutes later when the convoy turned right onto two lane black top. Cagney spun the wheel and the lurching vehicle smoothed out as its wheels left the track and gripped the tarmac. The little girl tugged at Green's sleeve and pointed to the sun. He looked up, the ever baleful golden orb had changed colour, now it was a dull red with its edges curiously indistinct. He turned back to the youngster to find she had wrapped her dress round her own and her brother's head.

Quickly Green grabbed the canvas cover for the Humvee and tied it shut, that done he started to wind his window closed, not fast enough to avoid a stinging blast of hot sand in his face. Cagney followed suit then groped in the dash pocket and pulled out two pairs of goggles. Green steadied the wheel while Cagney donned his and then slipped his own on.

The hissing, biting sand drummed its insistent tattoo on the Humvee's armoured skin. Fine sand found its way into the vehicle through every chink in its loose canvas cover. The Tank Transporter was only thirty yards in front but was visible only as a vague shadow and a glimpse of tail lights. Green delved into his pack and found a tee shirt. With the help of his bayonet he sliced it in two, handed one half to Cagney and wrapped the other half around his nose and mouth. The Marine braked to a halt to use both hands to tie on his makeshift mask. Satisfied with its fit he gunned the Humvee forward into the swirling yellow murk.

Driving faster than was prudent to catch up with the convoy, Cagney felt rather than saw that they had left the road. Green's shout, muffled by the tee shirt told Cagney that he too had noticed their detour. The howling wind and incessant thrash of sand on metal prevented any further communication. Cagney sawed at the big steering wheel, in vain seeking smooth tarmac, the heavy vehicle bumped and yawed over the rough ground. Cutting his speed to a crawl to avoid pitching headfirst into an unseen gulley, Cagney became aware of tail lights ahead and came to a sudden halt barely a metre from them. From the distance between the red lights it could only be the low loader with the Abrams.

Cagney tried the radio, but the storm ensured only a crackle came through the headphones. He killed the engine. They sat not speaking, the harsh staccato rattle of sand on armour plate making conversation impossible. The heat in the four wheel drive was stifling, the fine airborne sand finding a passage through every gap where canvas met steel. The storm continued unabated for an hour or more, its violence buffeting and rocking the Humvee; then little by little its ferocity diminished until the wind was little more than a whisper.

Green wound down his window and looked down the length of the Tank Transporter, something seemed odd. The tractor unit was skewed and it looked to Green as though a tyre had burst, though he could not be sure as a miasma of sand hung still in the air like a foggy day. Cagney opened his door and made to step out.

Green frantically undid his seat belt and dragged the Marine back into the vehicle.

"Over the top," he rasped, his mouth parched. "I think he's hit a mine"

Cagney frowned, and then nodded his understanding. The two men opened their doors and scrambled on to the hood of the Humvee then leaped the gap on to the trailer unit, steadying themselves with the tank's hold-down chains. Slowly and cautiously they made their way forward, Green checking the surrounding area and Cagney focussing in the distance seeking the rest of the convoy. They reached the tractor unit and peered inside. The driver was slumped over the steering wheel. The driver's door refused to open when Cagney tried it; he shouted to Green to try the door on his side and was unsurprised when a few moments later the Paratrooper confirmed that the man was dead. The two soldiers clambered back on to the low loader and met leaning on the glacis of the Abrams.

Taking a swig from his water bottle, Cagney wiped the top with his hand and offered it to Green. ,
"Keep an eye out for locals, Mikey, I'll get on the horn and get some support here."

Green pointed to a piece of metal next to the shattered wheel. "How unlucky is that? He's run over a British anti-tank mine that's been here since the Second World War." Cagney, with a relieved look, jumped down and walked towards the Humvee.

Seventy five yards away behind the low wall of a ruined building a man lay watching. Captain Mohammed Hassan of the Iraqi Republican Guard had felt and heard the mine explode from the underground bunker he and the scientist had shared for the last six months. His heart soared, here was a target that was heaven sent and its destruction would go a long way to compensate him for the many months he had spent in that stinking underground hovel, bullying and cajoling the team of scientists who were building their so-called wonder weapon. The team were no more, killed along with their guards when the supply delivery truck had been targeted by an American smart bomb, which had destroyed the truck and the dormitory situated beneath it.

The Captain remembered the night it happened six months ago. He and the team leader had been drinking coffee and discussing progress in the refectory during the small hours. They had been about to enter the long corridor which led to the dormitory when the bomb struck, destroying that section and entombing the lifeless occupants.

The ensuing months had not been wasted thought Hassan, as he observed the two soldiers in conversation. They had stayed underground - the complex was self sufficient - and listened to the war on the radio. The scientist had wanted to go home, saying the war was lost, but Hassan had locked the trapdoor to the surface and they had worked together to finish building the weapon.

The American would surely radio for reinforcements now that the storm was over thought Hassan, he would have to work quickly. He dropped to his belly and snaked his way back to the newly opened trap door. His head in the opening, he softly issued instructions. Despite the urgency, he controlled the desire to shout for the enemy were close and though few in number they would be nervous and alert. Unseen hands, trembling from the effort, passed up a tripod which looked as if it had started life supporting a light machine gun. Hassan quickly placed it on the ground beside him then reached again into the hole and with infinite care withdrew a heavy object which looked like a cross between a Vickers heavy machine gun, and the insulation seen on high tension electricity cables. The machine trailed an umbilical which led back underground. With a speed born of practice the Republican Guard mounted the device on the tripod, he crouched behind it and swung it to point at the Humvee. The tall American saw the movement and began to un-sling his rifle.

"Too late, my friend," purred Hassan, and pulled the trigger.

Chapter 4

Silent save for a sibilant hiss, the weapon streamed its invisible power towards the American where its effects became visible. Cagney staggered back against the Humvee, a gradual paralysis was numbing and weakening his limbs. He slipped to his knees, his M16 clattering uselessly to the ground. Before he slumped to the ground unconscious, Cagney noted somewhat abstractedly that he had been enveloped by ice blue phosphorescence that was flowing over himself and the Humvee like an eerie coloured fog. A jubilant Hassan traversed the weapon to the tank transporter and smiled happily as the blue miasma folded around the vehicle infiltrating every surface and cranny.

Hassan's joy grew as he saw the second soldier fall with a choking but unheard cry under the front of the Abrams tank. Swinging the weapon to and fro Hassan hosed the vehicles and their occupants with the invisible ray. He saw with alarm that the swirling sparkling mist was flowing back from the target towards him, the rolling grasping tendrils had an inexorable quality which he did not like. He released the pressure on the trigger, but his alarm turned to dismay as the weapon continued to fire. He turned to flee but the mist, with a seemingly calculated malevolence, overwhelmed him leaving him twitching and helpless as it poured over him and passed on flowing through the trap door eliciting a strangled yelp from below.

The glowing fog enveloped friend and foe alike until with a dull phut the device expired. A molten blackened substance dripped from the weapon to solidify on its tripod. The blue fog lifted: as it did so its phosphorescent light was displaced for a few seconds by a blackness and silence profound and absolute, yet witnessed by no one.

Mikey Green fought his way back to consciousness aided by an intermittent shrill, shrieking noise he could not identify. He forced his eyes to open and with a great effort of will, remain open. The shrill sounds continued to invade his ears. Putting his hand to his forehead he discovered a large bump which his woolly mind attributed to hitting the glacis of the Abrams as he fell. Some small recollection of mist or fog came to him as he tried to collect his swimming thoughts. His blurred faculties became clarity when he realised what the shrill urgent sounds were. Children screaming.

The chains which held the tank immobile provided Green with the means to haul himself upright. He grunted with the strain. Looking for the source of the sound, his glassy eyes slowly regained their focus. The scene he beheld galvanised him into action. Thirty yards away Cagney was being attacked by a man in uniform wielding a knife. An obviously dazed Cagney gripped his assailant's wrists preventing a deadly blow from being struck, whilst the two Iraqi children aimed ineffectual blows at the stranger. They were rewarded by kicks for their attempts to help the Marine.

Green trotted towards the melee, weaponless, as his AK was lying by the tank's tracks. As he ran he was oddly aware of something different around him, but with no time to dwell he ignored the feeling. Reaching the fighting pair he slammed his fist into the knife holder's temple knocking him to the parched earth. With a fully fit Sergeant Green the result would have been a foregone conclusion, but his recent traumas had robbed his punch of much of its power and with a snarl the fallen figure regained his feet and ran off.

After checking Cagney for injury, Green picked up the Iraqi boy from where a well aimed kick had thrust him. His eye was blackened but otherwise he seemed unharmed. The youngster flung his arms round the Paratrooper's neck and buried his head into Green's battledress tunic. His tears trickled down Green's chest and the Paratrooper could feel his undernourished body wracked with silent sobs. Feeling a prod in his ribs, Green turned, noting as he did so that he was in shadow despite the sun blazing down. The second thing he noticed was an AK47 muzzle pointing at him; in fact it was his own AK. It was held by the Iraqi girl who was smiling at him. Green returned the smile, his momentary terror vanishing, and took the proffered weapon.

The reason for the shadow became apparent as he looked beyond the girl. He nudged a still dazed Cagney and inclined his head.

Cagney swivelled to follow his gaze. "Where the fuck did that come from?" he asked a mixture of wonder and astonishment in his voice. A huge edifice of volcanic rock stood to the seaward side of their vehicles where before there had been nothing but the road and sand. It towered over the Abrams by ten yards and was fully sixty yards long.

"It's not just that," breathed Green in a mystified tone. "Look around, there's vegetation where it was bare rock and sand before" Cagney leaned into the Humvee but turned back a few moments later after trying the radio and finding no response to his hails. Green walked past the wrecked Transporter, which clearly had not moved, to the furthest extremity of the rock – several yards to the right of the tractor unit. He stared out to sea. His jaw dropped. "Oh fuck."

Cagney, his muzzy head still not functioning properly walked over to join Green. They stood together staring out to sea. Where before the Persian Gulf had been a mile distant with undulating sand hills and sparse grass between the sea and the road, now there was a steep beach leading to a sheltered horseshoe bay. Water lapped gently at the edge of the sand not fifty yards away. "Got any ideas?" Green asked softly. Cagney stared silently, taking in the scene but not understanding.

"I think, gentlemen, this may be my fault" The voice, educated and well modulated came from behind the two men. The two soldiers spun round, Green more slowly as the young Iraqi boy still clung to him. Facing them was a middle-aged bearded man in a soiled white lab coat. He looked unarmed. Cagney searched him anyway.

Green hefted the now sleeping youngster, saying, "I'll put matey boy in the Humvee; he can sleep on those wet-suits"

"His name is Rashid," said the stranger. "He is five years old according to his sister here, her name is Selima and she thinks she is seven"

"Well, Rashid," said Green quietly, "it's snooze time for you." He walked back, lay the child on a pile of wet-suits in the back of the Humvee and returned. "And you!" He looked accusingly at the stranger. "It's time for you to talk, me and the Lieutenant here are pretty bloody unhappy and want some answers"

"I will do my best to answer all your questions," he answered with gravity. His calm, dignified manner impressed both soldiers and they visibly relaxed. "My name is Doctor Mahmud Aktar," he went on, "but first we need to do two things, keep a watch for Captain Hassan who most assuredly will try to kill you, and secondly either bury your dead comrade or put him in the mortuary in the complex under our feet." Both soldiers looked astonished at his last sentence. "It's true gentlemen, there is a self-sufficient research complex built under here."

"You keep watch, Mikey," ordered Cagney. Green retrieved his binoculars from the Humvee and obediently hopped up on to the Abrams and crouched by the turret scanning the terrain.

Dr Aktar shouted up to the Paratrooper. "He is only armed with a knife; you will not be shot at."

Green grimaced, "Everyone and his dog has an AK in this country, so I think I'll keep my head down if it's all the same to you"

"I do not think you will be troubled," replied the Doctor enigmatically. With a great deal of effort, Cagney and the scientist managed to extract the dead Marine from his cab and, directed by the amiable Doctor, carried him to a wrecked building. They cleared away some rubble from the steel floor then Aktar slid some bolts and pressed a button. The floor, with two live men and one dead one, began a slow descent. The lift deposited them in a corridor, brightly lit by fluorescent tubes. Cagney cocked his rifle and looked around suspiciously.

"Fear not, Lieutenant, the people who are down here cannot hurt you, for they are long dead."

A trolley was conveniently placed by the lift and the men lifted the dead Marine driver on to the cold steel surface. With Cagney pushing and Aktar steering they came to a steel door at the end of the corridor which opened into a mortuary. The bearded doctor approached the fridge which occupied one wall of the room and selecting a door at random opened it. They lifted the dead Marine onto a tray and slid him in. Before Aktar could close the door Cagney looked inside, but apart from the driver the fridge was empty.

"Let's get back to the surface," said Cagney tersely. A few moments later they were walking back to the vehicles after bolting the lift door shut.

The vigilant Green waved as he watched them emerge from the ruined building, and then as they grew nearer motioned them to join him on the tank transporter. "No sign of your mate."

"My gaoler, I'm afraid, definitely not my mate," was the grave reply.

"Now," growled Cagney, "I have a dead Marine, a wrecked vehicle and the scenery has changed beyond all recognition; on top of that the radio airwaves are silent. You said it was your fault a little while ago." With studied politeness he added, "Now if you wouldn't mind I'd like some answers, please."

The Doctor sat on the giant spare wheel of the transporter and cleared his throat. "My name, as I said, is Mahmud Aktar, I am an Iraqi national. Three years ago I was conducting research at Cambridge University in England. It was a happy time, and my wife and two children who were with me liked England. One day I was visited by an official purporting to be from the Iraqi embassy who asked me to return to Iraq to work in Saddam's experimental weapons division. I demurred, saying that I was content where I was. He offered me an incentive."

"An incentive?" queried Green.

"Yes. Sergeant, an incentive. He told me that my brother who was an engineer in Baghdad was being watched and would be arrested and shot along with his family if I did not comply with his err . . . request"

Cagney gave the seated man a quizzical look. "So you came home?"

"Yes, Lieutenant, I did. My wife supports our sons in England with her teaching, for although Saddam employed me, he alas did not pay me. Upon my arrival in Iraq I was whisked here under conditions of great secrecy. The complex under our feet extends seventy five yards in all directions from that ruined building" He pointed to the structure holding the lift.

"A functioning petrol station was built on top of the complex to deflect any suspicion away from the construction. The petrol station was destroyed during the war by an aircraft which we believe targeted our delivery trucks, possibly mistaking them for tanks. The bomb also destroyed the dormitory killing everyone apart from myself and Captain Hassan"

"And this?" Cagney snapped crossly, indicating the changed terrain with a sweeping gesture. "Just what the hell caused this?"

"Ah," said Aktar softly. "We get to the crux of the matter"

Green was twitching with impatience, but said nothing.

Aktar continued, "My weapon did this. My team and I designed a particle beam projector which was supposed to destroy everything in its path. It was that weapon which

Captain Hassan fired at you." He glanced up, holding each man's gaze in turn. "The weapon is there." He pointed to the wall which had hidden Hassan and now concealed the scientist's invention. "I will show you"

The two soldiers followed Aktar as he carefully climbed down to the ground and walked with measured tread towards his invention. Seventy five hot dusty yards later the three men were gathered round the device. The soldiers regarded it with undisguised curiosity whilst the Doctor's demeanour suggested a worried man.

"What's the melted stuff on the tripod?" asked Green.

"It is . . . or rather was gold, it . . ."

"Hey hold on a minute, Doc," interrupted the American with some asperity. "Gold is an element, and you can't change it into something else no matter what you do to it."

The scientist shook his head sadly. "The gold insulated the particle accelerator, but the weapon was firing for longer than the gold could act as insulation and now it is no longer gold but another substance."

He picked up a blob of the melted material and handed it to Cagney who crushed it with his fingers and allowed the dust to trickle to the earth.

Green knelt and examined the device closely. "There's your problem, Doc, the trigger's jammed due to sand and too close tolerances."

"Ah, I see . . . thank you, Sergeant, you are most observant and, I judge from your comments, a competent engineer." The scientist looked with approval at Green. At the request of the Iraqi, Green and Cagney helped him lower the device back underground and closed the trap door. The three men walked back to the vehicles, Green had voiced his concerns over the children being left alone whilst the Republican Guard Captain was roaming free. Peering in the window of the Humvee, Green was gratified to see the youngsters sound asleep on a pile of wet- suits surrounded by equipment.

"So, Doc," said Cagney flatly, "You really haven't told us much apart from you think you caused this to appear." He slapped the basalt outcrop.

"Now, a little more information would be good or I might just ask the Sergeant here to shoot you."

The American's words, delivered with an ironic smile did not seem to perturb the Iraqi scientist in the least. He gave a wry smile. "I do not think the good Sergeant here is a murderer, Lieutenant, and that," he touched the rock, "has been here since the Earth was young"

"It wasn't here half an hour ago," interjected Green forcefully. "And this" he continued, kicking a wheel of the wrecked tank transporter, "has definitely not moved. So pardon my French, Doc, but what the fuck is going on?"

The Iraqi scientist looked uncomfortable and tugged nervously at his beard. He opened his mouth as though to speak then closed it again with no sound."

"We have moved," he said at last.

"Moved where?" chorused the two soldiers. Distant gunfire, like muted thunder, caused the three men to become warily alert, Green stared inland, Cagney searched the sky, but the Iraqi walked out of the shadow of the massive rock outcrop and gazed out to sea. There perhaps a mile away heading towards the bay were two vessels, they were sailing ships, each had three masts and both were carrying as much sail as was possible. The ship furthest away had cannon thrust through ports in the ship's side and a puff of smoke from one cannon followed by a report confirmed the source of the gunfire. Doctor Aktar heard the crunch of sand underfoot as the soldiers flanked him.

"Not where, gentlemen . . . but when!"

Chapter 5

"I need to think," muttered Green, his face ashen. "I'm going to clean the fifty, it's full of sand and we might need it soon." In sombre mood he walked slowly to the Humvee where even the smiling greetings of the now awake children could not dispel his gloom. Removing his binoculars from around his neck, Green hung them from Rashid's saying "Jimmy" and gently pushed the boy towards where Cagney was standing unseen, concealed by the outcrop. The boy trotted off happily to find the American. Green concentrated on stripping the big Browning whilst his mind raced. Focussing on the task of removing the sand from every cranny of the machine gun helped the young Para re-gather his thoughts. It was with a flash of guilt mixed with pleasure he saw that the ammunition belt he had placed at his feet had been brushed free of sand by Rashid's sister. He ruffled her hair affectionately. "Well done gunner's mate."

He carefully layered the ammunition belt in its box and fed it through the breech of the weapon. He decided not to test fire it as they only possessed two boxes besides the one on the gun.

Cagney's voice calling him roused Green from his introspection. The British NCO slid into the driving seat, plonked his rifle on the passenger seat and drove the Humvee closer to Cagney then parked it concealed by the rock from the sea. The Marine beckoned urgently to Green, his attention riveted on the scene unfolding in the bay. Green followed his gaze. The nearer, larger ship had come to a wallowing standstill five hundred yards away; its captain had swung the ship broadside on to its pursuer. Green wondered why the fugitive ship had not fired its cannon at its pursuer, he could see from the gun ports that it was well armed as befitted a ship which would have enemies. A movement caught Green's eye. He saw a small boat being lowered from the side nearest to shore and the opposite side to its foe. As Green watched he saw armed men boarding the larger ship when the two vessels touched. Green shot a questioning glance at Cagney. The American was oblivious; his borrowed binoculars were glued to his eyes following the drama before him. The sound of shouts, high pitched screams and the occasional shot floated faintly across the water.

"I can see women on the stern deck," shouted Cagney. "Hey, one of them is climbing down to the rowboat."

Green prised his binoculars from the Marine's unwilling grasp and peered at the ship. A woman in white was climbing down the steep side of the ship, hampered by her long dress. A figure beside her – *presumably a seaman,* thought Green, was helping her into the small boat; she gestured to someone still aboard to follow but to no avail. The seaman started rowing strongly to shore. Something fell or was thrown into the water from the ship.

"Was that a body, Mikey?" asked an anxious Cagney.

Green trained the glasses where he had seen the object hit the water. A little of Green's cheerfulness returned when he saw it was a dog, now swimming strongly towards the rowboat. "A body of sorts; the sort that has floppy ears and barks."

The seaman ceased his frantic rowing as the dog reached the boat and was hauled aboard almost capsizing the small craft with its flailing limbs and unbridled enthusiasm.

"They've got company," commented Cagney. Green swung the glasses in an arc, halting the movement as he saw a larger boat crewed by several men leaving the smaller vessel. Green handed the binoculars to Cagney who snatched them up greedily, hypnotised by the events.

Green, ever practical, shooed the children and scientist behind the huge basalt monolith.

"Stay out of sight," he instructed them. "Things might get messy." Green crouched by the rock, half hidden from the sea, Cagney stood alone watching. *Looking for all the world like a target* thought Green, with mild irritation.

The keel of the small boat ground into the sand, slewing sideways throwing the three occupants headlong into the shallows. The seaman picked up an oar and hefted it menacingly at their pursuers who were a bare ten yards behind them.

"Go, go," he roared at the woman, who lifted the hem of her dress above her knees and sprinted towards Cagney. Cagney lowered the glasses and shouted encouragement at the woman running barefoot through the soft sand. *This is like watching a movie on TV* thought Cagney, *in a moment the ads will start.* The ads did not start, the brave seaman with the oar was shot with a musket, and as he dropped to his knees he was slashed by a cutlass which lay his throat open and briefly reddened the surf.

The woman with her dog at her heels, realising she could not reach Cagney- her potential saviour - before she was caught, turned to face her persecutors and screamed, "Pirates." The dog, a large Dalmatian, leaped between its mistress and the leading pirate, barking furiously. The pirate, snarling obscenities at the dog, lifted his cutlass for a killing stroke. The action stirred Cagney from his hypnotic trance, and too late, began to un-sling his M16. *Bloody amateur* thought Green as he put a round into the pirate's chest. The man flew backwards to land at his fellow pirates' feet. The three remaining pirates halted, puzzled by the uniforms of the two comrades.

The oldest of the three urged the other two on. "Rush 'em lads, they be only one shot left, an' the Cap'n will reward 'ee for bringing him a white woman." Green thumbed the selector over to automatic and waited. The two pirates glanced uncertainly at each other, then lifted their cutlasses and charged towards Cagney. One step into their brief journey their lives ended as Green fired a short burst from his AK. The men tumbled to the sand in a bloody tangle of limbs. The woman rushed to Cagney who put a protective arm around her. *Bastard* thought Green.

The surviving pirate stood stock still, astonishment writ large on his villainous weather beaten face. Green rose to his feet and approached him. "Are you sure you're a proper pirate?" Green asked the suddenly listless man, "Because you haven't got a wooden leg or a parrot."

"Yes, he is a pirate," came the heaving sobbing voice of the woman who lifted her head from Cagney's chest," I saw him kill the midshipman who was only twelve years old."

"S'pose I'd better shoot you then," said Green baldly.

"Hold on a minute, Sergeant,"

Green heard the concerned voice of the American but ignored it and shot the man. The pirate dropped his cutlass and slumped to the sand near his equally unfortunate shipmates. "If you want to question someone, try him," Green pointed to the fifth pirate who had remained with their boat, and with some justification was looking alarmed. "I wasn't going to leave that dangerous old bugger alive," Green offered by way of explanation.

The Brit levelled his rifle at the man, noting as he did so that he appeared to be in his teens. "Come here," he bellowed. The man quailed at Green's summons, but encouraged by a round in the sand to his left, and then another to his right he trotted up the beach with, Green saw, an eager to please look on his face.

The lad halted, breathless from the effort. "Oi be not a poirate Zur," he gasped, his West Country burr accentuated by his fear. He pointed to Green. "Your dawg, Zur." Green looked down; the large Dalmatian was urinating on his leg.

"He likes you," smiled the woman in white. The dog gave Green an affable woof then sauntered off to its mistress, gazing at her with adoring eyes. Green was alarmed to see the same dog-like devotion on Cagney's face, for the handsome American had not taken his eyes from her since she had swooned in his arms – the same arms Green noted that were still wrapped around the mystery woman.

Green looked the woman up and down, mostly up as she was taller than he was. Despite her soaking he could see that she was breathtakingly attractive. *She would be* he thought, *in her mid thirties*, her wet dress clung to her, hiding little of her shape. She had the build of a runner, *no, a sprinter* he thought as he admired her lithe coltish long-leggedness which was softened by the gentle curve of her belly, a contour which said her youthful years were behind her. Yet her unsupported shapely breasts gave a lie to that thought. Green studied the woman's face as she clung tightly to the Marine. Her shoulder length auburn hair was plastered to her skull, yet oddly did not detract from her beauty, *and beauty she was without a doubt* mused the young Paratrooper. *Hmm,* he reflected, *her jaw was too wide, her chin a little too narrow, but mere details. Her generous mouth coupled with blue-grey intelligent eyes, elevated her beyond minor criticisms. Here,* Green speculated *was a woman who had grown into her loveliness, her tiny worry and laughter lines spoke of past experiences which lent her face character. She was* Green decided, *a woman who owned her beauty.*

The woman in white saw Green staring at her and reluctantly disentangled herself from Cagney's embrace. She stared in wonderment at their clothes and particularly their weapons. Clearing her throat she spoke, haltingly, but with an articulate, cultured tone, "Thank you both for saving my life, please let me introduce myself, my name is Philippa Somerville, and you have my eternal gratitude." She started a little as the Iraqi scientist and the children ventured into the sunshine. The little girl gave a small scream when she saw the pirates' bodies and ran to Green, clinging to him. Rashid, bolder than his sister plundered the corpses, gleefully holding up a pistol and a cutlass. Green hopped smartly to one side as he saw the waving flintlock come to bear on him. Swiftly he removed it from the boy's grasp. Rashid's face fell. Feeling tears were imminent Green called the dog over. Rashid dropped his cutlass and hugged it, being rewarded by a large lick on his face.

"What's his name, Mrs Somerville?"

"Please call me Philippa," she responded quickly, "and his name is Royal Russet McNaught." Green's eyebrows shot up, he knelt by the dog which was revelling in the attention of both children now. He pointed to the dribbling hound and said loudly, "Spotty Dog." The children, laughing, repeated his new name.

"As good a name as any," said Philippa gravely, "and who are you gentlemen, and where in heaven's name have you come from?"

Cagney reacted first, "This is Sergeant Green – Mikey, if he likes you – of the British Army's Parachute Regiment. Over there is Doctor Mahmud Aktar. Your dog's new friends are Rashid aged five and his sister Selima aged about seven. I'm Lieutenant James Cagney of the United States Marine Corps, at your service," he added gallantly.

"And where have you come from?" she asked again. The two soldiers and Aktar exchanged meaningful glances but said nothing. Green pulled a coin from his pocket and flicked it towards her.

She caught it adroitly at the top of its glittering arc, holding it up close to her eyes she gasped as she digested the information it gave her. Her voice was tremulous as she framed her next question, "This is real, not a fake?" Cagney held out his hand with a selection of coins on it, she shuffled through them with one elegantly manicured finger checking the dates.

"And if that doesn't convince you, have a look round there," Green inclined his head at the rear of the rock. A few tentative steps later she was facing the monstrous battle tank sitting on its trailer.

Awed beyond words she rejoined the group. "How has this happened?"

Taking a deep breath, Cagney replied, "The doc here who is a physicist can explain, unfortunately you'd need to be another physicist to understand. The bottom line is we're here by accident."

"And fortunate it is for me that you are here. Will you help me once more gentlemen?"

Cagney nodded before he could help himself, but Green was more circumspect. "What is it you want," he asked in a not unfriendly tone.

"My daughter was with me on board our ship. Can you get her back for me before those awful men take her away and I never see her again?"

The young pirate found his voice, "We need to take shelter, Zurs, Cap'n Scorponi is about to turn his guns on us." He gestured to the pirate ship which had disengaged itself from the merchantman and now was side on to them.

Raising the glasses to his eyes Cagney scrutinised the vessel, a figure on deck stared back at him through a telescope. The man, tall yet corpulent had an arm raised like a starter at a race. The arm fell abruptly. Horrified, Cagney bellowed, "Down, everyone," and dived pulling Philippa with him. The others followed suit with alacrity. A broadside boomed from the vessel, a cannon ball parted the air where they had been standing, another smashed into the basalt outcrop raining shards of volcanic splinters on the group, whilst another reduced the dead pirates to mere meat. Scrambling to their feet they beat a hasty retreat to safety behind the rock. Cagney peered cautiously round the edge, the pirate ship had turned slightly and its cannon could no longer bear on him. The tall figure had his telescope pointing at the shore again,

"Give him something to think about," urged Green. Cagney lay on the sand, snuggled the stock of his M16 into his shoulder and sent four quick rounds at the figure, Green, watching through his binoculars saw the telescope leap and spin and the corpulent figure shake a bloody fist at the shore.

"He's not happy," grinned Green as he raised his own rifle and fired five times. The bay echoed to the reports and the ship yawed slightly. "Must've hit the driver."

"Helmsman," corrected their young captive before he could help himself, Green gave him a dark look.

"He's leaving," announced the American as the pirate ship left the bay. "I wonder what the hurry is." The captive pirate waved an arm at the horizon where another vessel was in view.

"It be a British frigate, Zur, an' ee has the weather gauge on Cap'n Scorponi, e'll have to fight and. . ."

"How many men, you whatever your name is," Green interrupted, "are aboard the merchantman as a prize crew? And tell the truth or you'll be joining your mates on the beach."

"Moi name be William, Zur, an' about twenty men, Zur," said the lad, his fear palpable.

Cagney prodded him, "Hey, why didn't the merchant ship fire back? She looks well armed."

"The Cap'n got a man aboard as crew when she wuz in port, he spiked the guns when they put to sea." *Clever*, thought Cagney and trained the binoculars on the captured merchant ship. The prize crew were hauling up the anchor. He could see what looked like the passengers huddled on the aft deck. He handed the glasses to Philippa. "Can you see her?"

She fumbled with the unfamiliar instrument until Cagney placed her finger on the knurled adjuster and showed her how to focus it.

"Yes! Yes she's there," she exclaimed, "But they're setting sail, they will be gone in a few minutes."

"You up for this, Sergeant?" asked Cagney.

"Oh, I think so," replied Green cheerfully. He handed Doctor Aktar the flintlock pistol and cutlass, "Look after the youngsters, and if matey boy shows his ugly face, stick that in him," he tapped the cutlass.

Cagney dragged his flak jacket and helmet from the Humvee and put them on Philippa. Opening the passenger door he helped her in despite her protestations about lack of horses, whilst Green "helped" William in the side door with a boot up the backside. The Para manned the big Browning as the Marine leaped into the driving seat. He fired up the big diesel and a squeak of terror came from Philippa.

"Did someone tread on the cat's tail?" a question which earned Green a glare and a punch on the leg. Low moans emanated from the rear of the vehicle where William the ex-pirate huddled in the corner next to Spotty Dog who had decided to hitch a ride. Cagney gunned the engine and set off in a swirl of dust, he glanced at his passenger whose face was a mixture of astonishment and pleasure. He drove from behind the massive outcrop and sped round the bay and down the narrowing strip of land that connected "their" bay to the adjoining one on the blind side to the pirates. He coasted to a halt facing the bay as he reached the furthest point. They all climbed out bar Green who stood waiting with the spadegrips of the Browning in his hands.

Cagney took up a position to the right of the vehicle; he crouched in a firing position with spare magazines within easy reach. "I'll fix the guys in the rigging," he told Green, "and I want you to nail the guys on deck."

Green approved, he had the heavier calibre weapon which was better suited to his task. "We've got about a minute," Green informed them from his vantage point, "and they've seen us. A bloke in the rigging is shouting to his mates." The seconds ticked by slowly until the ship's bowsprit eased its way into sight fifty yards away from them. The pirate prize crew on board were relaxed, they were well armed and it would take a lucky musket shot to hit them from that distance. They gazed with curiosity at the strangely dressed men on shore but were unafraid.

Cagney opened fire first, there were only two men in the rigging and it took him five shots to send them cartwheeling to the deck. Green, swinging the silent Browning to and fro could see no one apart from the passengers on the aft deck. Something was wrong, to his horror he realised why. Several heads were bobbing up and down behind the third gun port from the bow – the pirates had unspiked one cannon and in less than a second it would line up on the Humvee. Furiously he depressed the trigger of the half inch calibre machine gun and concentrated his fire on and around the gun port, now with the ugly snout of a cannon poking out. The three inch oak of the gunwale concealing the men offered scant resistance to the large bullets. Four of

51

the five men serving the cannon were cut down, three by the heavy rounds and one from the oak splinters which pinned him to the deck. The survivor, suffering from a shattered arm, but with the bravery deserving a better cause, pulled the lanyard, the powder charge ignited and sent the cast iron ball hurtling towards its target.

The mayhem Green had created with the gun crew paid off, the delay in firing the cannon meant the ball did not hit the Humvee square on which would have destroyed it and ended Green's life. The cannonball smashed into the left wing of the vehicle above the front tyre. The impact lifted the armoured front and punched the heavy vehicle two yards to the left leaving Green dazed, with his head in the foot well and his feet on the steering wheel. Dragging himself up he could hear Philippa screaming her daughter's name, imploring her to jump overboard. The stern of the ship was about to pass them. Green could see that it barely had steerage way, as so little sail had been set, a tribute to the American's shooting. A slender blonde girl wearing a blue dress was attempting to climb over the stern rail; her efforts were being foiled by a pirate with a distinctive yellow bandana above his eyes. Green ignored the Browning, he could not tell passenger from pirate in the scrum that had formed on the aft deck, in any case the Browning was not an accurate gun and Green imagined Mrs Somerville would be unlikely to forgive him for shooting her daughter. She was in fact urging Cagney to shoot the man grappling with the girl, who Green gathered was called Francesca. It was a difficult shot and Green did not envy him. Cagney slid his finger in the trigger guard, as he watched; the motion of the ship was gradually causing Francesca's body to obscure her captor making a difficult shot virtually impossible.

Fate took a hand at this juncture; two people detached themselves from the melee on the deck and attacked Francesca's assailant. Cagney could see they were a woman and a man. He saw the man wore a red coat, a soldier maybe. They swayed to and fro in a macabre waltz until the combined weight of the newcomers became too much and all four toppled into the calm waters. The ship sailed on out of the bay, ignorant of its loss. Cagney stood and stretched, hefting his M16 feeling pleased with his performance. His smug contentment lasted all of a second.

"Help her please, James! She cannot swim," the heartfelt request from the tear-stained Mrs Somerville jolted Cagney from his self complacency. The Marine handed his rifle to Green then climbed over the rocks and down to the water's edge, swiftly he stripped to his pants and plunged into the water. His powerful over-arm crawl cleaved the water and propelled him towards the struggling figures.

Green cast a glance at Philippa; she cut an incongruous figure with Cagney's helmet falling over her eyes and the borrowed flak jacket dwarfing her. Green's binoculars hung from her neck, "How many people have we in the water, Mrs Somerville?" She lifted the field glasses, having forgotten they were there in the excitement. Focussing the lenses with a newly acquired dexterity she scanned the scene, concentrating first on Cagney. He was making steady progress towards the shore using a backstroke. He was towing what appeared to be a large blue jellyfish that could only be Francesca's dress billowing in the water.

Philippa dragged the binoculars away from them with a great effort of will and brought her attention to bear on the others in the water." James has Francesca," she shouted, a little deaf from the Browning's insistent thudding, "but there are three others, none of whom seem to be able to swim."

Green reached into the Humvee and grabbed his pack removing the rolled up polystyrene sleeping mat. He handed his AK and Cagney's M16 to Philippa who slung the AK over her shoulder and lifted the M16 to a firing position. He prodded William, and barked "Can you swim?" William shook his head miserably. "You're with me," he snapped and William obediently followed Green to the water's edge.

Green rapidly undressed and was about to enter the water with his makeshift float when he spotted Cagney's pistol in its holster, sitting on his clothes. Loath to trust William near a loaded weapon he slipped it from its holster and trotted back over the rocks to Philippa. She giggled at Green effing and blinding crossly as the sharp rocks hurt his feet. A very un-amused Green offered the pistol to her but encumbered as she was with two assault rifles and a magazine she could do nothing but shrug apologetically. Green impatiently thrust the pistol down her cleavage provoking a startled squeak from the blushing Mrs Somerville. Green's final instructions were to shoot William, "if he played up." William looked forlorn as the Para eased himself into the water. Green knew he was not a particularly strong swimmer and he was relieved the water was warm with only a very gentle swell. With his mat under one arm he propelled himself with an inelegant sideways doggy paddle using his free arm. Hearing splashing from his left, Green lifted his head to see another doggy-paddler alongside him. "Hello, Spotty Dog," he grinned, "we might just need you before long." The ill assorted pair made slow but steady progress, guided to their goal by much splashing and shouting. A short while and a lot of effort later Green trod water as he surveyed the strange scene. A middle aged lady was attempting to swim to shore, but a pirate – the one with the yellow bandana was clinging to her with a desperation born of fear. A bald be-whiskered man, presumably a soldier from his uniform jacket, was belabouring the pirate, with precious little effect from what Green could see.

"Unhand her you blackguard," roared the old soldier.

"Hi not sweem," bleated the pirate, who suddenly saw his salvation in Green's mat. He let go of the woman and tried to snatch it. Green was too quick for him and pulled it out of his reach then kicked him in the face. The mat was speedily pushed into the woman's grasp, who despite her exhaustion managed a polite "Thank you."

"Right, you young bastard," ground the red coated soldier, who took a deep breath and pulled the struggling pirate beneath the surface of the limpid water. Green saw a trailing piece of red material and was puzzled until it dawned upon him that the man possessed only one arm. Many seconds passed without either man reappearing as Green rested a weary arm on Spotty Dog. Enviously, he watched as the unknown female passenger in the distance slowly paddled her stately way to shore.

Green had virtually written off the soldier when with a huge splash and spluttering like an old Grampus the man surfaced next to him in an explosion of scarlet and foam. "Dead as mutton," he crowed, "that'll teach the swine not to hit women."

Despite the soldier's ebullience Green could see he was exhausted and would not last much longer without assistance. He pulled him closer and wrapped the man's fingers round the dog's collar. "Off you go Spotty Dog; hang on to him, Sir, he'll get you back to shore."

"Grateful to you m'boy, grateful," was the tired response. It dawned on Green with dismay that his own position was precarious, his strength was almost spent and he had drifted another thirty yards from dry land. Euphoric with relief as he felt a touch on his elbow he seized his would be rescuer only to find to his disgust and disappointment that it was the dead pirate who had floated to the surface.

"Fuck off," he shouted in sudden irritation.

"Hey soldier! Save your insults for the live ones," the transatlantic drawl in Green's ear was the most welcome sound the young Para had ever heard. An empty Jerry can was thrust into his arms, Green held it tightly, not even noticing the stink of Diesel fuel. Cagney slowly towed him to the shore where the flagging pair staggered on to the sand to applause from the small group. Francesca Somerville impetuously threw herself at Cagney who half heartedly tried to fend her off and look embarrassed as he caught a disapproving look from her mother who was still festooned with weapons and equipment.

A mischievous smile played on her lips. "Would you care to retrieve your guns Sergeant?" She smiled sweetly at Green who responded as she had intended him to by gently disengaging Cagney's pistol from her bosom, giving it a final and totally unnecessary jiggle as he did so. Her tone dropped to become sultry, her eyebrows arching deliciously, "And is your weapon still in good working order, Sergeant?"

Green deadpanned his reply, "Perfectly, Ma'am."

She passed him his AK. Green handed the pistol to Cagney with a wink. "Still warm."

After a moment the entire gathering were rocking with laughter, a reaction, Green thought to their brush with death and narrow escape. Cagney joined in the merriment but his relief was of a different variety. Introductions were effected as the two man dressed. The soldier was Colonel Bartholomew Trelawney of the Wiltshires, (whoever they were thought both Green and Cagney) the middle aged lady was introduced as Mrs Boscombe who the Colonel readily admitted he barely knew having met her and her sister only briefly on board.

Philippa held her daughter's hand, "My daughter Francesca who celebrates her seventeenth birthday tomorrow, and," she added ominously "had never been kissed until she met the Lieutenant here." Cagney spluttered his innocence of all charges and wondered if he would ever come to terms with the English disease of irony. The mooted purity of the pretty young girl caused the Colonel and Mrs Boscombe to exchange knowing looks, the raised eyebrows of the latter bringing colour to the girl's cheeks.

The new arrivals clustered round the military vehicle, aware that something was not quite right with the wondrous technology they were confronted with. They were however too stunned by their adventures to ask questions and were content to be led. Green surveyed the damage to the Humvee's wing, it had been pushed in by the glancing blow from the cannonball, jamming the steering and it could not be fixed without tools – tools he did not have, he thought glumly. He showed the damage to Cagney and the pair muttered together for a short while.

Cagney got to his feet, "Listen up, folks; we have an hour of daylight left to walk back to camp at the other side of that outcrop. It's about two miles, so setting off soon is good. I shall be staying here to keep an eye on our vehicle; Mrs Somerville will also remain as she has lost her shoes." Green repressed a smirk with difficulty, then grabbed a jerry can of water from the Humvee. He handed it to William to carry along with the holdall of AK magazines. Delving into the bag Green pulled out an old baseball cap with the Nike logo on it, he tossed it to the Colonel whose bald head was already suffering in the late afternoon sun.

"Before I forget," said Green, and picked up Cagney's helmet from where Philippa had left it. He turned it upside down and filled it with water for Spotty Dog who lay under the Humvee panting. "Sorry, old boy," he murmured, "almost forgot you." The shadows were starting to lengthen as Green gathered his little troop and the five companions trudged off, leaving the Marine with his thoughts, a dog and the beautiful Mrs Somerville.

The hour of daylight soon passed leaving Green and his companions in darkness a good half mile from their destination. Francesca and the Colonel were untroubled by the trek, despite their recent exertions. Mrs Boscombe struggled, her foot wear was unsuitable and her feet rapidly became blistered, yet she walked on without complaint, albeit slowly. The moon was almost full enabling Green to lead his flock without fear of losing his way. He saw the basalt outcrop looming near and offered encouragement to Mrs Boscombe. The whispered, "Thank you Sergeant," touched his heart, he called the Colonel over and handed him the AK, and then with an apology to the exhausted woman grabbed her hand and hoisted her over his shoulder.

The next two hundred yards to the tank carrier were as long as any Green had travelled. He deposited Mrs Boscombe as gently as he could against the giant wheel of the tractor unit, where she slumped without a sound. He shouted into the moonlit night, "Hey Doc, are you about? I need a hand." Small feet pattered near him, the gloom was punctuated by shrieks of "Mikey, Mikey."

Almost knocked off his feet by impact of the youngsters, he lifted the skinny children and hugged them.
"You fat little buggers," he laughed, "I'll have to put you on a diet."

Aktar arrived, a voice in the dark as a cloud blotted out the moon. "I am pleased you are safe, Sergeant, we followed your adventures from here and the children were worried."

Green placed the children on the ground. "We need light, food, a first aid kit and as many blankets as you can lay your hands on."

"We saw you coming and I foresaw this situation" returned the scientist, "bear with me a moment," The sound of a generator starting disturbed the silence then night turned into day as a pair of arc lights illuminated the scene. A frightened squawk came from Francesca followed by "Good Lor'" from the Colonel as their senses were assailed by the instant light and again as the monstrous armoured vehicle was lit. The Colonel stared open mouthed at the twenty first century war machine, vast, brutal, brooding and malevolent, made even more menacing by the deep shadows where the limited light could not reach.

"I'll answer your questions tomorrow, folks, but now, food and rest."

Doctor Aktar, with the assistance of his small helpers distributed blankets and thermos flasks of hot soup.

Green busied himself making a bed up for Mrs Boscombe and eased her into the coarse blanket cocoon, "I need to check your feet, Mrs B." He gently removed her shoes and frowned as he saw her feet raw and bloody. He rose to his feet "I wonder if there's a first aid kit in here?" he muttered to himself as he clambered into the big vehicle's cab. He fumbled in the half dark and shadows; his questing fingers found something behind the driver's seat easily identifiable as the driver's rifle. Pleased by his discovery but not satisfied, Green eventually found the first aid kit, a large box. Grunting he heaved it out of the cab, set it down at Mrs Boscombe's feet and returned to the cab for the M16.

"Will you take the first watch please, Colonel," he asked the officer.

"Certainly, m'boy," came the enthusiastic reply. Green checked the M16 magazine, cocked the weapon and put the lever to safe.

"Take this Sir," he offered the American rifle, "And I'll take that," he relieved the Colonel of the AK. Putting the AK over his shoulder he familiarised the officer with his new weapon then knelt to deal with Mrs Boscombe's injuries. He elevated her legs by inserting a rolled up blanket beneath them then proceeded to wash them with sterile water and gauze after donning thin latex gloves. He rubbed antiseptic cream all over her feet then bandaged them. The whole operation took ten minutes. The Colonel looked on approvingly and patted Green on the shoulder. "Wake me in two hours," Green told him quietly and strapped his watch to the rifle butt, not noticing the man's slightly baffled expression. The Paratrooper's last act before rolling into his blankets was to turn the arc lights to face outwards, lighting up the landscape and any possible threat. In the few seconds before sleep engulfed him Green dwelt upon his day; he had killed several pirates, suffered the effects of an Iraqi secret weapon, acquired two children and before sleep engulfed him he reflected to cap it all did not even know which century he was in.

As he watched Green's party grow smaller in the distance, Cagney became aware of Philippa's teeth chattering, for the temperature had dropped rapidly. He switched on the interior light for a moment and emptied his own and Green's pack. Sorting through the contents he gathered together a selection of dry clothing. A tee shirt from himself with a sweater and battledress trousers which belonged to Green.

59

"The nights are bitterly cold here, Philippa, you need to take off all your wet clothes and put these on." He handed the bundle to her. "I'll turn my back," he smiled.

She shook her head, "Th…thank you, James, but I will n…need some help…..I am so cold." She turned her back so Cagney could undo the fastenings on the back of her dress. After unfastening what seemed like fifty buttons her soaking dress fell to the ground. Cagney, trying to be businesslike but not quite succeeding, touched her skin. It was like marble. As quickly as he could he removed her undergarments, then grabbed a towel and quickly dried her body. A stab of desire raced through him as he wiped the moisture from her breasts; even in the deepening twilight he could see that she was very shapely. A few moments later she was clad in an assortment of military clothing. Cagney sat her on a wet-suit and rubbed her feet dry and sand free, then slipped on both his and Green's spare socks. Finally he dried Philippa's hair and placed the Sergeant's woolly hat on her head. A few strands of hair fell across her face, Cagney gently stroked them under her hat, an affectionate gesture that would have caused Philippa Somerville to purr if her teeth had not been chattering so much. He stood, and reaching down for Philippa's hands, helped her to her feet. She gazed up at the tall handsome American and touched his face, feeling the tremor that ran through his body as she did so. Pulling his head towards her and stretching on tip toe, she kissed his mouth. With her face against his, Cagney held her close in the darkness; he could feel and taste her tears as they traced a path down their faces. She pre-empted his question, "They're tears of happiness, James." She pulled away from him slightly, "We should not be doing this whilst we are enemies at war," Cagney felt her lips on his once more. "But," she went on, "everyone should commit a treasonable act once in their life. I am quite sure there is a law forbidding me to kiss a colonial rebel."

"It becomes known as the American War of Independence," he whispered, "you lose."

"I don't think I mind losing to you, James," she whispered back, "Even if you are a know all."

"Time to be practical," Cagney squeezed her hand. "I need to make a bed and get you warm." Aided by the very last of the twilight the Marine cobbled together a bed on the sand from mats, sleeping bags, a couple of old blankets and wet-suits for pillows. Satisfied he tucked Philippa in and then lay close to her feeling her warmth return. They talked and held each other in the darkness. There had never been a shortage of women in Cagney's life. He knew he was good looking and his future and stature as a doctor had been assured, drawing women to him. None of them had lasted; his interest in them had been short lived. This woman was different, he told himself, she was capable, confident, interesting and exciting. He never wanted this night to end, and yet he was nervous, worried even that she would leave him – not, he reminded himself that she was his in the first place. They talked on, him about his background and his plans to resume his medical training after the Marines. She spoke about her husband who had married his child's governess eighteen years ago after his wife and son had died of cholera. He was a Major who had been killed by a French bullet twelve years later leaving her to run the large estate in Dorset. The sea voyage had been her idea. Their daughter Francesca, she explained was being wooed by a neighbouring Squire who was much too old for her and needed to be discouraged. Two years away, touring the Empire was what was necessary to keep her headstrong daughter out of his clutches.

Philippa ran her fingers over Cagney's jaw, rasping her nails on the day's growth of beard. "Do you think you know me well enough, James?" she asked.

"Well enough," he echoed stupidly.

She giggled and shook her head in mock exasperation.

"Well enough to make love to me, you Colonial fool!"

Chapter 6

The hand shaking Mikey Green's shoulder was persistent, it needed to be, he had been sleeping like a dead man.

"I'm sorry, Sergeant," the apologetic voice of Colonel Trelawney was close to Green's ear, "I cannot stay awake for a moment longer."

It took a few seconds for Green to come to terms with his surroundings. Alert now, he thanked the Colonel who climbed into Green's vacated bed and instantly fell asleep. All was quiet apart the occasional sound of sleeping people; *dark too* thought Green and then it struck him there was a lack of noise from the generator. Worried for a moment, he shrugged as it occurred to him that the petrol had run out. Taking his sentry duties seriously the Paratrooper climbed on to the Abrams and switched on the night sight of the M16. Methodically he scanned the surrounding countryside looking for the heat signature of his main concern, the fugitive Republican Guard. Something living did register on the scope about a thousand yards distant. It was immobile whilst Green had it under surveillance and he had no means of knowing whether it was man, dog or sheep. Green considered sending a few rounds down that way, but thought better of it, it could be a local shepherd, and putting holes in him was not going to help their situation. He removed his watch from the rifle and strapped it to his wrist, four o clock. Dawn in half an hour he mused, already there was a faint gleam from the horizon.

Dawn arrived not in half an hour but in twenty minutes, it was still chilly, so Green let people sleep on. He reckoned after yesterday's adventures, a lie in would not go amiss. A rumble from his belly reminded him that it had been a long time since breakfast yesterday. *Yesterday,* he sneered to himself; the word had changed its meaning in the last twenty four hours. His stomach gurgled again, *it's alright for you, you don't have to think* he silently admonished it.

His hunger got the better of him and he decided to rouse Dr Aktar to find out what the food situation was. His eyes wandered from one makeshift bed to the next, trying to pick out the Doctor. The Somerville girl was easily identified by the cascade of blonde hair, a flash of scarlet confirmed the Colonel, a small bed must be the children and Mrs Boscombe lay swaddled next to the wheel. There were no more beds; the Doctor and William were missing. Leaping lightly down from the tank carrier Green narrowly missed Mrs Boscombe who did not stir. William's blankets, he noticed were neatly folded on the ground, not he mused, the behaviour of an escaping prisoner

For a moment the Paratrooper felt that his senses were betraying him, he could have sworn he had smelled fresh bread and coffee. He chided himself for being over imaginative; perhaps his stomach was doing his thinking after all. The notion made him chuckle. His nose twitched again as the same wonderful aroma made his mouth water. Green heard the sound of gravel underfoot from behind him. Turning he was relieved to find that both his mysteries had been solved. The Doctor and William were walking towards him from the direction of the trap door entrance to the underground complex. They were each carrying a tray laden with something steaming. The Paratroopers mood improved tenfold when he saw that his nose had not lied, fresh bread and coffee were always welcome whatever century a bloke was in! The breakfast smells woke the sleepers more surely than any alarm clock; conversation was at a minimum as hungry people tucked into the unexpected feast.

Doctor Aktar, at Green's urging moved away from the main party with him, they sat on a clump of coarse grass, eating and drinking. Aktar thought the soldier seemed ill at ease, though his first attempt at conversation was friendly.

"Thanks for this, Doc; your cave must be pretty well equipped." Green's attempt at humour did not deceive

Aktar, the man clearly was unhappy and the Doctor thought he knew why.

"No thanks are necessary, Sergeant, our cave, as you put it, is virtually self sufficient. There is always a six month supply of food for fifty men, which goes a long way when forty-eight are dead. Saddam's engineers tapped into an underground stream, so fresh water is always available. We have workshops, a kitchen and a large electricity generator but no dormitory or armoury courtesy of the United States Air Force."

The Paratrooper nodded but Aktar was not sure he had listened. "Can we get back?" the words spilled from Green.

"I think you mean forward," said Aktar, with an indulgent smile

"Don't bloody well patronise me," shouted Green, his anger shattering the morning, his outburst turning the heads of the rest of the party. "Can you get us back to where aircraft fly and toilets flush?"

The Doctor raised his hands in an apologetic gesture. "I am sorry, Sergeant, I did not mean to appear to be condescending, and yes we may be able to return, but not for a few days until I have checked and rebuilt my device."

Green's temper subsided as quickly as it had risen, the prospect of returning to a world he understood cheered him immensely. "Good stuff, Doc; do you need a hand with anything? I've got a background in spanners 'n' stuff. My life doesn't just revolve around shooting people you know," he added facetiously.

"Yes," said the Iraqi cautiously, "I may need your help; in the meantime can I prevail upon you not to shoot William? He was captured by the pirates, they only let him live because he is a carpenter and useful."

"Oh I think so; hey, do you have a sledgehammer in your workshop, Doc? I need to straighten out the wing of the boss' taxi." The humorous reference to the Humvee gave Aktar a glimpse of Green's human side.

"I shall find one for you," he promised. They rejoined the group who were finishing their breakfast.

The colonel who had slept late due to his extended guard duty shook Green's hand warmly. "Good morning m'boy, the ladies," he smiled at Francesca and Mrs Boscombe, "and meself would like to thank you most heartily for your actions yesterday . . .but we are dashed puzzled by many things." He gestured vaguely about him.

Green gave them a reassuring smile. "The Doc here will explain, I have some bodies to bury."

Francesca stood up. "Sergeant, Mama told me that a seaman from our ship died trying to defend her. Will you please bury him separately from the pirates?"

"No worries," Green assured her. He pulled a shovel from the tool box on the tank carrier and with a curt "You're with me," to William walked round the basalt monolith and on to the beach.

The scene had changed on the beach, the dead pirates were no longer in a heap but spread out. A suspicion was growing in Green's mind, a suspicion which hardened into a certainty when he stood over the corpses. Some had clothes missing; a tricorne hat was gone but most worrying of all, the pirate's weapons had disappeared. "Dig a hole and throw 'em in," he instructed William, handing him the shovel, "then drag that poor sod up from the water's edge and dig a hole for him away from this vermin. And make sure it's deep," he added. Lost in thought Mikey Green walked back to find Doctor Aktar in the middle of a deeply technical lecture on particle physics – at least Mikey thought that was the subject. A glance at the listener's slack jaws and glazed expressions told Green that the scientist was having a less than successful time attempting to explain their presence.

Without any preamble Green interrupted Aktar's flow. "We've got a problem, folks." He went on to bring everyone up to speed on the Republican Guard Captain Hassan, whom he strongly suspected of having obtained a firearm. "I think you'd better keep this," Green handed the M16 to Colonel Trelawney. The officer was looking very tired, but with a weary smile he assured the Para that he would stay alert to the new threat.

"Got a moment, Doc?" Doctor Aktar smiled and nodded his assent; in truth he had been pleased when Green interrupted his doomed explanation. Teaching, he thought ruefully, had never been his forte. The Paratrooper wanted boots and the sledgehammer; they walked together to the trapdoor and entered the underground complex where Green was surprised at how extensive it was. A visit to the clothing store provided boots and socks for Mrs Somerville, courtesy of the Iraqi army. When they reached the refectory Green tied the boot laces and slung them round his neck, as an afterthought he stuffed a sock in each boot. Grabbing a chair, Green sat down and motioned the Iraqi to follow suit. The two men chatted amicably about the logistics needed to keep their group fed, watered, healthy and secure. Green took a deep breath, "Tell me what you need from me so that you can fix your machine. William can do the cooking, fetching and carrying, Jimmy and yours truly will handle the security duties and with a little luck that will leave you with the time you need."

The scientist nodded sagely, "I will need your metalworking expertise, Sergeant, to fabricate a shield from gold sheet for the accelerator chamber. Can you do that?"

Green thought for a moment, "Yes I can do that, what gauge is the sheet?"

"That I do not know," admitted the scientist, "the technicians dealt with the actual construction of the weapon, but I do know where the sheet is kept." He led Green down a long fluorescent lit corridor to a workshop. The scientist opened the door and pressed a switch. The overhead tubes flickered reluctantly to life, flooding the room with harsh light. Green whistled, it was a large room and probably the best equipped he had ever seen. The scientist walked purposefully across the room, pausing momentarily to re-acquaint himself.

"Been a while, Doc?" enquired Green.

"It has been eight months since I entered this room, I do not trouble myself with the practical aspects of weapon construction," he added with a touch of pomposity. He pulled open a drawer in a wide steel cabinet; a frown creased his bearded face. Opening and closing the other drawers in turn, he leaned heavily on the cabinet, head bowed. "They are gone," he croaked, "all the gold sheets are missing."

"Hassan?"

"I think not, Sergeant, Captain Hassan was not a thief, he was fanatically loyal to Saddam. The sheets were probably stolen by a technician, or one of Captain Hassan's men." The Iraqi looked to have aged twenty years. "Without the gold sheet, Sergeant, we cannot construct an insulation shield for the accelerator chamber and the weapon will not function – we cannot go home." To the amazement of Aktar, the Paratrooper laughed out loud. "Is this an example of your British phlegm?" he said sourly.

Green continued to laugh. "No, Doc, it's an example of what the Parachute Regiment taught me – to improvise. Gold is used widely as a currency here, there will be plenty around. Me and the boss are the most heavily armed men on the planet so we are going to rob someone!"

The scientist looked aghast at Green, "You will steal from innocent people?"

The Briton seized Aktar by his lapels and pushed his face against the Iraqi's. "You bloody hypocrite," he said stonily, "you invented that damned contraption of yours which would have killed thousands and kept that bastard Saddam in power and yet you lecture me on morals!" He pushed the scientist out of the way and stomped out, snatching up the sledgehammer as he left.

Despite his brief loss of temper, Green was in quite a sunny mood as he strolled leisurely to the group of people he thought of as his flock. William was trotting back from the beach and they arrived at the Tank Carrier together. Everyone seemed in good heart; even Mrs Boscombe had managed a few tentative steps. Colonel Trelawney was perched on the Abram's turret holding his rifle so Green called him down to join the group. "I'll be gone for a couple of hours to retrieve our vehicle and bring back Lieutenant Cagney and Mrs Somerville, but before I go, I need to say one or two things. Firstly, I no longer regard William here as a prisoner, from now on he is a part of our little group and I trust him." William beamed at the unexpected change in his status and lost his hunted look. Green told them of the complex beneath their feet and how the supplies and facilities there would sustain them for some time. He warned them to be constantly on their guard, not only for the fugitive Iraqi soldier but also because it was a lawless part of the world. The arrival of Dr Aktar interrupted Green's discourse; the scientist had his arms full of Iraqi army uniforms which he placed carefully on the ground. "Help yourselves, folks" offered Green, "I want no one with sunburn." He looked meaningfully at Francesca whose bare arms and shoulders were looking vulnerable. "Everybody wears a hat, and make sure you drink plenty of water." Green removed his helmet and plonked it on William's head. "You were William the pirate but now you're. . ." a look of concentration spread over Green's battered face ". . . Badass Bill the sailor." Hoots of laughter split the air which woke the children who had fallen asleep after breakfast.

William blushed shyly and murmured to himself "Badass Bill."

The colonel shook his hand and said, "Welcome aboard" and Francesca gave him a peck on the cheek which caused his ruddy face to turn scarlet.

"Right then, Badass Bill, grab that sledgehammer, we're off to rescue the Lieutenant."

"From the glint in Mama's eye your Lieutenant may not want to be rescued," giggled Francesca.

"Best rush then," said Green, slapping William on top of his new helmet and pulling out his most prized possession, a red beret with paratrooper's wings on it. Cramming it on at a rakish angle, he strode off with William in his wake.

Although not an hour had passed since the sun had risen the heat seared the shoulders of the two men as they toiled on their journey, after some prompting from Green the west country lad gradually sketched in his life as a pirate in the six weeks since he had been captured. *Whatever pirate life was about* thought Green, *it certainly was not about glamour and romance on the high seas.* The tales William told of Captain Scorponi's cruelty surpassed anything in Green's experience – even when he had served in Bosnia. Green shuddered at the memory of that unhappy place. When asked about the fate of the crew and passengers of the merchantman or Indiaman as William called it, William's voice faltered, unwilling to talk about the horrors that awaited them. His own crew had been thrown overboard apart from two sail-makers and himself whom the captain had deemed to be useful. The two men halted and drank from Green's water bottle. The conversation turned to the local population, and more importantly to Green how affluent they were. In William's opinion there were no rich locals, they had been robbed blind by the pirates who came ashore whenever they felt like it and took what they wanted – including women.

"So what you're telling me," broke in Green, "is that there is no gold available in this part of the country because Captain Scorponi has it aboard his ship."

"Oh no, Zur, Cap'n Scorponi keeps his treasure locked up in his fort in case his ship sinks."

"Oh," said Green gloomily, "So he wouldn't mind us popping across the Persian Gulf or into the Arabian Sea to ask him for a bit."

The irony was lost on William. "No, Zur, the Cap'n has his fort just down the coast, about two days sail!"

Green was suddenly worried, he tried to pin down the distance to the fort but William's notion of distance was hazy. Green guessed at around ninety miles, close enough to pose a significant danger if the pirates decided to march up the coast and attack them. He shared his worries with William but surprisingly was reassured.

"The pirates have no 'orses, Zur, an' it be too far to walk." Green was unconvinced, and was still frowning when they arrived at the Humvee.

The two travellers halted thirty yards from the armoured vehicle, unnoticed by either Cagney or Mrs Somerville. Cagney had a jack under the front of the Humvee and was attempting to remove the front wheel; Mrs Somerville was sitting on the ground with her back against the vehicle. She had Cagney's rifle across her lap and Green's book of poetry in her hand. She was making noises of encouragement to the Marine as he grunted and swore whilst wrestling with the wheel. The two men walked into her peripheral vision; she looked up and saw Green. Her beautiful, happy smile of greeting almost made him melt. The American similarly had a grin like a Cheshire cat and pumped Green's hand in welcome. So much happiness was infectious, and it wafted away Green's worries like autumn leaves.

"We've got a new man on the team," he said, prodding the lad, and I changed his name from William the pirate to Badass Bill the sailor." Cagney clapped William on the back and Philippa rose to her feet and approached him. "Don't kiss him," warned Green, "your daughter did and I haven't had an ounce of sense from him since!"

"Nonsense," she said sweetly and kissed the youth on the cheek. Predictably his face turned crimson. ". . . and I will continue to call you William."

Kneeling by the wing of the Humvee, Green gripped the wheel and wiggled it, obediently it popped off and he leaned it against the vehicle. "Here's where I want you to hit, Badass."

"Sergeant Green," he felt Philippa's hand on his shoulder, "I absolutely forbid you to use that horrid name for William."

Green gave a defeated shrug, "OK, you win," he smiled.

William set to work with a will and the bay echoed with the clang of hammer on armour plate. At Green's prompting they moved away from the noise and sat on the sand. "I've got some news," announced Green, "the Doc reckons we might be able to get back to where we belong."

Cagney's response was muted. "That's good," he said slowly but Green felt the mood had chilled. Philippa's hand had stolen into Cagney's at the news and they exchanged looks.

"Let's not go overboard with the celebrations," said Green, his voice heavy with irony. The pair sat close, there was an awkwardness that Green felt he could almost touch, he ploughed on. "Our Republican Guard has managed to get a firearm, OK, it's only a musket but he is definitely a worry. Not as big a worry as having Captain Scorponi and his merry men in residence less than ninety miles up the coast. William here has been filling me in on our mate the Captain; he's been around a while, he's clever – a good sailor, and a bad, bad man. Think of Vlad the Impaler, if he had a naughty brother that'd be our Captain Scorponi." He added with grim humour. "And talking of our favourite pirate, guess what he's got that we need?" Cagney looked blank, shrugging his shoulders. *God save me from falling in love* thought Green *if it removes the power of rational thought I can do without it.* Aloud he said, "Gold, the Doc wants me to obtain a few ounces of gold so that I can fabricate a shield for his device and with a bit of luck we can all go home."

The clanging stopped and William joined them. "All done?" asked Green, with more cheer than he felt. William did not reply, just pointed to the horizon where a sail could be seen.

"Is that the pirate ship?" asked Philippa, her voice tremulous.

Cagney stirred himself into action, handing binoculars to William. "What do you think?"

William climbed onto the roof of the Humvee and after fumbling with the adjuster managed to focus on the distant vessel. "Can't tell, Zur, too far away." He dropped to the ground and returned the glasses to Cagney. Green checked the wing to see if the wheel had enough clearance to steer then wiggled the wheel back on to its studs. The wheel nuts had been carefully wrapped in rag by Cagney to keep sand from the threads Green noted with approval as he quickly fitted them then tightened them with the wheel brace. Green released the pressure from the jack and threw it in the back of the vehicle. They climbed aboard followed by Spotty Dog who found a comfortable seat on William. Cagney drove, Philippa alongside him, with the others in the back. They set off slowly, with Cagney gingerly testing the steering. "Seems OK, Sergeant."

Ten steady minutes of driving saw them back at the camp where mother and daughter shared a tearful reunion. At Green's urging, the Doctor managed to produce a ladder which the Paratrooper placed on the Abrams turret, William swiftly shinned up on to the huge rock to monitor the sailing ship. The two soldiers called Colonel Trelawney over to discuss tactics should the vessel prove hostile. "What's our weapon status, Sergeant?"

"One AK47 with fifteen magazines, the fifty has two and a half boxes, I found five M16 mags in the cab plus the one in the Colonel's rifle and whatever you have."

"Four and a half for me," said Cagney grimly.

Green grimaced. "Not a lot when we're facing two hundred pirates."

"Three hundred," came William's voice from above them.

Cagney laughed and with bitter humour said "What are an extra hundred bad guys between friends?"

Colonel Trelawney called their attention to the Abrams, "Can we not use this monstrous machine for our defence?"

Cagney looked at Green, "Over to you, Mikey."

The expression on Green's face was not encouraging. "The tractor's had it, it's not the blown tyre, I can change the wheel, but the sump is smashed and the oil has leaked into the sand. The Abrams has lost a track and an idler wheel. It won't move. There is the tank commander's fifty on the turret, but the ammo box is empty."

William's voice floated down to them, "It's a British frigate, Zurs," A sense of relief flooded the camp; even the children who could not speak English were infected by the general cheer. William shouted again. "An' she's sinkin'"

Chapter 7

It was a race between the allied soldiers to reach William and see for themselves. The agile American's long legs gave him the advantage and he was the first to stand alongside the lad. With scant ceremony he took the binoculars from him and zeroed in on the stricken vessel which had fought its way to the mouth of the bay. He passed the glasses to Green as the wind suddenly gusted, helping the struggling ship, Green saw it was listing badly and although his knowledge of sailing ships was sketchy he could see no damage to masts or rigging. Water was gushing from holes in the ship's side as the pumps worked overtime ridding the ship of its liquid burden. The wind gusted again, as it did so, Green felt suddenly giddy. He dropped to his knees thinking *it must be a touch of the sun,* to his surprise he found Cagney similarly crouched with steadying hand outstretched and a puzzled look on his face.

William glanced down. "It be the rock, Zurs, it moves in the wind." The young lad had taken the movement in his stride. A little shamefacedly, the twenty first century warriors rose unsteadily to their feet. The bow of the Frigate had just nosed aground with so little way on that barely a tremor ran through the ship. Sailors swarmed overboard laden with ropes and equipment and in response to shouted orders were gathered on the beach pulling the stern of the ship round so she lay parallel to the shore.

"What do you think, Boss, should we go down and say hello?"

Cagney nodded. "That sounds like a good idea, Sergeant; let's hope your countrymen are friendly." By the time the three men had climbed down to the Tank Carrier the camp was swarming with British sailors who were open mouthed in amazement, gazing in wonderment at the twenty first century technology. Their murmurs and whispering were silenced by a bellowed order.

"Bosun's Mate, disarm those men!"

Cagney swivelled his head to see a horse faced Lieutenant pointing at himself and Green; the Bosun's Mate gathered several sailors to him and advanced purposefully towards the Tank Carrier.

"Lieutenant!" Philippa's voice was whiplash sharp, "I strongly suggest you belay that order . . . unless you and your men particularly want to die." The sailors hesitated and looked for guidance from their officer who appeared troubled by the unworried expressions of the strangely dressed men. "Perhaps Sergeant, a demonstration?"

"Yes, ma'am, how many should I kill?" asked Green guilessly.

Philippa tipped Green a small wink. "I think just the Lieutenant would suffice."

"Yes, Ma'am," said Green tonelessly. Sweat poured from the English officer's brow as Green raised the AK to his shoulder, aimed at his chest then lowered the muzzle and fired half a magazine into the earth at the man's feet. A tell-tale stain appeared at the front of the officer's white breeches.

As the echoes of the automatic fire died away, a quiet voice broke the tense hush. "I am a little short of officers, gentlemen, and consequently I would be mightily obliged if you could forgive Lieutenant Caruthers for his intemperate behaviour and join me for some refreshment?" The heads of the entire company turned to the speaker, a man of middling height, aged around forty, dressed in the uniform of a Captain in the Royal Navy. An impish smile played on his lips as he surveyed the aftermath of the recent drama. "I am Captain Harry Fairbrother of His Majesty's Frigate Endeavour, and I am delighted to make your acquaintance." His arm made a sweeping gesture that encompassed the gathering. His smile faded and he stared stonily at Lieutenant Caruthers. "Take the men back to the ship, Number One, transfer the port cannon to the shore and lighten her. We will begin careening after the men have been fed. Give the men who were operating the pumps two hours rest. Oh . . . and, Number One," he added in a lowered tone, "change your breeches."

Caruthers issued orders and the sailors filed back towards their ship. He gave Green a hard look as he passed. Green spat at his feet knowing he had made an enemy.

Fairbrother turned to Philippa, "Despite your uniform, ma'am, I would hazard that you are no soldier."

"Indeed not, Captain! The Lieutenant saved me from a chill by dressing me in the Sergeant's spare clothing." She felt a wave of warmth as she recalled the previous night and the flush spread upwards from her throat to her cheeks. The sharp eyed Fairbrother noted it with interest.

She introduced herself and a small frown of concentration appeared on the Captain's face, then a smile, "I met your late husband Lord Somerville some years ago when we were transporting his regiment, a fine man, Lady Somerville."

"We do not stand on ceremony here, Captain Fairbrother, please call me Philippa, and let me introduce my companions." She introduced Francesca, Mrs Boscombe and the Colonel; Fairbrother looked with curiosity at the M16 over the Colonel's shoulder but said nothing. Philippa glossed over William's history, merely saying that he had been rescued from the pirates. Philippa's Dalmatian together with the children appeared from nowhere; the youngsters were picked up and hugged by Green, then deposited on the ground to follow Spotty Dog who was sniffing Fairbrother's leg. Philippa walked over to Green and Cagney and stood between them. She linked her arms through theirs and pulled them close. "These two handsome," Green flushed, "dangerous men are responsible for the salvation of myself, my daughter and my companions, furthermore they vanquished a band of pirates over ten times their number. This is Sergeant Mikey Green of Her Majesty's Parachute Regiment, and this," she smiled at Cagney, "is Lieutenant James Cagney, of The United

States Marine Corps." Fairbrother looked down, his expression aghast as Spotty Dog urinated on his leg.

"He likes you," said Green. He continued unabashed, "His name is Spotty Dog."

"I am honoured to meet you, gentlemen," said Fairbrother striding forward and warmly shaking them by the hand. He took a pace backwards and eyed the two men, *not sure about handsome* he mused casting a glance at the shorter man, but definitely dangerous.

Philippa, Lady Somerville interrupted his thoughts. "We have fresh coffee, Captain, and newly baked bread; can we tempt you to an alternative to your ship's fare?"

Fairbrother's face lit up; his private stock of coffee aboard the Endeavour had run out a week ago, and fresh bread was but a distant memory. "Delighted to accept, Ma'am."

Philippa released her hold on Cagney and gave brief instructions to William who hurried off to the complex entrance. Colonel Trelawney joined Mrs Boscombe sitting against the wheel of the tank transporter and Francesca wandered down to the ship. Philippa slipped her hand into Cagney's and trailed by the naval Captain and the Paratrooper they strolled to the rear of the tank carrier. Fairbrother looked over his shoulder with some trepidation at the seventy ton battle tank. There was a slightly uncomfortable silence when no one seemed to want to make the opening remark.

Philippa thrust her hand into Cagney's pocket, then put the half dozen coins she had grasped into Fairbrother's hand, "Would you give the Captain an English coin, Sergeant?" Captain Fairbrother looked intently at the collection and closed his eyes tightly; after a few seconds he opened them again. Philippa spoke, "It's not a dream, Captain; these men," she looked fondly at Cagney, "have come from another war, far distant yet in another sense close, and I feel for all your profound differences that you may be able to help each other."

William arrived beaming; he had enlisted Selima's help to carry the coffee, hot rolls and butter. Rashid trailed behind with Spotty Dog. Sitting on the Low Loader, Fairbrother saw the dog and hurriedly lifted his legs out of the way. The Royal Navy Captain was consumed with curiosity, but being a pragmatic soul decided that questions could wait until his belly was full. William turned to go but Cagney halted him,

"We may need your input, Badass, so have a seat . . . ow!" His exclamation was caused by Philippa biting his finger, a curiously intimate gesture which confirmed Fairbrother's suspicion about their relationship.

"William," she admonished firmly. Mildly aggrieved, as Philippa had sharp teeth, the Marine asked Green to brief Fairbrother on their situation.

"Not until he gives me my pound back," said Green lightly. Solemnly Fairbrother returned the coin. "From the top then," said Green, and for the next hour with frequent interjections from his listeners he related their adventures since his meeting with the American. His throat dry from what was for him an unusually long speech, Green finished his coffee which was now cold.

Fairbrother cleared his throat, levered himself from his seat on the Low Loader and stood up stretching his limbs. "Thank you, Sergeant; I freely confess that your presence here is something I am struggling to absorb but," he squeezed the paratrooper's arm "you are definitely real." He turned to address Cagney, "I am sure we will be able to help each other, I am particularly interested in Captain Scorponi and his villainous band of cut throats for I have been tasked by their Lordships at the Admiralty to seek out and destroy them. They have been a scourge in these waters for too long. You have seen that my ship is damaged, that damage was sustained when I engaged the "Scorpion"- Captain Scorponi's ship. We had the weather gauge and we outgunned him but," The Captain smiled ruefully, "the fellow had the damndest good fortune, after I had swept much of his rigging away with chain shot we were caught by a sudden gust which caused us to heel over and expose ourselves below the water line. That damned fortunate fellow managed to hit us twixt wind and water forcing us to devote all our attention to saving the ship rather than sinking him." He paused then exclaimed vehemently, "I do believe that accursed man is in league with the devil!" A young naval officer arrived to interrupt Fairbrother's tirade. "Ah, Lieutenant Rotherhithe, what news of our damage?" He added darkly, "I am expecting good tidings."

"Alas not, Sir, we have careened the ship and I believe we are pierced three times by ball, we shall see more as the tide ebbs."

"Thank you, Lieutenant," said Fairbrother heavily. His face etched with worry, he addressed them all, "I must hasten repairs to Endeavour, if the Scorpion manages to rectify the damage to her rigging that I inflicted he can sail into this bay and reduce my ship to matchwood with his cannon. You say his base is only ninety miles away?" this to William.

"Yes, Zur, but he bain't goin' there, Cap'n Scorponi uses a shipyard across the Gulf a days sailing away, Zur."

"Splendid, splendid!" Fairbrother clapped his hands with undisguised delight. "That will give us valuable breathing space: we will have the bounder yet! Now gentlemen, I must away to my ship." He smiled grimly, "I would be honoured if you would accompany me. We have much to discuss, a campaign plan to decide upon and not much time to do it in."

"Captain. . ."

Fairbrother touched his hat. "Yes, Lady Somerville?"

"A seaman from the Anastasia is buried here on the beach, he died defending me and I would be greatly in your debt if you would say a few words over his grave."

"It would be my honour, Ma'am," he replied gravely, "if you will allow me perhaps half an hour to make preparations?" He tipped his hat again then led the way down the beach to his ship. Cagney was amazed at the scene - tons of stores lay on the sand. The port side cannon, twelve he counted were being manhandled up the slope by sweating matelots. As the group neared the ship the first Lieutenant hurried over accompanied by a wizened little man whom Cagney judged to be well past retirement age. "Report, Number One?" rasped Fairbrother, struggling to conceal his dislike of the man.

"Holed three times by nine pound shot, Sir. Dryden can explain if you will allow?"

Fairbrother nodded affably to the old man, "Well, Abraham, what is your opinion?"

The old man knuckled his forehead, "Ten days, Sir, at the very least. When I can see more it may be worse."

"Thank you, Abraham," said Fairbrother gently, "carry on; I know you will do your best. You too, Mr Caruthers." Caruthers shot a venomous look at Cagney and Green as he hurried off to supervise operations.

"Trouble ahead," Cagney offered quietly to Green.

Fairbrother looked from one man to the other, "My hearing is excellent, gentlemen. You have indeed made an enemy, you need not fear him whilst I am alive, but if I should fall . . . be on your guard." He called over a carpenter, "Make a cross please, Jones, we have a funeral in ten minutes."

Green spoke, "Can you explain to me, Sir, what it is you are doing to your ship? I know little about the sea."

"Nothing would give me greater pleasure, Sergeant, than to educate a landlubber like yourself in what we are trying to achieve here." The genial smile and hand on Green's shoulder took the sting from the mild slur. Green did not mind in the least, Paras regard everyone not qualified to wear the winged red beret as a "craphat" though personally he thought the Captain's tricorne headgear was pretty cool.

Fairbrother continued, "I have beached the Endeavour because she is holed by cannon fire below the water line and she would have sunk had I not taken this action. We had blocked the holes temporarily, but in order to make a permanent repair we must elevate the holes above the water. The port cannon have been moved to the shore so that the weight of the starboard cannon makes the ship tilt to expose the damage. My shipwrights still will not be able to work on her until we lighten the ship by removing stores and let the incoming tide raise her when we will secure her with ropes to leave her high and dry as the tide turns." Fairbrother faced the two men. "You can see my problem; until the Endeavour is repaired and afloat my only effective defence are the guns I have brought ashore and they cannot defeat the massed broadsides of the Scorpion," he spat the name, "and Scorponi will know soon enough I fancy." He pointed to a small fishing boat gliding past the bay, its occupants gazing intently at the stranded ship. "Young William tells me that Scorponi pays the local fishermen well to keep him informed of events. I estimate his repairs and his sailing time will have him arriving here in three days, my carpenter tells me that ten days is the very best he can do before Endeavour is seaworthy. Things are looking bleak gentlemen and if you have any relevant thoughts on our situation I will be pleased to hear them."

"Maybe this could work," ventured Cagney. "We could assault the pirate fort and recapture the Anastasia, sail her back here, un-spike her guns and we'll have a weapons platform."

Fairbrother shook his head. "I cannot march my men ninety miles, assault a fortress and assuming we capture her sail her back before the Scorpion arrives and destroys us."

"I think I can do better than have us wear out our shoe leather, Captain, I can transport a small group of men to the fort in five hours or so."

"God's teeth!" exclaimed Fairbrother, "That certainly does put a different complexion on things.

William piped up, "The Anastasia won't be there yet, Zurs; the wind wuz agin 'em an' they not enough men to set the sails bein' as you killed most on 'em, Zurs."

The Captain walked over to a carpenter who was stripping copper sheet from the ship's bottom and borrowed his chisel, taking William by the arm he crouched at the water's edge in the wet sand. "Build me a model of the fort please, William."

The young carpenter set to with a will and a few minutes later a rough but accurate – or so William claimed- replica was constructed. The three men shot question after question at William to build a more complete picture of what they were up against. His interrogation revealed that the fort was square with walls of around twenty feet high; the seaward side had a deep water anchorage where a ship could berth against a jetty hugging the wall. There were two gates: one on the jetty and one on the landward side that William claimed was never opened whilst the Scorpion was at sea. It was manned by fifty of his most loyal henchmen who were well provisioned and armed but had no boats or horses. This William explained was to stop them leaving after plundering the locked cellar where Scorponi kept the proceeds of many years pirating.

Each wall was provided with two small cannon - chasers, Fairbrother called them which were loaded with grapeshot.

Fairbrother's face grew grim as he assessed the difficulties of taking the fort. "I fear, gentlemen, that a frontal assault using ladders would be doomed to failure, our only alternative is to use darkness as a cloak for our activities. Much as I dislike the confusion of night battles, it is our only viable option."

"I think we may be able to help you there, Captain." Green nodded in agreement with Cagney's words. "This," said Cagney patting the sight on his M16, "Can see in the dark and the Sergeant I believe has a pair of night vision goggles. Using these we can pinpoint the whereabouts of the sentries - William tells us that two are set at night and . . ."

"Can we kill them quietly though?" interrupted Fairbrother. "If we can achieve that and remain undetected I can lay an explosive charge against the gate and the element of surprise will be complete. With the noise of your carriage and your quick firing weapons we will carry the day."

William spoke up. "I can help there, Zur, oi can knock up a bow and arrows today and it bain't make a sound." He subsided blushing at his temerity at making a suggestion.

Fairbrother clapped him on the back. "Well said, young William, a capital notion." The Marine and Paratrooper glanced at each other and smiled their approval. Fairbrother's frown returned. "If, gentlemen, our venture is a success, and I emphasise it is a very big if, then we still have a large problem, he paused dramatically. "Even assuming I can sail the Anastasia into this bay with her hold full of pirate booty, her guns are spiked and useless if I cannot un-spike them quickly and transform her into a fighting ship the Scorpion can still follow and slaughter us all, for I cannot repair my ship before the Scorpion is battle worthy. . . Unless. . ." his expression became thoughtful, "unless," he repeated softly. The two soldiers waited. "How much does your monstrous cannon carriage weigh Lieutenant?"

Cagney thought for a moment, "The Tank weighs seventy tons, and the carrier around ninety thousand pounds so say . . ." he tapped his teeth with a fingernail, ". . . oh around one hundred and fifteen tons."

A sailor approached Fairbrother with a wooden cross.

"Ah, good, Jones, thank you, my complements to the first Lieutenant and will he assemble the ship's company by the grave?" He put his hand on Cagney's shoulder, "Would you inform her Ladyship we are ready to begin the ceremony?" Cagney strode off to find Philippa.

"A word please, Captain?" Green motioned to the officer and they walked out of earshot along the beach.

"You look troubled, Sergeant Green," observed Fairbrother.

"I am, Sir, very. I believe the Lieutenant intends to stay here when the rest of us return to where we belong, he's fallen for Mrs Somerville - not that I blame him and I reckon he's set his mind on returning with yourself in the Endeavour or in the Anastasia if we capture her."

A thoughtful look came into Fairbrother's eyes. "Yes, Sergeant, I can see your dilemma, he has much knowledge . . ." Fairbrother held up his hand to prevent Green speaking, "Sergeant, I do not wish to know, I am already familiar with devices and machinery I have no business to understand and should be beyond my comprehension. I feel I have seen far too much already."

"Yes, Sir," concurred Green gloomily, "He knows enough to turn your world upside down,"

Lieutenant Caruthers appeared at Fairbrother's side and saluted. "Ship's company assembled, Sir."

"Thank you, Number One, and, Sergeant," he added significantly, "leave it with me."

Green followed the British Navy Captain up the beach where the ship's company had gathered by the unknown sailor's graveside. Fairbrother spoke briefly to Philippa who replied too quietly for Green to hear. The Captain opened with a tribute to a young man whose name he did not know then went on to deliver the burial service. He finished and looked at Philippa, "I believe you wished to add something Ma'am."

Her tone low, she answered him, "Thank you, Captain, I will read a short piece of poetry." In a clear voice she began,

"They went with songs to the battle, they were young.
Straight of limb, true of eyes, steady and aglow.
They were staunch to the end against odds uncounted,
They fell with their faces to the foe.
They shall grow not old, as we that are left grow old:
Age shall not weary them, nor the years condemn.
At the going down of the sun and in the morning,
We will remember them."

Green stood to attention, aware she was reading from his own book. As Philippa reached "they shall not grow old" he followed the words with his lips remembering the many times he had heard them, written by a man, Lawrence Binyon not yet born. The faces of dead friends and horrors from places as distant from each other as Bosnia and Northern Ireland swam before him. Tears rolled unbidden down his cheeks and he felt the reassuring pressure on his fingers from Francesca and Mrs Boscombe as he reflected on the wasted lives that his profession had exposed him to. Fairbrother dismissed his men as Green's blurred vision filled with Philippa. She pressed his book into his hand and gently stroked the tears from his eyes.

"Soft bugger." The muttered words came from the Bosun's Mate of the Endeavour as he walked by.

Green un-slung his Kalashnikov and thrust it into Philippa's hands. "What's that you say, fat boy?"

The Bosun's Mate did an abrupt about turn; a happy smile broke out on his face when he saw the Paratrooper was unarmed. He walked slowly and confidently to Green who was a head shorter than him. The Bosun's Mate was the first Lieutenant's favourite and he ruled below decks using his fists and boots with a casual brutality. He faced the smaller man, "I says you soft bu..."

His words were cut short as Green's forehead hit his nose with a sickening click, Green followed up with a punch to the midriff knocking the air from the man's lungs. Taking a step back Green kicked the man's legs from under him; he placed a boot on the prostrate man's upper arm then grabbed his wrist intending to smash the elbow joint.

Green felt the pressure of Cagney's hand on his arm, "C'mon, Mikey, he's learned his lesson."

Reluctantly Green released his grip and the Bosun's Mate got to his feet shakily and shambled off. The Paratrooper walked after him and gave him an almighty kick up the backside sending him sprawling once more to hoots of derision and laughter from the watching sailors.

Fairbrother strode up angrily. "Get back to work, Sullivan you fool, and you, Sergeant, I would remind you that discipline is my responsibility." Fairbrother paused for breath then snapped, "Come with me!" and huffily stomped off out of sight behind the basalt outcrop.

Green moved to retrieve his weapon from Philippa who held it at high port, her finger on the trigger. She handed it to him, saying quietly. "It's cocked and the safety is off."

Green smiled his thanks, his estimation of her raised a notch or two as plainly she would have used it. The small group followed Fairbrother and found him leaned against the Tank Carrier, Green braced himself for a confrontation but was astonished to see the officer laughing. "'Pon my soul young man, I would have paid good money to see you trounce Sullivan, the man is an out-and-out bully and you placed your boot up his behind!" He pumped the smiling Paratrooper's hand. "I had to put on a stern face in front of the crew but getting out of their sight was imperative before I exploded with mirth." Still chuckling he climbed on to the Low Loader; he raised his hand to the barrel of the main gun and looked at Cagney, his face serious. "Will this fire?"

The Marine scrambled on to the Abrams, lifted a hatch and disappeared inside. A few seconds later the turbine engine fired up with a scream. Fairbrother prided himself on his self discipline; nevertheless he uttered a surprised squawk. Cagney's head emerged from the turret. "You'll be pleased to know, Captain, that there are enough shells in here to sink the entire Royal Navy, would you care for a small demonstration?"

"If you would, Lieutenant," said Fairbrother, his composure partially restored. The huge turret swung smoothly round until it was aiming inland, Cagney sighted on a distant hillock and fired the one hundred and twenty millimetre cannon. Fairbrother, shading his eyes with his hand saw the resultant explosion over a mile away. The turret swung back under Cagney's bidding and the Abrams' turbine died. The American emerged from the hatch with a grin like a child on Christmas morning. "Very impressive, Lieutenant," Fairbrother called up, "I do believe we may have found our salvation."

"What is it you have in mind, Sir?" asked Green.

"I intend Sergeant to move this vehicle the necessary distance so that this marvellous weapon can point out to sea and destroy the Scorpion when it arrives."

"You know how much it weighs?" parried Green.

"I do, Sergeant, but I have many strong men, as much rope as I need and most importantly, block and tackles. Now, Sergeant, can you replace that damaged wheel?"

Green climbed on to the Low Loader and quickly found what he sought, a large hydraulic jack together with a wheel brace. He kicked the spare wheel to check if it was inflated, happy with its pressure he jumped lightly onto the ground next to the Captain. "I can replace the wheel, Sir; may I borrow a couple of your lads and some stout wooden blocks?"

"Of course you may Sergeant" He walked to the extremity of the basalt outcrop. "Lieutenant Rotherhithe!"

The sweating young officer dropped what he was doing and doubled to his Captain. "Sir?"

"Oblige me by detailing two men to help Sergeant Green."

"Aye, aye, Sir." The Lieutenant trotted back to his ship shouting orders as he went.

"If you need anything my ship can provide ask one of these lads." Fairbrother nodded to the seamen Rotherhithe had sent.

A third seaman rushed up to Fairbrother. "Mr Caruthers' compliments Sir an' Mr Rotherhithe is taken bad."

"Lead on Turner, we shall see what ails our third Lieutenant." The Captain followed the seaman out of sight.

"Right then, lads," said Green to his new helpers. I'm Sergeant Green and you are?"

"Smith, Sir."

"Armitage, Sir . . . an' the lads be proper happy seein' as you gave Sullivan a right royal pasting." The faces of the seamen lit up with the remembered pleasure.

Green chuckled at the compliment. "What I want you to do, lads, is unload that lump of steel there," Green waved a hand at the jack. "And when you have done that get me three or four large blocks of wood." The seamen set to enthusiastically, hauling the jack from the Tank Carrier and then leaving at a brisk walk to their ship for the blocks Green had requested.

Green looked around for Cagney; he could hear his voice from somewhere near, echoing strangely. The words were indistinct but Green thought they must have been funny as they had produced a giggle from a female listener. Baffled, for he could see no one, he turned full circle - still no one. Cagney's voice again, still with that hollow quality, Green frowned with concentration, frustrated by his inability to solve the mystery. A clang from the Abrams told Green all he wanted to know, he climbed onto the turret and stuck his head in the hatch. He laughed at the sight he beheld and the occupants looked up. The clang he had heard was Cagney swinging the breech block. Mrs Somerville was clutching a hundred and twenty millimetre shell to her bosom and was attempting to load the cannon.

"Don't you get oil on my best sweater," he remonstrated gently, grinning. "Can I have a word with your instructor?" Philippa, grimacing with the effort thrust the shell into the breech and looked up at Green with a satisfied smile on her face. She put her hand up to Green and he hauled her through the hatch in one swift fluid movement, there was a grunt from Cagney as Philippa's booted foot used him as a climbing aid. Green put his arm around her to help her balance as they stood astride the turret. "Do you walk on all your men?" he asked mischievously as Cagney emerged rubbing his head. Without waiting for a reply He hopped down from the Tank; taking his mobile phone from his pocket he snapped the pair as they sat on the Abram's turret. Philippa's baffled expression turned to awestruck when Green handed her the phone and she gazed at the image. Taking his own phone from his pocket Cagney showed her how to take photos and videos. Impulsively she snatched it from him and slid from the turret to the glacis plate and then to the Low Loader.

With a girlish giggle she promised to be "back soon."

"Special girl," ventured Green.

"Special doesn't even scratch the surface, Mikey, how about winning the lottery, losing the ticket and not caring because it's not important if she's near to me?"

"Lucky man," said Green and meaning it. He made a sweeping gesture at their surrounds, "Any thoughts boss?"

Cagney looked pensive. "I think Fairbrother is right, we need to protect his ship until she's repaired and can look after herself. Whether he can pull this," he rapped his knuckles on the turret, "the distance we need to swing the gun and fire out to sea is a big ask. We can make life very uncomfortable for Scorponi with the fifty and our light weapons but sooner or later we'll be overwhelmed by his cannon and manpower advantage."

"Pretty much my assessment too; we also need to relieve him of his ill gotten gains sharpish. If he gets his rigging sorted quickly he might go back to the fort and stick it all under his hatches - so no gold and no going home." Green concluded gloomily. Green's two seamen had returned and were waiting by the tractor unit looking at him expectantly. "I'll get this wheel changed," he looked at the sun, "what time do think it is?"

Shading his eyes Cagney looked up. "'tween two and three I guess- too late to drive down the coast today I reckon."

Green pursed his lips. "What sort of speed can we make on this track?"

The American gazed into the distance at the cart track meandering along the coast. "No better than twenty miles per hour," he hazarded, "so we're looking at a five hour trip, how are we for fuel?"

Green walked to the Humvee and looked at the fuel gauge. "Around half a tank and one full jerry can. His eyes came to rest on the tractor unit, "You could siphon some from this while I sort the wheel out," Cagney made eye contact with the Paratrooper and saw mischief there. "You know how to siphon? Stick one end of a hose in the fuel tank, suck like crazy on the other end 'til you get a mouthful of diesel then put the pipe in the can," A sly smile played on Green's lips.

Dwelling for a long moment on the effect his mouth stinking of diesel fuel was likely to have on intimate moments with Philippa, Cagney offered his own solution. "How 'bout you do it and I'll promote you to Colonel?"

Green mulled over the offer. "Well, Lieutenant Sir, thank you for your kind offer but I feel this might be the ideal opportunity for William to demonstrate his loyalty to the common cause." Laughing at his own duplicity he handed his AK to Cagney, "Look after that whilst I'm under this beast." He crawled under the tractor unit calling for the seamen to push the jack in after him. Levering it under a main member he instructed Smith to pump the handle and Armitage to slide the wooden blocks to him. Smith watched as the tractor gradually lifted and he swapped astonished glances with his shipmate. His voice stuttered to life,

"How does it work, Sir?"

Struggling to manoeuvre the heavy blocks under the axle, Green's muffled shout came back to him. "Hydraulics."

Mystified for a moment, Smith assumed the air of a man entrusted with a great secret, with a conspiratorial glance he whispered to Armitage, "dry bollocks."

Green wriggled out from beneath the vehicle, he quickly showed the sailors how to unscrew one wheel nut then left them to remove the rest.

"All progressing smoothly, Sergeant?" Captain Fairbrother had returned from his ship with a party of twenty men weighed down with ropes and equipment.

"Yes, Sir, the wheel will be replaced in a few minutes and then I shall show your men where to attach their ropes."

Armitage shouted to Green that all the nuts were off and between the three of them they removed the damaged wheel and replaced it with the spare, bolting it on tightly. Green showed the First Mate which chassis members to use then directed his little team to remove the blocks and lower the vehicle.

Fairbrother let his team get on with their work then together with Green strolled to where Cagney was happily listening to an animated Philippa. The Captain tipped his hat to her. "Lady Somerville."

She broke off mid sentence and held out Cagney's phone. "Your ship, Captain, accurate in every detail."

Fairbrother gazed spellbound at the photograph, he smiled then became serious. "You show me magical things, Ma'am, but these pretty pictures will not save our lives. If the Scorpion sails into this bay before we can bring your cannon to bear on her we will all be slaughtered! Their prospects so baldly put cast a cloud over the group. "I think, Lieutenant, your plan has much to commend it; we will attack the fort before the Anastasia arrives there then capture her and sail her back here where she can be armed and at least you will not be incommoded, Lady Somerville, for you can sail in her after we defeat this dastardly pirate."

Philippa smiled sweetly at Fairbrother who flushed slightly. "I am grateful for your kind thoughts, Captain." Green noticed that she had stopped short of accepting his offer.

"Captain," the voice was Cagney's, "might I respectfully suggest that we postpone our raid until tomorrow? At a rough estimate I think we can reach the fort in five hours but that will leave us travelling in darkness and that's a risk too far." His fingers drummed uneasily on the Humvee's hood.

"What do you think, Sergeant?" Green was surprised to be asked but flattered nevertheless.

"I agree with James, Sir, even travelling at twenty miles per hour we can suffer much damage if we leave the track." The figure of twenty miles per hour caused Fairbrother's eyebrows to lift skywards. Green continued, "We need to carry more men for a successful assault; we can squeeze six inside . . ."

"There I think I can help," interjected Fairbrother, "I will have my sail makers throw rigging nets over the vehicle so we may carry perhaps several more?"

He looked expectantly at Cagney, who inclined his head in grave assent. "The weight isn't a problem Sir, so long as they can hold on."

"You underestimate my crew, Lieutenant," came the confident reply. "They may not be the most sophisticated of souls but they have altered sail whilst beating round the Horn, I assure you this task is well within their compass!" His face darkened, "However, I must take my leave of you, albeit temporarily. My third Lieutenant Mr Rotherhithe has been struck down by a mysterious malady and I must lend my presence forthwith before my surgeon bleeds him to his grave."

Philippa looked over at Cagney. "James, would you attend? . . . Captain Fairbrother, James has much experience in medicine; he may be of some assistance."

Fairbrother gave a wintry smile. "I genuinely hope so, Ma'am, for my surgeon has a propensity for assisting his patients to shorten the journey to their maker."

They found Rotherhithe lain on a trestle table beneath a canvas awning on the beach. Pale and sweating he clung to Francesca's hand, grimacing with pain. The ship's surgeon, a short grimy figure, his frock coat covered by a bloodstained apron, stood over Rotherhithe. A short knife clasped in his hand, he lifted it to the light and unhappy with the blood and rust he saw spat on the blade then wiped it on his apron. Taking a swig from a bottle in his pocket he reached for the young Lieutenant's arm seeking an appropriate vein. Wheezily he said, "I shall bleed thee now, young Sir, and release the bad humours within thee."

Rotherhithe braced himself. Fairbrother looked over at Cagney and gently raised one eyebrow; he was rewarded by an almost imperceptible shake of the head. Fairbrother placed his hand on the surgeon's shoulder, "One moment, Mr Squires, with your permission I will ask Lieutenant Cagney to examine our Third."

Cagney stepped forward and Squires stalked off with a harrumph. "If I might have a few moments alone with Mr Rotherhithe, Sir?" The group moved to a discreet distance with an agitated Francesca hovering midway between. The minutes ticked by as they waited for Cagney to return, the murmur of his questions in the distance together with his inspection of the young officer's abdomen heightened the tension. At last the Marine walked over to the silent group. "I believe your Mr Rotherhithe has an inflamed appendix which is likely to kill him within forty eight hours," Cagney paused, "but we can't have that so I will take it out in the morning." Only Green seemed unperturbed by the news and the realisation came upon Cagney that everyone else expected him to operate without anaesthetic and the young officer not to survive. Aghast at his own insensitivity he hastened to inform them all about the procedure.

Fairbrother was the first to react. "Am I given to understand he will sleep all the way through the operation and suffer no pain?"

"Yes, absolutely, he will suffer some discomfort for a number of weeks afterwards but that's usual."

Philippa touched Cagney's arm. "You are such a thoughtless brute, James, come, tell Nicholas. I suspect he will be mightily relieved to know that he is not to die on the morrow." Chastened, the Marine spent the next fifteen minutes with Lieutenant Rotherhithe detailing his forthcoming treatment.

Green nudged Philippa. "Don't be too hard on Jimmy; it's difficult for us all right now."

She put her arm through his. "Walk with me, Sergeant." They strolled back to camp passing the work party assigned to move the Tank and its Carrier. Green marvelled at how industrious and well organised they were. Already four thick manila ropes complete with block and tackle were attached to the tractor unit and the sweating crew were furiously hammering iron anchor spikes into the rocky ground. They walked the length of the basalt outcrop and sat on the sand, in the shade of the rock and out of sight.

Philippa opened, "You and James will be in great danger tomorrow and I am very worried."

Green shrugged. "We're both soldiers, well trained, well armed and in my opinion James is a brave man."

Philippa frowned. "Yes, Sergeant, I believe you and agree, but I am sorely afraid he will behave impetuously and be killed as a result." She gripped Green's arm tightly. "I want him returned to me safe but he feels he must prove to you and others that he does not lack courage and is fit to command – he is a driven man." Green patted her on the hand, even to the Paratrooper it seemed a particularly ineffectual gesture and Philippa saw it as such. "Please look after him, Mikey, I love him."

Green spread his hands in a helpless gesture. "The assault will be planned for as little risk as pos . . . ."

"We plan to marry," she blurted, "I have a large estate and money; we can be happy!"

Green laid his back against the giant rock and let his head rest against its unyielding solidity, he closed his eyes for a moment and then looked intently at Philippa. "I'm not sure you've thought this through, there are many implications to your decision."

"How so?" she demanded angrily, red spots forming high on her cheeks.

Green sighed heavily. "James has knowledge which could literally change the course of history; his medical training alone, if he chose to use it, could save millions from death and disease."

"Is that such a bad thing, Mikey?"

"Not in itself I suppose, but it's too early; modern medicine is developed during the First World War. James is a modern American; he's not like us Brits who keep our cards close to our chests. He's generous and big hearted; the medical procedure he plans for tomorrow will make him famous and you will never be able to hide far enough away from people and governments who will be greedy for his knowledge and the power it would bring them." He raised his eyes to her downcast face. "There is an alternative you know." Philippa's face brightened but she was prevented from replying by the arrival of Spotty Dog who affectionately bowled over her seated figure and licked her face.

"Always knew you were a pushover." The transatlantic drawl identified the speaker. Philippa lifted Spotty Dog's ear from over her eyes and squinted into the sun. Cagney was a black silhouette with the sun's late afternoon rays bursting around him. "I leave you alone for half an hour and you're on your back with a tongue in your ear." She smiled and knew Cagney was smiling, knowing it warmed her. The Marine became serious. "I need an assistant to give me a hand removing the young Lieutenant's appendix tomorrow. Do you feel like volunteering, Sergeant?"

Green pulled a face. "Mmm, not sure that's a good idea, Boss, if we're both gowned up and disinfected we'll be away from our weapons and I'm not comfortable with that."

"Do you not trust your countrymen, Mikey?" asked Cagney mildly.

"Just being cautious, Boss, and besides," he gave Philippa an encouraging look, "I'm not pretty enough to be a nurse."

"You're not pretty enough to be a goddamned gargoyle for that matter," offered Cagney cheerfully.

Green laughed until his sides ached. "A face for radio," he eventually spluttered.

"Who is radio?" asked Philippa.

"I'll let James explain," smiled Green. "I'm heading to the workshops downstairs; I've an idea that might help us when we attack the fort tomorrow." He sauntered off leaving Cagney and Philippa together. As he ambled towards the underground complex Green spied the teams of men tasked to move the Tank and its carrier. He made the short detour to sound out their success. Five long iron stakes had been driven into the earth twenty yards from the tractor unit as anchors for the ropes with their block and tackles employed to reduce the effort needed to move the vehicle. Files of fifteen men each were pulling on the hawsers in the manner of tug-o-war competitors. To Green's surprise the men burst into song, a sea shanty the rhythm of which coincided with each heave on the ropes. He noted that the sweating men had moved the vehicle perhaps six inches. As he watched one team fell backwards in unison as the anchor spike was torn out of the earth from the colossal strain. All the men ceased pulling and waited whilst the ship's carpenters straightened the spike with hammers and laboriously drove it back into the ground under the supervision of the First Mate.

He nodded a greeting to Green then walked over to him, his expression grim. "Six inches in two hours, the stakes keep tearing free."

The Para grimaced sympathetically, he was conscious of a vague thought hovering at the back of his mind which was causing him a degree of disquiet, he couldn't put his finger on it but he knew it was important and it bothered him.

Green gave the man an encouraging slap on the shoulder, then made his way to the complex entrance his stocky figure throwing long shadows courtesy of the late afternoon sun. The baleful eyes of Lieutenant Caruthers burned into Green's oblivious figure as he climbed down the ladder and into the bunker. Caruthers turned back and glared at the work party hissing his displeasure at their lack of progress – a performance that was witnessed by Philippa and Cagney.

"That arrogant bastard is going to be a problem," said Cagney quietly.

She nodded her agreement. "I spoke to the Captain, the First Lieutenant has money and influence, his family make muskets and cannon by the thousand. He would like nothing better than to see you dead and to learn the secrets of this." She tapped Cagney's M16.

"Looks like I'll have to watch my back very carefully," was Cagney's grim response.

"I will watch it too," said Philippa lightly in an effort to brighten Cagney's mood.

"You'd better have this then," The Marine pulled his pistol from its holster, cocked it and handed it to her. "That's the safety catch; it's on at the moment. Flick it there," Cagney's thumb showed her how, "and you're ready to blow holes in people." Cagney nudged the lever to safe. Philippa slid the weapon into the leg pocket of her borrowed battledress pants. The couple watched the snail like movement of the Tank Carrier for a while and then followed Green to the entrance to the underground complex. They climbed down the ladder and walked along the long corridor, passing one work shop where Dr Aktar was working on his device. They gave him a cheery wave and were rewarded by a brief smile before the scientist resumed his labours. The sound of a machine tool humming drew them to the neighbouring workshop where they found Green operating a lathe. Ignorant of their presence they watched him withdraw a cylinder from the chuck and hold it up to the light.

"Is that what I think it is?" asked Cagney. The Englishman jumped at the unexpected sound and instinctively reached for his AK lying on a nearby bench. "Relax, Sergeant, we're the good guys!" Green smiled ruefully and handed the cylinder to Cagney who examined it carefully, "What have you packed it with, Mikey?" Green pointed upwards where a ceiling tile had been pushed aside to reveal fibre glass wadding. Cagney grunted his approval, "Cute, beats a bow and arrow, never took you for the Robin Hood type anyway."

"Too right, sport," agreed Green as he reached for his Kalashnikov and deftly stripped it then carefully tightened the barrel in the lathe chuck, "Just cutting a thread on this so I can screw it on." He pointed to the metal cylinder in Cagney's hand.

"What is it," asked Philippa, her curiosity getting the better of her.

Cagney smiled indulgently at her. "It's like this, Honey…"

Philippa's finger prodding his chest abruptly halted his flow. "Do not ever, ever, patronise me again James-know-all-Cagney or I will put my eighteenth century foot into your twenty first century backside!"

"Erm . . . it's a silencer," continued Cagney lamely, he shot a glance at Green who had his back turned thread cutting but who's shaking shoulders told a tale.

"And what pray does it silence, James?" She replied archly, the question hung in the air.

"It silences this," Green waved the AK's barrel in the air between the embattled pair, a huge grin still on his face.

Philippa turned her head and looked coldly at Green. "If, Sergeant, you are amusing yourself at my expense I would remind you I have two feet." His grin vanished instantly and he busied himself assembling his assault rifle, hurriedly he plucked the silencer from Cagney's hand and screwed it on to the muzzle of the AK. The Para cocked the weapon, raised the butt to his shoulder and aimed at the large block of wood supporting an anvil at the far end of the workshop. Green squeezed the trigger and the block jumped backwards a hand's width, the loudest sound in the room was the clack of the rifle's bolt returning.

Philippa's reserve broke and she laughed delightedly to the relief of both men. "Will you make one for James' rifle?"

"Won't work unfortunately" said Green. "The bigger rounds in this," he tapped the AK, "are subsonic; the rounds in James' popgun are supersonic and impossible to silence."

Philippa toyed with his words for a moment. "Are you mocking my ignorance, Sergeant?" She spoke sternly.

Green raised his arms in a defensive gesture. "No, definitely not, Mrs S . . . err Philippa." Green's discomfiture brought the germ of a smile to Cagney's lips which disappeared without trace as Philippa's eyes momentarily came to rest on him. Green went on, ". . . I can quieten the report of either weapon when the bullet leaves the muzzle by dissipating the gases into an absorbent material." He lifted a piece of glass fibre insulation. "What

I can't do is silence the round as it breaks the sound barrier."

"The sound barrier?" echoed Philippa.

Cagney pulled a full magazine from his pocket, ejected a round and handed it to her, his face was contorted with the effects of concentration. He took a deep breath. "When we speak the sound our voices make travels through the air at around seven hundred and sixty miles per hour if I remember correctly." He looked across to Green for confirmation. "As this bullet leaves the barrel of my M16 it travels faster than that speed and makes a loud crack as it does so."

Green took up the explanation. "This round," he placed the AK bullet next to Cagney's, "is bigger, heavier, and most importantly slower, slower in fact than sound," he concluded. Philippa licked her dry lips, her mind struggling to absorb the concepts which were commonplace to these two men but were akin to magic to her. Green pressed home his advantage, "Back home we can travel under the sea and flying is a daily activity for millions of people – in fact I could travel from England to Australia in around twenty four hours."

Philippa's eyes found her lover's; his expression endorsed Green's words. "My country has sent men to the Moon and back several times." Philippa's jaw dropped. "But neither we nor the Brits can cure the common cold," he laughed. Cagney's humour went some way to restore Philippa's composure though in truth she was still shaken. "Come on, let's find the pharmacy then I can brief you on the duties of a surgeon's assistant."

"You'll need this," Green reached to the rear of the bench for a powerful flashlight, "The lights are down in that section of the bunker, the power is on for the fridges and sockets, but no lights I'm afraid. As Green spoke the lights in the workshop died to leave them in a Stygian darkness, ten seconds later they flickered to life again. "The Doc tells me it happens occasionally, sometimes for a few minutes," volunteered Green. Concern was etched on Cagney's face,

"What troubles you, James?" prompted Philippa.

"I'll need to operate on Lieutenant Rotherhithe in the sunlight tomorrow, I planned to use the pharmacy but that is totally without lights, and if I operate," he paused, "say in here, I run the risk of the lights going down when I am up to my elbows in young Nicholas!"

"Makes sense," agreed Green.

"You just about done down here, Mikey?"

"Sure, Boss."

"Can you rig up lights and a generator so the towing party can work during the night? We'll search the Pharmacy for the drugs and equipment I need for the procedure tomorrow . . . Oh, and tell our patient he's nil by mouth." *That'll cheer him up* thought Green as he made his way to the trap door ladder, he half turned looking over his shoulder at the wavering torch beam and smiled as he watched Cagney's arm drape itself protectively around Philippa.

The heat even at twilight hit him as he emerged from the bunker. The towing party were seated enjoying a well deserved rest and food, Green noticed the Tank and its carrier had moved over a yard he sauntered to the First Mate to offer a "well done". A sweating matelot offered Green a pewter tankard, Green thanked the man and took a large swig. The beer he was expecting turned out to be rum; the fiery spirit made him gasp and his eyes to water provoking a gale of affectionate laughter from the gathered seamen.

"Got some news for you boys," he announced, "I'm setting up lights so you can work tonight." Some good natured grumbling greeted Green's words but the men knew their salvation lay in moving the Tank to where its firepower could be harnessed. The Para offered encouraging words, "If you lads can pull this far enough so that big bugger. . ." he pointed at the Abrams cannon ". . . can traverse, I promise you that pirate ship is going down." Hoots and cheers rose from the group who Green saw were a tough looking bunch of hombres. He busied himself setting up lights and fuelling the generator then left as the twilight finally died to find the Captain of the Endeavour. His search led him to the beach where the rest of the Endeavour's crew were gathered round a fire eating and talking. Green's eyes probed the darkness and dancing shadows seeking the Captain's distinctive tricorne hat. A shadow deeper than the rest moved towards the Paratrooper,

"Would you be looking for me, Sergeant?" Fairbrother's voice competed with the crackling of the fire and the background chatter of his relaxing men.

"Yes, Sir, I am," said Green quietly, "Might I have a word about tomorrow's schedule?"

"By all means, Sergeant," Fairbrother's reply was equally quiet. The Naval Captain took Green by the arm and led him away from the fire's patchy illumination; the two men seated themselves in the soft sand and made themselves comfortable.

Green opened, "James is going to operate on Lieutenant Rotherhithe at first light; he thinks it will take him around two hours which will give us plenty of time to drive down the coast to the fort. If it suits you we can check it out in daylight then put an assault plan together for the night."

"Excellent, Sergeant, my carpenters have draped your vehicle with boarding nets which should ensure we arrive with a full complement. The first Lieutenant has detailed several men for our assault force and they are resting tonight rather than towing your . . .err . ."

"Tank," supplied Green.

"Thank you, I have taken the liberty of having my carpenters build a wooden scaling ladder – I believe it will be more suitable than your metal one." Green thought of the extendable alloy ladder that he had obtained from the Iraqi stores and knew Fairbrother was right, the rattles would have given them away. Fairbrother went on, "I shall be coming with you, and," he added firmly "I shall command; I trust that sits well with your good self and the Lieutenant?"

"I doubt he will have a problem with that, Sir . . .if I might make a suggestion?"

"Most assuredly,"

"I would like to take Colonel Trelawney along, he knows more about taking defended fortifications than we do so I think he will make a useful team member."

"A sensible suggestion, Sergeant, I trust we will be taking William too?"

Green nodded forgetting Fairbrother could not see him.

"Yes, Sir, William is the only one of us with first hand knowledge of the fort and he's a sound lad."

"Then we are agreed, Sergeant, bye the bye are there any developments with the Lieutenant and Lady Somerville?"

"Yes," said Green, his tone gloomy, "more complications, I haven't spoken to James yet but Philippa tells me they are to marry."

"Marry, by George!" cried Fairbrother in astonishment, "your Lieutenant does not let the grass grow under his feet I will say that for him." His voice dropped, "I say, he's not a blackguard is he?"

Green smiled in the darkness. "No, Sir, he is not, I regard him as an honourable man. I feel this is more her Ladyship's doing."

"Interesting," murmured Fairbrother with a small chuckle. "If he is a victim of her Ladyship's charms I dare say he is a willing victim but nevertheless I may have to thwart her wishes for I will not allow my world to be thrown into disarray . . . not even for love."

"My thoughts exactly, Sir," concurred Green. "In the meantime we have a great deal to occupy us, I'm getting my head down now, Sir, I reckon it'll be a big day tomorrow and I want to be fresh."

"I share your sentiments, Sergeant, I too need to sleep. I will bid you good night." The two men rose and walked away from each other, Fairbrother to his bed on the sand and Green to where Lieutenant Rotherhithe's bed was illuminated by a small lantern. The young officer lay quietly, his face and upper body a sheen of perspiration. His eyes moved as they followed Green's approach, he raised a finger to his lips and Green saw Francesca sleeping by his side on an Iraqi issue blanket, her arm draped across Rotherhithe's chest.

"First light tomorrow," whispered Green." I had mine out when I was twenty and I lived to tell the tale." He patted the man reassuringly on the leg and wandered into the dark. His path took him to the opposite end of the monolith to the vast Leviathan that was the Abrams on its wheeled carriage. He trod carefully; he knew their little party had moved their sleeping quarters here to avoid the noise and light of the towing party. The last thing he wanted to do was to tread on a sleeping body.

"Hey, Mikey," the American's voice came softly out of the darkness. "Take a couple of steps to the right then come forward – unless you want to spoil William's night." Green realised that the Marine was looking at him through the night sight of his M16 and the thought unnerved him slightly. He headed slowly towards the American's voice until he bumped into him. Cagney's words were soft in Green's ear, "The Colonel's got first watch, he's on the Humvee, William second, you want third or last?"

"I'll do both," breathed Green. "You have a big day tomorrow operating and driving; I'll kip on the trip."

There was a pause as the Marine considered the offer until a female voice behind him said, "He will accept your kind offer, Sergeant, and," she added firmly, "I will let him sleep." *Don't believe it* thought Green as he carefully made his way to the Humvee to have a word with the Colonel before bedding down nearby.

Chapter 8

Despite the night being uneventful, Green slept fitfully and was almost pleased when William roused him for his watch. Taking his blankets with him he climbed onto the roof of the Humvee and scanned the perimeter of the camp with his Night Vision Goggles. Movement within the camp caught his eye. Concerned for a moment, he relaxed when he saw Spotty Dog wandering aimlessly. He had been banished from lying next to his mistress since a sleepy Cagney had discovered a cold nose where he expected a warm Philippa to be. Green gave a low whistle and the hound loped over, giving a noisy impression of Bambi on ice as it scrambled through the open door of the vehicle. The dog whined softly as it tried and failed to climb through the gunner's aperture to join Green on the roof.

"Quiet, you hairy, fat bastard," whispered Green urgently. The dog whined again so Green hauled it unceremoniously through the hole where it settled happily with its head on the Paratrooper's leg. Green smiled wryly to himself as he heard Cagney snore in the distance. *I'm two centuries away from where I should be, the Boss has pulled the best looking woman in the Universe and I'm cuddling old Spotty Dog here.* The Humvee rocked slightly as Rashid climbed up to Green who wrapped his blanket around the skinny form. "Can't sleep, eh?" The next hour was spent fruitfully teaching Rashid a few English phrases until the little lad fell asleep.

As the first rays of the sun streaked the horizon, Cagney left Philippa's warmth. Picking up his rifle, he smiled as he saw the strange trio sleeping soundly on the roof of the Humvee. Spotty Dog raised its head at the approach of the American and gave a half-hearted growl. Unimpressed,

Cagney reached up and stroked its head whereupon the dog licked his hand.

"Make your goddamn mind up."

"He's not keen on sharing," yawned Green, stretching.

"And I'm not keen on cuddling hairy Limey hounds," retorted Cagney. Rashid lifted his head from the Dalmatian's flank and rubbed sleep from his eyes. Cagney ruffled his hair. "Hey, how're you doing, kid?"

Pleased with the attention which he had rarely enjoyed in his short life, Rashid smiled beatifically and said in a passable gangster drawl, "You dirty rat."

Cagney took a step backwards stunned, his mouth agape then his characteristic reserve left him and he put his head back and laughed until his ribs hurt, yanking the Para from the Humvee he put his arm around Green's neck and pulled his head towards him,

"You little Limey bastard, I could hear you chatting last night, now I know what you were saying." Green's muffled laughter erupted from Cagney's chest area; he dragged himself free, his chest heaving.

Rashid stood up, stretched, patted his empty belly and to no one in particular said, "Look at me, Ma, top of the World."

Green ran away leaving Cagney with tears rolling down his cheeks. He lifted the youngster down and at Rashid's urging performed the same task for Spotty Dog who seemed to have forgotten his earlier enmity. He felt Philippa's arms encircle him from behind,

"You are much too happy for a man who has just left my bed!" With much difficulty Cagney explained the humour of the movie references. Philippa's face showed the pleasure she felt, "I do believe you have finally learned how to laugh at yourself, James Cagney; you owe Sergeant Green a very large debt of gratitude."

Cagney dwelled for a long moment on the truth of Philippa's words. "I suppose I can be a bit of a stuffed shirt sometimes."

"Not to mention pompous," chided Philippa, "but a better and healthier man now I feel."

The pair walked to the beach in search of Lieutenant Rotherhithe.

Nicholas Rotherhithe had not moved since the night before; he lay dry-mouthed with fear, holding Francesca's hand tightly. Despite Cagney's assurances yesterday and the Marine's relaxed demeanour today, his apprehension was clear to all. Cagney and Philippa did their best to allay the young officer's trepidation but with little success.

The tension diminished noticeably when Green trotted up with two seamen in his wake carrying what looked like a table top. His noisy good humour was infectious. "Morning Nick, morning Frankie." He looked over at Philippa. "Hello, Pip."

She took two deliberate paces towards him and smiling sweetly put her lips to his ear.

Green blanched and swallowed hard. "Right err, Philippa it is then." To Cagney, "The Captain has donated his dining table to stick our patient on, I've dropped the ramps on the Tank Carrier so they're level and we can span them with the table. The towing crew are having a break 'til you're done." He indicated the tired seamen sprawled in the sand asleep.

"That's cool, Mikey, I'll show these guys how I want the table and if you can show the Lieutenant to the showers and give him a hand I'd be grateful," he paused, "I want him cleaner than he's ever been before in his life."

"No worries, Boss; can your man walk or is it a stretcher job?"

"I can walk, Sergeant," broke in Rotherhithe. Green reached down and clasped the man's hand, and with Francesca pulling his other hand they hauled him upright. The group set off on their short journey, Cagney and Philippa unencumbered in the lead followed slowly by Francesca and Rotherhithe who was helped by one of the seamen. The other seaman, Armitage, dawdled deliberately as he bent to pick up the table.

"Here, let me give you a hand," said Green helpfully.

Armitage jerked his head slightly and Green knelt pretending to examine the table. "The First Lieutenant has put a pair o' bad buggers in the lads who's a goin' to the fort, Casey and Jorgenson – don't turn your back on 'em if you knows what I means, Sir?"

Green smiled wolfishly. "Don't worry mate, if they so much as look at me the wrong way they're dead men. And thanks."

The pair rose to their feet, picked up the table top and marched in step to the Tank Carrier catching up with Cagney and Philippa as they reached it. Cagney had a pleased expression as he assessed the progress of the towing crew – the tractor unit was no longer in the shadow of the rock. "Another few yards and we can swing the main gun out to cover the bay."

"Must say I'm impressed," replied Green. "By the time we're back from our little jaunt they'll have pulled it clear and we will definitely be in business."

Leaving Cagney to build his makeshift operating theatre Green took Rotherhithe's arm. He had escorted him with the help of Francesca almost to the bunker entrance when the waddling puffing ship's surgeon caught them up and positioned himself in front of them, halting their progress.

"Piss off," said Green brusquely.

"I . . ." began the man.

"Sorry, my mistake," said Green his tone unchanged; the surgeon's face brightened. Green raised the muzzle of his AK until it was level with the surgeon's chest. "I meant piss off or I'll shoot you."

The sweating, portly little man scuttled away. "The Captain will hear of this," came breathlessly over his shoulder.

"Pompous little fart," spat Francesca.

Green could feel himself warming to the teenager. "You reckon I should have put a hole in him then Frankie?"

"Too much paperwork for Nicholas," she answered sweetly, "but if you really cared, Mikey, " Rotherhithe frowned at her familiarity, "you could shoot him as my birthday present." She leered at Green but could not hold the expression and burst into a fit of giggles. At last they reached the trapdoor; Rotherhithe looked askance at the ladder leading downwards.

"I've got a better idea." Green led them to the damaged building with the lift and they soon descended from the heat of the early morning to the coolness of the underground complex. Sending the lift back to the surface Green grabbed the wheelchair he had placed there earlier. Rotherhithe subsided into the seat with obvious relief and Green pushed him along the corridor to the shower room, a large communal area which would have been familiar to soldiers and sportsmen the world over. He switched on the showers – a line of six behind a wall and checked the operating gown still in its sterile wrapper that Cagney had taken from the pharmacy and left there. Green un-slung his rifle. "If you would like to wait outside, Miss, I'll help the Lieutenant to . . ."

"No, Sergeant, thank you but it is you who are leaving; I will attend to Nicholas' needs." The firmness in her voice reminded Green of her mother.

"Fine by me," he shrugged and walked down the corridor to the workshop where he carefully repacked his silencer. After around ten minutes he wandered back up the corridor to the shower room. Pushing the door ajar he was about to stick his head in when the two piles of clothes he saw, together with the sounds from within made him change his mind. *So that's what she meant when she said attending to his needs* he mused, chuckling as he closed the door.

"Something amusing you, Mikey?"

Green turned to find Philippa facing him. "Laughing at my memory," he explained, "forgotten the towels, do you know where they are?"

"I will help you look," she offered. "Just how long does it take a young man to wash himself?"

"He's in some pain," ventured Green lamely.

A touch of asperity crept into Philippa's voice. "I cannot find that daughter of mine; have you seen her?"

Green solemnly shook his head. "I think the laundry is this way." He strode down the corridor praying for Philippa to follow: to his infinite relief she did so.

"I'll give that girl a piece of my mind for disappearing when she is needed."

"You all ready up top?" asked Green.

"Almost," she replied, "Will you be long with the Lieutenant?"

"He'll be up as soon as he's dry." *And as soon as he's got his breath back,* he thought wryly. They found the laundry cupboard and Green returned to the shower room with his largely decorative towels. He turned as Philippa reached the top of the ladder and cast an appreciative eye over her behind. "Lucky sod," he grumbled. Green knocked on the shower room door and walked in. A barefoot Francesca approached him and kissed his cheek.

"Thank you, Sergeant, you are my hero."

He thrust a towel at her. "Do NOT go anywhere near your mother until your hair is dry and you . . ." he pointed accusingly at Rotherhithe, " . . . if her mum gets wind of this your balls will be going the same way as your appendix!" He pulled the wheelchair to Rotherhithe, "Get on." They left Francesca. It was the work of a few minutes to reach the Tank Transporter where Cagney and Philippa were gowned and masked, waiting by the makeshift operating table. "Hop up there," he prompted Rotherhithe. "If you have enough energy left," he added slyly. An apprehensive Rotherhithe lay on the newly scrubbed and disinfected table where Cagney slipped a cannula into a vein on the back of his hand followed by a syringe filled with morphine. He depressed the plunger slightly and the young officer slid into unconsciousness. Taping Rotherhithe's eyes closed, Cagney then swabbed his abdomen with disinfectant. Satisfied with his efforts Cagney then reached over to a dish filled with disinfectant, his fingers delved into the liquid emerging with a scalpel.

Shaking the drops off, he glanced at Philippa standing by Rotherhithe's head. "Remember what I told you yesterday, when his eyes stop moving he has moved to a level of unconsciousness where he will feel no pain and I can begin the procedure. Your job is to watch his eyes and tell me if they start to move, then I can administer more morphine and deepen the level of anaesthesia."

Philippa's brow was furrowed with concentration. "Yes, I understand and you want me to watch his breathing?"

"Please . . . keep his air way clear." Cagney searched for and found his incision point. "The base of the appendix should be under here." He placed the point of the scalpel on the lieutenant's skin drawing a minute amount of blood, drawing the blade across he opened the first layer of the abdominal wall. As the blood trickled down Rotherhithe's abdomen an incredulous voice said, "Ee bain't moved." Cagney's eyes flickered right; there was a semi circle of men three or four deep surrounding him about twenty feet away, Fairbrother was in the front circle. Putting aside his irritation at being watched, Cagney concentrated on the task in hand.

Philippa's voice louder than normal, nervous, "The Lieutenant's eyes moved."

Cagney depressed the morphine plunger and paused until Rotherhithe's eyeballs ceased their wandering. He pressed on, the scalpel sliding slowly and accurately. Cagney glanced up at Philippa. "I've made two incisions at right angles, this muscle. . . " he ran his finger along it, "is the internal oblique and I have cut it along its length . . ."

Cagney became aware of a commotion; the ship's surgeon had forced his way through the ranks of seamen and was remonstrating, bottle in hand with his Captain. Fairbrother lay a restraining arm on the Surgeon's arm but tearing it free the man strode over to Cagney and bellowed in his face, "You Sir! This is an abomination." Even through the surgical mask Cagney could smell the sickening stench of rotting teeth and rum. Fairbrother leaped forward as the Surgeon drew a deep breath to continue his drunken tirade.

"Mr. Squire," grated Fairbrother, "if you do not return to the ship this very moment I assure you that you will be hanging from the yardarm within the hour." Squire blanched and, mustering as much dignity as his drunkenness would allow, walked unsteadily back through the seamen. Fairbrother tapped the nearest man. "Make sure he does not return, use whatever means necessary." The seaman smiled happily, he had suffered in the past from Squire's drunken quackery and he was looking forward to a little retribution. Fairbrother spun slowly and glared at the audience, silently daring them, all avoided his angry eyes. He turned to address Cagney. "My apologies, Lieutenant, please continue."

"Thank you, Captain," said Cagney calmly and resumed his work. After another reminder from Philippa that Rotherhithe's anaesthesia needed to be deeper, Cagney administered more morphine then entered the peritoneum, but not before drawing Philippa's unwilling gaze to his actions.

Within a few short minutes the offending organ had been identified, tied off and removed. Cagney held it high for Philippa's benefit but the audience of seamen interpreted it as a triumphal gesture and greeted it with cheers and clapping. The men's reaction served to remind Cagney that Rotherhithe was a popular officer. The appendix was placed in a steel dish and the Marine proceeded with closing up his incisions, stitching slowly and carefully. Forty minutes later the young officer was pronounced "good as new". Rotherhithe recovered consciousness shortly afterwards and the contented audience dispersed.

After delivering his human cargo, Green stepped away and joined the growing band of onlookers. He kept half an eye on the bunker entrance and was unsurprised to see Francesca emerge, her hair flopping on to her shoulders in damp, tangled ringlets. Quickly checking that Philippa's attentions were engaged in her new duties, Green intercepted Francesca as she hurried to join the throng, her concern obvious.

He took her arm and with some reluctance she followed him. "Let's go to the beach, you don't want to see your boyfriend's insides do you?"

"Why not?" she countered, "he certainly knows me inside and out!"

Green's mouth dropped open at her brazen reply and reflected that she would probably have been pushing a pram on the council estate where he had spent his early years.

"Let's visit the ship until your hair dries," he encouraged, "no sense making waves," he added vaguely. They spent time looking at the ship and chatting to crew members until Francesca's patience expired and she stalked back to the camp with Green trailing unhappily behind her. At least her hair is dry he thought with relief and her formidable mother would not guess she had shared a shower with her young lover.

When they reached the Tank Transporter only Rotherhithe and Philippa remained. Cagney had disappeared underground leaving her to hold Rotherhithe's hand until the effects of the anaesthetic wore off. Rotherhithe was mumbling incoherently, his head and eyes moving constantly as he attempted to make sense of his situation. His wandering eyes found and held Francesca; she rushed to his side and he clasped her to him.

"Thank you, thank you," he mumbled, "I so did not wish to die a chaste man!" Philippa's mouth formed the perfect "O" and Green closed his eyes in silent entreaty. A few moments later he carefully opened just one to see mother and daughter tearfully laughing and hugging each other. He caught Philippa's eye, she shrugged and slowly walked over to join him. She put her arms around his neck and Green held her tight then pulled away slightly.

"I surely do not repel you, Mikey."

He shook his head, smiled sympathetically and handed her a tissue. "Not usually but you've got snot on your lip."

She wiped her face. "Oh, you so bring a woman back to Earth, Mikey Green!"

Green smiled sadly. "You're going to have to let go all over again – and permanently if you want to keep James. Your little girl grew up today and you handled it pretty well." Privately Green was of the opinion that Francesca had dipped a toe in those particular waters once or twice before but he diplomatically kept his thoughts to himself. Out of the corner of his eye Green saw Cagney striding to the Humvee. He had changed from his operating garb into his battledress and Green's confidence grew as he took in the helmet, M16 and determined expression of the Marine.

Philippa followed Green's eyes and relaxed her hold on him, taking half a step towards Cagney. The Paratrooper gripped her wrist, holding her back. "Keep your goodbyes low key; I want him good to go, not worrying about the girl he left behind!"

She gave him a brief nod and hurried to join the Marine. By the time she reached him, Fairbrother had assembled the members of his crew chosen for the assault team. At a word from him they climbed on to the rigging nets draped over the Humvee and busied themselves getting secure. Each man had a musket, some two, and all had a blade of some kind.

With a light heartedness she did not feel, Philippa squeezed Cagney's hand. "Come back soon, and look after the Sergeant." Without looking back she returned to Rotherhithe to supervise his recovery.

Cagney and Fairbrother walked round the Humvee checking each man's hold. Green joined them.

"Happy with our human baggage, Lieutenant?" asked Fairbrother.

"Looking good, Captain, we'll stop every hour to give your guys a break. I've stowed the keg of gunpowder and the chow your cook gave me, Mikey's put water in there. Hey, William…" The youth started, "…we fuelled up?"

"Yes, Zur, and three cans on top." He pointed to the roof of the vehicle then pulled a face. "It don't taste too good that diesel though." Cagney and Green exchanged looks and with difficulty kept their faces straight.

A seaman trotted up and handed a sword in its scabbard to Fairbrother who thanked and dismissed him. "The sabre you requested, Lieutenant; we looked long and hard in our armoury for it." He held it out and Cagney took the proffered weapon, sliding the blade halfway out and checking the edge.

"Sabre?" said Green doubtfully.

"The school I went to had fencing on the sports curriculum." Cagney grinned suddenly his face looking younger. "Never thought it would come in useful."

Green had a sudden thought. "Can we do a roll call, Sir? I'd like to put names to faces."

Fairbrother lined his men up including the First Mate who greeted Green with a wink. Green paid particular attention to Jorgenson and Casey when they spoke, but his face gave nothing away. Jorgenson, the Dane, was a huge brute of a man, his battered face the evidence of many a bar room brawl. Casey was a Londoner, barely out of his teens but with the look of a hardened killer. Green rated him the more dangerous of the pair. The men, at a word from their Captain, climbed aboard the Humvee.

"Are we ready, gentlemen?" asked Fairbrother. "I suggest the Sergeant drives, Lieutenant, you have had a trying start to your day. The Sergeant has briefed me on your quick firing weapon so I will man that whilst you rest." His tone brooked no argument so the three men clambered aboard, Cagney and Green in front with William and Colonel Trelawney in the rear with a seaman. Fairbrother stood idly swinging the big machine gun. Green started the powerful diesel, put his left hand down for the gear lever, forgetting it was on the right, and slowly pressed the gas pedal to oohs and aahs from his new passengers. The Humvee bumped down the rutted track past the end of the rock where the ship's company had assembled to give them a rousing send off. Green glanced at the cheering throng and their smiling faces, even Lieutenant Rotherhithe was there in his wheelchair flanked by Philippa and Francesca. He caught Green's eye and raised his hand in weak salute. Fairbrother, on impulse, cocked the Browning and fired a few rounds into the air, driving the crowd into a frenzy of applause.

He crouched down into the Humvee interior. "We will not fail these fine people," he thrust his arm between Cagney and Green, "my hand upon it gentlemen!" Green lifted his hand from the wheel and found it clasped by the Captain and Cagney. *He's right!* he thought exultantly, *we can't fail.*

Chapter 9

The dusty miles rolled under the Humvee's wheels. The sun blazed down with an unrelenting malevolence despite Green estimating it could be no more than nine o clock or so. The first hour passed; they had driven through several villages, the inhabitants of which fled at their approach.

Cagney shouted up to Fairbrother, "You guys ready for a break?"

Fairbrother's face appeared, dusty with red rimmed eyes. "Splendid idea, James."

Feeling somewhat remiss, Cagney handed the officer a pair of goggles from the dash as Green cut the engine and the Humvee coasted bumpily to a halt. Men leaped to the ground, cursing as their stiffened limbs refused to respond. At Cagney's prompting, William unloaded a can of water which was welcomed greedily by the crew. When five minutes had elapsed Fairbrother clapped his hands and they all boarded. The Captain had ordered his men to rotate their positions on the vehicle to ease the strain on their bodies and he joined Cagney in the front of the Humvee leaving Green to man the Browning. Fairbrother's hand appeared at Green's waist holding his borrowed goggles; Green thanked him briefly and put them on.

As the vehicle lumbered into motion he swung the machine gun so it pointed at Jorgenson's back. The Dane was clinging to the hood of the Humvee; he shifted his position and caught sight of the long perforated barrel aimed at him. Green stared unblinkingly at the man, wondering if he should fire a round and blame it on a misfire. He weighed his options as Jorgenson's eyes widened. It would remove a potentially dangerous problem but they had a small assault force and they might need the man's undoubted fighting ability soon. Jorgenson's shoulders sagged with relief as the barrel of the Browning moved to point skywards then he flinched as he saw Green's cold stare. *That little pantomime should give the sod something to occupy his mind*, speculated Green with grim relish.

The raiding party halted on three more occasions to drink and stretch. After the last stop Cagney drove more slowly and as they approached the crest of each new hill he halted the Humvee short of the crest with a man being sent to peer over. At an earlier stop there had been a conference when this tactic was decided upon. The fort was in a valley running towards the coast, and if the party wanted to keep their presence secret they must avoid driving over the brow of a hill to be in full view of the fort's occupants.

"Caution," as Fairbrother emphasised, "will be our watchword."

Their wary approach paid off. As they drove up yet another hill, Fairbrother sent a seaman ahead to reconnoitre carefully the other side of the escarpment. He ran back in a state of excitement, the words bubbling from his mouth. "It's here, Sir . . .the fort I mean." The seamen disembarked, chattering volubly.

Fairbrother quelled the noise with a raised hand. "Lieutenant, would you hide the vehicle in the copse there?" His outstretched hand indicated a small group of trees a hundred yards from the track. "You men follow him; I want branches and brush over it so it is not visible from this track." He pulled a telescope from his jacket with a flourish. "I shall see how the land lies."

Green looked askance at his light blue coat, shiny epaulettes and tricorne hat. "Hang on a minute, Captain, let's get you sorted."

"Sorted?" queried Fairbrother, a trifle crossly.

Green was stripping off his camouflage battledress jacket and had already woven leaves and vegetation into his helmet netting. "Put these on, Sir, and remember you'll be looking into the sun which might reflect on your lens and give us away."

117

"Hmm," Fairbrother's momentary irritation evaporated as he saw the sense of the Para's advice. He donned the proffered items then walked to a spot on higher ground. Dropping to his knees he crawled between two boulders and, after carefully shielding the lens with his hand, watched the fort for several minutes.

Sliding back from his observation post, Fairbrother regained his feet and rejoined his crew at the Humvee. Calling over Colonel Trelawney and the soldiers, he issued instructions. "Off you go in turn, gentlemen, to observe our objective, then we will meet and plot its downfall."

There was an air of suppressed excitement around the camp; any movement which might be seen from the track was forbidden. A constant watch was kept on the fort but the occupants seemed to exist in a state of listless inactivity. Each watcher noticed however that there were always two men on the firestep behind the battlements acting as sentries. Green kept an eye on Jorgenson and Casey; they stayed apart from the rest of the crew, or the crew shunned them, Green was not sure which.

In the last hour before darkness fell Fairbrother motioned the three soldiers to follow him and walked a short distance from his men. "Shall we finalise our plans gentlemen?"

The four men made themselves comfortable sitting on the sandy soil. "In essence my intentions are these; we will approach the fort shortly before dawn when the defenders will be sleeping their soundest and the sentries will hopefully be at their least attentive." Fairbrother paused. "Are we happy so far?" His audience voiced their agreement. "The sentries," he went on " must be killed or this whole operation will fail dismally and what is more, they must die silently for if the garrison is alerted our assault is doomed to failure. You two . . ." he pointed to Green and Cagney, ". . . have devices which allow you to see in the dark, so one of you shall be tasked to silence the sentries. Now! Which one of you has the greater expertise in these affairs?"

"It's got to be you, Mikey," Cagney said reluctantly.

"Not a problem, Boss, I'm not boasting but I am more experienced than you at this stuff."

Fairbrother gave him a searching look. "And the killing, Sergeant? I know you have a weapon which can kill silently, but can you get in close and take a man's life? . . . .I need to know you can or I will assign one of my own men."

Green returned the Captain's look with a steady gaze. "I don't enjoy killing, Sir, but I don't flinch from it when it's necessary." The firmness in Green's voice reassured Fairbrother.

Colonel Trelawney spoke up. "I can see a problem." Fairbrother gestured to him to continue. "The firestep is a yard wide; the Sergeant's rifle is powerful. If the sentry is shot from outside the walls, the bullet will carry him over the firestep to topple into the courtyard below . . . noisily."

"Thank you, Colonel," said Fairbrother, "and your thoughts on the Colonel's observation?"

"I need to get over the wall and inside, then make sure they go down quietly," said Green. "The seaward side has the most shadow so I'll go in from there . . ." he paused. ". . . The problem I'll have is when we're in the lee of the wall with the ladder; we won't know if the sentry is above us on that side of the fort . . . hmm." He sank into silence.

"Got it!" Cagney's words jerked the three men from their own thoughts; they all looked at him. "It's around two hundred and fifty yards to the fort from here and we can see clearly with the night sight where the sentries are. When they meet to shoot the breeze on the landward side I'll lift both arms up and if you're monitoring me with your NVG's you'll have a window when you can get the ladder up and scale the wall. Even if the sentries are looking at me they will see nothing unless they have infra red vision."

"Brilliant, Boss!" The Paratrooper's grin spread from ear to ear.

"Excellent, James," breathed Fairbrother, "and I shall not ask what infra red is. On to the next stage, and it is indeed an exercise in simplicity. Once the sentries are disposed of I will have my men push your vehicle over the brow of the hill and down the gradient until we are near the fort. It is then we place our keg of gunpowder by the gate and set the fuse. When the gates are blown apart you Lieutenant will start the . . .erm"

"Engine," prompted Cagney.

"Yes, quite, and we will drive in with lights afire and all guns blazing." Fairbrother drove his fist into his palm. "There are fifty men in there and we are many fewer; we must cut them down. Do not – and I emphasise NOT be squeamish or they will overwhelm us and I assure you they will show us no mercy whatsoever!" Fairbrother looked questioningly at the group. "Yes, Sergeant, what is it?" as he spotted the Englishman's raised finger.

"We should take some of the large rocks from here and place them around the charge; it will direct the blast inward to the gates."

"A well made point my boy, by George! I wish you could sail with me on all the voyages I command." In spite of himself the praise made the Para's chest swell with pride.

Cagney spoke up, "Do I take it, Sir, you will be operating the Browning?"

"Browning? . . . .oh, the quick firing weapon, yes I will, Lieutenant. Unless . . ." his eyes twinkled in the darkness ," . . . you would prefer me to drive your carriage?"

Just in time Cagney recognised the irony in Fairbrother's voice and answered only with a chuckle.

"If there is nothing else, gentlemen? I will brief my men."

"Can I choose my men for scaling the wall, please, Captain?" Without waiting for an answer Green said, "I'd like William and Casey."

A note of displeasure crept into Fairbrother's voice. "Ah Casey, our fugitive from the gallows; a very useful man with a knife I believe. You may have him. Sergeant.

But will I bring him back? was the thought uppermost in Green's mind. Aloud he said, "A saint is no use to me, Sir; I'll take your gaolbird."

"Quite, quite," murmured Fairbrother soothingly. He rose to his feet and joined his men. Presently the three soldiers could hear his calm, authoritative voice as he briefed them. Green took the opportunity to bring Cagney, William and the Colonel up to speed on the doubts he harboured over Jorgenson and Casey. He admitted to them both that he had almost shot Jorgenson with the Browning and blamed it on a misfire.

The Colonel made them laugh with his typically British understatement when he blandly said, "You're not keen on the chap then?"

In accordance with Fairbrother's orders the raiding party tried to get some rest until the time came for the assault. Most were too keyed up to sleep and just lay quietly. Green lay in the sandy hollow he had scooped out for himself; his helmet was by his side and his head rested on a rolled blanket. He tugged at his flak jacket and adjusted it to an almost comfortable position; he considered taking it off but instead resigned himself to a little discomfort. Sleep eluded him as he listened to the sounds of the night. The occasional noise of a sleeper intruded but always in the background were the clickings and whirrings of insects and the distant cough of an unknown animal. He drifted off into an uneasy slumber to be woken what seemed a few short minutes later by Cagney shaking him.

"Time to saddle up, soldier."

The pale moonlight revealed William standing behind the Marine, a short bow and quiver of arrows slung over his shoulder.

Green shambled sleepily to his feet and rubbed his eyes clear of debris as Cagney returned to the Humvee. "You ready to rock, William?"

"Just show me the bad guys, Boss."

Green shook his head sadly. "Too much American TV," he grumbled. William looked blank.

"Blame me," chuckled Cagney emerging from the gloom with Casey near. Green's nostrils reacted to the man's rank aroma of stale sweat, he could smell something else too – fear, it was all around him. Men were making unfunny jokes with their mess mates and constantly fiddling with their weapons. With a start he realised some of the fear he was smelling was his own. He concentrated on his own preparations and felt his apprehension ebb slightly. After filling his pockets with magazines and placing his water bottle on the ground he jumped twice on the spot – nothing rattled.

"Now, you two," he ordered. William's arrows fell out and Casey's musket balls rattled. "Stuff some rag in there and try again." Green tried to keep the edge from his voice, unwilling to reveal his own anxiety. The men jumped again, this time silently. "Good, go fetch the ladder, we're off in a minute".

Green felt Cagney's presence in the gloom. "How're you doing, Mikey?"

"Pretty OK," Green responded.

Cagney moved close. "Don't take any chances with Casey; use this sooner rather than later." He pressed a Marine issue combat knife into Green's hand; the Paratrooper slid the knife with its sheath into his pocket.

Green licked his lips; the burnt cork he had darkened his face with tasted acrid. He paced restlessly, impatient to start the mission. The ladder and his men had arrived and Green tapped his foot as he waited for Fairbrother to give him the nod.

As if on cue the Naval Officer appeared at his side and shook his hand. "Good luck Sergeant; our ultimate success lies in your very capable hands."

Cagney gripped his arm. "Be safe, Mikey."

Green tried to put his senses on high alert. His small crew waited, ladder at their feet. "Right you two, you know the score – we head to the beach from here. We can't be seen from the fort until we reach it. When we're there we keep to the shadows in the dunes and move only when the moon is clouded out."

The three men picked their way carefully through the rocks and scrubby vegetation. Green scanned the track with his night vision goggles before they crossed it. He did not expect any travellers at night but it was good field-craft to check.

They reached the beach in good time and rested in the shadows. Green raised his goggles to his eyes and checked the battlements for movement – nothing. Quietly he urged his troops onward when a passing cloud dimmed the weak moonlight. They paused as the cloud drifted on, revealing the moon. They were less than fifty yards from the walls. Green lowered the goggles and yard by yard scrutinised his target area, the seaward side of the fort. There was a jetty which ran the length of the wall, it looked paved and about three yards wide. After what seemed like hours, more cloud covered the moon. Green surveyed the battlements again and saw nothing, no movement and no sentries though from his low angle they could be there and still not be seen. He turned, traversing the NVG's up the hill seeking Cagney. Back and forth he swung them in a slow methodical arc, *ah, there he was*, he could tell it was the Marine by the shape of his helmet and the outline of his M16 at his shoulder. Another, shorter figure was beside him, *makes sense* thought Green. Cagney could watch whilst the other man signalled. The figure had his arms by his sides so the sentry on the wall must be too close to their scaling point.

Green lowered the goggles and blinked; he raised them again, *was there movement? Yes!* The man next to Cagney was waving his arms; he had an oddly shaped head which after a moment Green deduced was Fairbrother's tricorne hat. Green tapped both men. "Let's go."

They rose from the shadows and trotted up the sloping beach until they were walking on rock. Green slowed deliberately, they could not afford to stumble and alert the sentries. Though his senses screamed out for speed he again slowed his pace until eventually they stood in the lee of the wall. The three men buried themselves in the shadows at its base. Leaving them, Green sidled towards the corner of the fort then looked round searching for the Marine. After what seemed an age he finally focussed on him. The tall figure was watching through the night-sight of his M16; Green traversed right, Fairbrother was motionless his arms held rigidly by his side. Green's nose twitched; the rich aroma of pipe tobacco wafted by him. Slowly, very slowly he lowered his goggles to the limit of the strap around his neck until they rested against his chest. Without moving his feet he craned his head backwards so he could see the battlements at the top of the wall. There was a scrape from behind him; his head movement had caused his AK to touch the wall. To Green's tortured nerve endings it sounded deafening.

Holding his breath and feeling sure the unseen smoker could hear his heart pounding, Green inclined his shoulders away from the wall then with infinite care un-slung his assault rifle and cradled it in his hands. He looked up, not daring to release one hand from the rifle to use his goggles. His eyes registered a shape jutting from the embrasure which was at odds with the uniformity of the castellations. Green stared hard, trying to make sense of the scene in the gloom. The wind came to his aid, puffing and tugging an unwilling cloud from the moon's face. Suddenly he understood; the odd shape was the man's hand holding his pipe, the indistinct shape to the left must be the sentry himself. Green knew he had to make a decision, should he shoot the sentry now – he knew the bullet would fly almost vertically and not throw the man into the courtyard, but it was a difficult shot, the target was only twenty feet away but the bulbous silencer made it impossible to use the AK's sights. Green had just made the decision to wait until the sentry moved away when the figure leaned through the battlements and cleared his throat preparing to spit. *Now or never!* Thought Green and after sliding the catch from safe to fire aimed and shot in one movement. The muted cough and metallic clack of the AK's bolt were drowned by the lapping of the water against the jetty. Green hugged the wall again, heart pounding wildly. There was no sound from above and a quick glance revealed no change in the man's silhouette. Had he missed? How could the sentry not have felt the wind from the round as it passed him?

A slight rattle came from the cobbles at Green's feet; he cautiously looked down to see a minute red glow, it was the sentry's pipe. A persistent tapping sound entered Green's consciousness and he felt something touch his shoulder. He reached round and his fingers returned sticky – he sniffed and recognised the smell of blood. He looked upwards again; the sentry was slumped, his head and arm resting on the wall..

Swiftly Green walked the half dozen paces to his men. "He's dead; get the ladder up right by him." The men, quickly yet quietly, did as ordered and Green shinned up the ladder, leaving his rifle with William. The ladder squeaked a little but that could not be helped. Resting his goggles on the dead man's shoulder he searched anxiously for the other sentry; there was no sign of him on the wall opposite where the landward gate was. Frantically Green swivelled his head left – nothing again.

The voice came out of the darkness, near. "You're a quiet me old shipmate; can ee see a mermaid out there?" Green tried to answer - even a grunt would have allayed the man's suspicions but Green's throat was dry with fear and all that emerged was a croak. Green crouched down as the man approached, laughing quietly. He almost panicked, he had no weapon, he had left his rifle with William. In a flash of inspiration he remembered Cagney's knife. He slid his hand into his pants pocket – there it was, tucked behind a magazine. His fingers closed on it as the sentry's silhouette appeared above him; he tried to ease it out but it had snagged on the magazine. Desperately he tried to drag it free, the ladder swaying ominously, until with a jerk both knife and magazine emerged together, the magazine spiralled to the cobbles to land with a clatter. The noise finally aroused the sentry's suspicions and he was in the act of un-slinging his musket when Green sprang, wrapping his left arm around the man's head whilst his right reached up with Cagney's knife. The man's cry of alarm was choked off as the knife found its target. Green fell back as his scrabbling feet sought the ladder's rungs; his foot caught it and pushed the ladder in a silent arc until it fell with a small splash into the water. Clinging to the dying man, Green attempted to climb over him to grab a handhold on the wall; he had almost succeeded when his efforts pulled the man over the parapet to impact on the jetty with a dull thud. Green's flailing hand miraculously found a rope to cling on to and he grabbed it thankfully. Too late he realised it was the first sentry's pigtail and as he swung from it the blood and gore from the man's ruined head made it slip from his fingers and he fell.

Green's training as a paratrooper had been thorough and painstaking so it was second nature to bend his legs slightly to take the sting from his descent. He was not to land on level ground, however; his left leg landed on the dead pirate pitching him to his right and smashing his knee into one of the jetty's cobblestones. The cry of agony died on his lips as he lay still hugging the injury and breathing heavily.

"Are you alright, Sir?" William whispered hoarsely in his ear. Green gritted his teeth; wave after wave of shooting pain came from his knee,

"Help me up, Will, my leg's bust." Casey stood watching in the gloom. "You, too!" The two men hauled Green upright on to his good leg, tentatively he straightened his right leg then gingerly put some weight on it. Green hissed from the pain and for one awful moment thought the nausea was going to make him faint. William caught him as he swayed. Several deep breaths later Green was back in control and he took a couple of cautious steps. Painful but do-able he thought grimly. He reached out to William and retrieved his rifle. "Find the ladder; we're going in – and be quick about it we're running out of time!" Green hobbled to the wall and leaned against it, resting his damaged leg whilst his men searched for the missing ladder. Time passed on leaden wings as Green, fuming with frustration, waited.

William appeared from the shadows. "Got it, Sir; it was in the drink."

"Good lad," he whispered; he could barely speak his throat was so dry. "Get it against the wall then sprint up the hill and tell our gang that the sentries are done for and we're good to go." The ladder positioned, William set off at a steady trot.

Green turned to Casey. "Steady the ladder, when I'm over the wall follow me." Awkwardly Green placed his feet on the rungs; by pushing himself upwards with his good leg and dragging his injured limb he laboriously made his way to peer over the parapet. William had placed the ladder in the next embrasure to the dead pirate. Cautiously he raised his goggles and surveyed the courtyard below him. The embers of a dying fire made them white out for a few seconds but not before he had been able to discern the sleeping figures around it, about twelve to fifteen he estimated. As he watched one figure rolled over then lay quiet. He moved the goggles away from his eyes to obtain a truer measure of the darkness; without the artificial aid the gloom was stifling. Glancing up he saw masses of cloud covering the moon and heaved himself over the parapet. He crouched silently on the firestep waiting for any kind of reaction from below to indicate he had been seen; the occasional snore and grunt reassured him that all was well.

A light scrabbling sound and gentle thud from behind him confirmed Casey's arrival; he pulled the man close wondering as he did so when the man last had a bath? *Probably never,* he told himself. Quickly he gave the man his orders, "Stand up and walk slowly round to the far wall, they'll be expecting someone up there so don't worry if you're seen, when you're there stretch your arms up as if you're yawning." When Casey had confirmed his orders Green sent him on his way, walking slowly as instructed like a bored sentry would. Green kept a wary eye on the sleepers below but none moved. He assumed the rest of the garrison were in the rooms underneath them which were

127

part of the fort's design on this the seaward side of it. That aspect pleased Green; when the Humvee burst through the gate their enemies would be in front of them not to the side and definitely not above, thought Green, for the stairs that gave access to the battlements were on the landward side and anyone who wanted to reach the battlements via those stairs would meet Sergeant Mikey Green and that would be the end of the matter.

Green rose stiffly to his feet and removed his helmet – *pirates don't wear helmets* he reminded himself. He walked slowly to meet up with Casey who he could just see leaning idly against one of the castellations. Slipping his AK from its slung position on his shoulder he held it across his chest, the distinctive magazine and bulbous silencer were too different from the outline of a musket and would have given him away even in this murk. The pain from his injury had diminished a little but still caused the Para to grit his teeth as he tried to walk as normally as possible. Every few steps he glanced in as casual manner as possible at the sleeping figures. None were stirring – so far, he worried. Green looked East at the horizon; was that the first glimmer of dawn the other side of the hills? He hurried, his painful old man gait with its dragging foot scraping causing more noise than he liked. Eventually he made it to where Casey was standing.

"They be coming," Casey murmured. Green stared over the battlements and saw the Humvee, engine off, cruising to a halt as it left the slope and encountered level ground. The scene darkened as clouds drifted and Green raised his goggles. The crew were pushing the Humvee towards the side of the fort; they were still around a hundred yards away but Green nevertheless could hear the squeaking of the suspension as the seamen laboured to move it closer. Concentrating hard, he could see they were making good progress. His senses sharply attuned, Green heard another noise – a scraping. He swung round with difficulty on his one good leg to survey the courtyard.

He felt Casey's hand on his arm. "It be William, Sir." Casey's other hand was pointing urgently downwards at the base of the wall outside. Puzzled, Green peered over to be confronted by the grinning face of William who had carried the ladder round and climbed up to them.

Bending his face close to William's Green spoke softly, "Get back to the Captain and tell him not to come any closer; they're too noisy and they'll wake the buggers." He jerked his thumb over his shoulder. "Tell him to blow the gates as soon as he can." The youth nodded and slid down the ladder. Green watched him run to the Humvee. Cagney's head snapped up and Green could see him nodding rapidly, looking straight at Green he put his thumb up. The Humvee was now fifty yards away, facing the side wall of the fort away from the gate. Men scurried from the vehicle, all of them laden. Two seamen carried the keg of gunpowder whilst the others struggled with rocks of varying sizes. Colonel Trelawney stood apart looking carefully around using the night sight of his M16.

Green dragged his eyes away from the scene; he needed all to remain quiet in the courtyard. Even now if the garrison was alerted it could all end in disaster for the assault force. He groaned inwardly when a dull clunk came from the gate as a careless seaman from the Endeavour dumped his load. Green cursed but the sleepers below seemed oblivious. He stared balefully at the figures wrapped in blankets, knowing that he dare not use his NVG's as his silhouette would have been at odds with the sentry's normal outline. He stared harder then felt a touch on his arm to alert him. One man had shrugged off his blanket and shambled sleepily to the sidewall of the fort giving the pair a casual wave. The man stood close to the wall and Green could hear a trickling noise.

Green spoke softly to himself, "That's it, son; you have a leak and go back to bed like a good little pirate." The man yawned hugely, pleasing the Para; *we've got away with it,* he thought jubilantly. A loud scraping noise came from the gate and the man cocked his head in a listening attitude.

"Just forget it," was Green's low urgent whisper to himself. "It's only a rat." The pirate's body language relaxed as though convinced by the Para's whispered urgings and had almost reached his bedroll when another louder noise emanated from the gate. Curiosity overcame his lethargy and he walked closer to the gate and stood silently listening. Green tried to maintain his bored posture, staring aimlessly into space. His silent prayers for the raiding party to be quiet seemed to have been answered for the wakened sleeper started to amble back to his bed. Almost as an afterthought he glanced up at the "sentries" and waved. At that moment the cloud drifted away from the moon and a shaft of light illuminated the Para with his assault rifle, the curved magazine a stark contrast to a much longer one shot musket.

The pirate paused for a moment, his befuddled senses not quite taking in the scene. His slow reactions were his undoing. As Green fired from the waist the man spun and went down on one knee. He looked up at Green his face wreathed in bafflement. All was quiet, the AK's muted cough and clack as the bolt returned had not been heard. The kneeling man opened his mouth so Green, this time with the AK at his shoulder shot him again before he could shout. Though the pirate subsided soundlessly to the sandy soil, it did not matter. Green's luck had run out; the second shot caused his makeshift silencer to burst at its seams and the Russian rifle emitted its customary bark. Sleeping figures awoke and reached for the weapons that were never far away from such men. Green calmly unscrewed the now useless silencer and with a tidiness born of training slipped it into his jacket pocket. He would have crouched into a firing position but his knee had stiffened too much, so Green leaned back against the parapet and fired short bursts into the milling figures below. One pirate, braver or perhaps more fortunate than his shipmates, almost made it up the stone stairs to the firestep before Casey thrust a bayonet into him then booted him back down the stairs with a savage kick.

As he changed a magazine, Green became acutely aware of musket balls slapping the wall behind him; one even plucked at his sleeve. Casey lay prone on the firestep either dead *or sensible enough to keep his head down* thought Green whimsically. The magazine went home and Green cocked the AK, ducking as a ball whined past his ear he forced his injured leg forward and slid down the wall so he sat on the firestep. His questing hand found his helmet by his side and he quickly slipped it on. Sliding down as low as he could he fired two or three round bursts at the musket flashes that were coming from the windows and doors of the buildings that hugged the sea facing wall.

Green knew his situation was becoming desperate; if the fort's defenders charged across the courtyard and swarmed up the steps as he was changing magazines they were dead men. With an insouciance he definitely did not feel he shouted to Casey, "Can you see the cavalry on the horiz . . .?"

The explosion at the gate drew the breath from Green's lungs and deafened him. The air filled with debris and dust, Green thought wildly, *I'm deaf and blind and don't even know if the bad guys are coming for me, my senses are so shot away.* A roaring in his ears complemented by bright lights forced their way into Green's confused world. The staccato thudding of the Browning added to the cacophony and confirmed the arrival of the cavalry in the shape of the Humvee and its motley crew.

Struggling to his feet, Green gave Casey a boot in the ribs. "Get up you little tosser." He looked down at their small assault force; Cagney was standing by the vehicle, his M16 targeting the muzzle flashes. Fairbrother on the Browning was methodically moving the big machine gun from building to building causing death and destruction in an orderly and regular manner. The pirate's return fire was faltering and Green felt confident this particular skirmish was nearly over. He ran a practised eye over the raiding party; one seaman lay unmoving, the Colonel, despite having one arm, was aiming and shooting from a kneeling

131

position. Whenever there was a pocket of resistance Fairbrother turned the Browning's power onto it. The Endeavour's seamen were adding to the combined firepower with their muskets. Green peered closer, searching for Jorgenson amongst the shooters; the big man was not visible.

Green's eyes flicked to and fro searching for the Dane; behind him Casey's eyes followed his movements glittering with a mixture of hate and avarice. The First Lieutenant had promised him much if Green did not return and he had not forgotten the boot in the ribs Green had just given him. Green lifted his NVG's from the battlements behind him and scanned the shadows in the gate area. *There!* Jorgenson was crouched by the smashed gate some distance to the rear of the Humvee; Green thought he saw some movement behind the Dane but could not be sure. He focussed again on Jorgenson who had lifted a musket to his shoulder and was carefully taking aim. A baffled Green swung with his goggles to see what the Dane's target was and thrust them impatiently to one side as they whited out from the glare of the Humvee's headlights. His own Mk one eyeball however could see that there was only one possible target; with dread in his heart he saw that it was the American.

Green heaved his rifle round but even as he did so he knew he was too late as the flint descended into the pan of Jorgenson's musket with a brief flare. He had not taken account of William though, for even in the act of firing the sprinting form of the youngster had driven his shoulder into the bigger man forcing the musket up and the ball to fly wide. Green's jubilation was short lived; the errant musket ball had hit Fairbrother who slumped tiredly into the Humvee, pulling the butt of the Browning down with him, leaving the silent weapon pointing impotently at the sky. A raging Jorgenson regained his feet and stood over William who lay winded on the sandy earth, his bow and quiver of arrows strewn next to him. The Dane lifted his musket to club William who raised his arm defensively, then the fury on Jorgenson's face turned to a look of surprise as a single

132

shot from Green entered his back. The musket fell from his nerveless fingers and he crashed to the ground. William's grateful eyes flashed upwards to his benefactor, who, thanks to a combination of his injury and the recoil of his rifle, had stumbled backwards and now sat on an embrasure.

William watched aghast as Casey, with a feral snarl, drove his bayonet into Green's chest, pushing him over the wall. Hypnotised by the scene, William saw Green's dying act was to fire his rifle; the flames from the muzzle ended at Casey's belly catapulting the man into the courtyard where he lay still, his lank hair dark against the sand. Cagney's first inkling of the drama behind him was when the Browning ceased its angry bark. In fact the little battlefield was quiet − too quiet thought Cagney with alarm. The barrel of the big machine gun was pointing at the moon; Fairbrother was hanging from it, his sleeve caught up by the cocking handle. Only muskets were firing now; Cagney could see Colonel Trelawney struggling to change a magazine, reminding him that his own needed changing. He fumbled in his pockets to find them empty. Cursing, he remembered his spare magazines were in the footwell of the Humvee and he took a step towards the vehicle to retrieve them − too late. He realised he had run out of time for the surviving pirates, emboldened by the cessation of automatic fire, had emerged from cover and were charging towards his small band howling with rage and frustration.

Cagney looked up, his eyes seeking Green; the battlements were empty. His men were looking expectantly at him for leadership. Anderson, the First Mate, his eyes wild and voice hoarse gasped, "Sir!"

Cagney knew he had to act very quickly or they were all dead men.

Chapter 10

As Green plummeted from the fort wall, his life saved from the bayonet thrust by his flak jacket, a voice inside him said *this is going to hurt*. A large bush clinging to the outside wall was his saviour. Its harsh spiny branches cushioned the initial impact and then threw him to one side where his helmeted head crashed into the sandy soil. For long moments he lay unmoving, his senses scrambled by the severe blow. The noise of the battle on the other side of the wall penetrated the woolly edges of Green's mind although the concussion prevented him from gathering together the strands. An instinct within that wanted him to live shouted down all other inputs and forced Green to concentrate all his efforts into survival. Grunting with pain, he hauled himself to his feet and the injured animal that was Mikey Green staggered haltingly across the barren rocks to the foothills in the distance that offered a safe haven from the noise and violence.

Captain Giuseppe Scorponi stood on the deck of his ship the Scorpion. He spoke the name aloud to himself, "Scorpion." A seaman took a step towards him under the impression that his Captain was speaking to him; Scorponi's glare convinced him otherwise. "Scorpion," he murmured again. He had changed the name of the ship after he had captured her; it amused him to move the letters of his own name around to make a venomous creature that men feared. He tried to remember her original name but failed; it took an effort of will to remember his own name. "Giuseppe," he whispered. It had been thirty years since anyone had called him that. He recalled that day in the merchant's warehouse in Palermo where he had been bedding the owner's daughter – *Giancarla – yes that was her name.* Her father had caught them and young Giuseppe aged fifteen had killed him with his knife. A thrill ran through his corpulent body as he relived the moment. His mouth twitched, the nearest he ever got to a smile – the daughter had tried to scream so his long-bladed stiletto had done its bloody work with her too, but not before he had enjoyed taking her again. Long ago pleasures, he sighed to himself and pleasures that had forced him to flee Sicily to a life at sea where his intelligence and hard work brought him steady promotion until at twenty five he was First Mate of a merchantman. He had promoted himself to captain by the expedient of slitting the officers' throats as they lay sleeping off the evening's wine. Twenty years ago he mused; twenty years of pirating and smuggling which had made him a very rich man – riches which he meant to enjoy and to do that he needed to survive, which he very nearly had not when they had been surprised by the British frigate. Scorponi knew it was as much luck as his own seamanship which had crippled the frigate. The British and to a lesser extent the Dutch were drawing a noose around his activities now they had driven the Portuguese from the area. He bellowed an order to clap on more sail; the sails were new and drew well. Sailors fearful of his wrath, *and rightly so* Scorponi thought with a smirk, sprang into action. He watched the seamen scrambling like so many monkeys, scurrying up the rigging to set more sail. The professional sailor within Scorponi assessed their skills; as good as the accursed Royal Navy he opined silently.

He ran an eye over the new rigging the small shipyard on the Persian side of the Arabian Sea had provided – provided at a price, he thought with a scowl. Still, he could afford it, though the work had cost almost all of his ready cash including providing a brothel for his men to stop them deserting. Their journey to the shipyard had taken only one day thanks to the prevailing winds which would have hindered the Anastasia with her small prize crew and the work less than twelve hours. He had not used the brothel himself; no, he breathed, he had promised himself the

135

pleasure of the two English women. His spies had informed him they were mother and daughter and the surge in his loins would not be denied much longer when the Scorpion had berthed at her destination – the fort. The Anastasia would be waiting for him there with the blond daughter fresh and untouched; for the men knew they would pay with their lives and slowly if their captain were denied his prize. Scorponi debated his options, as the ship sailed onwards; he would abandon the fort, take his treasure aboard along with the garrison. The Anastasia would fetch a pretty penny after he had put a larger prize crew aboard and sailed her to a port where he knew he could sell her.

The aching throb from his hand reminded him he had unfinished business; the middle finger was missing, smashed off by a bullet from the strangely dressed men. He held his damaged hand up to the light; it was splashed with black where he had cauterized it by dipping it in molten tar – the memory of that agony fuelled his desire for revenge. The bullet that had caused the injury resided in Scorponi's pocket; it was a 5.56 millimetre round from Cagney's M16. After it had smashed his finger it had killed the helmsman – in fact a curious Scorponi had dug it from the man's chest before he had breathed his last. Scorponi's fingers stroked the largely undamaged round and he marvelled that something so small could kill and be accurate at such a range. Fishermen from a village along the coast from the frigate had sailed across the Arabian Sea informing Scorponi of its plight to be rewarded handsomely. Scorponi sighed with pleasure; he knew ships and before the British frigate was seaworthy he intended to sail into its bay and destroy her along with everyone there – no, not everyone, he mused, the tall Englishwoman, the girl's mother, he would save her. His mood was restored by the prospect and his face twitched with the rictus of his smile.

Scorponi turned full circle slowly, letting his eyes rest for a moment on each member of the crew. Without exception they avoided his stare. They were in a subdued mood he thought with satisfaction as he focussed on the sailmaker sitting on the foc'sle repairing old sails; the man would never speak again, Scorponi had personally cut out his tongue as a punishment for his attempted desertion and the crew were fearful of his continuing anger. The fool had hid in the dockyard hoping the Scorpion would sail without him but Scorponi knew all the hiding places and the fool losing his tongue served as a reminder to the rest of the crew that their captain was as cunning as he was ruthless.

"Land ho!" The cry from the crows' nest lookout interrupted his thoughts and the delicious feeling of anticipation grew within him. He paced the deck impatiently his pig-like eyes unblinking in their ferocity whenever they alighted on a seaman he considered to be slacking. Every few minutes he barked questions at the lookout, "Can you see the fort; are there sails?" until after twenty minutes the terrified man hailed the deck,

"Fort in sight."

"Can you see masts?" roared Scorponi, his anger spilling over when the lookout replied in the negative. He stamped round the deck cuffing and kicking all within reach; the men knew all to well what the consequences might be for a miscast glance. The Scorpion entered the fort's bay; there was no sign of the Anastasia. Scorponi levelled his telescope at the fort's walls and hissed – death had visited this place and left its mark.

Cagney's training took over; he knew all the modern weapons were out of action and his brain worked at lightning pace. "Colonel, take William, get on the battlements." The old warrior trotted up the stairs with William in his wake who picked up a musket from a dead seaman without breaking stride.

Cagney slid his sabre from its scabbard, raised it above his head and sprinted towards the pirates, screaming as he ran, "With me, Endeavours!" The frigate's seamen, their numbers depleted by four, charged after him with First Mate Anderson in the van. Cagney met his first pirate head on; he was a small man carrying a musket tipped with a long bayonet. Cagney eased inside the long weapon and smashed the sabre's hand guard into the man's face leaving it a bloody mess. He switched his attention to the next man who was wielding a cutlass. Cagney turned the cumbersome weapon aside with an effortless wrist movement – all the lessons from his school's fencing academy returning. The sabre was much heavier than the sword he had held at school but now he was a bigger, stronger man and the blade felt like a toy as he slashed the man across his neck. "Have that, you bounder!" he cried triumphantly and then to the great surprise of friend and foe alike he burst out laughing. "Goddamn! What am I saying? Bounder!" He punctuated his words with thrusts and slashes, driving his opponents back. He laughed again. "I am not a Limey; I am a Marine! Lieutenant James Cagney United States Marine Corps and you guys are going down."

Despite his outward ebullience Cagney knew the fight was not going well. He, Anderson and the few surviving seamen were fighting back to back surrounded by, he estimated, twenty pirates who saw victory within their grasp. An Endeavour seaman collapsed to the sand, a bayonet jutting from his chest; his assailant died by Cagney's blade as he desperately tried to withdraw the long blade. *This is only going to end one way* thought Cagney frantically as he parried first a bayonet then a cutlass away from his body. Cagney's strength was ebbing as the pirates sensed their advantage and pressed home their attacks with renewed vigour, another of the Endeavour's seamen went down and the pirates raised a cheer. The echoes of their voices had not ended before there was a crack and then another; two pirates fell to the earth, one screaming. Cagney risked a glance over his shoulder; Colonel Trelawney had cleared his rifle's jam and was coolly aiming and killing individual pirates. Three pirates spotted the new danger and sprinted to the battlement steps; only two reached the foot as the Colonel cut the third man down. The two survivors scrambled halfway up before they were met by a musket-wielding William who despite his smaller stature had the advantage of standing higher up the steps. He thrust his bayonet into the nearer man and tried to withdraw it as the suction held it firm. Colonel Trelawney was screaming at him to twist the blade in order to free it but before he could act the second pirate on a lower step slashed William's arm with the tip of his cutlass. A panicked William dropped his musket and fell back as the pirate pushed aside his dying comrade to reach the prostrate lad only to be wafted back as though by a giant hand as Trelawney put a round into him, realising even as he did so that the magazine had emptied.

The old soldier that was Colonel Trelawney did not even glance at the melee of whirling steel and screaming men in the courtyard below as he focussed his efforts on changing the magazine in his M16. He gripped the stock firmly between his knees and slipped in a fresh magazine. William scrambled up to him and cocked the weapon for the older man as Sergeant Green had showed him then stood in front of the taller officer. The Colonel rested the rifle on William's shoulder and calmly began killing Cagney's opponents. Lifting his sabre for yet another desperate parry, Cagney did not even have breath for screaming abuse at the pockmarked giant trying to impale him on a bayonet. He thrust the musket to one side, only to find the man let it drop from his fingers and raised his hands. Astonished, Cagney took a step backwards fearing a ruse but no, the pirates were surrendering, throwing their weapons to the sandy soil. Cagney kept his sword aloft unwilling to believe what was happening; blood and gore trickled from the blade down his forearm and dripped from his elbow. He risked another glimpse over his shoulder to see Colonel Trelawney his face impassive gazing down the barrel of his rifle at the vanquished men. Cagney tried to speak but his voice was barely a croak from the constant screaming. First Mate Anderson and the Endeavours left standing herded the dozen pirates into the corner of the courtyard where they left them sitting.

Cagney strode to the Humvee and gently removed Fairbrother's limp form. He cocked the Browning. "Mr Anderson!" The First Mate ran over. "Take over this gun and if any of them move, kill them." Cagney turned as though to move away then turned back; with a bleak smile he placed his hand on Anderson's shoulder and spoke softly, "I will need these men if we are to capture the Anastasia, so don't get an itchy trigger finger." Anderson gave a nod and wondered how the Marine had divined his intentions. After retrieving his discarded M16 together with his spare magazines the tall American strode into the centre of the courtyard. He stood still then swivelled his head taking stock of the situation. They had done well, he thought, as he surveyed his bloody and exhausted troops. They too were elated and noisily congratulated each other as they relived the battle. Their red-rimmed eyes and sweat-streaked, blackened faces emphasised the strain. Cagney counted up, shocked at the number of casualties. With a rush of horror he suddenly realised that his friend was missing, he looked round seeking William. He bellowed the lad's name and William who was gathering up captured weapons trotted wearily to him. "Where is Sergeant Green?" he demanded.

William's tearful face told Cagney what he wanted to know even before he spoke. "Mikey's dead, Sir, Casey stuck a bayonet in him an' ee went over the wall." The blood drained from Cagney's face and he put a hand on the Humvee to steady himself.

Anderson glancing down spoke quietly, "Straighten up, Sir; the lads be looking to you for leadership."

With an effort Cagney gathered his senses together. Calmly he said, "Take two men, William, and bring the Sergeant's body in here." William walked towards the group of Endeavours and spoke earnestly to them; two seamen detached themselves from the group and accompanied William to the gate. One of them kicked the body of Casey as he passed and spat on it; the body groaned. Walking over to the renegade seaman, Cagney gazed down at him.

Casey's eyes fluttered open to see Cagney above him, his stare pitiless. "Water."

Cagney knelt by the man, unscrewing his canteen as he did so; he splashed a little on the man's lips. "Well?" he asked softly.

"I'm dyin,'" croaked Casey. Cagney looked at the man's exposed intestines already black with flies and nodded. "It was the first Lieutenant," said Casey weakly. "He wanted you and the Sergeant dead; said he'd make me an' Jorgy rich men. Ee wanted your rifles . . ." the dying man coughed, blood spraying and guttering from his mouth. Casey drew a gargling breath, "Ee wanted your woman too. . ." he gave a gurgling cough and giggled. "Ee's goin ter be unluck . . ." the head lolled as his blood soaked into the sand. Cagney stood and looked at Anderson who had placed a seaman on the Browning then walked over.

"I heard that, Sir, but it won't make no difference, Mr Caruthers has too much influence."

Cagney looked stonily at the First Mate and patted his M16. "His influence won't stop this, will it, Mr Anderson?"

Anderson chuckled dryly. "No, Sir, I reckon you be right there."

The two men walked towards the Humvee where Cagney examined Fairbrother, exploring his bloody head after washing his hands.

"How is he?" murmured Anderson,

"Not real good," answered Cagney as he inserted a saline drip into Fairbrother's arm. "Can you rig up an awning to keep the sun from him please?"

Pounding feet interrupted the men as William ran towards them and halted breathless. "Sir, Sir, it be the Sergeant, ee's not there . . ." he paused winded. "No body, Sir," an' no blood," he added significantly.

"Look after the shop, Mr Anderson," ordered Cagney and followed William. The young man was hopping from foot to foot with impatience and had only just stopped short of tugging Cagney's sleeve. Despite his eagerness to find out what had happened to his friend, Cagney adopted a relaxed demeanour as he ambled after William. These men were looking to him for leadership, as Anderson had reminded him, and officers in the United States Marine Corps were supposed to look cool under stress – *even if they did not feel it.*

They halted outside the walls. William pointed upwards where Cagney could see the strap from Green's NVG's on the battlements. "Ee fell from there, Sir."

Cagney's eyes followed a vertical line downwards which ended in a large spiny bush; he took a step closer and examined it closely. "Not big enough to conceal a man," he thought aloud.

"An' no blood, Sir," added William.

Cagney peered again at the bush and saw something gleam within its spiny foliage. He crooked his finger at William and pointed. William carefully inserted his musket lengthened by his bayonet deep inside and after several attempts reached down, grasped an object and held it up for Cagney's scrutiny. "Mikey's silencer," he breathed, noting as he spoke that it was split. "And you're sure there's no blood on or under the bush?

William shook his head vehemently. "No, Sir, no blood nowhere." Mystified, Cagney peered at the ground for any kind of trail "Ground be too hard, Sir, for any tracks," volunteered William.

"I can see that!" snapped Cagney testily. William's face fell and Cagney put his hand on the young man's shoulder. "Sorry, William, I'm on edge. Mikey is my closest friend."

"Mine too," said William brightening, "an' I know he's alive."

Cagney looked dubious. "You saw him take a bayonet in the chest, William."

"I know he is," repeated the lad . . . "I just know"

Cagney stood still in the early morning sun frowning with concentration. "Let's have a look on the battlements," he said at length. William nodded eagerly and they walked back to the gate, now hanging off its hinges.

Cagney halted and faced William; he held his hand out to the lad who looked confused. "Take it" ordered Cagney and solemnly shook his hand.

"Well done today; if you hadn't held those pirates at bay whilst the Colonel reloaded we would all be dead now. Well done and thank you, William." Sensing the young man's embarrassment, Cagney slapped him on the back. Striding together they entered the gate and climbed the stairs to the battlements. "Hold on to those," grunted Cagney, as he retrieved Green's NVG's and handed them over. There was a clink from underfoot and William plucked a shard of steel from beside Cagney's boot. Cagney lifted it from William's outstretched hand and looked closely at it. "A broken knife blade?"

"No, Sir," hooted William, delightedly pointing at the foot of the courtyard wall, "that's Casey's musket and the bayonet be broken!" William rushed down the stairs and retrieved Casey's musket then dashed back to Cagney who had negotiated the stairs in a more leisurely manner. He handed the sliver of steel to William who matched it triumphantly to the bayonet. "Casey must've missed and hit the wall and the Sergeant just fell," he offered.

Cagney just smiled, having made an intuitive leap he felt was well overdue. "Mikey was wearing a flak jacket . . . a sort of armour," he explained. "He must have hit his head in the fall and found somewhere to hide." The First Mate approached them and Cagney greeted him with a smile. "Organise a search party, Mr Anderson, if you will; it seems Sergeant Green is alive and I want him found."

"No time, Sir." Anderson shook his head, his expression worried, "There's a sail on the horizon and we need to prepare.

Chapter 11

"You're right, Mr Anderson." Cagney did not like what he was saying but in his heart he knew it was the right decision. "Can you identify her?"

Anderson shook his head again. "Too far away, Sir, we've about three hours before she enters the bay and about an hour before that when we can see who she is." He sucked his teeth. "She can only be Anastasia or Scorpion; there are no other big ships in these waters."

"Best get started then, Mr Anderson; can we spare William to search for the Sergeant in the meantime?"

The First Mate nodded reluctantly. "Don't be long, my lad." William turned before Anderson had finished and was trotting eagerly towards the gate. "Take two muskets and water," bellowed Anderson at William's retreating form.

The two men sat on the ground with their backs against the Humvee. Anderson opened, "What's your plan, Sir?"

Cagney pursed his lips. "If it's the Scorpion, then we leave – and quickly. If it's the Anastasia then we get the prisoners on the battlements – are they secure by the way, Mr Anderson?"

Anderson's head inclined slowly. "In leg irons, Sir, two by two and Clark on the big gun. . . " he jerked his thumb over his shoulder at an Endeavour manning the Browning ". . . has them covered."

"Good, the prize crew on the Anastasia should be taken in by seeing their mates on the battlements and as she docks . . ."

"We kill them," interrupted Anderson.

"Quite right, Mr Anderson; we will kill them with our modern weapons. I can't afford to lose even one more man from our depleted forces and when we go aboard, Mr

Anderson, I want no prisoners taken. Let me be quite clear about that."

Anderson nodded sombrely, a droplet of sweat running down his nose onto his shirt. "I agree, Sir . . . and this lot?"

Cagney's eyes narrowed. "When they have served their purpose as bait you have my permission to hang them," he said harshly. As he hauled himself wearily to his feet, Cagney reflected on his new found ruthlessness and surprised himself by not caring. If he left these pirates alive when they departed, Scorponi would bolster his crew with their number and also gain valuable intelligence. "Yes, hang them, Mr Anderson," he repeated, "and hang them from the sea wall on the outside so Scorponi knows we mean business!"

Anderson leaned on the Humvee and levered himself upright; despite his tiredness he still had work to do. He looked at Cagney with a new respect in his eyes; he had once harboured reservations about Cagney's leadership qualities and ability to fight, but not any more. He held his hand out then changed it to a hurried salute. "Beggin' pardon, Sir . . ." the hand was proffered again, "but I'd be honoured to shake your hand . . . his nervousness made him stammer, "I . . .I mean we would have been dead men today if it weren't for you, Sir."

Cagney took Anderson's hand and shook it warmly. "Your words mean a great deal to me, Mr Anderson, thank you . . . now shall we see what riches this villain Scorponi has hidden away?"

They walked together to the corner of the courtyard where a small building leaned against the walls; there were at least three chains and padlocks securing the solid looking door. All the Endeavours gathered round, bar Clark on the Browning who was keeping a vigilant watch on the prisoners.

"So, lads," said Cagney easily, "are we going to let a few chains stop us getting to fat boy's treasure?" His words brought guffaws, chuckles and vehement nos from the sailors. "No, indeed" laughed Cagney, milking the drama. "Simmons here," he indicated a brawny short sailor, "has found a key that fits." The men laughed with Cagney because Simmons was holding a sledgehammer in his meaty paws. Cagney stepped back. "Do your stuff." The courtyard rang as the big hammer rose and fell; after a dozen blows one padlock burst to general applause and a tired Simmons handed the hammer to a crewmate.

Cagney touched Anderson's shoulder. "I'll be on the battlements, keep me informed." He walked past the Humvee on the way to the stairs offering an encouraging word to the gunner as he did so. Loping up the stairs his mind was working quickly trying to formulate alternative strategies which depended on the identity of the ship sailing in. Marching to the sea wall he brought his binoculars to bear on the distant ship. *Not so distant now,* he thought with alarm, *the wind must have changed.* "Mr Anderson!" the First Mate caught the peremptory tone and hurried over gazing up at the American. "Get your butt up here; the wind has changed and these may be the bad guys." Anderson responded with alacrity, running across the courtyard and up the stairs. A slightly breathless Mate arrived at Cagney's side; Cagney handed the binoculars to him. "Well?

Anderson's shoulders sagged with relief. "It's the Anastasia and she'll be here in half an hour." He returned the binoculars as a cheer erupted from below when the final chain sheered.

Cagney flashed Anderson a bleak smile. "Let's get below and spoil the party."

The comrades ran round the firestep, pounded down the stairs and jogged to the treasure room from whence there were whoops of joy. Anderson stuck his head through the door and roared, "Everyone out!"

The sailors spilled out, all with something shiny clasped tightly. Anderson went round them all, tearing trophies out of hands and throwing them back into the room.

"We've got visitors," snapped Cagney. "Get the prisoners on the sea wall and tell 'em they'd better look happy or they're dead men." The prisoners, with Cagney's warning ringing in their ears, were herded up the steps to shuffle their way to the sea wall and welcome the ship. Cagney gathered his men together as William walked through the gate and joined them.

"I couldn't find the Ser . . ."

"Later," Said Cagney gently, aware that even a few days ago he would have snapped at the boy. *I'm changing,* he thought and enjoyed a small inward smile.

"Listen up, guys; this is what I want and you are gonna make it happen for me." He paused for effect and looked at each man individually. "We open the gates to the jetty, that rabble up there are going to cheer as though their lives depend on it – and believe me it does. Colonel Trelawney . . . " the old soldier looked grimly determined, "I want you in the left corner of the sea wall with your M16 and dressed as a pirate . . . now who is the best shot here?" Cagney scanned their faces; William raised his hand and Cagney thrust his own M16 into his arms, "You're in the right corner of the battlements – keep your weapon low and out of sight. When her sides grind against the jetty I will fire up the Humvee and drive through the gate with Mr Anderson on the Browning. I estimate they can only have twelve or so men left and they will be on deck working the ship. I want them shot before they can get below decks. William, get on the parapet and shout down if the ship is close."

William, clasping his rifle, hared up the steps and ran round to the sea wall standing away from the prisoners. "At the mouth of the bay," he shouted. "The wind's dropped," he said laughing. William's news pleased the sailors but their smiles puzzled Cagney.

His expression alerted the First Mate. Chuckling he said, "They'll have to lower a boat and tow her in, Sir; we can shoot them like fish in a barrel."

Cagney nodded thoughtfully "How many men will they leave on board the Anastasia, Mr Anderson? Given that they are down to maybe twelve."

Anderson cocked his head to one side and paused for a moment, scratching his sandy head reflectively. "Ten in the longboat, they'll leave a helmsman and probably one guard for the prisoners."

Cagney thought hard, his brow furrowed. He did not have much ammunition left for either the M16's or the Browning – how to minimise expenditure? The solution came easily and quickly to him, the pirates had met the Browning before and were well acquainted with its devastating firepower, just pointing it at the men in the longboat should be enough to quell any thoughts of resistance. With that in mind he issued his orders and the men moved to their positions. The Colonel, now in a gaudy shirt and sporting a straw hat courtesy of the pirates' slop chest stood on the parapet, his rifle held low, partnered by William in the far corner with the shackled prisoners between them. The gate was opened and the Humvee parked unseen from the sea with Anderson getting brief instructions from Cagney on the finer points of the heavy machine gun.

He hopped down from the vehicle and walked over to the sea wall to give his last instructions. "Remember, guys," he looked first at Colonel Trelawney then at William, "let them get near enough for you to waste the guys on the Anastasia, then cease fire 'til I say." He glared at the sullen prisoners chained by the ankle two by two, "You bastards better start cheering and waving right now or I'll come up there and use this." He half pulled out his blood-stained sabre as a warning. The captured men began shouting and waving, half heartedly at first then with more enthusiasm as Trelawney levelled his rifle at them. Cagney sneaked a look through the open gate. The merchantman was, as Anderson had predicted, being towed by a rowboat – the Mate had called it a pinnace. The rowers – Cagney counted ten - were working hard but were making very slow progress due to the sheer weight of the ship. They paused before their next surge and then began rowing again. Cagney was puzzled why the pinnace crew were working so hard when they had all day to row at a steady pace to the jetty. Anderson joined him, so he asked the question, to be told the ship needed to dock before the tide turned and made the pirates' job impossible. Cagney took another peek, the pinnace was about thirty yards from the jetty, its crew making a final sweaty effort. He and Anderson climbed aboard the Humvee; the First Mate cocked the Browning and waited imperturbably. Cagney checked the key was in the ignition at least three times. His fingers drummed on the wheel, *what was keeping the Colonel and William? Surely the two men on the Anastasia were in their sights by now – and if they didn't shoot in the next few seconds there would be ten pirates on the jetty and life would become very difficult.* Two rifle shots almost as one rang out; Cagney fired up the big diesel and drove through the gates on to the jetty. The men in the pinnace ceased their efforts and looked around in consternation to find the Browning, a nemesis they thought they had seen the last of, pointing its ugly fluted snout at each one of them.

All eyes were on Cagney as he strolled round the Humvee and lounged against its armoured side. His voice rang out across the water. "So guys we meet again; it seems to me we've got the drop on you so weapons overboard and keep rowing." The pirates muttered amongst themselves for a moment then began dropping weapons into the bay. A brief argument flared aboard as one pirate ignoring his shipmates protests pulled a pistol from his belt and fired at Cagney. The ball flew well wide of a ducking Cagney but it was all the excuse the First Mate needed; he fired three short bursts, the heavy machine gun bucking in his large hands.

Cagney surveyed the dead and dying men aboard the sinking pinnace. "Notice anything, Mr Anderson?" Cagney's arm swept in a small arc encompassing the scene. Anderson's look of satisfaction turned to one of bafflement and he shrugged half apologetically. The pinnace is sinking Mr A and with it the towrope - you got any thoughts on how we get that goddamned ship alongside the dock now?"

Anderson's shoulders sagged as he realised the significance of his actions. A slow smile stole across Cagney's face. "I may just be able to save your hide; how long before the tide turns?"

A crestfallen Anderson looked at the tide mark on the jetty and then at the sun. "Very soon, Sir, less than half an hour."

"We'd better get our asses into gear then, Mr Anderson."

Anderson looked blankly at his officer. "They don't have a boat here, Sir, to take up the tow."

Cagney chuckled and went to the front of the Humvee, stooping he unhooked a wire hawser with a carabiner on the end. "Get a hold of this please." Anderson did as he was asked, looking perplexed. Cagney climbed into the driver's seat and fumbled around until his fingers found what they sought. Anderson jumped as the winch whined into action and the hawser un-spooled itself. He walked along the jetty until the entire forty yards of the hawser were laid on the cobbles. He turned to see Cagney stripping his uniform off then, down to his shorts, he padded over to the older man, took the proffered cable and jumped into the water. Cagney's sidestroke carried him to the pinnace which had filled rapidly with water and was about to disappear beneath the surface. Reaching with his free hand, Cagney unhooked the towrope from the painter and thrust the wire hawser through the loop. It took four attempts to clip the carabiner back onto its own wire to finish the job. Satisfied, Cagney swum back to the jetty where Anderson leaned down to haul him from the water with one brawny heave. They both stared over the water as the pinnace sank leaving dead men bobbing on the surface.

Cagney hopped into the Humvee without bothering to dress and reversed into the fort, taking up the slack on the hawser. He braked to a halt and climbed out stubbing his toe as he did so; he hopped cursing as Anderson approached looking grave.

"Sorry for opening fire, Sir, I . . . "

"No, Mr Anderson," interrupted Cagney his smile warm despite the pain from his damaged toe. "I meant to frighten them with the Browning so they could do the hard work for us but, hey! I should have taken you into my confidence and it's me at fault, not you!"

"Thank 'ee, Sir." Anderson's hand came up in involuntary salute. "With your permission, I'll get the prisoners down into the courtyard and make them secure."

Cagney nodded briefly and started to dress; already the day's heat had dried his body. A thin layer of pirates' blood was encrusted on his shoulder; he wiped it off with an indifferent shrug. Clad once more in his uniform he climbed in the Humvee and slowly took in the slack on the wire hawser. The wire and manila towrope rose slowly from the water until it twanged water off as it became taut and the Humvee shuddered. Cagney slowed the winch then gradually fed in power. The cable again twanged musically as the winch turned and the Humvee, all four wheels locked, began its inexorable slide towards the jetty's edge. *Dumbass* he laughed to himself and shut the power off. The entire raiding party gathered round the vehicle joined in the laughter.

Colonel Trelawney was in a jovial mood and flushed with victory. "By George, Sir, I did believe for a moment we were walking home!" Anderson took advantage of the break to volunteer that the prisoners were secure in their own gaol.

Cagney climbed from the Humvee and addressed his men. "OK, guys, our priorities now are to dock the Anastasia, release the prisoners from below decks and sail her back to the Endeavour before the Scorpion turns up. Nothing . . . I repeat, nothing," he emphasised his words by slapping the hood of the Humvee, "is to hold us up, not treasure hunting," he stared about him meeting eyes, "and not searching for Sergeant Green." He gave William a stern look, receiving a hurt one in return. Crisply he issued orders and a baulk of timber was thrust under the Humvee's front wheels. Remaining with the vehicle, Cagney sent his troops

151

to the jetty to receive the Anastasia. The docking itself went as smoothly as Cagney could ever imagine. Slowly but irresistibly the Humvee's winch pulled the bow of the merchantman to nudge the jetty where the manila tow tope and the winch cable were separated and the rope looped over a bollard. An Endeavour seaman nimbly vaulted onto the ship and trotted to the yawing stern where he found a heaving line and threw it ashore. Willing hands pulled the stern in until she lay snug against the jetty. Cagney looked at his men; they were exhausted and needed a lift, *so be it* he thought *I'll give them one*. He beckoned the shipboard seaman who hopped to the jetty. "OK, guys, a job well done!" he smiled conspiratorially. "Maybe we'll leave the crew and passengers where they are for the moment; the less they know the better . . ." he tapped the side of his nose, "I reckon we've got some treasure to have a look at." Grins broke out on all faces apart from William's. As the group walked round to the breached strong-room Cagney had a quiet word with him. "Off you go, William; see if you can find Mikey." The grateful youngster trotted off, still holding Cagney's rifle. "Mr Anderson." The Mate turned. "Please get everything out of there and lay it on the ground here." Anderson and the surviving Endeavours began enthusiastically dragging chests from the darkness - most were too heavy to carry - whilst Cagney stood, a picture of nonchalance, chatting to Colonel Trelawney. After ten minutes work there were six chests and numerous sacks sitting in the baking heat with Anderson and the seamen standing expectantly, sweat dripping from their brows.

Cagney cleared his throat. "Tell me, Mr Anderson . . . " he trickled his fingers through the gold coins in the nearest chest, "how many of these coins . . ." he held one up gleaming in the sun, ". . . would be a year's pay for a seaman in this man's navy?"

Anderson picked up a handful and let them spill carelessly until just two remained on the palm of his calloused hand. Cagney raised his eyebrows in surprise and

Anderson, a sardonic smile smearing his features, nodded. "Yes Sir, that is how we are valued."

"Not today, Mr A; give yourself and your shipmates a pay rise . . . I think fifty of these should buy you a beer or two? Can I rely on you to allocate the same amount to the families of our dead comrades?"

"You can, Sir," answered Anderson promptly. "There may be a fly in the ointment though, Sir."

Cagney scowled. "And that would be?"

"If me an' the lads turn up with pockets full of gold Mr Caruthers will have us flogged as looters – after 'e 'as pocketed the gold." Earnestly he added, "You can't protect us once we're aboard the Endeavour, Sir."

Cagney smiled; his teeth very white against his tanned face. It was not a very nice smile, Anderson noted, and for a brief – very brief - moment he felt a pang of sympathy for the First Lieutenant – a man he loathed.

Cagney spoke softly his voice just above a whisper, "When we return to the Endeavour, Mr Anderson, that goddam' son of a bitch Caruthers is a dead man."

Anderson smiled happily. "If I might offer a piece of advice, Sir?" Cagney inclined his head almost imperceptibly. "The crew will be loyal to the Number One - it's the discipline of the service; bribe them, Sir. A couple of gold coins each and they won't care if you keel haul the bastard!"

Cagney laughed, this time with real humour. "Oh, I do like a practical man, Mr Anderson! Now this is what I want. Get our dead lads sewn into canvas, they can be buried at sea; give the troops their gold and don't forget the dead guys – the rest of the gold coins go into the Humvee." Cagney paused and scratched his buzz cut. "Get this lot . . ." he indicated the other chests overflowing with a king's ransom "Into the Captain's cabin . . . lock it and bring me the key, and last of all throw that scum in the bay." His sweeping gesture took in the dead pirates littering the courtyard.

Anderson saluted. "Aye, aye, Sir."

Cagney stood and stretched. "Colonel Trelawney, with me, please; let's release the prisoners from the Anastasia." The two men walked to the jetty leaving Anderson shouting orders at his men. As they walked, Cagney glanced at the old soldier and then looked himself over. Trelawney had changed back into his uniform jacket and his baseball cap. Cagney marvelled at the contrast; the eighteenth century officer with a twenty first century assault rifle – *which he looked to have been born with,* thought Cagney - and himself with a bloodstained sabre.

The old man caught the glance and returned it with a quizzical smile. "May I say, Lieutenant, that command suits you and if I might make so bold you now have a certain swagger in your step that suits you even more."

"So what do you think to my new found ruthlessness, Colonel? I haven't always been this way," he admitted, a touch embarrassed by the soldier's praise.

The old soldier faced him, his tone mild. "I believe you have come to a time where individual bravery and decision-making are perhaps more prevalent than in your own age . . ." he put up his hand to halt Cagney's reply ". . . I know of your time from Dr Aktar, it rewards efficiency and a better understanding possibly. I think a brutal hand is often better rewarded in these – my days, but . . ." Trelawney placed his hand on the American's shoulder ". . . do not abandon your compassion, my boy – it sets you apart from the likes of Caruthers and Scorponi."

Any further conversation was halted by a muffled thumping from the Anastasia; the two comrades waited until the ship yawed closer to the jetty and then took a long stride aboard. Trelawney, who knew the ship well, led Cagney to the hold where together they slid back the hatch.

Cagney took an involuntary step backwards as the nauseating stench wafted upwards; he steeled his senses and peered down into the darkness.

"You're all safe; the pirates are dead." An excited babble broke out below and people began to emerge into the unaccustomed sunlight. Cagney counted thirty in all, of which twelve were crew. He recognised the features of a middle aged lady who he assumed was Mrs Boscombe's sister. "Captain?" he called out.

"Dead, Sir," replied a seaman, "And our Number One."

Another man emerged slowly from the hold, peering suspiciously around him as though suspecting a trick. A tall, thin middle-aged man with a receding chin, he fiddled constantly with his horn rimmed spectacles. He approached Cagney, more confident now. "I am in command; I am Lieutenant Courtney Twill. I was below when the pirates attacked," he added by way of explanation.

"Hiding!" grunted a seaman behind him contemptuously.

Courtney Twill flushed angrily, his voice reedy and shrill. "That is not true . . ."

"You're wrong, Courtney Twill," interrupted Cagney impatiently. "You're not in command – I am. You lost this ship and I recaptured her with a little help from my friends, some of whom, Mr Courtney Twill, are dead now." Cagney heard a murmur of approval from behind the thin officer. He pushed the protesting Third Lieutenant aside and addressed the crew. "Mr Anderson, the First Mate from His Majesty's frigate Endeavour will be aboard shortly; you will obey him." He spoke louder and quelled the chatter his news had provoked. "This ship will be sailing up the coast to join the Endeavour. You will be leaving in the next half hour. Any longer," he added soberly, "and the Scorpion may be sailing into this bay and we don't want to meet her do we?" A chorus of nos greeted him.

Cagney stood legs apart on the deck and cried, "Are you with me lads?" The crew and passengers cheered their rescuer loudly with the exception of Courtney Twill who stammered about the ship needing to return to India. Cagney did not even deign to answer, merely pushing him aside as leaped on to the jetty. He strode rapidly into the fort. "Mr Anderson!" His shouted summons echoed off the walls. Anderson rapidly appeared by his side. "Get the bodies and the booty on board; you are in command of her."

Anderson's face showed his pleasure. "I want her out of here in half an hour . . . and take no notice of that goddamned chinless wonder who thinks he's the boss!"

Walking over to check on Captain Fairbrother, Cagney could hear frenzied activity behind him as Anderson goaded his new crew into action. Lifting the flap of the awning, Cagney felt Fairbrother's pulse and was pleased to find it strong and steady, the Captain's chest rising and falling with an encouraging regularity. Relieved, he retrieved his medical bag from the Humvee then washed the Captain's head wound with sterile water. Fairbrother had lost a fair amount of blood *but the drips should keep shock at bay.* Cutting the Captain's fair hair away from his temple he could see and feel what appeared to be a depressed fracture. "You need a hospital, my friend," he said quietly then hung another drip from the upturned musket and regained his feet. The courtyard was empty apart from himself and his patient though he could see figures in the rigging of the Anastasia. The murmur of discontented voices from the pirate prisoners floated to his ears; sucking his teeth he reflected upon Colonel Trelawney's words about compassion then walked to the landward gate to call for William.

Avoiding the rubble from the explosion he took the few steps outside the walls as William's disconsolate figure trudged towards him. "No luck?" he asked unnecessarily.

William shook his head miserably. "He has to be near, Sir, being as he hurt his knee falling off the wall getting in." He handed Cagney his rifle and magazines as a seaman hurried towards them.

"Mr Anderson's compliments, Sir, an' we're ready to cast off."

"Thanks," acknowledged Cagney. "You guys can give me a hand getting the Captain into the Humvee." A few moments later Fairbrother lay in the back of the vehicle, his saline drip hanging from the Browning and two chests of gold for company.

A worried-looking Anderson walked through the sea wall gate, his pace increasing as he saw them. "I'm ready to cast off now, Sir; the tide is in our favour and there's a breath of wind. Just time to hang these buggers," he added cheerfully.

Cagney looked uncomfortable, mindful of the Colonel's words. "Put them in the hold, Mr Anderson, they may come in useful." Anderson's expression changed to one of perplexity but he held his tongue. "I'm sure Mr Anderson could use an extra hand, William, so get aboard the Anastasia and ask the Colonel to join me for the journey home."

William shook his head. "No, Sir," he said quietly. The two men stared at him in astonishment. William looked up defiantly and spoke firmly. "No, Sir, I be stopping 'til I find the Sergeant; he's my friend."

"He's my friend too, William," said Cagney gently, he hesitated, "I suppose I can wait a couple of hours while we look . . . "

Anderson interrupted, "Beggin' pardon, Sir, but you b'aint got two hours to spare – you need to be back at the Endeavour bein' as you're the only proper officer . . . it's true," he stammered, "Mr Caruthers 'as seen no action much an' ee's a coward any road an' Mr Rotherhithe is sick still." Cagney stared at him. "You needs to get back, Sir," his voice fierce, "We needs you to command."

Cagney stood silently, torn between searching for his friend and his duty. "Quite right, Mr Anderson," he said quietly, his features anguished, "and thank you for reminding me of my duty." The American reached into the Humvee, pulled a jerry can of water from it and handed it to William along with his M16 and magazines. "Take these and keep on looking for Mikey. When Scorponi turns up keep your head down until he's gone – I'll be back when Scorponi is dead. . . or I am," he laughed. Moving to the driver's door he leaned in and emerged with Green's backpack then reached back in stuffing it with gold coins from one of the chests in the back of the vehicle. A sudden

157

thought struck him and he delved into the jacket of the unconscious Captain, removing his telescope. "Take this, too; the Captain won't mind," Cagney climbed into the Humvee with the returned Colonel after shaking hands with William and Anderson then drove off. A happier William trudged to the hills weighed down with gold and water, Cagney's rifle and Green's NVG's slung around his neck.

Anderson watched the Humvee disappear over the top of the ridge with the red-jacketed Colonel manning the Browning and then ordered his men to hang the remaining pirates from the sea wall – a task they performed with alacrity and much good humour.

Chapter 12

It took only two hours to find Sergeant Green though William would have been the first to admit that luck was on his side. Lugging the jerry can of water had become tiring and irksome, so spotting an overhang which would provide cooling shade and a hiding place, William wriggled under the rock only to find the niche occupied by the unconscious body of his friend. Despite his joy, William approached Green with much circumspection; he softly and deliberately placed a hand on Green's rifle and only then shook the man's shoulder, gently at first then with more vigour. He was rewarded by a small moan and a muttered obscenity. Encouraged, he pulled Green into the sunlight and lifted the AK from his limp hands talking all the while as though to a sick child. With an effort William manoeuvred the Para into a sitting position and splashed water onto his face. Green moaned again and William saw movement in his closed eyes. Reaching into Green's pack he found a torn tee shirt which he soaked with water then sponged away the debris which was gumming Green's eyes closed. First one then the other opened and closed, unused to the bright light. His glazed look slowly dwindled as William leaned forward and put a cup of water to his friend's parched lips.

Green focussed into the distance over William's shoulder. "Trouble," he croaked.

William looked behind him; the Scorpion, a black flag with the skull and crossbones flapping at the masthead was just nosing into the bay.

The Scorpion's crew were terrified; never in the years they had sailed with Scorponi had they seen him so angry. None dared risk more than a sideways glance at him. They too were angry; as their ship had sailed into the bay, its bluff bows had bumped aside the bodies of their shipmates thrown in the sea by Cagney's orders. Worse was to come, as the Scorpion forged slowly on the crew could see clearly on the wall of the fort what they had suspected from afar; another dozen of their shipmates blackening in the sun, hanging from the ropes which had choked the life from them. All were eyeless courtesy of the ever present vultures which flapped clumsily away as the Scorpion slid alongside the jetty. The crew swarmed ashore with drawn blades and cocked muskets; Scorponi strode through the gate without a qualm – the vultures had told him the fort was deserted.

Walking quickly to the landward gate, he briefly examined its remnants. Turning to survey the courtyard, his face was white with fury, pig-like eyes mere slits in his bloated face. Something shining in the sand caught his attention, two swift paces later Scorponi was on his knees inspecting his find. Rising wheezily to his feet, suspicion clouding his eyes he held it to the light, the object was a brass cylinder. Plucking from his pocket the bullet that had removed his finger and killed his helmsman he offered them together. The round fitted snugly into the cartridge case, suspicion hardened into certainty. The tall man who had shot him with the uncannily accurate musket – this was his doing. Scorponi put his head back and howled, the primeval sound causing the bravest of his men to quail. All had seen the broken chains on the treasure room where their accumulated wealth had been stored; they waited for their captain to tell them what to do next for they were paupers to a man if they could not recapture it.

The pirate crew gathered round Scorponi who still shook with rage; his harsh voice cracked the air. "The men who did this are with the British frigate that is careened down the coast, less than two days sail . . . get aboard, we are going to kill them and we shall have what is ours!" The men began to file aboard. Scorponi called his Lieutenant, a small villainous looking man with a cast in one eye. He waved at the door to his booty room and growled, "Gomez, see if they left anything." His orders were more in hope than expectation as the man kicked away the stone that held the door closed. Ever suspicious, Scorponi wondered why the thieves would close the door after they had ransacked the room. As Gomez swung the door towards him he noticed a length of twine tied to the bottom and tightening. His eyes followed the twine in the gloom to what looked like a musket; there was a click and a flare in the musket pan. Gomez tried to shout a warning but the open keg of gunpowder which Cagney had placed next to the musket exploded killing him. Thirty yards away Scorponi was dashed to the earth by the blast. Men rushed back from the ship drawn by the explosion to see their Captain hauling his bulk upright. Without a backward glance Scorponi stalked wordlessly to his ship; within minutes the Scorpion was inching away from the jetty to begin its voyage of retribution.

Green and William watched as the Scorpion, clapping on plenty of sail in the light airs, sailed from the bay. They had kept a very low profile whilst the pirates were in the fort and had been hopeful that the explosion had killed Scorponi when they saw him fall. Green guessed accurately that it had been a booby trap set by Cagney. The pirate Captain's survival disappointed them both. A scowl haunted Green's normally cheery face. "If I'd been fit I'd have gone down and shot that fat sod," he grumbled.

William thought for a moment. "If you'd been fit, Sergeant, you wouldn't be here in the first place."

"Just thinking aloud," said Green defensively, "and call me Mikey!"

During the pirates' brief occupation of the fort Green had asked William to bring him up to date with events. After a few questions William realised Green had no recollection beyond the journey over, so he slowly told the story of their adventures. The news of the capture of Scorponi's gold cheered Green immensely and the retelling of Cagney's bravery and leadership pleased him equally. "Always knew he had it in him," he observed laconically.

William had heard third hand from one of Endeavour's seamen about Caruthers' treachery; Green's fingers grew white clenching the barrel of his Kalashnikov when the death bed confession of Casey was relayed to him. "We need to get back ASAP," he spat as he struggled to his feet, almost falling as he took his first faltering step. The Para hissed with pain as he took his second step, his arm reaching out to garner support from a concerned William.

"There's a crutch in the fort, Boss; I'll nip down and get it."

"No owner then?" gasped Green as he leaned against a rock.

William thought about the one legged cook Anderson had hung from the battlements. "I don't think he'll mind," he replied seriously. The lad trotted down to the deserted fort leaving Green with a puzzled expression. A half hour elapsed before a sweating William returned with a crutch for Green who tried it and pronounced it sound.

"We can buy a donkey at the first village," opined William.

"Buy?" queried Green crossly, the pain from his head and knee making his mood sour.

"With this," said William, smiling as he nudged Green's gold-filled pack with his foot.

Green's habitual grin returned at the prospect of a ride. "Good stuff mate . . . and tidier than shooting the owner."

The pair slowly began their journey home as the sun low on the horizon lit them: a limping Green with his crutch and his Russian assault rifle across his chest and a heavily laden William with a rucksack of gold on his back, a jerry can of water in his left hand and his right clasping his borrowed M16. Darkness followed a brief twilight which had seen the comrades settle down in a sandy hollow off the trail. William was worried; the Sergeant had not once complained but it was obvious that he was struggling. Their progress had been painfully slow. Before sleep overtook the exhausted pair William persuaded the older man that he would walk to the village alone in the morning and return with a donkey for his injured friend. Despite the night chill the two men slept soundly and woke at first light; the thought which had haunted the dimly lit corridors of Green's mind moved to his consciousness as he sat up.

"Shit!" William looked at him. "The Tank Carrier won't move. By now the compressed air in the tanks will have leaked away and locked the brakes on." William frowned struggling to make the connection; he started as the realisation hit him and bit his lip, "That's right" said Green Grimly "The Abrams' cannon won't be able to traverse and cover the bay. Scorponi will be able to sail in and do as he likes."

It took twenty minutes of stretching and painful massage before Green could walk a few steps with his crutch. William filled his pockets with gold coins and with Green's cheerful advice to "Make sure it's got a leg at each corner" ringing in his ears he headed off down the trail.

Five minutes later Green looked up as William hurried back. "There's a camel train coming, Mikey."

With assistance from William, Green climbed a large boulder and asked the lad to throw up his telescope. Green focussed the glass on a dust cloud about a mile away. "You're right lad; armed men, women, children, dogs, and about thirty to forty camels."

"One hump or two?" quipped William causing Green to lose his balance and slide down the boulder to land at William's feet in a dusty cursing heap. Concerned, William offered the Para his hand to get up.

Despite his pain Green was laughing. "One hump or two? You cheeky sod – listen, this is how we're going to handle this." William listened intently to Green's short but thorough briefing and was then sent to a place of concealment forty yards the other side of the trail after helping Green back on to the boulder – this time with rifle and pack. The young Para waited patiently, rifle across his knees and pack of gold coins next to him.

The camel train approached at the walking pace dictated by the women at the rear on foot. There were seven riders leading the train of roped together camels – all were armed with muskets slung across their saddles. At fifty yards the lead rider noticed Green sitting nonchalantly on his boulder and raised his arm. Everyone halted at his command. The riders gathered round one man to whom they seemed to defer and although Green could hear nothing he noticed he was pointed at several times. After several minutes the discussion seemed to have achieved some kind of consensus, thought Green, and the whole train moved slowly forward until its leaders were ten yards from Green's position and halted again. Two large dogs bounded forward and barking furiously tried to climb the boulder on which Green was sitting. Their scrabbling feet made no impression on the rock and they fell back snarling. The leader of the Arab camel traders stared at Green impassively as Green smiled benignly back at him. Feeling that this had gone on long enough the Paratrooper pointed at the dogs; there was a crack and one dog was bowled along the sandy soil to lie twitching, the huge exit wound from William's M16 round visible. The Arabs looked around them seeking the unseen threat. One man raised his musket but lowered it as Green raised his left hand and wagged an admonishing finger. If he had raised his right hand the man would have been shot from the saddle by William.

Green yawned hugely and theatrically; reaching into his bag he withdrew a shiny gold coin which he held aloft to glint seductively in the sun. "Morning." He offered the deeply suspicious men a bright smile. "I'd like to buy a camel or two please." Dark glittering eyes and silence was the only response. Green again using his left arm pointed at a camel behind the riders. The leader, who Green could see was an old man, growled something guttural to the nearest rider who wheeled his beast and cantered to the rear of the column then returned driving a teenage girl. "Nice try but no cigar," laughed Green shaking his head and pointing at the leader's mount. The man laughed harshly in return and ordered a camel brought forward. Green held up three fingers thinking they had better have a spare mount and threw the coin to the Arab leader. One of the group slid from his mount, picked up the coin then handed it to the old man. He looked closely at it then bit it, a satisfied smile appearing on his face. He held up five fingers. Two more camels had been driven up to join the first. Green swept an arm over the three and held up five fingers; the Arab smiled sadly and opened his hand three times. Green smiled equally sadly. "You thieving old sod," he remarked with no particular malice and opened his hand twice. The old Arab obviously enjoying himself wagged a finger gently at Green then mimicked Green's gesture and wiggled two extra fingers. After a suitable pause the Brit nodded and tossed eleven coins to a tribesman who had walked cautiously to the base of the boulder. "Saddles," said Green, indicating the leader's own. More bargaining followed and five more coins went to swell the old man's purse. Green pantomimed the fitting of the saddles and it was done for him.

"Thank you," smiled Green; he pointed to the dead dog and tossed a coin to the old man who nodded graciously and spoke to the dismounted tribesman who walked off and returned moments later with the girl the old man had offered earlier. The young Para's puzzled look brought a smile to the grizzled face of the old man; he barked something to his followers and the camel train majestically wended its way past the seated Green. An older woman disengaged herself from the column and hugged the girl, giving her a cotton bag. The woman rejoined the group and the train disappeared into the distance.

Green checked with the telescope to see if the old man had left a straggler to rob him of his gold but no, they were indeed all gone. He whistled William out of hiding and the lad wandered slowly over, his eyes glued to the girl all the while. "It's a girl!" snapped Green crossly, "You never seen one before?"

"A few," admitted William, "but I don't normally buy 'em." He paused thoughtfully. "Was she dear?"

Green's face darkened. "I didn't bloody well buy her," he snarled. "She kind of came with the camels . . ." he finished lamely. Privately he blamed himself for buying

165

three beasts; he had intended one as a spare but the old boy must have thought one was for the girl. The girl, alarmed by Green's raised voice burst into tears. Green glared at William. "Now look what you've done." He slid down the boulder landing gently on the earth then limped to his new purchases which eyed him with undisguised contempt. Untying the nearest beast, he attempted to impose his authority upon it by looking it hard in the eye; the camel spat at him and stretched its jaws in an unhurried yawn. A girlish giggle reached Green's ears from behind him which did nothing for his mood, blighted as it was by the green slime down the front of his battledress. For the next five minutes he tried everything he could think of to make the camel lower itself so he could climb aboard. The beast looked down at him with a supreme indifference.

William's voice floated to him, suffused with laughter. "P'raps . . . p'raps if you threaten to shoot it, Mikey?"

Green glared venomously at the lad whose laughter was too far gone to contain. The girl took pity on him eventually and strode to the camel. She shook her head vehemently at the Para. "No neldon airybastid!" She turned her attention to the beast and snarled harshly in its ear whereupon it sank to its knees with a world weary sigh. She motioned him aboard and Green meekly did as ordered; he was just settling himself in after painfully catching his injured knee on the wooden saddle when the camel rose without warning; rucksack, crutch and rifle clattered to the ground as he fought the rolling motion. As the camel reached its full height the girl handed him the reins and his possessions. The disparaging look he received from her took him back to his basic training at Aldershot and his ever critical training Sergeant.

William, who had a natural affinity with animals, felt at home on his camel as he and the girl followed the cursing Paratrooper on the long journey home. William was happy, he had a pocket full of gold, the respect of Green and Cagney and there was a pretty girl next to him.

166

He smiled broadly as Green's voice drifted back to him promising to "Puke on your neck if you can't walk straight!"

Chapter 13

Cagney had hoped to approach the camp unannounced but he was to be disappointed; the noise of the big diesel and the cloud of dust it raised from its wheels alerted the camp when they were half a mile away. By the time the Humvee had rumbled to a halt a crowd had gathered to greet them. The Tank Carrier, Cagney was appalled to note, had barely moved since their departure. Colonel Trelawney, aching from long hours standing was about to dismount but stayed where he was at a word from the American.

Reaching for Trelawney's M16, Cagney eased himself stiffly from the Humvee's cab to be surrounded by a milling chattering mob; he fired a round into the air causing an expectant silence. "Good news guys . . . " the breath was knocked from him as Philippa threw herself into his arms, oblivious to the stares and chuckles from the seamen. He gently disengaged himself from her embrace. Philippa looked up at his tired, lined and dirty face and saw a changed man – grimmer, utterly self-assured *and more attractive if that were possible.* " . . . We were successful, we captured the Anastasia, killed the pirate garrison, and relieved Scorponi of his treasure . . ." Cheers echoed round and smiling faces exchanged happy looks. ". . . at a cost; six dead," he listed the seamen's names, "your Captain badly injured and the Sergeant missing." Faces fell, for Green and the Captain had been popular.

Cagney recognised the old carpenter who had informed Fairbrother about the cannon damage to his ship. "Hey, Abraham, can you rig up a bed and shade for Captain Fairbrother?" He waved a hand to the rear of the Tank Carrier "Somewhere there is good." The carpenter hurried away after saluting. Cagney looked about him, "I want four strong men." Almost everyone stepped forward and Cagney chose the nearest four. "OK, guys, you'll find two chests in the back of the Humvee, carry one to the Tank Carrier." Cagney held Philippa tight. "Hey, Honey, will you hand five gold coins to each crew member for me? I've got business to sort."

"Business?" queried Philippa, noting his set angry expression.

Cagney nodded slowly. "Yeah, I guess you could call it business, I'm gonna kill that sonofabitch Caruthers."

She placed a warning hand on Cagney's arm. "Wait."

The tall Marine gave an almost imperceptible nod and stood like a statue whilst men filed by, each one becoming richer by over two years pay. It took over half an hour for the entire ship's company to be paid; Cagney peered into the chest – still half full, plus the other chest, plenty there to build a shield for the Doc's weapon he estimated.

As the last man was paid Philippa lifted her head; she looked at Cagney and her eyes flicked right. His head turned to follow them. Caruthers, the Bosun's Mate and two seamen stood twenty yards away, the First Lieutenant's face a mixture of anger and surprise. Cagney strode towards the group un-slinging his rifle as he did so and cocking it. The two seamen started to lift their muskets as he approached then lowered them when they saw the expression on his face. Cagney halted five yards away from Caruthers and stared at him with contemptuous calm.

Swallowing nervously, Caruthers broke the silence. "You will oblige me Lieutenant by explaining why you are giving the King's gold to the ship's company?" Cagney remained silent. His voice croaky, Caruthers continued, "Those coins were captured by a naval expedition and thus belong to the cro . . ."

"You bastard," grated Cagney, "you gutless murderous bastard – you sent Casey and Jorgenson along to kill Mikey and me; it's your fault the Captain's dying." He lifted the M16 until it was level with Caruthers' chest and addressed his escort "Step aside, guys; this is on auto and I'll blow you all away if you stay where you are." The men, despite a despairing look from Caruthers, obediently moved away leaving the First Lieutenant isolated. The two seamen lifted their muskets once more.

The clipped authoritative voice of Trelawney cracked the air. "I believe dropping your weapons would be a more acceptable option." He emphasised his words by swinging the Browning's ugly snout to cover them. Two muskets clattered to the earth.

"Say your prayers, buddy boy," ground Cagney, his finger tightening on the trigger.

"I will not allow this!" The voice, tight and pained, came from behind Cagney. Nicholas Rotherhithe walked haltingly around the Marine and stood between him and Caruthers. Swaying unsteadily, his face sheened with sweat it was clear that the Endeavour's Third Lieutenant was using his last reserves of strength. His voice was weak but firm. "I say again, Lieutenant Cagney . . ." he faltered slightly ". . . I will not permit you to harm the First Lieutenant."

Cagney glowered at the young officer. "You listen now and listen good, son; this asshole tried to have me killed – the Captain got my bullet and my best friend is missing thanks to him."

"Is this true?" Rotherhithe spoke without turning.

"Absolute poppycock" spluttered the red faced Caruthers but his words carried little conviction to the ears of his listeners. Cagney's eyes never left Caruthers.

"Well, Colonel?" Rotherhithe lifted his eyes to the old red faced soldier whose finger was poised inside the trigger guard of the heavy machine gun. "Oblige me, Sir, with an honest answer if you would be so good." Rotherhithe stumbled slightly and Philippa hurried to support him.

"Lieutenant Cagney speaks the plain unadorned truth, young Sir." Trelawney's tone was scornful. "Casey's last words were to damn Mr Caruthers."

Caruthers' features glowed with a manic, frightened rage and spittle flew from his lips as his words spluttered out, "The ravings of a dying man; I will see to it that you can never show your face in London society again – my family has influence!"

Trelawney looked untroubled. "You blustering, bullying braggart, Sir; my colonial comrade who stands before you is worth a hundred of your ilk. Begone before my other friend . . ." He patted the Browning meaningfully, ". . . speaks to you!"

A frightened Caruthers, realising that that he had been thrown a lifeline, snapped petulant orders at his men and flanked by them stalked back to the ship.

Cagney lowered his rifle, the rage within him ebbing as the treacherous officer disappeared round the basalt outcrop. With a wry expression he spoke to Rotherhithe, "Jesus! You Limeys sure stick together; you'll never know how close I came to letting daylight into you."

"And undo all your good work, Lieutenant; no. there was never any risk." whispered Rotherhithe and fainted into Philippa's arms. Cagney grabbed him by the shirt front and with one sinewy forearm lowered him to the ground. Philippa marvelled at the strength of the man . . . *her man.*

Cagney shouted for Abraham who scuttled over. "Make Mr Rotherhithe comfortable near the Captain, please." The old carpenter called over a couple of idlers who were admiring their coins and placed the young officer with Francesca in attendance next to Fairbrother. Cagney walked slowly over with Philippa, "Looks like I'm stacking up your officers, Abraham."

The carpenter paused in the act of setting up an awning. "Aye, Sir, . . . and maybe there's one officer who needs to be stacked under the soil!"

"Soon, if I have my way," returned Cagney quietly.

Abraham reached out and held the American's forearm and just as quickly withdrew it. "Beggin' pardon, Sir, but ee's cunning an' mad." He tapped his head in emphasis. "Ee won't rest 'til you be dead."

Cagney gave the old man a grateful smile. "Thank you, Abraham; for sure I'll be covering my ass. Hey, bring me up to speed on this. . . " He slapped the ramp of the Tank

171

Transporter. ". . . It sure ain't moved much while I've been away."

"The wheels 'ave locked, Sir," said Abraham, leading Cagney to the Tractor unit. The old man pointed to the wheels nearest the outcrop and Cagney saw they had been lifted and now rested on copper sheets greased with tallow. Abraham looked uncomfortable "W'em used the dry bollocks machine . . . beg pardon, ma'am." He tugged his forelock. "At least that's what the Sergeant called it."

Cagney's brow furrowed then he smiled broadly. "I think you mean hydraulics Abraham; but, hey, an easy mistake – I want you to lift this wheel . . ." he kicked the right-hand front ". . . and remove it. Can you do that?"

Abraham nodded quickly. "Yessir, I'll get the lads who done it before and we'll have it off in a jiffy." The old carpenter trotted off shouting names.

Cagney felt Philippa's hand slide into his then standing on tiptoe she kissed him, wrinkling her nose afterwards. "You smell, James Cagney." She smiled anyway

"I'll take a shower when I've got these wheels spinning." He led her towards the bunker. "I wanna have a word with the Doc, tell him his gold is here and grab some tools to get this thing mobile."

"Tell me about your adventures," she urged.

"Sure" he replied; "Let's get downstairs then I can fill in both you and the Doc." They found Aktar in the workshop working on his device with the children watching him listlessly. His own mood was subdued as he greeted them. "I am pleased to see you back unharmed, Lieutenant. Sad news about Sergeant Green. The children are heartbroken."

Cagney frowned. "Hell, Doc, Mikey's missing not dead and I'll be going back to get him when I've settled up with Scorponi. The scientist quickly relayed the news to the children whose faces immediately were wreathed in smiles. Cagney scowled again. "Hey, Doc, what made you think Mikey was dead?"

Aktar smiled grimly. "The First Lieutenant Caruthers came down here yesterday . . . I warned him that Sergeant

Green would be likely to shoot him but he laughed at me. His words were – "you have seen the last of your precious Sergeant."

The Marine was thin-lipped with anger. "We got back less than an hour ago, Doc – he arranged one of his men to kill Mikey, here let me bring you up to speed." Cagney spent the next fifteen minutes recounting his adventures to his attentive audience, finishing with a request for tools. Philippa who had overheard men from the raiding party praising Cagney's central role and bravery felt a warm admiration for his glossing over his own contribution and giving credit to others. Five more minutes saw the pair blinking in the harsh sunlight as they stood by the Tank Carrier where Abraham and two crew members stood waiting. Cagney dropped the heavy toolbox to the earth and nodded amicably to the new men. "You know how to take the wheel off?"

The shorter of the two answered in the affirmative. "Yessir, the Sergeant showed us how."

"Go to it, guys; make it happen!"

The sweating, straining men quickly lifted the wheel of the tractor unit and removed the wheel after dropping the chassis on to sturdy wooden blocks. Cagney inspected the hub assembly and rapidly came to the conclusion that the brakes were held in the "on" position as a failsafe due to the lack of air in the pneumatic system. With a little detective work he was able to identify the bolt which forced the brakes off when the vehicle was due maintenance and after selecting the appropriate ring spanner turned it so the wheel could rotate. Cagney grunted with satisfaction as he spun the hub on its bearings. "Get the wheel back on and we'll free the others in turn" He raised his voice, "Abraham!" A pleased-looking Abraham who had been monitoring the progress from a distance hurried over. "We're back in business; sort your towing teams out, this . . ." he slapped the tractor unit ". . . will be rolling in a couple of hours."

The short Middle Eastern twilight was fading when Cagney freed the final wheel of the giant vehicle. As he levered his exhausted body from beneath the vehicle, Abraham's skinny arm hauled him upright. The Marine glanced sideways at the assembled towing team, bubbling over with enthusiasm for the job ahead. Cagney rested his arm on the cab; he had never in his life been so weary – not even at boot camp where a large percentage of officer candidates dropped out due to fatigue.

"Better stand your men down, Abraham," the old man's face fell. "We have no light, my friend; the Doc just told me the gas for the generator has run out, let your guys get some rest. We'll move this at first light tomorrow." Abraham nodded agreeably and led his men to the beach to sleep. Cagney cleaned his hands, thought briefly about a shower but decided sleep was his priority. Stumbling with fatigue he made his way to his blankets. He lay down next to Philippa who draped her limbs around his exhausted body,

"I have made a decision, James; I am returning with you for a new life in the future," she whispered;

"Good," he murmured and a contented Cagney drifted into a dreamless sleep.

They came for Cagney in the darkness before dawn. Men loyal to Caruthers armed with Marlin spikes and cudgels. Philippa had left a sleeping Cagney to enjoy an early shower, a modern habit she happily embraced. Some instinct within the American stirred him from the black depths of his fatigue and for an instant he saw shadows looming over him before a Marlin spike glanced off the side of his head. Two burly seamen dragged the semi conscious Marine to the ship whilst the Bosun's Mate located Cagney's rifle by his blankets. A muffled grunt and thwack told him that Colonel Trelawney had been similarly dealt with and the Bosun's Mate, grinning in the dark, followed his men carrying the limp Trelawney. A half hour later Philippa was emerging from the shower room when she heard the crash of a cannon; puzzled she walked towards the entrance of the bunker, drying her hair en route. As she neared the ladder a head appeared in the dawn lit aperture.

The face was familiar; it was Abraham the carpenter who had helped James with the wheels.

"Come quick, Lady Somerville!" he panted. "The Number One, ee's about to hang Mr Cagney and the Colonel" His head was yanked back and she heard a strangled cry from outside. Philippa sped up the ladder, cursing as she barked her shin on a rung; she emerged into the pale cold early morning to see the Bosun's Mate repeatedly punching Abraham whose blood-coated face was unrecognisable.

"Stop that, you despicable excuse for a man!" Her words, withering and scornful, penetrated Sullivan's thick skull; he turned to face her, laughing derisively. Reaching into the pocket of her borrowed pants, Philippa's hand emerged holding Cagney's pistol. Her thumb snicked the safety to off. Sullivan saw the weapon in Philippa's unwavering hand and his confidant look faltered. Weighing his options quickly, he sprinted hard, and desperately threw his body at her. Philippa stepped coolly to one side, leaving the Bosun's Mate to crash to the earth; before he could even look up she shot him twice. Sullivan shuddered, then died.

"Hurry, Ma'am," mumbled Abraham through his smashed lips.

Shakily she gathered her thoughts and urged her body into action; leaping over Sullivan's body without sparing it a glance she sprinted past the Tank Transporter to the edge of the basalt outcrop, gasping as she absorbed the scene before her. Cagney and Trelawney were standing by the beached ship each with a noose around his neck, their hands bound behind them. Philippa's eyes followed the rope from Cagney's neck over the yard arm and down into the ready hands of two burly sailors. Young Lieutenant Rotherhithe she saw was pleading for the men's lives; his voice, high with anxiety, came faintly over the still morning air. Caruthers was laughing in his face and haranguing the junior officer, alternately shrieking and giggling until eventually he lost patience and pushed the ailing man who fell over onto the sand. There was a murmur of discontent from the assembled crew sitting on the sand which was stilled as the First Lieutenant barked an order. Philippa's eyes flicked to Caruthers' henchmen and realised why the crew were so passive – three swivel guns were aimed at the ship's complement as they sat there on the beach. Caruthers it seemed was not willing to rely solely on Naval discipline to impose his will on the seamen, he was threatening them with the swivel guns which would dispense bloody mayhem if they made a move to rescue the captives. Caruthers looked at his men holding the killing ropes and gave them a curt nod; the men, two to each rope, began to haul.

Mikey Green was in a reflective mood as he adjusted automatically to the camel's rolling gait; he longed for a seat that did not move on this his second day in the saddle. Yesterday had seen him and his companions spend ten hours driving their unwilling beasts forward with breaks as they passed through villages to buy food for themselves and fodder for the animals. At the girl's urging they had bought Arab clothing – a good move, thought Green; it was cooler and attracted less attention. He and William had kept their modern weapons outside their new attire and this overt demonstration of firepower had served to keep nosy villagers and passing travellers at a respectful distance. Green estimated their journey would take maybe until the end of the day as the camels seemed disinclined to travel at better than walking pace. Despite his discomfort it was, he reminded himself, an improvement on using his own two legs. His injured knee had seized up again during the cold night and he had willingly swallowed his pride as William and the girl had helped him climb aboard his camel which he had less than affectionately named Bastard. The girl, William had smugly informed him, was called Leila; Green was baffled how William had discovered this as the girl seemed reluctant to speak to anyone but himself and William knew not a word of Arabic. Green was still not sure how Leila's presence had come about but had happily resigned himself to letting her undoubted camel handling skills and ability to haggle with villagers smooth their path home. His thoughts drifted back to late afternoon the previous day; they had spotted two ships near the horizon several miles apart. Despite the distance William averred that they could not be other than Anastasia and Scorpion and although the following ship was a good distance behind its quarry he estimated the Scorpion's better sailing qualities would enable her to catch the Anastasia before she reached the doubtful safety of "their" bay and the Endeavour.

Unknown to the land-bound pair, Anderson, the First Mate of the Endeavour and now Commander of the Anastasia, was of a similar opinion. He had ordered the ship further out to sea to catch a breeze; he had caught a rather gentle air which even now filled his sails unevenly. It was the same Zephyr which was even-handedly bringing their relentless pursuer closer by the hour. He raised the glass to his eye for what seemed the hundredth time; the gap between the ships had not narrowed since his previous check. A puzzled frown marred his features for he knew with an unshakeable certainty that the Scorpion was a faster sailor. He concentrated on the Scorpion's sails; had Scorponi reduced sail and slowed? It certainly seemed so. Anderson tapped his teeth thoughtfully unable to see any rationale for Scorponi's actions then realisation dawned – Scorponi was shepherding them into the bay like a mangy and particularly vicious sheepdog. The villain was unwilling to assault them at sea, perhaps fearing a fire which would send his stolen treasure to the bottom of the sea. Scorponi, he reasoned, wanted all his enemies in one place where he could destroy them with his broadsides or board them at his leisure. He hoped the pirate captain may just have bitten off more than he could chew. If only the brave and resourceful American could move his monstrous cannon carriage to where its gun could bear upon the Scorpion. And if his Colonial friend failed? A rueful smile played on his lips and he shrugged to himself; at least he would die amongst friends. He laughed aloud with real humour; surprising and pleasing the worried crew members. The morning he felt sure would bring an end to this . . . one way or another *and sooner rather than later,* he mused, as the wind picked up and the ship's sails bellied out. Anderson staggered slightly as the big ship heeled over, carrying as much sail as was humanly possible. *We'll have the last laugh yet,* he vowed grimly to himself.

William reined in his camel alongside Green; his face had lost much of its cheer as he fretted about what they might find when they reached camp. He and Green had discussed the situation at length last night in the moonlit darkness; although his friend had been outwardly confident that Scorponi would "get his head kicked in" William suspected that Green was trying to buoy his spirits – but no matter how many times they aired various scenarios both men knew their friends' survival depended on Cagney moving the Tank Transporter so the Abrams cannon could dominate the bay. Green in turn was of the opinion that given his head Cagney could manage the situation; *but would he be allowed to by Caruthers?* As his camel plodded on, Green worried; he knew his worrying would alter nothing nevertheless his concerns were etched upon his face. He looked across at William; no words passed but each man felt the determination of the other.

Chapter 14

Cagney's feet were beginning to leave the ground as Philippa opened fire. A pistol is not an accurate weapon even at relatively close range and Philippa was fifty yards away; nevertheless the nine millimetre rounds smacking into the ship's side were close enough to persuade the two would-be executioners to drop their ropes and dive for cover. After four rounds, one of the swivel guns swung round and opened up on her. She caught the movement and stepped back smartly behind the rock as the grapeshot lashed the basalt already scarred by Scorponi's earlier broadside. *What to do now?* Her shots had bought the two captives a few more moments of life but Caruthers' men were already pounding their way up the shelving beach towards her. Desperation gave her thoughts wings; she dashed to the Humvee, diving through the open door and into the driving seat. Holding the wheel, frowning with concentration, Philippa strained her memory as she frantically tried to recall Cagney's routine. *Key! – Yes key,* her fumbling fingers found it and the big diesel thrummed into life; what next? Her frenzied thoughts were not allowing her to remember clearly. *On the floor,* she looked down at the pedals and pressed the brake *no, no, no, the other pedal!* She depressed it, the engine roared and the vehicle rocked a little but did not move. She lifted her foot and looked up to see a seaman not a dozen yards away rushing towards her – *the stick! Yes,* she recalled now, *the stick in the middle.* Carefully she moved the gearshift into D as Cagney had done. Nothing happened, then with a flash of inspiration she realised the floor pedal would need depressing again. As her foot moved to find it, a tattooed arm was thrust through the window, the gnarled fingers grabbing her hair.

"Not so fast my beauty." The sailor's excited face rubbed against hers; his stubble scored her cheek and his sweat mingled with her own. The foul stench of his rotting teeth reeked into her mouth as her foot found the accelerator and stabbed it. The Humvee lurched forward, its tyres scrabbling as it veered to the left scraping its armoured flank down the unyielding Tank Carrier. Her attacker's body was smeared away with a squelch and an anguished wail, his severed arm still entangled in her hair. Wrestling the wheel with a strength borne of determination, she wrenched the Humvee away from the huge vehicle and drove hard past the end of the outcrop where she sawed the wheel to the left and found herself staring at the sun as the Humvee lurched on to two wheels then slammed back down. The impact knocked the breath from Philippa and jarred her foot from the pedal.

She jabbed her foot hard down again then sped towards the ship, the Humvee bouncing over the sand, agile crew members leaping to each side as she carved a lane towards Caruthers. A swivel gun fired and starred the armoured windshield; unblinking, she moved the steering wheel a touch, ending the gunner's life by simply driving over him. Almost too late she saw Cagney standing in her path but he stepped nimbly aside as the careering steel chariot narrowly missed him and hit the First Lieutenant amidships. His head slammed down on the hood and his desperately questing fingers found a grip. Caruthers' mad unblinking eyes held Philippa's from two yards away as he tried to drag his shattered body on to the hood. Philippa screamed as she spun the wheel to the right and drove the Humvee into the calm waters of the bay. She lifted her foot from the pedal as the vehicle shuddered to a halt then slid herself on to the sand and stared at Caruthers, trapped under the steel front of the heavy vehicle, his head several inches under the surface of the water. His fingers reluctantly released their hold on the hood as bubbles trickled from his open mouth and the madness slowly left his eyes. An arm was wrapped around her shoulders and she turned to see Cagney, newly released by the crew. One eye was closed but his grip was firm. He gave her a crooked smile, his free hand investigating the rope marks around his neck.

"If we ever get back . . ." Philippa looked at him expectantly, her heart melting ". . . no way are you driving my Corvette."

Philippa laid her head on Cagney's chest; great heaving sobs racked her body as Cagney murmured soothingly in her ear. He gently disentangled himself from her embrace and spoke to Francesca who had come to her mother. "Take your mom back up to camp, Honey; I'll be up just as soon as I've organised these guys." Arm in arm the two women walked slowly up the beach and disappeared behind the outcrop. The American knelt by the side of Nicholas Rotherhithe who looked grey with pain, "You're the ranking officer now, Lieutenant," Cagney pronounced it the American way. "Guess I'd better start calling you Sir.

Rotherhithe managed a tight smile. "You are in command now, *Leftenant*, I fear I will be of little use for some considerable while," he whispered in return. Cagney called over two passing seamen and instructed them to carry the third Lieutenant back to his bed in camp. Rising to his feet wearily, the Marine looked full circle around him – no one was doing anything apart from gazing at him expectantly waiting for his orders. Cagney reached his full height, straightened his shoulders and calmly returned the stares of the men around him- *his men,* he reminded himself with an inward smile. He noted the men looked confident and unperturbed by their situation, which was dire by any standards, and Cagney knew deep within himself that their confidence was in him and his leadership *and he would deliver!* The diffident officer he had been – *how many days ago was it?* - was gone forever, never to return. The crew felt it and so did he. Cagney opened his mouth and started bellowing orders, comfortable in his new role.

A throat was cleared behind him and Cagney turned slowly to find a very battered Abraham standing before him. "You ain't looking real good, sailor." Gently placing his hands on each side of the old man's jaw, Cagney eased it from side to side. Abraham grimaced then reached a gnarled hand into his mouth and pulled out a tooth which he cast down on to the sand with a lopsided grin. "Get your towing team together, Abe, take as many men as you want but do it quickly!"

The old man hurried off and Cagney reflected that he had sent an obviously injured man back to work without a second thought. He shrugged; Abraham would be as dead as the rest of them if the Scorpion arrived before the bay was commanded by the Tank's gun. Colonel Trelawney was organising the gun crews, arranging the Endeavour's cannon so they all could fire across the waters of the bay. Cagney cocked his head to one side and listened to the hurly burly noises on the beach; men chaffing each other and cursing good-humouredly as they put their backs into their work. A comforting noise. His ears caught a rumbling in the background and with a start he realised it was the Humvee ticking over gently, its high level exhaust and inlet allowing it to do so despite having its nose buried in the clear waters of the bay. *Try again*, he thought as he settled himself into the seat, selected reverse and fed the power in. Obediently the all-wheel-drive vehicle tracked back from the water. Cagney beckoned to a sweating Colonel Trelawney, now reunited with his M16. "Let's hurry things along, Bartholomew . . ." Trelawney blinked his surprise at the use of his first name. ". . . We'll hook up each cannon to the tow hitch and I'll drag them into place."

Trelawney smiled his approval. "Might I suggest carrying powder and shot inside the vehicle, Sir?"

"You got it, Colonel, and no Sir needed, remember you outrank me!"

The Colonel shook his head vehemently. "You are in command, Lieutenant – and I SHALL address you as Sir as long as that may be." A movement in the water caused their eyes to shift; the body of the first Lieutenant had floated to the surface no longer held down by the armoured vehicle. "Shame we cannot kill him again," grunted Trelawney, gingerly touching his raw neck where the rope had abraded his skin.

Cagney called over a passing crew member. "Grab a couple of guys and take the dead into the bay and sink 'em – use the rowboat" He paused. "He looks pleased" said a mystified Cagney in a lowered tone to the old soldier.

"So he should" replied the Colonel with a knowing look, "He will be richer by a considerable degree when he has rifled the Lieutenant's pockets!"

Cagney shouted at the man, who was dragging the body from the water, "Share the profits with your buddies."

As Colonel Trelawney's men were tying a cannon to the Humvee's tow-hitch, Cagney watched the sailors roping the dead men together. The men who had been loyal to Caruthers had been beaten to death by the rest of the crew.

Abraham appeared at the Marine's side. "We be ready to pull now, Sir."

"Go to it, sailor and make 'em sweat!"

Abraham touched his threadbare forelock and headed back. He had taken no more than two steps when he halted to address the sailors on burial duty. "There be a couple more behind yon rock . . ." he paused looking thoughtful, ". . . well one an' a half!" he cackled.

"Jesus! My girl sure has been busy" muttered Cagney, half to himself. He spent the next hour at the Colonel's behest towing cannon round the bay, depositing each one above the high tide mark spaced out to provide a good field of fire. He left each cannon with ample powder and shot. His task over, he watched as the Endeavour's boat returned from dumping the weighted bodies far out into the bay. Calling the crew chief over he noticed a telescope jutting from his pocket; Cagney deduced it had recently been the property of the first Lieutenant. With a pang of guilt he recalled he had not set a watch. In consternation Cagney looked out to sea, half expecting Scorponi to be sailing into the bay. The sea was empty; barely a breath caressed the calm waters. The sailor stood before Cagney waiting his bidding and with his heart still pounding at his own lack of foresight he sent the man to keep watch from the top of the outcrop.

Still chiding himself for his carelessness, the Marine drove the Humvee up the beach and into camp. He noticed the gore congealing on the driver's side of the vehicle but his mind had moved on to his next problem and questions could wait. Parking up, the American walked past Fairbrother and Lieutenant Rotherhithe being tended by Francesca. She smiled and called a greeting but a preoccupied Cagney neither saw nor heard; his attention was entirely focussed on the Tank Carrier and the towing party which at present were standing around watching as anchor spikes were being driven into the ground. Abraham was supervising, his voice waspish with irritation. He jumped as Cagney approached unseen, placing his hand on the old man's shoulder ."How goes it, old friend?"

"The spikes be tearing out!" Abraham snapped crossly – his disappointment acute.

"OK, let's try this" soothed the American, his tone encouraging. "I'm gonna help you out with the winch on the Humvee and maybe between us we can move the beast that last few yards." He ran back to the Humvee leaving the carpenter baffled; a sailor from the raiding party explained the working of the winch to him. After Cagney had manoeuvred the heavy vehicle into position the same sailor raised his hand to Cagney to show he was lifting the winch cable. Cagney nodded then pulled the lever to un-spool the wire. The seaman walked to the Tractor unit then crawled beneath it to hook the cable to a frame member. Gaining his feet, he gave the American the thumbs up. Reversing the winch, Cagney took up the slack until the Humvee shuddered as he held the drive. "Your move, Boss." Cagney's cheerful smile brought a grin from the old man's bruised features. The teams formed up amid much spitting on hands as they took up the slack on their ropes. Cagney's eyebrows lifted as Abraham began a sea shanty; the men following suit after a few bars and Cagney revved the engine to coincide with the emphasis as they strained. To the Marine's surprise and pleasure the huge vehicle moved three inches at each pull helped by the Humvee's winch. In no time at all the Carrier and its monstrous cargo had travelled two yards as the singing men, aided by the growling diesel, converted effort into territory. As Abraham exhorted the sweating men to greater toil an anchor spike bent then swiftly uprooted itself. Too late Cagney caught sight of the falling men and before he could step off the gas to lessen the load the winch seized. Relieved of its burden the big diesel roared in protest and the wire hawser drooped to rest on the parched earth.

"We're not done yet, boys!" Cagney injected a note of cheerful optimism into his voice as he selected reverse and took the Humvee back until the hawser tightened again. As Abraham chivvied his men to drive the spike back into the ground, Cagney stepped from the Humvee to survey the scene. On the beach the red-coated Colonel Trelawney was striding from cannon to cannon spread in an arc above the high tide mark on each side of the Endeavour. Raising his eyes and shading them with his hand, he took in the lookout perched on the outcrop and made a mental note to send a hat and water to the man. His gaze dropped to the Tank Transporter; there was movement at the rear and with a feeling of relief he saw one of the figures was Philippa helping her daughter with the injured pair of Fairbrother and Rotherhithe. Cagney's eyes were instinctively drawn to the sea and the beach. The sea was empty and the activity on the sloping sand was relaxed as all possible preparations had been completed. *No,* he thought with a start, *not quite complete* he had forgotten the cannon aboard the Anastasia. He called Abraham; the little man trudged over to the Humvee. "How are the guns on the Anastasia spiked?"

The old man answered with assurance, "They be spiked with copper or brass rod, Sir . . ." he scratched his head pensively, ". . . but they be the very devil to get out, Sir."

"We'll see about that," replied Cagney, suddenly cheerful. He motioned to a nearby sailor, "Go find the Doc; ask him for battery drills with an assortment of bits and see if he's got a gas welder with a cutting torch?" The man stumbled repeating the orders so Cagney scribbled in his notebook and gave him the torn out sheet. "Give him that and hurry back with the answer." Cagney turned his gaze back to Abraham. "Who's your best gunnery guy, Abe?"

Abraham pointed his skinny arm at the shelving sand where Colonel Trelawney was deep in conversation with a member of the Endeavour's crew. "That be 'im, Sir." Cagney grabbed a man standing close, unashamedly eavesdropping and sent him to ask the pair to join him. The team hammering the spike into the ground ceased their labours and nodded to Abraham who gave Cagney a grim smile, "W'em ready to 'av another go, Sir." Cagney took the few strides necessary and hopped into the driving seat, twisting the ignition key; the engine thrummed into life. Selecting reverse, he listened to the renewed shanty, catching the changed cadence when the men pulled and gunning the engine to suit. The singing grew in volume as the Tank Carrier moved a little on each occasion. Their voices swelled and the diesel roared in time. The smell of burning rubber filled Cagney's senses at the same time as Abraham lifted his hand to call a halt. Cagney lifted his foot from the gas; the diesel rumbled to idle. Trotting over, the old man pointed to the Humvee's wheels. Scrambling out, Cagney saw the vehicle had dug itself in as it had moved to softer ground and it now was resting on its axles. Looking hard at the Abrams, Cagney's eyes told him they were tantalisingly close to achieving their aim, another yard and a half would see the turret able to traverse and command the bay. The worried frown that was about to form changed to a confidant smile as he felt the dismay of the towing team. With a moral- boosting grin which transformed into an elaborate yawn he casually asked Abraham and his sailors to dig the Humvee out. Abraham immediately began barking orders which his men scurried to obey. In a voice designed to carry and convey an insouciance he certainly did not feel Cagney announced he was "going for a stroll". He gestured Abraham towards him and placed his head next to the older man's with an easy informality. His face lost its confident mask and his voice gained a low urgency. "Quick as you can, my friend, I'm depending on you." The old man's eyes lit with understanding and he nodded briefly.

Cagney sauntered towards the Abrams as Colonel Trelawney and his gunnery assistant strode towards him from the beach, from inland came Aktar with the messenger Cagney had despatched to find him. They all met by the cab of the tractor unit. Aktar looked askance at Cagney's battered face but was reassured by the American's impish grin. "I'm OK, Doc; you got the gear I need?"

Cagney's demeanour was infectious and the Iraqi smiled. "Yes, Lieutenant, I have placed the drills and welding equipment at the base of the lift." His curiosity got the better of him, "What do you intend to do with them?"

Cagney turned to Trelawney's companion. "Abraham tells me you're the Gunner's Mate." The man nodded nervously. "The Doc here will show you the equipment you will use to un-spike the Anastasia's guns when she arrives . . ." he looked pointedly at Aktar ". . . then we'll have a weapons platform to blow the Scorpion out of the water."

Trelawney caught Cagney's eye. "Is all not well with this, Sir?" He placed a hand on the cab.

Cagney gave the soldier a quizzical glance. "Could be better, Bartholomew and I'd be happier with a backup plan." With a word Aktar hurried off for Cagney's promised equipment. Cagney sent the Gunner's Mate to help him.

"Nevertheless you seem pleased, Sir" offered Colonel Trelawney,

Cagney dropped his veneer of cheerful confidence. "It's an act, Bartholomew; we need that ship and soon." He sighed and a frown clouded his face. "We need the Anastasia's cannon – I can un-spike them in a couple of hours with our modern gear . . ." Trelawney listening attentively nodded. "Or . . ." Cagney thrust his fist into the palm of his other hand, ". . . I need the Abrams out from behind this goddam' rock! Right now we ain't got either and I'm worried."

Trelawney nodded sympathetically, noting the strain on the American's damaged face. The Englishman's eyes twinkled and the ghost of a smile tugged at the corners of his mouth. "Oh, I think a little perspective is due here, Sir; only hours ago we had been beaten senseless and we were on the brink of having our necks stretched rather further than I would have liked. I do believe we are in a somewhat happier position now . . .Sir." He raised his eyebrows and gave the American a gentle smile. The tall Marine laughed out loud at the soldier's faultless logic.

"Sail on the horizon!" The lookout's bellow caused everyone within earshot to stop what they were doing and look up.

Cagney climbed on to the Abrams turret. "Which ship, man?" he shouted, trying vainly to keep the anxiety from his voice. The lookout lifted his telescope again and focussed for long moments. Cagney tapped his foot impatiently cursing the man under his breath.

The man spoke hesitantly without taking the glass from his eye. "She be the Indiaman, Sir . . . the Anastasia."

"Good, good," grunted Cagney, his relief palpable as he started to clamber down.

"Wait, Sir." Cagney sensed the tension in the lookout's voice and paused his descent. Squinting hard, the lookout fine-tuned the magnification then lowered the telescope and faced his commanding officer, his face drawn. "The Scorpion, Sir; she be right behind her . . .no more than a league or two back – I couldn't see at first," he added apologetically. Cagney thanked him calmly, noting that the man staggered slightly as the rock moved in the freshening breeze.

Leaping lightly to the earth, Trelawney forestalled his announcement. "I heard, Sir. I should return to my gun crews if I may?"

"Go, Colonel, go," muttered Cagney abstractedly. "Give my guys digging out the Humvee the hurry up as you pass."

Deep in concentration Cagney started as a hand slid into his.

Philippa, looking remarkably composed, smiled up at him. "The Captain has woken and is anxious to speak to you." She led him to the rear of the low loader where Fairbrother and Rotherhithe lay near each other.

Fairbrother's smile was weak but his eyes were bright. Philippa arranged pillows to help him sit up and held a cup of water to his lips. The liquid splashed on his hollow cheeks; trickling down his stubbled chin. "I hear we are expecting visitors, Lieutenant." Cagney knelt hesitantly by the sick man, wanting, needing to be active with his troops. Briefly he told Fairbrother their situation. "Will you have enough time to un-spike the Anastasia's cannon?" croaked Fairbrother. Cagney shook his head grimly. "Then your own cannon is the answer, James."

"It's not looking real good right now," said Cagney, levering himself upright.

Fairbrother leaned his head backwards and stared up at the vast edifice behind him. "Remember. . ." he rasped drawing on his last reserves, ". . . mountain and Mahomet, James, mountain and Mahomet." Drained from the effort his eyes closed and he slumped tiredly onto the bed.

Cagney grunted, unwilling even to try to decipher Fairbrother's cryptic words. Looking down at the sleeping man he felt more than a tinge of jealousy, sleep was what his battered, exhausted, body and mind needed more than anything in the world right now. Squeezing Philippa's shoulder, he stalked back to the Humvee; *mountain and Mahomet!* he snorted derisively to himself. As he left the shadow of the rock Cagney's eyes swivelled, drawn like a magnet to the sea. The ships were less than a mile away, with little distance separating the two vessels. With an effort he wrenched his gaze to the Humvee; the sweating crew had dug ramps for him to drive either forwards or back. He chose forward. The willing diesel punched the vehicle from the ruts on to rocky, firmer ground. Leaping from the seat, Cagney collared the nearest sailor. "Unhook from the Tank Carrier, wrap the hawser around the cross member a few times to take up the slack then make secure again." The sailor ran to the transporter cab and did as he was bidden.

"Off we go again, guys," shouted Cagney to the towing crew who had picked up their ropes and were poised. Singing began again, noisier and more urgently with the big diesel providing the chorus. Abraham stood in front of the men singing and gesturing like Satan's very own conductor. The Tank Carrier moved a little, encouraging the men and then again, three inches on each heave. Seven times the straining sinews and bunched muscles moved the one hundred and twenty tons nearer their goal. On the eighth the ever-faithful engine roared to the red line but without any corresponding movement from the other end of the towing wire. Cagney knew with a dreadful certainty that the gearbox had given up the ghost and the Humvee would not move again. Scrambling out, almost against his will he stared out to sea. Half a mile separated the Scorpion from the bay.

A sudden thought burst in on Cagney and he sprinted to the Tractor Unit. "Keep the weight on, boys!" he yelled at the disconsolate crew. Throwing himself into the cab, he selected what he thought was low gear and reached for the ignition key; *maybe . . . just maybe* he could use the starter motor to pull it that last yard or so. He turned the key and the starter whined and moved the vehicle a few inches – miraculously the engine started despite being starved of oil and his heart leaped but it seized solid just as quickly. In a paroxysm of haste Cagney almost fell from the cab and vaulted on to the Abrams. The Tank had moved forward enough for its cannon to cover the spit of land which divided the bays but the Scorpion was already beyond the limit of the turret's traverse. They had failed and Scorponi. who was only a quarter of a mile from the entrance to the bay, was going to swan in, destroy their laughably few cannon on the beach then kill every single one of them. The towing party had wandered over to the Tank Transporter and stood in small groups, grim-faced talking desultorily – they knew just as well as Cagney what their failure meant.

Cagney called the lookout down, his work was done. The man knelt briefly as the breeze lifted to keep his balance on the trembling rock. Sliding down the ladder he brushed past Cagney who gave the huge basalt monolith a malevolent glare. "So you beat us after all, you goddam half-assed mountain," he muttered, hating the inanimate object as much as he had ever hated anything in his entire life. His movements laboured, Cagney slowly climbed down from the great Battle Tank knowing he was going to have to order these men to fight and inevitably die. Stepping heavily from the Low Loader to the sandy soil, the Captain's cryptic words echoed in his head; puzzled, he beckoned Abraham. "Hey Abe; what does mountain and Mahomet mean?"

A brief twitch of the carpenter's battered face suggested a smile. "Why it be a saying, Sir, it means if Mahomet can't go to the mountain then the mountain must go to him . . . or mebbe the other way round"

Cagney strode round the cab of the tractor unit and placed a hand on the warm smooth surface of the outcrop conscious of valuable time ebbing away. "Well, this is the only mountain we got and it looks pretty permanent." Abraham stared at him curiously. The sun had almost reached its zenith and he stood half in and half out of the rock's shadow. Cagney watched the old man's face illuminated by the sun then darkened as the shadow moved. His hand felt the rock shudder a little like a sleeper disturbed. The American looked up at the sun with his hand shading his eyes – he blinked in the relentless glare then his eyes were relieved as the swaying bulk of the rock placed him in shadow. Turning back to face Abraham again the carpenter was astonished to see a broad smile on Cagney's face. "So that's what the Captain meant."

Abraham leaned forward to catch the softly spoken words. "Sir?"

Cagney took a long stride and gripped Abraham's shoulders. "Send a man . . .no, two men to the Colonel on the beach; tell him to turn his cannon around to fire at the base of the rock."

Abraham looked perplexed. "W'em be defenceless, Sir!"

"Just do it!" snarled Cagney, "and double shot the guns – they fire on my signal." Two idlers listening to the exchange volunteered their services and rushed off to the beach. Cagney spun on his heel; *they had a chance*. Maybe only a small one but better than waiting to be slaughtered. The tall Marine felt animated now, a new vigour coursed through his veins. He caught Abraham's eye who was watching him cautiously. "Move the Captain and Mr Rotherhithe away from the lee of the rock Abe; if it slides I want them safe."

"Slides, Sir?"

"Yes, slides, my friend." Cagney grinned manically with real humour "We're gonna shoot at the base of this oversize pebble and roll it down the beach."

Enlightenment dawned on Abraham's face. "Do you really think we can do it, Sir?"

Cagney laughed and wagged his finger reprovingly. "Failure is not a cool word around this neighbourhood, Abe." The American's enthusiasm was infectious and the old man cackled. "OK, Abe, get your men on the beach to help the gun crews – get them armed 'cause some bad guys are bound to get ashore – then come back, I'll need you here."

"James."

Cagney looked at the girl he loved, her grey eyes level with his. "I got twenty seconds to say this, Honey; I want you and Francesca up country away from here and safe but I can't let you." He shook his head regretfully. "If our guys see you high tailing it outa Dodge they'll think the battle's lost – so it looks like you're staying put."

Philippa's eyes twinkled and the corners of her mouth turned up. "Idiot." she murmured. "Go lead your men, James. Be my hero." She kissed him quickly and Cagney sprinted off, his sabre catching his leg and almost upending him. "Idiot" she repeated shaking her head with a small smile. A grinning Cagney ran to the Humvee then climbed on to its roof. All the Endeavour's cannon were aimed at the base of the basalt outcrop and every eye was upon him. The gun captains held their smouldering fuses ready, some whirling them to keep the tip glowing more fiercely. The two ships were on the verge of entering the bay; the Anastasia a hundred yards out and the Scorpion the same distance behind. Cagney waited for the wind to gust; he planned to stay his hand until the rock had swung forward like an inverted pendulum with its summit overhanging the beach before he gave the order to fire. Both ships, pursued and pursuer were almost becalmed, their sails flapping listlessly.

"C'mon wind. . . " whispered Cagney to himself ". . . blow, dammit, blow." Pursing his dry lips he managed to scratch up a few notes – a traditional sailor's way to conjure up a breeze. Despite himself, a smile crept across his face; with his hands thrust deep in his pockets and whistling tunelessly he knew he must be cutting the very picture of nonchalance. Colonel Trelawney waved from the beach but after a moment's hesitation Cagney kept his hands where they were – a wave might well be interpreted as the fire order. The American piped a few more notes but nothing. *Wait a moment;* the Scorpion's sails were billowing out, to be followed seconds later by the Anastasia's. Cagney slowly lifted his hands from his pockets leaving his arms by his side. *The wind would be here in a moment . . .yes! Here it was* – it ruffled his hair and pushed him a little. *Good.* Cagney looked closely at the monstrous basalt structure and concentrated – *yes!* There was the movement. He raised his right arm whilst looking behind the rock; its shadow was magnified over the Tank and its Transporter . . .was it still moving? *Yes, just.* He concentrated on the rock's shadow picking out a depression on the very edge of the umbra. The shadow was motionless; the huge bulk had moved as far as it would go and now its thousands of tons were girding themselves for their return journey. The depression emerged into sunlight again and Cagney dropped his arm. The cannon roared in crashing unison; splinters flew from the base of the primeval monument and he saw a couple of gun crews duck as the cannon balls ricocheted from their colleagues weapons. One cannon had refused to fire despite its captain reapplying the fuse to the touchhole. The black gargantuan tottered on the edge of falling for second after long second until Cagney was convinced their efforts were in vain. He looked right and saw the Scorpion entering the bay, its gun ports open like rotting black teeth. BOOM! Cagney jumped as the reluctant cannon fired and hundreds of thousands of tons began their relentless march.

Chapter 15

Cagney's restless eyes could see no movement in the rock, so focussed their attention on its shadow which would magnify any movement and was steadily diminishing to expose the Tank and its carrier to the bright sunlight. He concentrated on the front of the rock; a shadow was gradually growing on the beach under it as it tilted with growing speed. Dry mouthed with awe at the grandiose spectacle, a spellbound Cagney watched as the ebony colossus finally crashed onto the beach with an ear-splitting, booming thunderclap. Clouds of hurtling sand spat and billowed from around its edges. The sand and the impact's reverberations reached Cagney as one; half blinding him and forcing him to his knees in order to steady himself. He raised a hand to shield his already slitted eyes and gawked hypnotised as the rock turned over once more with less pace and reduced violence then, with the groaning effort of an old man trying in vain to leave his seat, it rolled forward once more until its bulk was vertical, then subsided backwards with a thump amongst the clouds of sand.

Leaping down from the Humvee, Cagney sprinted towards the Abrams, still rocking gently on its carrier from the shuddering of the miniature earthquake. Philippa was waiting by the glacis plate and with a heave Cagney launched her up to the turret, now with a clear field of fire. The Marine followed her up then lowered her through the commander's cupola, cursing the stinging in his one good eye as he did so. A few seconds later the Abrams' turbine engine screamed into life. Standing in the turret, Cagney looked down at Philippa in the gunner's seat with her hands reaching for the controls; he tapped her on the shoulder,

"You're shooting; I can't use this." He indicated the binocular targeting viewfinder. "Need two eyes," he explained, pointing to his closed left eye. Lifting his head up, he looked into the bay; through the swirling sandy mist he could see the Scorpion marginally behind the Anastasia.

"Traverse left," he shouted above the whine of the engine. The huge turret with its 120mm high velocity cannon rotated smoothly. Looking down he saw Philippa's face pressed against the gunner's viewfinder; the cannon swivelled, resting momentarily, it seemed to Cagney, on the pirate ship before continuing the few degrees until it pointed at the Anastasia. "You've overshot" screamed Cagney, "traverse ri . . ." The concussion of the Abrams' main gun drowned his plea as the Tank rocked on its suspension from the recoil. Across the bay the high explosive shell entered the merchantman's hold and exploded within.

An aghast Cagney watched Anderson cutting the ship's boats free and ushering the crew and passengers into them knowing they would float free when the ship sank which it did less than a minute later leaving the top of the masts above the waves to show its final resting place. Cagney ducked into the turret,

"Jesus, Honey! You sunk the wrong ship! Reload and traverse right." Philippa raised her eyes guiltily and lifted another HE round from the rack near her. Aboard the pirate ship Scorponi and his crew were stunned; the demolition of the basalt monolith had caused consternation but the appearance of the iron monster above the beach appalled and terrified them. They heard the demonic whine of its turbine and men who had never before entered a church crossed themselves. When the Anastasia was targeted and sunk, a few optimistic souls thought deliverance might be at hand but then they stood hypnotised as the giant turret turned and the long barrel was again pointed at them. The pirate crew could not hear Cagney's quiet words "Fire when ready," but saw the telltale puff of smoke as the shell left the gun and felt the simultaneous concussion in the bowels of their ship as the round exploded beneath them. The Scorpion began to settle immediately, its deck listing ominously to port. The panicked crew were galvanized into frantic activity and small groups began launching the ship's boats with little regard for their shipmates. Frequent squabbles broke out and not a little blood was spilt as the crew fought for the available spaces. Scorponi ignored it all. Bending swiftly he picked up a large cork float and calmly waited as his ship sank beneath him. Carefully avoiding becoming entangled with the rigging he floated up then climbed until he sat in the cross trees of the mast which protruded a few feet above the water. Scorponi cursed as his telescope slid from his pocket and fell with a small plop into the water. He settled himself comfortably, hiding under a sail. There was a small bag of diamonds hanging from a cord about his neck and enough gold secreted on his person for his immediate needs. Once darkness had fallen, he could swim around the headland into the next bay to make his escape. The swim held no terrors for him – unlike most seamen he was a strong swimmer and he had the insurance of the cork float if tiredness struck.

Philippa looked up apologetically at Cagney. "I am so sorry, my love; my finger slipped on the trigger."

Cagney, in truth, had not recovered from the shock of the Anastasia sinking. He felt guilty for the lost lives of the pirate prisoners in the ship's hold but said nothing.

She brightened. "I have found these in a locker." She held up the end of an ammunition belt for the Browning. "Are these bullets for your . . .um . . . rat-a-tat-tat gun," she finished with a small smile. Reaching down Cagney took the heavy belt from Philippa's outstretched arms and layered it in the empty ammunition box of the Tank commander's machine gun on the cupola. He fed the belt through the breech and cocked the Browning then ran his good eye down the ugly fluted barrel into the bay. He counted ten boats from the Scorpion, each crowded with men and pulling strongly towards the shore. Switching his gaze, he observed Colonel Trelawney haranguing his troops to turn their cannon around to target the incoming boats.

Cagney took a moment to assess the situation; he did not know much about cannon but thought they would find it difficult to hit such relatively small targets. Lining the Browning up on the nearest boat he depressed the trigger, seeing the bullet splashes in front of the boat he walked the rounds in. The men who survived the onslaught threw themselves into the water as Cagney had intended. A grim smile crossed his face; the few pirates who could swim and managed to struggle ashore would be easily dealt with by the Colonel's men. Aligning the sights on a second boat was less easy as the turret turned as he was drawing a bead; adjusting his aim, he was thwarted again as the turret rotated a little and the main armament depressed then fired. The pinnace to the right of his intended target simply disappeared in a bright flash. The Abrams rocked from the recoil. Cagney looked closely – no swimmers, no boat! The Endeavour's sailors on the beach cheered the destruction of each small vessel and abandoned attempts to manoeuvre their own heavy weapons. At a word from Trelawney they waited at the water's edge with cutlass and musket in hand for the remnants of the Scorpion's crew who were capable of staggering ashore.

As he lined the Browning up on yet another boat, Cagney felt a moment of unease about dispensing death so easily, almost casually. He could see the faces of the pirates and how they quailed as they saw the big machine gun swing towards them. Spraying a few rounds near their boat caused the panic stricken men to abandon their small craft, leaping frenziedly into the limpid waters. Elevating the muzzle, a short burst ruined the boat and eased his conscience. Philippa, he observed, with mixed emotions, shared no such compunction as pragmatically she blew two more boats to shreds with the Abrams' main gun. She desisted only because the long barrel would depress no further leaving only two boats from the small flotilla which had left the Scorpion. Cagney squinted again down the barrel of the Browning and decided the Colonel and his men could cope with mopping up the remaining pirates.

The red coated figure was determined not to allow a single armed man ashore and so used his borrowed M16 to pick off several of the boats' occupants until the rest leaped into the water to escape the accurate fire. The bedraggled, beaten men who stumbled ashore surrendered without a fight to the Endeavour's crew. Cagney scanned the pitifully few survivors searching for Scorponi's bulky figure; there was no one amongst the prisoners who remotely resembled anyone of the pirate Captain's build.

Cagney crouched down into the turret and with disappointment in his voice informed Philippa, "I'm going down to the ship; stay here 'til the area's safe." Philippa looked up and Cagney impulsively wriggled his body down in the confined space to kiss her. He banged his head on the breech of the cannon and cursed, offering her a rueful smile,

"You lanky, gangling, clumsy, colonial oaf," she laughed. "Go now before you damage yourself beyond repair." Levering himself out of the steel confines, an ebullient Cagney leaped down to the earth. Down the sloping beach he walked, stopping at the edge of the fallen giant lying on its side in the sand. Its reduced height had removed much of its threatening, overpowering bulk and he felt curiously saddened at being the architect of its demise. Cagney stroked its warm side and reaching down picked up a shard of basalt splintered by the Endeavour's cannon. Placing the gleaming splinter in his pocket he walked on. Everywhere he saw pockets of seamen talking excitedly; most offered their congratulations. His broad smile encouraged some crew members to extend their hand to him. Cagney walked on until he reached the beached Endeavour then halted. There was a twenty yard corridor between the ship and its large new companion; he touched the rock again, reflecting that one more roll would have seen the Endeavour crushed beneath it.

"A damn' close run thing, what?" Trelawney's voice spiked his thought train - the old soldier wore a grin stretching from one peeling red ear to the other - he reached for Cagney's hand and shook it firmly. "An inspirational move, Sir." His eyes flicked to the fallen giant.

"Bartholomew, I'd surely like to take credit but it was the Captain's idea and, hey, you made it happen with your gun crews."

Trelawney tilted his head to one side and looked quizzically at Cagney. "With all due respect, Sir, I have heard more sense coming from a horse's arse." Trelawney's words, softly but firmly spoken left the American open mouthed. The red coated figure prodded the marine in the chest with a long, bony finger. "This is your victory, James; do not attempt to credit others. You and you alone are the driving force behind our triumph!" Cagney coloured; Trelawney continued. "The prisoners are being clapped in irons as we speak and shortly, Sir. I do believe a few words to the men might be in order."

"Sure thing, Colonel," returned Cagney, "Have them gather round."

Trelawney frowned. "With respect, Sir, no! Do not diminish this occasion: you will address your men ,and I emphasise YOUR men, from atop the . . .um . . .Abrams!" Trelawney patted Cagney on the shoulder and instructed the nearest man to pass the word for the crew to assemble by the Tank. The two soldiers separated by age and ages trudged up the beach. Philippa watched the two men from her vantage point on the Low Loader. She had just straightened up from pushing Cagney's diving equipment under the Tank from where Cagney had thrown it in preparation for the raid on the fort. Dr Aktar had observed her with a puzzled expression and his sense of bafflement increased when Philippa noticed him and put a finger to her pursed lips in the universal signal for quiet. The children had emerged from underground with the scientist and Spotty Dog appeared from wherever he had been hiding and bounded onto the Transporter to join his mistress. As the two soldiers approached, Philippa, in the corner of her eye, saw the First Mate Anderson with his crew and passengers coming from the other direction. Anderson's face was a mixture of anger at the loss of his ship and wonder at the displaced outcrop. Philippa hopped off the Transporter, rushed to Anderson and clasped his hands fervently,

"Oh, Mr Anderson! I do so beg your forgiveness." The Mate's jaw went slack. "It was I, Mr Anderson, who sank your ship . . .I made a dreadful mistake." Breathlessly she continued, "Were any of your people hurt?"

Somewhat mollified he answered slowly, "Why no, Ma'am, but the men are not rich and the prize money would have meant much to them."

She smiled sweetly, disarming the man. "Fear not, Mr Anderson; James' vehicle is awash with gold and I assure you it will be shared amongst the crew."

"Thank 'ee Ma'am," said Anderson, the scowl vanishing from his face. Cagney had overheard the last of the exchange – he looked right, seeking his diving equipment; he could see the masts of the Anastasia and knew the Captain's cabin full of booty was under only forty feet of water.

About to offer a solution, he felt Philippa's nails dig into his wrist and discerned a warning look in her eyes. She reached up and pulled his head close putting her lips to his ear. "No diving."

Despite his face reflecting his puzzled thoughts, Philippa's stern expression and raised eyebrows only emphasised her words. Trelawney's clipped tones interrupted his thoughts. The old soldier was standing by the Abrams with his arm aloft waiting for the hubbub to die down. He glared down at Mrs Boscombe who was chattering volubly, newly re-united with her sister oblivious to the irate officer; her sister caught the Colonel's eye and touched her sibling's arm, halting her in mid sentence. Trelawney's icy stare was wasted on the short-sighted lady who smiled happily back at him. He cleared his throat. "Harrumph, Lieutenant Cagney will address you now on the day of our great victory . . ." A roar of approval rent the air as Cagney strode towards Trelawney who gave him a helping hand onto the makeshift steel rostrum.

The Marine looked down at the sea of smiling faces. His characteristic reserve evaporating as a broad grin spread across his lean face. "It's been a good day . . ." More cheers and clapping made him pause. ". . . A very good day in fact. I want to thank you all for your contribution to our victory. There's been a downside to today – we lost the Anastasia; but mistakes happen . . ." He treated Philippa to a small sad smile. She guiltily glanced away. He pointed to the Humvee. "But there is enough gold in there for everyone to leave here rich. And that's what's gonna happen." Delighted sailors swapped looks and began thinking how to spend their new-found wealth. Cagney lifted his arms to quell the murmuring. "Tonight, people we are gonna have us a celebration . . ." he paused theatrically ". . . with good food and enough drink to float the Endeavour." Cheering again broke out and the Marine let the emotion wash over him. "Anyone not royally drunk tonight will be shot by the Colonel here!" A cold silence dawned; Cagney scanned the faces of the subdued men. "Jesus guys; it's a joke!" Smiles broke out once more. A voice filtered from the rear of the gathering. Cagney lifted his hand to shade his eyes and saw Nicholas Rotherhithe, looking pale with his arm around Francesca, her blond tresses falling on his shoulder. Heads and eyes turned to the pair,

"Three cheers for Lieutenant Cagney!" came the ringing tones. Cagney gave a deprecating shrug and made to jump off the trailer;

Colonel Trelawney's fingers entwined themselves in the back of his battledress and hauled him back. "Enjoy the moment," he hissed.

Cagney stood stock still soaking up the applause from the whistling, cheering crowd. His eyes found Philippa and locked on to hers; taking a deep breath, the young American Marine felt utterly complete. Philippa saw his smile fade away and knew he was thinking of his missing friend.

Ten miles away Mikey Green was trying to make his mind up which hurt most, his knee or his backside. Green and "Bastard" the camel had negotiated an uneasy truce. Three times the surly beast had reached its long neck round to bite Green's leg; on the final occasion it had found Green's bayonet waiting for it. "Bastard's" bloody muzzle and the Paratrooper's sore elbow from his subsequent violent ejection from the saddle had convinced both man and beast that a temporary armistice was an option worth taking up. The three camels with their mismatched trio of riders plodded on in the baking sun. Green had called a halt earlier when he thought he could hear gunfire or explosions. William had cocked his head to one side and concurred with Green's assessment. They had speculated in a desultory manner about how the unseen drama had been played out and then nudged their beasts into life to continue their slow march onwards. Their apprehension was building but, as Green had pointed out, they really had nowhere else to go. William had not understood the Para's assertion that they would "drive off that bridge when they came to it" but desperately wanted to rejoin his friends and see familiar faces. The girl said nothing; her eyes had flicked from one man to the other, understanding no words but hearing the low tones and catching their mood.

An hour passed, then two; Green was about to call a halt for a drink when they crested a rise and saw the battlefield before them. There was a surreal, unfamiliar look to the scene which Green was at a loss to explain until William gasped, "The rock 'as fallen over, Mikey!"

Green stared for many moments and with a queer smile said, "I reckon it might have been pushed, mate."

It was William's turn to be flummoxed. "Pushed?"

"Yes mate, pushed; I think Jimmy boy found he couldn't move the Tank so he moved the rock. What a clever boy," he finished, admiration in his voice. "But did they win?" he continued soberly pulling out the telescope and lifting it to his eye. He moved the instrument about trying to analyse the scene.

"Well?" grumbled William.

"Can't tell." The Paratrooper frowned with concentration. "There are two ships sunk in the bay and the Abrams cannon is pointing out to sea but we're too far away to identify the people.

"You think Scorponi got ashore and won?" queried William anxiously.

"Could be," replied Green moodily. He injected an artificial lightness into his voice. "Right, this is what we'll do; you two can wait here while I amble down with my Arab gear on looking like a local. If the good guys won you can follow. If Scorponi won then it's going to get messy." He reached for his pack full of gold coins. "Here take this; it will give you a start in a new life."

William's eyes narrowed at being excluded from whatever danger Green wanted to shield him and his anger grew. "Fuck off," he said, slowly and distinctly.

Green's eyes popped and his mouth hung open. He swallowed. "You can't say that to me!"

William nudged his camel closer and moved his face to within inches of Green's. "Fuck off . . ." he paused ". . . shortarse!"

"Shortarse," echoed the girl as she trotted her beast ahead of them both.

Green thoughtfully patted his camel's neck. "Giddy up, Bastard; I think we're outvoted. The beast for once did as it was ordered and lumbered forward. There was silence bar the clopping of the camels' outsize hooves; William could tell Green was thinking hard and his suspicions were confirmed when a loud thwack coincided with a stinging pain at the back of his head. He whirled in the saddle to see a grinning Green waving his crutch.

"That's for the shortarse!"

Cagney leaped from the Tank Carrier and headed to Philippa. "I need to talk to Nicholas, Honey." She slipped her arm through the American's and they threaded their way through the milling throng until they reached him. "How're you doing, sailor?"

Rotherhithe smiled sheepishly. "I may not have been a great help during the battle, Sir, but I believe I am sufficiently recovered to organise tonight's victory celebrations." He called over a passing seaman, "Assemble three teams of six men each; you will be visiting nearby villages to buy fresh meat on the hoof – remember, Smith, I said buy, not steal." Rotherhithe, a concerned look on his youthful face, glanced back at Cagney, "Considering you have won a great victory, Sir, you seem unhappy."

Before Cagney could open his mouth Philippa spoke. "James is worried about Sergeant Green, Nicholas; his mechanical carriage is damaged and the Sergeant is injured many leagues distant."

Rotherhithe looked thoughtful. "I would gladly sail the Endeavour along the coast to the scene of your raid but she is sorely wounded. However, as time is of the essence we do have a pair of skiffs which will bear canvas and I will sail at first light on the morrow to seek our brave friend."

Cagney took a deep breath. "Thank you, Lieutenant, I'll leave you to sort the details while I sleep for about a year," he laughed and sat wearily on a convenient boulder.

"No you don't," smiled Philippa as she hauled him to his feet ignoring his protestations of fatigue. "You are going to sleep until we eat this evening . . . which will be when, Nicholas?"

"Dusk is my estimate, Ma'am."

"Very well." Scooping up blankets which were lying on the ground she added, "Wake us when food is ready, we will be in the Humming . . . err thing." She pointed at the Humvee and with her arm through Cagney's, who was stumbling with tiredness, they headed to it. Third Lieutenant Nicholas Rotherhithe prided himself on his organisational skills and within minutes the former battlefield was bustling with activity. The cook and his

205

helpers were building cooking fires in anticipation of the returning foraging parties, sailors busied themselves.

He called over the First Mate Anderson. "My commiseration on the loss of your first command, Mr Anderson."

Anderson smiled ruefully. "These are strange times, Sir."

"Strange indeed," murmured Rotherhithe. "You must know upon our return we will be called before their Lordships at the Admiralty to explain our adventures – any thoughts on that, Mr Anderson?"

The First Mate gave the young officer a speculative look. "That sounds like officer's work to me rather than an innkeeper's."

"Innkeeper's?"

"Aye, Sir; I have enough money – more than enough thanks to Mr Cagney to buy an inn, find a wife and settle down away from the sea."

"Hmm." Rotherhithe's voice was full of youthful disapproval," I cannot believe the Navy will be entirely happy with your decision but for myself I do not blame you, Mr Ander . . ."

Francesca interrupted him, "Promise me, Nicholas, you will turn a blind eye; I will accompany you to their Lordships."

Rotherhithe clasped Anderson's hand. "I cannot do as I am ordered, Mr Anderson, but I can promote you to Third Lieutenant so you may resign your commission with a clear conscience when we dock . . . now, I do believe the men deserve their rum ration, *Lieutenant* Anderson."

"Double, Sir?" queried Anderson, smiling broadly and nodding by way of encouragement.

"Oh, by all means!"

The Mate was spinning on his heel when a thought crossed his mind; he turned back. "Beggin' pardon, Sir, but bein' as you're Captain now. . ." He spoke at some length and as his words trailed away Rotherhithe gazed at Francesca. "What a capital suggestion; as soon as the

Endeavour is seaworthy it shall be done!" The trio wandered round the busy site chatting to and encouraging men who were in various stages of intoxication.

Rotherhithe collared a rather worse-for-wear Abraham to construct a dining table for thirty. "That is if you can build it without sawing off your arm, Dryden?" Abraham assured him that it was well within his compass.

"Ah, Captain Rotherhithe!" The voice was from behind him. Rotherhithe turned slowly, his stitches dragging, to find Professor Aktar accompanied by the Boscombe sisters. Rotherhithe's face betrayed his pleasure at his new title. Aktar was in jovial mood as he flirted clumsily with the ladies. "I have access to a large kitchen in the complex below if you can obtain some meat?"

Rotherhithe beamed. "There is your answer, Doctor." He grinned as he lifted his arm, Aktar saw in the distance several seamen herding sheep and goats towards the camp. "Speak to the cook; he will butcher the beasts and bring the cuts to you."

Chapter 16

Two men watched the activities of the bustling crowd with grim concentration. Captain Mohammed Hassan, late of Saddam Hussein's Republican Guard was two hundred yards away. The gold and weapons he had taken from the dead pirates had enabled him to buy food from a nearby village. When the Frigate sailed he planned to make his move on the allied soldiers. He was not sure how or why events had taken the turn they had but once the soldiers were dead he was sure the scientist could be persuaded to take them both back. Out in the bay, seated on the cross-trees of the Scorpion's mast, Captain Scorponi was also keeping a careful eye on proceedings through a chink in the sail that concealed him. He too had his plans.

The afternoon wore on with the busy, happy throng enjoying the carnival atmosphere. Abraham and his fellow carpenters had built a trestle table to seat thirty with a variety of objects masquerading as chairs.

Rotherhithe clapped the wizened old chippie on the back. "Address yourself to your victuals and rum, Dryden; your labours are done for today."

As the daylight bled into dusk, Rotherhithe tentatively approached the Humvee containing the sleeping pair. He tapped on the armoured side and called Cagney's name. "Dinner in fifteen minutes, Sir." He was about to repeat his call when he noticed the vehicle was rocking with a regular motion on its springs. "Ah" he said softly to himself and retreated quietly to join Francesca who was setting cutlery.

"Are they roused?" she asked brightly,

"They needed no help from m,." he replied pointedly, with a small smile.

Francesca giggled as she helped Mrs Boscombe set the table. Looking over Rotherhithe's shoulder she pointed.

"Visitors, Nicholas" Rotherhithe shaded his eyes to see a mile away, shimmering in the heat haze, three camels and their riders. One of the riders was observing them through a telescope.

Green put the instrument down and grinned at William,

"Looks like the good guys won, my lad!" William beamed in return and saw mischief in Green's face. "Cover your face; we're visiting locals – let me do all the talking." The trio plodded on.

Cagney felt alive; the three hours sleep and shower had rejuvenated him. Not three, he reminded himself with an involuntary smile. Philippa had stolen the last half hour to enjoy him and had giggled like a schoolgirl when Rotherhithe's knock on the Humvee had interrupted them. The memory must have generated another smile for as he sat at the head of the dining table Philippa squeezed his knee and gave him a knowing look. Cagney ran his eye over his dinner companions; Trelawney and Anderson were flanking himself and Philippa. The American had insisted on the veterans of the raid sitting close despite naval protocol placing his senior officers there. Rotherhithe had shrugged it off good naturedly and sat at the foot of the table with Francesca in conversation with the Anastasia's passengers and the Anastasia's Third Lieutenant Courtney Twill, who was drunk. Anderson was chatting amiably with Professor Aktar – an amazed Cagney listened to them discussing their common passion of beekeeping. The two Iraqi children sat on the other side of Aktar saying little but eating lots and passing chunks of meat down between them to a very happy Dalmatian. At the table head Cagney was in a relaxed frame, at one with the world. He surveyed the well-stocked table illuminated by ship's lanterns in the fading light. His hand for a change was not gripping a weapon but a silver goblet full of wine – the goblet had come from Captain Fairbrother's cabin as indeed had the wine. It was not the Californian red he preferred but given the circumstances it would do. Above the hum of conversation around the table he could hear the crew

209

singing; they were gathered around a campfire some fifty yards distant. *Some thick heads tomorrow,* he smiled. His smile faded as discordant tones from the foot of the table jarred against the cordial mood. Cagney was unsurprised at the source; Courtney Twill the Third Officer of the Anastasia was subjecting the diners closest to him to a mewling, sullen tirade. Cagney caught references to "eating with damned natives and lower orders who are promoted above their station." He glanced at Anderson who had coloured and looked distinctly uncomfortable.

"Beg pardon," he muttered, "Best I leave the table"

"Remain seated, Mr Anderson!" Cagney's voice, low and fierce reached the newly promoted man and he subsided, his face the colour of beetroot. Rotherhithe cast an uneasy glance at Cagney; Courtney Twill's drunken voice was becoming shriller as he warmed to his task. The background hum died as Cagney rose to his feet strode round to Courtney Twill and yanked him to his feet where he stood swaying as he tried to focus on the American.

"How dare you? You colonial upstart," he brayed petulantly, spraying wine. Cagney was in the act of pulling his arm back to punch the man when he felt hot breath on the back of his neck and smelled a musky overpowering odour.

"Greetings, Effendi." The words harsh and accompanied by an extravagant hawking and spitting came from behind the angry American. Cagney whirled round, forgetting about Courtney Twill and looked up to find himself facing a short man on a large camel. In the gloom he could see the man's two companions on their beasts behind him. The Marine took a step backwards as the nearest animal attempted to make a meal of his battledress tunic. The short man ,with only his eyes visible through his Arab headdress continued, after touching his forehead and chest and bowing slightly, his voice rough and halting.

"In the tent of my forefathers it is written that a brave warrior from a distant land would win a great victory and his tribe would cry loudly in triumph. Yea, even the harem forgive him for his small part which causes much laughing when he looketh away." He concluded piously, "I, Mustapha Swift'un have spoken."

Cagney stood slack-jawed with astonishment; his mouth opened then closed without speaking. Turning his head to Philippa he said incredulously, "Did this guy just say I have a small dick?"

Anderson nudged her and nodded at the "Arab's" footwear. She saw the British Army boot and gasped. Subduing the almost irresistible temptation to smile, she spoke, her voice clear in the stunned silence. "Welcome, O Mustapha Swift'un; thou speakest ill of my brave warrior for I, his bint have seen him. Yea, as he was born, and he is made as a baboon and maketh the harem wince when he desireth them." She set her hands apart in the manner of a fisherman describing his catch by way of emphasis.

Cagney's jaw dropped once more as Philippa's words faded away to be replaced by Mrs Boscombe's stage whisper. "Lucky girl!"

Cagney felt himself flush in the twilight. Mustapha Swift'un's companions "couched" their camels which subsided wheezing and groaning. The two riders alighted and moved into the light; Cagney was surprised to see one of them was a teenage girl. He turned his attention back to see the short rider noisily try to emulate the others and make his camel kneel. Cagney knew no Arabic and consequently was startled to hear the word bastard repeated amongst what sounded like guttural nonsense. The girl snapped an order bringing the camel quickly to its knees, surprising the rider who tumbled headlong to Cagney's feet, muttering and cursing. Philippa's Dalmatian padded over, buried its muzzle under the Arab's headdress and began licking his face.

"Hello, Spotty Dog," said the fallen rider.

Cagney blinked, his senses arrested and astounded by the phrase spoken in an unmistakeable Yorkshire accent. He reached down and yanked the rider's hood back to reveal the Paratrooper's head. "You little Limey bastard!"

he exclaimed, lifting the Englishman off his feet and shaking him.

"Hello, big boy," replied Green with a huge grin. Within seconds the Paratrooper was surrounded by well-wishers, slapping his back and shaking his hand. William stood shyly on the periphery of the celebrations until Green hauled him close. "This is the bloke I've got to thank!" William handed Green his crutch and looked away embarrassed.

Anderson thrust a goblet of wine into his hand. "Well done, my lad!"

Green grinned wolfishly at Philippa. "Don't I get a hug?"

She threw her arms around him and ruffled his hair, unashamedly delighted. "You are a villainous creature, Mikey Green! You simply wanted to thrust your nose into my cleavage!"

Spot on, thought Green, aloud he said, "Furthest thing from my mind." Cagney raised an eyebrow. "Yeah, alright, I lied."

"My cleavage too!" squealed Francesca wrapping her arms around him. *Rude not to* thought Green happily; squeezing her pert bottom as he did so.

She squealed again. "Oh, Nicholas, did you see what that naughty man did?" She draped herself around the young officer and in a little girl voice said "I suppose you will have to fight a duel over my honour now?"

Rotherhithe quickly calculated his chances of surviving the suggested encounter and responded pragmatically; he spun Francesca around patted her rump by way of invitation and smiled at Green. "Please do help yourself, Sergeant."

Francesca pouted and giggled then stamped on Rotherhithe's foot.

Green's eyes narrowed. "Where's that sod Caruthers?"

"The sea bed, Mikey," replied Cagney soothingly.

"Good man!" said Green approvingly taking a swig of wine and smacking his lips.

"Not me, Buddy." Green looked over to Colonel Trelawney. Cagney shook his head and nodded in Philippa's direction. "Ran him down with the Humvee when the bastard was stringing up me and Bartholomew – sit down I'll fill you in."

"Hang on a mo," muttered his friend walking to the shadows and emerging with the Arab girl. "Hey, Doc, have a chat to Leila and make her feel at home." Making himself comfortable at the table after piling a plate full of food, Green turned to Cagney. "I'm listening Boss; talk me through all this." He waved an arm airily. The only reply was Cagney's steady breathing.

Philippa reached to the table and held up a ship's lantern to reveal Cagney, his chin on his chest sound asleep. She smiled, half her features in shadow. "James has had the longest day a man can endure, Mikey. Mr Anderson, will you and William ensure James finds his bed please?" The two men helped Cagney to his feet and taking the lantern assisted the shambling, exhausted American to his pile of blankets thirty yards away where he subsided into a deep, untroubled slumber. Philippa lifted another lantern from the table and took Green's arm, leading his limping figure to the low-loader where the camels were tethered. They sat. "I have a great deal to tell you Mikey but first of all, I am returning with you to your time – I need to be with James."

"Cool," was Green's response; his camel at the limit of its tether nuzzled his hair gently. He reached up and scratched its muzzle affectionately.

"Does he have a name?"

"Bastard." he replied simply.

"Ah," said Philippa. There was a longish pause where she fidgeted, demonstrably uncomfortable. Green waited patiently. "Will I fit in?"

"Piss off you smelly bugger!" said Green equably, "Not you, Philippa."

"In your time, Mikey, will I be a freak who people stare at?"

"Men will stare at you," he admitted with a chuckle; "but men have always stared at you – and you might get more attention than you want if your driving doesn't improve!"

"James told you of that?"

Green squeezed her hand. "You're a bit of a star, lass; you'll fit in no bother. Now tell me all about the stuff I've missed." The Englishwoman smiled with relief and recounted events since the raiding party's return.

When she got to the point of the Anastasia's sinking, Green interrupted. "Are you telling me there is a King's ransom of gold and jewellery in the Captain's cabin under forty feet of water?"

"Shh" she admonished him fiercely.

Green whistled softly. "You know what James' particular skill is, don't you?"

Philippa moved her head closer to the lantern so Green could see her set expression. "I have no desire to travel over two centuries arriving as a pauper!"

"I can see a problem." Green spoke softly. "If I was in Rotherhithe's place I'd blow the cabin apart with gunpowder – yes it can be done," he emphasised as he saw her doubtful face. "His gunners can make a waterproof fuse, then he can use grappling irons to trawl up the goodies that are exposed."

Philippa looked thoughtful. "But will he want to?"

Green looked perplexed. "Eh?"

Philippa gave a low throaty chuckle. "Nicholas Rotherhithe wishes to take my daughter up the aisle and in doing so will inherit my considerable estates. She paused dramatically, "I do believe Nicholas and I can come to an accommodation whereby his inaction here will result in him becoming a very wealthy man upon his marriage."

Green had a sudden vivid insight. "Did you sink the Anastasia on purpose?"

There was a significant pause; *very significant*, was Green's thought. "Would it bother you, Sergeant, if it made you a rich man?"

"Probably not." admitted Green slowly. The awkward moment was broken by the arrival of Professor Aktar; unusually for him he was smiling,

"Ah, Sergeant; I have conducted a lengthy conversation with your newly acquired companion Leila and to use a very apt metaphor you appear to have caught a tiger by the tail." A scowl crossed Green's face in the darkness; he sensed the Iraqi was enjoying himself. "Apparently her uncle who sold you these camels . . ." he waved a hand at the snuffling beasts " . . . was overjoyed to unload her to you as he regarded her as a troublesome influence in his camp by refusing to marry his second son."

"Bloody hell," groaned Green, "That's all I need - a stroppy teenager blighting my life!"

Aktar replied with a smugness of manner. "Alas, Sergeant, if ill temper were her only vice you would be counting your blessings." Aktar laughed heartily causing Green's frown to deepen. "She has formed a err . . . shall we say, romantic attachment to you . . ."

"Not a hope!" snapped Green, "Tell her I'm married."

Aktar's smile broadened. "I already tried that tack; and with deep regret . . ." he spread his arms wide in a "not my fault gesture" ". . . I must tell you she is prepared to accept the role of second wife."

Green looked at Aktar's face with the remnants of a smug smile on it and knew the man's deep regret was a veneer. He looked daggers at him.
"Lucky for you we no longer kill the bringer of bad tidings," he said coldly. "Bastard!" he exclaimed. The camel, under the impression he was being summoned, ambled closer knocking the scientist to the ground. "He gets jealous," laughed Green, the spell of his short temper broken. He helped the Iraqi to his feet. "Look, help me out here, Doc . . . can't I just sell her?"

"Mikey Green." The sharp, peremptory tones rang out from behind him, "You will not sell that poor girl . . . especially as she loves you," she added mischievously.

The scientist rubbed his hip ruefully. "I will do my best, Sergeant, but she is a strong minded girl and as such is unlikely to heed my advice that, as we are likely to have our atoms scattered throughout the universe shortly, she will be wasting her affections."

Philippa and Green shared a glance; the Englishwoman spoke first, her tone wary. "Would that you are being unduly pessimistic, Professor."

"Or would it be realistic?" added Green.

Aktar scratched his head pensively and moved a little further from Bastard. "If my calculations are correct, the margin for error is small . . . very small," he repeated. "But I will double check them," he offered with an apparent lack of irony. He wandered off, intercepting the children and Spotty Dog who were intent on visiting the Paratrooper. "Bed, my little ones," he said in Arabic; Green guessed the meaning and waved at the youngsters who disappeared into the gloom.

"Still fancy a bit of century hopping then?" asked Green, trying to take the sting from the scientist's words.

"Where James goes I will follow." She said without hesitation, picking up the lantern and leaving, after kissing Green's cheek. He watched her walk away, the lantern swaying in the darkness then, with some difficulty, climbed into the cab of the Tank Carrier, wrapped himself in his Arab robes and fell asleep almost immediately, stretched out on the bench seat.

Green slept late and would probably have slumbered on if it were not for the succession of pebbles thrown through the cab window, the fifth of which struck him a light blow on the temple. Rashid had been sent to find him with his breakfast but had been unable to open the heavy door of the cab. Rubbing his head, Green opened his eyes and ducked away from the next pebble. He sat up and stuck his head through the window – a pebble impacted on his forehead with a solid dink. Rashid shrieked with laughter and stamped his foot excitedly. Grunting with stiffness and pain, the Para eased himself down to the earth to be presented with coffee and a fresh roll.

"Good Mikey morning," beamed the little lad who scampered into the cab to retrieve Green's crutch.

"Good lad," smiled Green. "Let's have a sit down shall we?" The pair made their way to last night's table where they were joined by Cagney and Philippa. Greetings were exchanged. Something moved on the Endeavour catching Green's eye he turned his head to see a hanged man swaying from the mast in the morning breeze. He pulled a face. "Suddenly I don't feel so hungry."

"It's how they do things in this part of town, Buddy; he's the last one – young Nicholas has been busy since early."

Green drank his coffee slowly and adjusted his position to ease the pain in his knee.

"Show me," ordered the American. Green obediently lifted his trouser leg until his cut and bruised leg saw daylight. Cagney manipulated the Para's leg and probed the damaged area with his fingers. "Cracked or broken patella," he announced eventually. "That's kneecap to you," he added unnecessarily. "My advice to you as the nearest thing to a doctor you're gonna get in these parts is to limp for a while until we get home or our atoms are scattered throughout the Cosmos – in which case you can ignore my advice!"

"So Professor Doom and Gloom's been spreading a little light relief eh?"

Cagney yawned and shrugged. "Hell, we got no place else to go, Mikey, so I guess we relax and try to be a tad laid back about it." They spoke at some length about their journey home and in particular the explaining they would have to do upon their return. "Fairbrother will die unless he has surgery soon." said Cagney abruptly. "What do you guys think; should we take him back? I can't do any more for him." Green and Philippa nodded in unison. "OK, team, that's settled." The Marine looked relieved to have shared the decision. "Can you start work on the Doc's device,

217

Mikey? The gold coins are in the Humvee but it's bust so I'll detail some guys to carry them for you." He went on to describe the vehicle's demise.

Green was sceptical. "The fluids in the auto box boiled, that's all; it should be OK now they've cooled." And so it proved; the armoured vehicle started and drove without a problem to the elevator at the complex.

The two soldiers manhandled the chests of gold coins from the Humvee to the elevator floor and thence down to the cool confines of the underground complex. Much sweating and straining saw the chests moved to the workshop where Green wanted to work.

Breathing heavily, Cagney lifted himself onto a bench and sat down.

"Got a problem, Mikey."

"Wassermatter?" grunted the Brit, sweat cascading down his face.

"Captain "hang 'em high" Rotherhithe has come to me with a proposition."

"Oh' aye?" said Green non-committally.

Cagney went on, screwing his face up, "It seems he's all eaten up about inheriting Philippa's estates with Francesca – he seems to think I should get them when we marry."

Green shook his head in resignation. "You're going to be two centuries or more away," he said reasonably "so that's a non-starter."

Cagney went on, "He suggested that when the Endeavour leaves I should dive on the Anastasia and recover Scorponi's treasure."

"Top bloke," asserted Green with some feeling. "Call it your dowry!"

"What bothers me . . ." the American ploughed on doggedly, " is the crew of the Endeavour will be stiffed out of a lot of money and I feel I owe them."

Green shook his head again, this time in exasperation; he limped over to his friend and prodded him in his chest. "Listen, you – you're too damned decent for your own good. The crew will get a pittance; the British Admiralty will get the lion's share of what may be several million pounds and do you know what their Lordships will spend that money on, eh?" He gave Cagney no time to answer. "Ships, ships of the line, frigates maybe and they'll send them to the US of A except it isn't the US of A, it's a colony fighting for its independence. Several ships extra may mean it stays a colony - not a good scenario," he concluded.

"Good point," said Cagney thoughtfully. "Whose side you on, Mikey?"

"History's," was the bullish reply, "and maybe mine if I'm honest."

"OK, Mikey," said Cagney lightly "I'll tell Captain Bligh he's got a deal."

Turning his attention to the blueprints of Aktar's device, Green made a swift calculation of how much gold he would need for its shield. "If it makes you feel any better, James, I'll only need a few ounces of this . . ." He let the coins trickle through his fingers. " . . . so you can give the rest to the crew."

A happier Cagney left to give Rotherhithe his reply and Green began preparing a hearth to melt the coins into sheet, a task which would occupy him until the early afternoon. When he emerged from the coolness of the bunker into the scorching heat, the campsite was virtually deserted bar Mrs Boscombe who sat by Captain Fairbrother's unconscious figure, wafting flies away, and a lookout from the Endeavour's crew perched on the Abram's turret with a telescope. Green passed the time of day with him then wandered on down to the beached frigate. All around the ship was frantic with activity as the ship's company worked hard to repair her. Even the Anastasia's passengers were lending a hand, he noted with interest.

A flash of scarlet drew Green's attention; Colonel Trelawney was sitting on a keg away from the frenzied anthill around the ship. The Paratrooper strolled towards him, acknowledging many a nod and friendly word from crew members.

Trelawney greeted him with a warm smile and firm handshake. "Good afternoon m'boy." He nodded at the hive of activity "Things are progressing, what?" Chatting to the old soldier, Green gleaned the information that four more days would see the Endeavour seaworthy and yes, the Colonel was bored with his own lack of input.

Green craned his neck around. "Where's the Boss?"

The Redcoat rose to his feet and walked out of the frigate's shadow; he pointed into the bay. Shading his eyes with his hand, Green could see a pinnace with his three friends aboard. A couple of seamen manned the oars; they were collecting the substantial flotsam from the sunken vessels. Peering intently the Paratrooper could see them all struggling to manhandle a waterlogged sea chest over the dipping gunwale of the small craft. Their difficulties gave him an idea. Waving both hands above his head he tried to attract the attention of the salvage crew; his movements caught Philippa's eye and she tugged Cagney's sleeve. Green made an unmistakeable come here gesture with his arm; Cagney lifted his hand in acknowledgement.

The seamen resumed their seats and began the pull back to shore where the boat was met by Green and Trelawney. As the boat nudged into the sand the seamen began bringing their "catch" ashore.

"Got an idea, Boss; it'll make life easier for you."

"Shoot" was Cagney's response

"I saw you struggle there lifting that chest. There are two boats here about the same size, let's get William to make a crude catamaran by nailing lengths of timber between the hulls; then building a structure in the middle I can hang a block and tackle on." He paused for breath his enthusiasm brimming over "We'll be able to lift heavy stuff from the water easily."

"Seems like a lot of work, Mikey," said Cagney mildly.

Green stared intently at his friend. "It will make an excellent and very adaptable salvage vessel!" ground the shorter man placing much emphasis on "very adaptable."

"Ah" said Cagney at length. "Good thinking, Mikey; you heard the guy, William. Go to it!"

"Good afternoon, Mikey," Philippa stepped lightly from the boat without getting her feet wet, reaching for his hand to retain her balance. "You look positively underdressed without your monstrous cannon over your shoulder."

Green instinctively felt for the AK; its absence made him feel oddly vulnerable. "Can't believe I left it in the workshop," was his weak response.

"I'll fetch it," offered Trelawney "I will feel useful once more." He turned and trudged up the beach his boots dragging through the soft sand.

"Anything I can do, Mikey?" asked Cagney.

"Mmm," pondered Green "Will you take the skiff and tow in any timber you think might be useful?"

"Aye, aye, me old shipmate," said the American using the worst Cockney accent since Dick Van Dyke's efforts in Mary Poppins.

Green gave Philippa a blank look. "If he says that again do I have your permission to shoot him?"

Her face was grave. "Most certainly! I may even do the deed myself."

Unabashed Cagney pointed to the matronly figure of Mrs Boscombe's sister bending over "Avast behind!"

Philippa and Green exchanged appalled looks. Still in Long John Silver mode with his face screwed up in a horrible eyeball-rolling, leering grimace Cagney seized her in a fierce grip. "Do 'ee know why pirates be called pirates?" without giving her chance to reply he growled, "They just arggh." And lifting her off her feet bit her neck, eliciting much squealing from his victim.

Green collapsed to the sand laughing weakly, tears streaming down his cheeks. *How preposterous,* ran through his mind, *an American two hundred odd years away from where he belongs doing his impression of actor Robert Newton's Long John Silver in Treasure Island – a movie yet to be made of a book not yet written.* He dried his eyes and joined in. "Arghh, Jim lad!"

The Marine hauled him to his feet where both men doubled with mirth. Philippa was laughing despite herself, not understanding but happy that they were happy.

"Go on, get me some timber," spluttered Green pushing his friend away who took Philippa's arm and ambled towards the skiff.

"Right then, Badass Bill!" William brightened at the use of his forbidden nickname. "Let's do a bit of catamaran building." Three long hours work later they stepped back to survey their handiwork.

"What do you think, Mikey?"

"Admirable," came the youthful voice of Rotherhithe, unseen. "A trifle unsophisticated but very purposeful – if its purpose is salvage?" Through Rotherhithe's outwardly cheerful demeanour Green detected an undercurrent of annoyance, maybe jealousy. In a low voice he went on "I suppose I could clap both you and the Lieutenant in irons and engage my men in the salvage work on the Anastasia. Their Lordships of the Admiralty would be most pleased!"

The cold look he received from the older man unnerved him. "Just remember who saved your life and who's taking out your stitches soon, Nicky boy; one slip of that scalpel and your balls will be rolling down your trouser leg!"

"Err . . . quite so," stammered the young officer. "Please excuse my poor attempt at humour, Sergeant." White-faced the newly promoted Captain walked uncertainly back to his ship.

Grabbing his rifle from the catamaran courtesy of Trelawney's kindness, Green strode to where the skiff had just nosed ashore for the sixth time. Green related Rotherhithe's words to Cagney; Philippa listened intently. There was much amusement as Green mentioned his threat

"Best not carry it out," he cackled. "Doubtless he'll want to be a father one day."

"Yes, he is," murmured Philippa absent-mindedly.

"Is?" from Cagney. A very long silence followed. Philippa blushed and nodded.

"Fertile girl," said Cagney in a tone of wonder.

"Fertile family," she corrected, looking meaningfully at her midriff.

Cagney licked his dry lips.

"Am I hearing you correctly, Honey?"

His wife- to-be slowly inclined her lovely head. "Happy?"

"Sure am, Honey." With a grin like the proverbial Cheshire cat. He grew serious for a moment. "You sure about this?"

"Not absolutely, James, but we both know our own bodies and our intuition tells us much."

Green held out a hand to his friend. "Congratulations, mate." He kissed Philippa's smiling face. "I suppose you're going to name junior after me – it will need a Godfather?"

She lifted her salt-streaked hair from her grimy face with an even dirtier hand. "I rather think we will . . .James . . ." Cagney looked expectantly at her, " . . .at the Christening . . .do you believe the vicar will approve of our child being called "Little, Limey and Bastard?"

"Right" said Green with mock severity. "I shall take my undervalued self away from you family folks; I'll catch you at dinner tonight after a bit of fabricating in the workshop."

Philippa leaned on Cagney as his arm wound itself protectively around her shoulders. "Any thoughts, James?"

He pursed his lips his brow furrowed. "How about Harry, Michael, Bartholomew, Badass Bill Cagney? You think the vicar will buy that?"

She spun in his arms and stood on tiptoe to kiss him. "The first three are acceptable, you Colonial upstart . . . Badass Bill . . .mmm . . .we may have to get a cat!

Chapter 17

Over the next three days Cagney barely saw Green who spent his time underground in close collaboration with Dr Aktar fabricating a shield for the scientist's device. Fairbrother remained in a coma; his day to day care being provided by the Boscombe sisters who seemed pleased to have a task to occupy them. Following a request from Rotherhithe, Cagney used the Humvee to drag the cannon he had so carefully dispersed along the beach back to the ship. The work on the Endeavour progressed smoothly under the supervision of Rotherhithe and the newly promoted Anderson. The men worked quickly and with enthusiasm, needing no encouragement from their officers. Their disappointment at being denied the pirates' spoils was assuaged by Cagney distributing what remained of Scorponi's gold coins after Green had taken what he needed.

The afternoon of the third day found Cagney and Philippa paddling around the bay on the makeshift catamaran. The morning had brought an unexpected surprise as they had neared the Anastasia; a sea chest had bobbed to the surface from the shattered hold of the sunken vessel and using the block and tackle Green had set up the pair had lifted it aboard. The faded stencilled letters identified the owner as a Captain B C Trelawney. Cagney smiled as he recalled the old soldier's delight at seeing his chest; he had opened it and with obvious pleasure had held aloft the dress sword his regiment had presented him with on his retirement.

Cagney dragged his thoughts back to the present. "Hey, Honey, let's head over to the Scorpion – I'll dive on her." Philippa did not demur as she saw Cagney's boyish enthusiasm bubbling up and they paddled over to ship, making fast to the protruding mainmast. Stripping to his shorts Cagney dived deep; Philippa watched through the limpid water as his powerful strokes took him down to the deck of the sunken pirate vessel. Peering closely, her face close to the water she saw Cagney reach for something and then again. With bubbles streaming from his mouth Philippa watched Cagney growing larger as he neared the surface. With a gasp Cagney's head emerged into the air, shortly followed by his hands holding a flintlock pistol and a cutlass. "Souvenirs for the guys back home," he spluttered, spitting out sea water. She took them from him as he dived again reappearing a few moments later with more weapons throwing them over the side of their small vessel. "Last time," he panted, "I've seen something." Taking two huge breaths he drove down to the Scorpion's deck, spending longer than before. Philippa's eyes followed his hand as it stabbed downwards near a cannon returning with something small. Intrigued she watched his movements as he propelled himself from the depths; his fist emerged first holding an ornate brass telescope. Taking it from him she held it to the light as he clambered aboard, shedding water, his face animated. Saltwater trickled down her arm as the brass tube emptied; ignoring it she looked at the inscription "*G Scorponi Capitano*"

"To the victor the spoils," she said simply handing it over to Cagney who lifted it to his eye and focussed on the Endeavour five hundred yards away.

If Cagney had turned the telescope to the rocky divide between the bays near to where the Humvee had been several days ago he may have caught sight of the instrument's former owner who was patiently spying on their activities. Scorponi's anger, never far from the surface, was growing, as was his desire for the woman. He growled, the noise deep in his throat as he watched the couple kiss and his corpulent body stirred as he saw the tall man's hand steal inside the woman's shirt.

"Wicked man," she murmured fondly and pointed up the Scorpion's mast. "Now there is a fitting memento of your victory."

Cagney followed her gaze until his eyes reached the skull and crossbones flapping listlessly at the masthead. "My pleasure, Ma'am." Cagney withdrew his hand but not before squeezing gently, causing Philippa's eyes to widen. Standing up, the Marine pulled the boat closer to the mast then hand over hand climbed the rigging until he reached the flag which he cut away with two swift strokes of his diving knife. Scorponi ground his teeth in mortification as the flag – the symbol of his power and domination, was taken down for the last time. The flag safely tucked under his arm, Cagney made his way slowly back to the boat; with a wolfish smile he spread the flag along the bottom of the small hull. "Looks mighty comfortable to me." Wriggling out of her borrowed clothes, Philippa agreed.

Green smiled as he looked away from the happy pair; he returned Rotherhithe's telescope to him. "They seem very much in love, Sergeant." Green nodded silently, pleased for Cagney – *and envious* – he told himself. If they got back safely to their own time he promised himself he would tell Elizabeth Harding exactly how he felt about her. Her image swam into Green's head and he swallowed with apprehension, more at leaving himself vulnerable than at the perilous journey they were to undertake.

Rotherhithe broke into his reverie. "I think all preparations are complete for our friends and, equally importantly. there is a high tide tomorrow to re-float the Endeavour."

Green looked down at the ship, mostly obscured by the fallen monolith. "Your blokes all done?"

Rotherhithe blew out his cheeks. "A little caulking and the replacement of the copper sheets along her bottom; I will sail her outside of territorial waters where my authority as Captain cannot be challenged and then I can perform the ceremony. Would you like to be the one to inform the Lieutenant and her Ladyship?"

Green shook his head vehemently. "Not me, Nick, old son; you're the Captain. You make the offer!"

Rotherhithe shrugged. "It will be one of my less onerous duties, Sergeant, and I look forward to it." A movement on the beach drew Green's attention.

Cagney was pulling the catamaran out of the water with the aid of a passing sailor; he waved to Green and Rotherhithe and padded barefoot and shirtless up the beach towards them. "Catch," he shouted as he neared the pair; Green plucked a flintlock pistol from the air examined it carefully with professional interest and thanked Cagney with a smile. A breathless Philippa arrived in Cagney's footsteps.

Rotherhithe tipped his hat to her, "Ma'am, Lieutenant, I shall refloat the Endeavour on the morning tide, shortly before noon tomorrow. May I invite you both aboard to be my guests on her sea trials of perhaps . . .two hours?"

Chapter 18

The Endeavour was finally lost to sight as it passed over the horizon. Cagney climbed down from the turret of the Abrams – the highest point of the camp since the rock had been toppled. He shifted his glance to his companions; all six were long faced, a contrast to the celebrations of yesterday. Leila and William had decided to return to the twenty first century; Leila because she literally had nowhere else to go and William because he could not take his eyes from her. Cagney stroked the unfamiliar ring on his wedding finger. Philippa and he had sailed from the bay yesterday as Rotherhithe's guests, ostensibly to enjoy the frigate's sea trials but as soon as they had travelled three miles or so Nicholas Rotherhithe had asked Cagney if he would like him as Captain of the Endeavour to perform a marriage ceremony for them both. They had happily accepted the offer to huge cheers around the ship. Green had presented them with rings cast from pirate gold – *just how romantic is that?* Francesca had surreptitiously carried aboard her mother's white dress, freshly laundered and Colonel Trelawney had pressed upon Cagney his own retirement sword then refused to accept its return after the ceremony muttering, "Wedding present, m'boy, wedding present." Green had recorded the entire event on a camcorder normally used to send progress reports to Saddam Hussein.

He called up to Philippa, his tone gentle, "Come on down, Honey, it's too dam' hot up there."

She stumbled down, red eyed from crying. "I shall never see her again, James." She turned her anguished face to his. "I did not know there could be such sorrow."

Cagney brushed her tears away. "She's alive, happy and well – and when we get back we'll find out how many great grand-children you have to be proud of."

Cagney became businesslike. "There's time for a couple of dives on the Anastasia; you want to come with me or keep an eye on Captain Fairbrother?"

She sighed, "I will sit with Harry," and wandered listlessly away.

Green stumped over giving an encouraging smile as he passed her. "Your air tanks are full; I found a compressor in a workshop so you can dive as often as you want. You need a hand on the boat?"

Cagney discerned a slightly hunted look about his friend. "Your girlfriend pestering you?"

Despite Cagney's amused expression, Green glared. "It's like having a sodding shadow, Jim; I even found her in my bed this morning after I got pissed at your wedding bash last night!" Cagney chuckled unsympathetically. "It's not bloody funny!" raged Green. "William wants to take her off my hands but will she as much as look at him? Will she hell! The problem is she's only safe with us – we can't give her a few quid and send her on her way – and where she goes love-struck William follows!"

"Talk of the devil," said Cagney, his eyes flicking left as Leila appeared at Green's side with a mug of coffee. Green ignored her and picking up an armful of tools with difficulty, limped heavily down to the catamaran. Cagney followed, after a kind word to the unhappy girl, placing his wet-suit and tanks carefully in the boat. The two men pushed off, rowing steadily to the wreck site tying up to the rearmost mast.

"You OK on air at this depth?" queried Green.

"Never a problem, won't even need much in the way of decompression." Cagney spat in his face mask and swilled it with sea water then tried his regulator valve; it gave a small hiss and met with his approval. He glanced across at his friend who was lowering a large steel hook into the water using the block and tackle. The rope went slack.

229

"Hook's resting on top of the Captain's cabin . . . I think," said Green, peering into the depths. Cagney grunted his acknowledgement as he struggled into his wet-suit. Green clambered over to Cagney's hull to help him strap his tanks on. After a final check, Cagney sat on the gunwale and entered the water backwards, a coil of rope over his shoulder, a pry bar in one hand and a flashlight in the other. Several powerful thrusts from his flippers took Cagney to the roof of the Captain's cabin; he examined the skylight and was about to break the glass when he realised the whole structure doubled as a hatch. *Of course; that's how the captain's furniture is lowered in.* The dogs which battened down the hatch were quickly released and he "swam" the hatch down to the quarter deck then finned back. Grabbing the lifting hook he yanked once on it, angling his head backwards to see the shimmering figure of Green sending more rope down. Cagney dropped the hook into the cabin and dived through the hatch, followed it. The light was murky in the cabin and Cagney prudently paused to let his eyes adjust. Anderson and his men had dumped the chests and sacks mostly in the middle of the room. Swimming to the nearest, Cagney inserted the bar under one end and lifted it enough to tie a loop around it; dragging the bar out he repeated the process with the other end of the chest. A brightly coloured fish swam in front of his mask startling him; he brushed it away with an irritable gesture and ran another rope beneath the chest, along its length this time. Reaching for the hook, he worked it beneath all three loops then yanked on its rope. The rope tightened as Green recognised the signal and began hauling. The gloom deepened as the ascending chest blocked the light from the hatch and Cagney had momentary misgivings in case it jammed and trapped him. His worry was short lived as the chest passed through the aperture with room to spare. Grabbing a sack, Cagney followed the chest's upward path until his hand clasped the boat's gunwale and fresh air filled his lungs. Green's fingers searched for a purchase in the coarse material then hauled the sack aboard in one fluent movement.

"Had enough?"

Cagney nodded wearily. "Plenty of time tomorrow . . .catch." He passed up his weight belt and with a shrugged effort removed his air tanks which Green lifted aboard.

"Give me your hand, you weary old bugger," laughed Green. A grateful Cagney accepted readily and a few seconds later was sitting in the boat. The heavy sack was plonked in front of him on the boat's ribs with Green looking expectantly on, eager to see the contents.

Cagney played for time and stared at the Paratrooper's cheekbone. "I'll take those stitches out when we get on shore . . . they're about due."

"Bugger my stitches . . .!" fumed Green, "…open the bloody thing." Cagney lifted his hand and made to inspect the stitched cut; Green pushed his hand away and slapped the Marine on top of his head. Cagney laughed and slid his diving knife from its sheath; reversing it he offered it to Green who took it whilst delivering more insults. Impatiently he slashed at the thin rope securing the neck then turned it upside down. The contents clanked and tinkled as they cascaded onto the boat's planking. Green whistled as the late afternoon sun was caught and refracted by the casually upended treasures. His wide eyes travelled over the gold and silver plate, candlesticks, a jewel encrusted crucifix and many other precious items together with many gold coins. Curiously, he picked up a jewellery box but was unable to open it and replaced it in the sack with the rest of the items. No words were spoken, both men rendered speechless by so much wealth at their fingertips.

They rowed slowly back to shore where two planks left on the beach were utilized to slide the heavy chest into the Humvee which Cagney had fetched from the camp. Cagney slammed the rear door and the two men climbed in for the short journey back around the fallen outcrop. Cagney parked by the Tank Carrier. A suntanned William climbed down stiffly from the Abrams' turret where he had been on watch all day.

"Fill Badass in our day willya, Mikey? I'm heading for a shower; the salt water's making me itchy." Philippa approached pale and unsmiling, but to Cagney's eyes looking more composed than she had been earlier. He stroked her hair affectionately. "Shower time, Mrs Cagney." She gave a small smile at the use of her new name. He raised his eyebrows suggestively. "Sure could use a hand to wash my back." She flushed as she always did at the easy informality Cagney had brought into her life and slipped her hand into his, matching his step. Spotty Dog trotted at her heels and howled mournfully as they reached the ladder and disappeared downwards.

Green, with Rashid in one arm and Selima in the other, bellowed at the grief-stricken dog, "Get over here you smelly fleabag!" Its unhappiness a transient affectation, it bounded over. Rashid wriggled from Green's grasp and hugged the dog; his sister pulled a contemptuous face and said something in Arabic to Green who smiled and shrugged.

"She says her little brother is a small, smelly dog." A tired looking Aktar gave Green and William cold drinks; Green shared his with Selima who shuddered with delight as the lemonade went down.

"What's the story, Doc?"

"Steady progress," a satisfied expression on his lined face.

Green noticed the red rimmed eyes. "You been up all night?"

The scientist did not argue. "The software is almost ready; we can attempt our return when your salvage efforts are complete."

Green looked intently at him. "How do you rate our chances of a successful trip?"

Aktar gave an eloquent shrug. "We arrived here by accident – I am attempting to recreate the conditions which generated our movement through time." The scientist tried to smile but failed. "I believe my device created a wormhole; my theory- a tentative one at best- suggests both ends are fixed physically but not in a temporal sense." Aktar sighed. "But we really have little choice, Sergeant, we cannot stay here and . . ." he gave a small sad smile, ". . . I miss my family."

"I'd like to meet them," said Green placing Selima on the ground. "Fat little monkey," he beamed at her. Aktar translated the comment, the girl laughed and looking up at Green asked him a question. Green raised his eyebrows at Aktar.

"She says will you be her daddy?"

Crouching down, leaning heavily on his crutch, Green ruffled the little girl's hair and nodded vigorously, smiling as he did so. "Yes." She smiled in return and spoke again.

The corners of Aktar's mouth turned up. "She says can you sell Rashid and buy her a dog instead?"

Four miles away Giuseppe Scorponi sat at the table in the one roomed hovel he had bullied from the family of a fisherman. The displaced family now huddled in a half-roofed lean-to with their animals. Scorponi frowned with concentration, racking his brains to devise a strategy whereby he could recapture his treasure. He drummed the fingers of his good hand on the table adding up the points in his favour; the British frigate had gone and the three heavily armed men who remained were ignorant of his presence. His fingers stopped their monotonous tattoo – those were his only advantages.

A harsh male voice came from outside where the fisherman's wife was cooking; *fish stew again* thought Scorponi with disgust. The voice was loud, authoritative, demanding food. Scorponi lifted his cutlass from its resting place on the table and hefted it menacingly. Silently he moved to the doorway and stepped out, holding the weapon before him. The newcomer stepped back and levelled a musket at the pirate captain. Scorponi's cunning, porcine eyes assessed the man dressed in Arab garb, a dark unshaven face. The army boots and olive green drab beneath his burnous caught his attention; Scorponi tightened his grip on the hilt of his cutlass. Doubt entered his mind. The stranger was thin, poorly nourished and ill at ease, not like those confident swaggering pigs who had stolen his treasure. The man looked over his shoulder with a hunted expression. Scorponi decided to gamble and lowered his sword. "The enemy of my enemy is my friend," he said softly in Arabic. He watched as the muzzle of the musket wavered uncertainly. "Bring us food, quickly!" he snarled at the woman who hurriedly slopped the stew which would have fed her family into two bowls. Head lowered, she scurried into the hovel and placed the bowls on the table along with wooden spoons. Scorponi cuffed her as she passed. "Bread too, you old hag!" The stranger seemed indifferent to his treatment of the woman. *Good*, thought Scorponi and leaned his cutlass against the wall inside the room. The man warily followed him in then, placing his musket beside him, sat down and attacked the food with a ravening enthusiasm. Scorponi sat opposite and pushed his own bowl to the hungry man. "Eat my friend," he said silkily.

The stranger moved his empty bowl aside then stared at Scorponi. "You're the pirate captain." Scorponi nodded slowly. "I heard the sailors from the British ship talking about you when I lay hidden."

"And you are?" Scorponi cocked his enormous head to one side but his eyes never left the man's face.

The man stood and hefted his musket. "I am Captain Hassan of the Republican Guard." He pushed his chest out in a failed attempt to boost his air of self importance. Scorponi had seen such demonstrations of stiff-necked, haughty behaviour before and had usually flogged it from the owners before throwing them overboard. He curtailed his natural inclination to strangle Hassan and bade him sit. He needed this popinjay as his ally – albeit temporary – and he would need careful handling.

"I think we may be able to help each other, Captain; it does me good to see a brave man with undoubted fighting ability." The flattering words almost stuck in his craw for he saw before him half a man, a bully and a soft-handed clerk- a cruel, intelligent and ruthless character nonetheless. Hassan's calculating eyes gazed back at the pirate. A lifetime of clawing his way up the hierarchy of Saddam's elite corps had taught him to trust no-one, but this bumptious peasant would prove useful in his quest to kill the allied soldiers and return home. "What is it you want?" he asked the corpulent figure before him, dominating the small room.

Scorponi's porcine eyes, set deep within their rolls of fat, narrowed. "I want what you want, Captain; the deaths of the men who dress as you do
. . ." he pulled aside Hassan's burnous to reveal the olive drab beneath. ". . . I want the return of my treasure . . ." his arm spread in an extravagant gesture ". . . though I will share it with you."

"Agreed." Even in the failing light Scorponi could see the burning intensity of Hassan's eyes like the missionary he had once nailed to his own beloved cross.

Scorponi licked his fat, red, shiny lips. "I want the woman; she must not be harmed."

Hassan shrugged indifferently. "She is yours." Scorponi lit a lamp as dusk merged with darkness and the two men talked on, scheming and planning.

Hours later, Scorponi stood and indicated a pile of straw in the corner of the room. "Sleep, my friend. I will wake you before dawn and we shall watch our enemies and seek their weaknesses. We will be rich and I . . ." he concluded softly, leering in the gloom, " . . . I will be satisfied."

Hassan lay his head down and his tired body was engulfed in a restless sleep. He dreamed of returning to his own time with the weapon and the scientist as trophies; he would present them to Saddam as his own triumph and the dictator would be able to change history at will.

Governments would fall and all would pay homage to Iraq and the Arab world – or suffer the consequences.

Mikey Green was not enjoying his food; a steaming bowl of mutton stew which had been prepared by Leila in the underground Kitchen. He glanced round at his dinner companions; without exception they were tucking in and making complimentary comments which Aktar was translating for the girl. She placed her hand on Green's who shook it free with a scowl. She hurriedly left the table, her eyes filled with tears, and walked into the darkness accompanied by Spotty Dog.

Philippa's voice, gently chiding, came from across the table. "You could be a little kinder, Mikey." Green's scowl transferred itself to her but he remained silent, instead watching her hand as she toyed with the jewellery box Cagney had salvaged from the Anastasia. She caught her breath; her questing fingers had located the hidden catch and the lid flew open. The contents glittered in myriad beguiling ways under the flickering lantern as Philippa's forefinger pushed and prodded gold and precious stones around the sodden velvet.

One particular object caught her attention and she lifted it twinkling to the light. "From what James tells me you may have a use for this upon our return." Green's interest was piqued; he looked at the object- a diamond ring. His eyes flicked from Philippa to Cagney and back.

She placed the ring in his hand. "Tell him, James."

"Tell him what?" said Cagney with an air of assumed innocence, shortly followed by a yelp as Philippa jabbed the back of his hand with her fork.

"Now!"

"Captain Elizabeth says she fancies you to bits . . . that's what she whispered in my ear." He rubbed his hand ruefully. Green's face lit up; taking his ID tag from around his neck he threaded the ring on the chain then looped it back over his head.

"So, life worth living again, soldier?"

Green took his fork and stabbed Cagney's other hand. "Bastard," he said equably as he lifted a sleepy Rashid on to his knee and ate his stew.

"When we get back . . ." Green looked up from his empty bowl. ". . . we're going to have big problems." Cagney continued, "Firstly . . ." he held up a finger, ". . . I reckon the Marine Corps and probably the Parachute Regiment are gonna take one look at our treasure chests and scream "looters" at us!"

Green grimaced. "Good point."

"Secondly . . ." Cagney's middle finger joined his index in a Churchillian gesture. ". . . the CIA are gonna be howling to get a hold of the Doc's device and I'm pretty sure your spooks will too."

Green banished thoughts of Elizabeth Harding from his mind. "You're right;" he said firmly, "I'd be happy if it was destroyed when we got back . . . but. . . " he looked at Aktar ". . . the Doc here could build another then we're back to square one!" The atmosphere around the table was sombre; the only sounds were the surf and Rashid's sleepy snufflings.

Aktar cleared his throat. "I will have to die . . . that is the only answer."

"My thoughts, too," said Green in a level tone

"It is agreed." Aktar's voice was barely audible. There was a chorus of protests from around the table at the two men's conclusions.

"Unless . . ." all eyes turned to the Paratrooper, ". . . unless the Doc can ride a camel?" Puzzled frowns greeted his remark, not least from Aktar.

A smiling Green explained. "If you can ride a camel, mate, when we get back you can clop off into the distance and all of us here will lie through our teeth and swear you were killed in the pirate attack!"

A relieved expression spread across Aktar's bearded face.

Cagney introduced a cautionary note with a caveat. "The Doc's disappearance won't prevent out spooks from copying the Doc's toy though; I. . ."

Aktar broke in, "My device is simple enough; anyone with a workshop could copy it but the programs to run it, together with the research are unique and irreplaceable. If they were missing the device would never function."

Cagney's expression showed clearly he was unconvinced. "Our spooks can throw billions of dollars and the best brains at this; what makes you so sure that your guys are better than our guys?"

The scientist gave Cagney a reassuring smile. "An enormous coincidence occurred when we were attempting to test fire the weapon; we encountered failure after failure until we had a power cut – a cut literally of only micro seconds but the time gap brought about a surge in the accelerator chamber and fired the weapon successfully . . .but . . ." he paused dramatically, ". . . when Captain Hassan attacked you that was the first occasion when the cutting of power was incorporated into the software on a repetitive basis to create an enduring surge in the chamber . . ." he spread his arms eloquently ". . .with the result that you see around us."

"So we wipe the program and bury your research then, Doc – problem solved, eh?"

"Quite so, Sergeant. Succinctly put if I might say so. The research is not bulky."

Philippa joined the debate. "Can we not also bury the larger part of the treasure if you are convinced your superiors will confiscate it?"

"I'm cool with that; what about you, Boss?"

"Sounds like a plan . . . and a good one."

William raised a hand tentatively. "What will happen to me when we arrive in your time – will they separate me an' Leila?"

"Will you stop bloody well fretting about that girl?!" snapped Green. "She doesn't even give you the time of sodding day here. . ." a malicious smile spread across his features, ". . . anyway, our boffins . . . you know blokes like the Doc here, will want to examine you . . . and . . ." he added with cheerful spite, ". . . the only way they can do that properly is to open you up and have a rummage about inside and then put you on display in a zoo"

William's jaw dropped, his eyes appealed to Cagney, but found no sympathy there. "Hey it's not all bad news, Buddy Boy; Mikey n' me will get a cut of the gate fee and on a good day . . . the gawkers will throw you a bone or two!" William subsided in stunned silence. The night air was rent by two howls of pain. Rashid woke in alarm to see Philippa holding on to the ears of both soldiers forcing them to stand up. He slid off Green's lap to the earth, giggling.

"Truth, now! Tell William!"

"You'll be part of the Royal Family, arghh stoppit," squawked Green.

"And a private jet," wailed Cagney. Philippa released her grip with a final painful flourish.

"What's a jet?" grinned a suddenly cheerful William.

"I'm getting my head down," said Green grabbing his crutch and limping off into the darkness towards the transporter cab. "When am I on watch?" The words came floating over his shoulder in the gloom.

"You're on third," shouted Cagney, "shorter stints tonight, Philippa's taking the last." Cagney stood and stretched. "Get the kids bedded down, William; I'll wake you in a couple of hours." He kissed his new wife and walked across to the Abrams which he climbed then settled himself comfortably on the turret. Cagney was relaxed but alert, regularly scanning the land beyond the camp. The American did not mind sentry duty; he could reflect upon a good day's work and his new found happiness. Nevertheless he was pleased to hand over to William after his allotted time had elapsed. The young man had risen uncomplainingly from his bed and now sat atop the turret, swathed in blankets against the cold night air. In accordance with Cagney's orders, William paid close attention to the scrubby hinterland but nothing moved apart from the hobbled camels as they grazed.

If William had chosen to look out to sea he might have seen the sail of a small fishing boat as it eased its way into the adjoining bay until it nosed on to the strip of land separating the inlets with a small sandy crunch. Were there a moon, Scorponi and Hassan, the occupants of the boat, might have noticed the tyre tracks of the Humvee left there after the confrontation with the prize crew of the Anastasia. Scorponi quickly removed the mast and the two men, making no more noise than ghosts, carried the small boat bodily up the sand and hid it amongst the rocks. They walked, sometimes clambered, until they reached a point opposite the masts of the sunken merchantman where they hid, waiting patiently to watch their enemies.

Rising from his haunches Cagney peered down at the unconscious Captain Fairbrother in the early morning light.

"How is our Captain, James?" Philippa's expression was worried as she studied the gaunt, stubbled face.

She thrust a mug of coffee into the outstretched hand. "His pulse and respiration seem OK." He addressed the silent prone figure, "C'mon Harry stay with us a little while longer 'til we can get you to an operating room."

"What are your intentions today, my love?"

"Dive and dive again; some of the chests have moved to the edges of the cabin so it will take longer - I'll probably need short decompression stops. Philippa's face clouded over so Cagney patiently explained about nitrogen in blood and the problems with "bends."

"It sounds dangerous, James."

Cagney laughed it off. "It's my job, Honey; I'm thorough and I know it inside out!" He looked around. "How's our lovesick teenager?"

Philippa wrinkled her nose. "Not overly infatuated this morn; she spat at Mikey by way of a greeting!" She sighed and switched topics. "Who will be your companion this fine morning?"

Cagney looked upwards at a sky of burnished steel and again at Philippa's fair skin. "Probably Mikey." She pulled a disgruntled face. "Hey, don't get all sour on me, Mrs C; you don't have the strength to manhandle the chests as they emerge from the water . . .and you need to conserve your energy …" his eyebrows lifted suggestively, " . . .I've got plans for you later."

"I may be in the mood . . ." she turned to walk away and after a few steps paused, looking over her shoulder with a coquettish smile playing on her lips, ". . . and then again I may not."

"Goddamn women," muttered the American under his breath.

"I heard that!" Her laughter tinkled softly as she walked away.

Cagney turned his attention to the job in hand and walked the fifty yards to where Green and the children were feeding titbits to Green's camel. "You good to help me dive today? . . . I can take Badass this afternoon." The Para's pleasure showed in his face and Cagney walked slowly to the beach followed by Green, leaning heavily on his crutch. Passing the Abrams, Cagney called up to William to inform him of his change of duties after lunch. William acknowledged the news with a wave and a cheerful grin.

The pair shoved the catamaran into the water and rowed to the sunken Anastasia. The Marine's rowing experience far outstripped the inept Green's and progress was erratic. In between grunting with the effort and each cursing the other man's navigational skills the two men discussed the perilous trip home. Cagney was amused to discover his friend feared the encounter with Captain Elizabeth Harding more than their dangerous journey.

He laughed again as Green provided a very dubious rationale. "It's like this; if my atoms get scattered round the universe I'll be dead . . ."

"With you so far, Einstein."

Green frowned, resting on his oar and choosing his words carefully. ". . . but if I crack on to Dizzy Lizzy and she laughs at me, it'll be like dying . . . but . . ." his face contorted with concentration, ". . . as I see her most days it'll seem like dying over and over again . . .see what I mean?"

"You think too much, Mikey, and anyway she has a weakness for ugly little bastards like you so what have you to worry about eh? You got any more confessions you want to run by me?"

Green yawned. "While we're at it yeah, I don't really need to be here. Those "works" Nortons have a round tube above the engine - they built a frame specially- a fake would have a flattened tube to accommodate the cambox" he yawned again, stretching." You can identify the bikes from that; I just came along 'cause I fancied a change of scenery."

Cagney shook his head in disbelief. "Start rowing!" A deal of effort later saw their unwieldy craft tied to the rearmost mast of the sunken ship with Cagney donning his diving gear aided by Green. Lengthening the tether, they manoeuvred over the Captain's cabin where Green dropped the lifting hook. A satisfied smile creased his face as he saw the hook drop squarely through the skylight of the cabin. Green peered intently through the water at the drowned vessel, seeing the occasional brilliance within the cabin as Cagney moved his flashlight about in the confined gloom. Cagney's gently sculling figure emerged slowly from the aperture, paying particular attention that no part of his equipment snagged on the perimeter. The top of his head changed to his face as he looked upwards and Green caught the "pull up" hand gesture. Moving to the block and tackle, Green cursed the awkwardness his damaged knee imposed upon him then took up the slack and slowly hauled on the rope as Cagney guided it through the skylight. Steadily he increased his effort until the sea chest broke the surface. Slowly, his muscles straining despite the reduction gear, the chest left the water, increasing in weight. The makeshift salvage vessel settled lower in the water reducing its freeboard. Having raised the chest to where he wanted, Green tied off the rope and moved the sliding wooden platform he had helped William to construct beneath its gently swinging mass. Moments later the chest sat square amidships.

Quickly stripping the rope loops from the chest, Green tied them to the hook with string and lowered the hook again to the waiting Cagney who vanished in to the cabin. The operation was repeated, more quickly this time as Green became more adept in his role and a second chest joined its fellow on the boat. About to drop the hook again, Green saw Cagney hovering midway between the ship and their boat. *Of course Cagney was decompressing.* Green waited patiently in the burning late morning sun wishing he had brought a hat. Ducking his head in the water to cool it Green found himself facing an ascending Cagney. A tired arm handed up a weight belt followed by air tanks; a brawny heave later saw Cagney aboard shaking his head like a spaniel spraying Green with droplets.

"Let's . . .let's have a change," gasped Cagney. Green shrugged. "To the Scorpion," continued Cagney, untying the boat from the Anastasia's mast. The heavily laden craft inched its way to the sunken pirate ship where they tied up again. Cagney beckoned Green, then pointed down at the drowned vessel. "There!" His finger jabbed. Green leaned forward, pressing his face close to the water; he could discern something glinting on the mast near the deck. "Try this." Cagney handed over his diving mask and helped Green achieve a snug fit. "Stick your face under water and have another look."

Green did as instructed, pulling his head from the water when his breath grew short. "It's the ship's bell," he grinned. "You going down for it?"

"Nope, you are," he told the astonished Green. "If you want that bell hanging in your hall you can go for it yourself! . . . you up for it?" Green was so excited he could barely speak; he nodded enthusiastically and listened carefully for the next fifteen minutes as Cagney ran through the dos and don'ts of diving. "There's enough air in the tanks for a short dive but not enough for me to work in the Anastasia." Cagney helped Green into his diving equipment with a single-minded attention to detail, finishing off by fitting flippers and strapping a dive knife to Green's calf.

"OK, let's go through the basics again." After satisfying himself that Green was familiar with the rudiments of diving he put his thumbs up then pointed downwards.

Green slid backwards into the limpid waters of the bay and swam steadily down to the ship, trying to remember Cagney's instructions – steady, even breathing, straight legs, let the flippers do the work. Pausing as he reached the ship's rail, Green reversed his body and gazed up at his instructor, his shimmering image haloed by the midday sun thirty feet above him. A small brightly coloured fish swam close to Green's mask, staring insolently at him; Green waved at it in sheer joy. *How could this be? An ordinary lad from a town in the North of England diving on the best preserved pirate ship in the entire world.* Gathering his thoughts, Green swam to the mainmast, avoiding anything that could entangle him; he reached for the ship's bell and with Cagney's diving knife cut it free. The bell was much heavier than he had imagined and pulled him down. Remembering Cagney's advice he straightened his legs and sculled powerfully with his flippers; little by little he ascended, determined that he would not be beaten. After what seemed a very long time Green realised he had bitten off more than he could chew and was about to swim back to the ship when he heard a splash and saw the lifting hook a yard or so in front of him. Making a last muscle-burning effort, he managed to hook the bell on; relieved of his burden he swam easily to the boat where Cagney helped him aboard.

"How was it?"

Struggling to regain his breath Green did not answer straight away. "Brilliant!" he eventually wheezed. "Absolutely bloody brilliant!"

Cagney lifted the bell down from the block and tackle. "Jeez that weighs some! I'm not surprised you struggled – you did real well to bring it up. Sorry pal . . ." he grew serious, "I really didn't think it was so dam' heavy." He turned the bell over in his lap until the rough texture of the engraved name came in sight. Cagney grabbed a rag from the bottom of the boat and rubbed the letters, peering intently as they became more clearly defined. "Egalité," he read slowly. "Guess this was a French ship before she was captured." He held the bell up; the newly polished area glinting in the sun.

"You sure you don't want this?" asked Green, "after all you sank her."

"Not me, Mikey; I couldn't use the binocular targeting system." He pointed to the bruising around his eye . . . an' I'm sure Philippa won't want it, she loathes pirates."

Green leaned back in the boat relaxing in the sun. "You know, every time her name comes up you grin like a village idiot."

Cagney laughed out loud. "Well thank you kindly, Sergeant Sigmund Freud!"

Shading his eyes from the sun Green lobbed a flipper at the Marine's head. "S'true, you useless lanky git."

Cagney snatched the flipper from the air. "Hell, Mikey; I'm happy . . ." he pointed to his face, ". . . this grin ain't just for show y'know . . .I feel like a jigsaw that has finally been completed – just waiting for that last piece – and now it's slotted in."

A faint shout echoed across the bay. "Lunch, I reckon," said Green, spotting Philippa's waving figure. Twenty minutes later a bemused Philippa listened for the third time to the Para babbling on about his underwater experiences while Cagney was in the complex replenishing his air tanks. "You fancy having a go then, Will?"

William shook his head firmly. "I'll just pull the rope."

"Saw a mermaid down there," said a straight-faced Green.

William's jaw slackened. "Really?"

"As God's my witness," Green went on, his face a mask of frank, honest, decency. "Young she was . . .didn't have a top on either." He added slyly. "Big girl, too!" He cupped his hands for emphasis; Rashid mimicked his gesture.

"A fine father figure you will be, Mikey Green," said Philippa sternly. "That young man will be running a bordello by his teenage years thanks to your tutelage!" Green wagged his finger severely at the youngster who giggled in return. Rising from the table, Philippa walked round to William. The seated youth felt Philippa's arms around his neck and her face next to his. He blushed and trembled. She pointed an accusing finger at Green. "That man is a charlatan; if he told me it was raining I would open a window to check . . . do not believe a single utterance of his."

She released William who croaked, "No, Ma'am."

"Philippa," she corrected, ruffling his hair playfully before she gathered up the lunch plates and walked over to check on Captain Fairbrother.

It was late afternoon before a weary Cagney called a halt to diving. The air tanks had been refilled twice when they had reached shore after ferrying their priceless cargo there. Now only one chest lay in the corner of the Captain's cabin forty feet below the calm waters of the bay. Green had met them at the water's edge with the Humvee; he had helped them load chests and sacks into the vehicle then driven up the sandy beach around the fallen outcrop into camp.

Philippa could not conceal her concern when she saw Cagney; she stroked the raw skin of his face where the mask had rubbed. "Shower, food, and sleep for you," she ordered. "Have you almost finished?"

"One chest left!" ground Scorponi. Tomorrow we will strike and we will have what is ours."

Hassan eased his cramped limbs. "Have you a plan?"

"I have," purred Scorponi. "I will be hidden, wrapped in sailcloth on the yardarm of the merchantman; when the tall one is under the water I will reach down and dash his helper's brains out.

Hassan pointed to the huge man's cutlass. "Using that would make sure."

"Idiot!" spat Scorponi, "if blood is spilled in the water the diver will see it and my advantage is lost."

"Ah," said Hassan.

"But if he comes to the surface ignorant of my presence I shall send him to the bottom permanently."

"And my part?"

The pirate captain could hear the uncertainty in his ally's voice. "You will kill the guard in the camp. Tonight when they are eating they do not set a guard and it will be their undoing for you will hide in their camp – you tell me there are bushes large enough to conceal you?" Hassan nodded. "You will conceal yourself and watch the two who come to steal my treasure. When you see me strike then you must kill the man they leave behind." Scorponi prodded Hassan's musket with a pudgy forefinger. "You will use this; it is not an accurate weapon so you must get very close . . .close enough to use it as a club." Hassan could feel the menace exuding from the man along with the nauseating stench of his obese body which caught in his throat making him want to vomit.

He started to rise, needing to move away. but Scorponi pushed him down. "Not yet; it is not yet dark and they have not called the sentry down for food."

"One chest left," groaned Cagney stripping off his wet-suit. There was a thud as the final chest from the afternoon's haul slid down the makeshift ramp from the Humvee and joined the others on the parched earth. "Oi! Mr and Mrs, get yourselves over here." Green had opened the chest and was rummaging inside it.

Philippa entwined her fingers with Cagney's and pulled him over to where Green and William were whistling and gasping in turn at their discoveries. "Come," she murmured, "it is not every day we can gloat over a pirate hoard!" Cagney heard a low exclamation from Green and turned to see him sitting on an unopened chest with a medium-sized, finely made wooden box on his lap.

Opening it, the Paratrooper held up a pair of matched pistols. Wordlessly he handed one to Cagney who whistled in turn as he saw the craftsmanship. "Duelling pistols." He rubbed flecks of rust from the barrel with a finger. "You need to get these oiled."

Green nodded enthusiastically. "I'll do it when I've eaten." He placed the weapons on a blanket in the back of the Humvee. The four were joined by Aktar who emerged from the complex along with Leila and the children. More and more chests were opened to the sound of gasps, giggles and the occasional awed silence. Finally only one remained closed: large, black and leather bound. The heavy lid was prised open and eight pairs of eyes peered curiously in. Nestling amongst the sodden straw were six sheets of what looked like lead. Green leant in and with some difficulty wriggled out the smallest. He balanced it on the chest.

"I believe the sheeting conceals a painting," said Aktar, examining the object with a keen eye. He indicated a crease in the sheet. "Sealed with wax. May I borrow your bayonet, Sergeant?" Green slipped the assault rifle from his shoulder. Aktar picked delicately at the wax until he could unfold a corner; the others followed. A framed image emerged of a mother and child; peering closely at the bottom right of the picture the scientist shook his head slowly. "I am not familiar with the signature."

Cagney followed his lead, his face close to the painting. "Me neither but it's undamaged by sea water because it's wrapped so thoroughly . . ." he looked up, ". . . and you don't do that to a five dollar print!" He refolded the lead sheet and placed the painting in the Humvee.

The children and Leila had become bored with sifting through the treasure; even the adults had reached the point where they were satiated with the abundance of riches.

Green lifted up a small but heavy bag of silver coins and handed it to Aktar. "You'll need these to live on – and buy a flight to England to join your family."

"You are ever practical, Sergeant - and I am grateful."

"Right guys . . ." Cagney interrupted his own words with a yawn, ". . . take a memento each but remember they're likely to be confiscated. We'll bury the rest tomorrow." Reaching down and grunting, he lifted a sack of ornate gold plate which he casually deposited in the Humvee. "A token offering." He smiled. "And at some point when the fuss has died down, we dig it up!"

"Dinner," said Philippa firmly, "is in fifteen minutes, so you must shower quickly." Cagney shambled tiredly away. "Lights, my little ones." The children scampered off, returning with lanterns which she lit.

In the shadows beyond the light a figure carrying a musket ghosted by.

Green placed his hand on Aktar's shoulder. "All ready for the big jump?"

The Iraqi offered him a bleak look. "The program is loaded, the research is in a filing cabinet by the elevator and if our journey is successful I will wipe the program with a flick of a switch . . ."

"And then hop on a camel and vanish in the direction of Baghdad airport."

"Two camels, actually; I will take Leila . . .I have relatives who will care for her."

Green's relief was palpable. "Take whatever you need from here and sell it, she'll need money."

Aktar held a thoughtful expression. "I will do so."

A damp and glowing Cagney interrupted them; his arms were laden with plates of steaming food. "I got hijacked by the ladies . . ." he jerked his head back over his shoulder at Philippa and Leila who were similarly encumbered. "Philippa discovered the microwave; she doesn't believe me when I say it's not witchcraft."

"Where I'm from they still burn witches, most Saturday nights and every other Wednesday!"

Philippa cast a sidelong glance at the Para as she sat down at the table; she patted the seat next to her. "Now, Mikey; you must know I love and admire you, but when your expression assumed a childlike facade of blameless moral rectitude my natural inclination is to see you as . . .remind me again of that phrase please, James?" Cagney whispered in her ear. "Ah yes; lying, Goddam' asshole!"

"Asshole," repeated Rashid. Green put a hand to his open mouth in mock horror, prompting a fit of uncontrolled giggling from Philippa. Cagney smiled to himself, relieved that Philippa had put behind her, even for a little while, the loss of her daughter.

Green changed tack. "I found a sandy hollow out in the scrub; we can deepen it then bury the chests – and the Doc's research. There are a couple of distinct features we can triangulate from so we don't forget where it is."

William cracked his knuckles nervously. "I don't know how you can be so cheerful, Mikey? I'm so scared about tomorrow I can hardly speak."

Green's smile faded. "Try this, Will." He looked around at his friends. "Put your hand up if you're not scared witless about our little jaunt tomorrow." Nobody moved.

"You're not alone, William," Philippa's voice was low, "we are all fearfully apprehensive." They talked on, ironing out any problems which might come up the next day. Green left them to visit the workshop where he could clean and polish the ship's bell and his duelling pistols. Eventually everyone drifted off to bed bar William who sat atop the Abrams on first watch. Hassan watched him for a while until he too fell into an uneasy sleep. Scorponi waited until later when the darkness was deepest then sailed round the headland to the wreck of the Anastasia. He climbed the short distance to the yardarm where he settled himself as comfortably as he could, wrapping spare canvas around himself then watched the boat he had stolen from the fisherman float gradually out to sea on the ebb tide.

Chapter 19

At first light in the camp, sleeping bodies stirred. Cagney, seated on the turret of the Abrams wondered if the others felt as he did – fear in his heart and a hollow, empty feeling in the pit of his stomach. His companions' troubled faces confirmed his suspicions and if he had looked in a bush nearby he would have discovered a cramped and dirty Captain Hassan who was similarly afflicted. Out in the bay hidden on the yardarm of the Anastasia Scorponi suffered no such misgivings; the madness that generated his lust, greed and cruelty left little room for fear. He looked forward to his day.

Cagney swung his body down from the Tank and rapped on the roof of the cab; muffled obscenities from its occupant greeted him. Cagney leaped to the earth determined to be cheerful even, or especially, if it was going to be his last day on earth. A crutch slid from the cab followed by a cursing, dishevelled Paratrooper. Muted greetings were exchanged.

"Get your ugly self over to the breakfast table, soldier; I'll remove your stitches after I change Harry's drip and catheter."

Green limped over to the quiet gathering and helped himself to coffee. "Well, it's been an adventure!" His forced light-heartedness fooled no-one; his companions remained silent, occupied by their own thoughts.

Cagney ambled across, medical kit in hand and wordlessly snipped and removed the stitches from Green's cheekbone. "There you go, Buddy Boy, irresistible to beautiful women all over again!" Green's fingers explored the new contours of his face.

Selima slid from her seat and approached Green running her fingertips over the scar. "Ugly, Mikey."

Green prodded her gently on the nose then pointed a finger at his face. "Handsome." She shrugged and looked at Aktar for guidance; the corners of his mouth twitched and he said a few words in Arabic.

The little girl shook her head slowly then threw her arms around Green's neck. "Ugly" she whispered. The tough Paratrooper felt his eyes prick with tears as he realised the youngster and her cheeky brother meant more to him than all the treasure he was surrounded with.

He rose from the table in confusion. "Time to get digging," he muttered, stomping off to the Humvee.

It took four trips to carry the chests and sacks to the sandy hollow of Green's choosing, two hundred yards from the camp. There were only two shovels so Green stood guard most of the time doing occasional shorter shifts until his injured knee forced him to stop. Philippa sat with the unconscious Fairbrother, chatting to him and holding his unresponsive hand. The children, unaware of any tension, ran circles around the camels with an excited Spotty Dog.

Hassan lay thirty yards from them, weighing up his options; he had listened carefully to the conversation of the foreigners both last night and this morning. As an ambitious officer in Saddam's Republican Guard, learning English was to gain a valuable asset. He knew the men were burying Scorponi's loot but did not care. A makeshift plan was forming in his head; he could club the woman with his musket - and the teenage girl if she interfered, then climb on to the American Tank and turn its heavy machine gun on to the soldiers. In the end his courage failed him. He had never fired a machine gun – his father's patronage and influence had had secured him a commission in the Intelligence Corps – and if he did not kill the soldiers with his first burst of fire from the unfamiliar weapon they would surely stalk him with their rifles and take his life. No, he told himself; let the fat peasant pirate slaughter two of the three and he, with the advantage of surprise, would kill the other. His heart quailed at the prospect of a confrontation with the British soldier and his fervent hope was that the youngest man would be the one to remain in camp. He looked at his goatskin water container – only about a quarter of the foul-tasting liquid was left. Hassan consoled himself with an inward sneer that at least the fat pig hiding on the ship was in a similar situation.

Scorponi was not only uncomfortable, he was worried. Everything he had planned would fall apart if the strangely dressed men with their hideously accurate weapons decided to not to salvage the final chest. The prospect of failure tormented him. Peering through a slit in the sail his sense of unease increased when the Humvee left and did not return.

Philippa halted in the middle of a sentence as she heard the growl of the Humvee's diesel engine. She turned her head to watch as the vehicle crunched to a halt at the rear of the giant Tank Carrier. Cagney and William emerged, laughing and joking at Green's expense; as they drew near she heard them mocking the Paratrooper's slow pace as he leant heavily on his crutch.

Ignoring the dirty sweat-streaked pair she walked quickly to Green, taking his rifle from his shoulder. "Put your arm around me, Mikey; they should be ashamed to have worked an injured man so hard!"

Green touched an imaginary forelock then slipped an arm around her. "Yes Ma'am," he whined. "The Master . . ." he pointed an accusing finger at Cagney, ". . . ee sed ee'd 'ave me flogged!"

"Yes, and I will help him, Sergeant, if you do not remove your hand from my bottom immediately!"

"Pure accident! Never noticed!" protested Green, with a transparent lack of sincerity. She helped him to a seat and laid the AK on the table. Cold drinks appeared as if by magic, courtesy of Leila and the children. Rashid leaped on to Green's lap, causing a muffled curse as the little lad's foot caught his injured knee.

"Hey, invalid!" Green involuntarily looked up. "I'll take William diving; you're about as much use as a trapdoor in a canoe!"

Cagney's words caused consternation for Hassan, who feared the alertness of the smaller soldier. Cagney reached into his pocket and passed Green two painkillers. "Take 'em - you look like you could use 'em." Green swallowed them gratefully.

"C'mon, Will. It'll be midday in a couple of hours; let's get this done before we roast!" He handed his mask, flippers and knife to the lad. "Meet you at the boat when I've picked up the tanks." He disappeared down the ladder as William walked to the boat. Green jogged Rashid on his good knee, making him chuckle.

Philippa placed her hand on Green's. "Will the British Army allow you to keep the children, Mikey?"

The happiness left Green's face. "They'll make it as difficult as they possibly can because they're a shower of bastards!" Green's camel, grazing a short distance off, pricked up its ears hearing its name. "Not you, Bonehead!"

Cagney appeared with his air tanks in one hand and Philippa's only dress in the other. "Sure be good if you wore this." He held it out to her, "we're heading into a war zone . . ." he explained, ". . . wearing an Iraqi uniform is a way of getting shot!"

"True enough. . ." Green agreed, ". . . no wet-suit today?"

"Not down there long enough to get cold." Cagney shook his head. He strode unsmiling to the beach, his long legs eating up the distance. The pair remained seated watching the salvage boat being rowed strongly to the sunken Indiaman and then surprisingly veer past it as though on a whim, and halt fifty yards further on when it reached the wreck of the Scorpion. Its Captain ground his teeth in frustration and gripped the long wooden stave with which he intended to smash the young man's skull. His faithful stiletto was tucked into the Arab robes he had taken from Hassan. He loosened the Kaffiya – the long Arab scarf cum headdress; it had kept him warm during the night but was causing the sweat to pour from him now. He suffered in silence; it would not be long before they anchored beneath him and his weapons could do their bloody work. In the

254

back of his mind he worried about Hassan's ability to kill the limping soldier; if he failed the soldier would simply turn his quick-firing weapon on to himself or even the huge cannon now lying dormant on the iron monster. Scorponi shook his oversize head free of such doubts and looked forward to the killing - and to the woman. A movement from the catamaran shifted his pig-like eyes; the tall one had surfaced, holding something shiny.

William took the proffered sextant and helped Cagney aboard. "Souvenir," he said, spitting out sea water. They rowed back to the Anastasia and settled over the captain's cabin in the motionless waters of the bay. William dropped the steel hook whilst Cagney put his mask on. The Marine slid into the water and finned effortlessly downwards. At a tug from below William paid out more rope and sat patiently with his hand resting lightly on the rope waiting for the signal to haul. The brooding, corpulent malevolence that was Scorponi waited impatiently six feet above the water, silently urging the ungainly craft to drift close enough for the killing blow. Slowly, almost imperceptibly the tide inched the boat and William closer to the Sicilian; he eased the stave free. The movement, slight as it was, caused the sailcloth to rustle. Scorponi froze and held his breath but the noise was drowned by the flapping of the sails and William heard nothing. Scorponi breathed again; now the boat was almost directly beneath him.

A bored William looked over the gunwale seeking Cagney; he noticed the boat had drifted a little but was not unduly worried. Idly he watched multi-coloured fish dart about the ship's deck forty feet below. His eyes changed their focus to the surface of the water to see the reflection of his face. *No! Not his face.* He frowned, puzzled until the image cleared and the huge bestial face of Scorponi stared implacably back at him. Recoiling in horror, William stretched out for his M16. His fingers frantically clasped it and lifted the weapon but the stave, swung with Scorponi's immense strength, swished past his head, dashing the rifle into the water and breaking his lower arm as it deflected.

William fell forward smashing his head on the gunwale. His broken arm hung limp in the water as he lost consciousness.

The follow-through of Scorponi's powerful blow caused him to lose his grip on the yardarm and his massive body hit the water head first and disappeared beneath the surface.

Cagney was mildly irritated that his tug on the lifting rope had gone unanswered; his eyes flicked towards the surface – the boat had drifted out of position. Maybe William was waiting so he could manoeuvre the craft until it sat square over the cabin to give him a straight lift? He swam on and upwards, passing under the boat, its shadow blocking the sunlight for a moment. Baffled because there was not the flurry of paddle movement he expected, his perplexity hardened into concern as an M16 spiralled downwards through the water a yard from him. Urgently Cagney kicked upwards but was met by an explosion of bubbles and noise as Scorponi's body plunged into the water and his massive head crashed into Cagney's own.

Captain Hassan had seen Scorponi fall from the yardarm into the water; his consternation turned to dismay when his ally failed to reappear. He swallowed hard, fear gripping him. His eyes moved to his left; the children were playing with the dog near the camels. The two women – he spun his head – were sitting on the Tank Carrier mending a dress; the soldier crouched by the unconscious man talking to him. *Now was his best chance,* but fear gnawed at him and stayed his hand. Hassan delayed.

The soldier's rifle was across his shoulder and he leant heavily on his crutch as he began to rise. *It must be now, NOW* when the man was at his most vulnerable. Hassan cocked the musket with an audible click; the soldier did not hear. Spotty Dog did however and bounded to the bush growling furiously. Green struggled to his feet unperturbed by the dog's histrionics. He limped towards the bush, his soothing words having no effect on the excited Dalmatian. As he got within ten yards it dashed into the middle of the bush and bit something; the barking was replaced by a very human scream. Green slipped the AK from his shoulder with a rehearsed ease but his crutch caught in a hole and the weapon dropped, dangling from its sling on the crutch. From the corner of his eye, Green could see a dishevelled unshaven man in olive green rise from the deep undergrowth and level a musket at him. Green's frantic, questing fingers found the trigger guard of his weapon and he lifted the heavy rifle, clicking off the safety as the man fired.

A dull boom filled the Para's ears. The muzzle of the musket which had been pointing unwaveringly at Green's chest a moment earlier dropped a little when Spotty Dog sunk its teeth into Hassan's ankle and the half inch ball flew low. It entered Green's thigh; plunging through muscle until it encountered his femur which it smashed whilst simultaneously expanding, then stopped, having exhausted its kinetic energy.

Green spun, consumed with agony as his leg gave way beneath him. As he crashed to the ground his hand closed in rictus pulling the trigger and the Russian assault rifle began its yammering. The first two rounds thudded harmlessly into the earth but the rest of the burst stitched across the Humvee. Twisting as he fell, Green lay with the weapon beneath him.

Kicking the dog away, Hassan, howling in triumph rushed the short distance to where Green lay, desperate to possess the AK - a gun he knew well - reaching the prostrate, helpless man he lifted the musket to finish him off, and brought it down with all his strength. The young Para knew his time had come, his luck had finally run out, as he saw the iron-shod butt of the heavy weapon descending.

The sprinting Leila threw herself across Green's body. Hassan's musket, driven by his vindictive fury and all the power his lean frame could deliver crashed down, pulping the back of her skull. A snarling Hassan started to pull her twitching body off Green then he staggered and dropped to one knee as a bullet from Philippa's pistol entered then left the fleshy part of his shoulder. A second round whistled past his ear as he picked himself up and ran into the scrub.

Philippa dragged the dead girl from Green; wincing as the sightless eyes met hers.

"Shoot the bastard . . ." hissed Green through gritted teeth ". . . use the AK." She tried to ease the weapon from beneath him. "Pull the bloody thing . . . don't mind me!" She tore it away, and standing, aimed at the fleeing man. The three rounds remaining left the barrel, hurtling a good ten feet over the fugitive's head. Philippa knelt by Green, placing the rifle on the ground and tearing the material round the wound site. "Reload!" he grunted, his lips drawn back. She swivelled her head back and forth, urgently seeking a new magazine. "Here!" The word came in a short agonised gasp; he patted the pocket of his uninjured leg and only just cut off a scream as she scrambled across him, dragging the magazine out with fumbling fingers.

Digging deep into his reserves to combat the pain, he snapped the new magazine in; Philippa slung the rifle over her shoulder then resumed her attempts to examine Green's wound. She looked closely; the blood welled slowly from the hole. "In my bag . . . the Humvee . . . dressings." Philippa ran to the vehicle and returned with Green's rucksack; she rummaged inside and found one she thought looked about the right size. The children gathered by Green's side, tearful and silent. "Get the Doc . . . the Doc." He pointed to the trapdoor; the youngsters sped off and disappeared down the ladder.

Philippa opened the dressing with her teeth. "I need to lift your leg, Mikey." Aktar's head appeared from the trapdoor, looking around suspiciously.

"Over here!" Philippa's peremptory tones brought him quickly across. "Lift Mikey's leg in order that I might apply this dressing." The next few moments were almost as bad as being shot for Green as the two ends of his broken femur grated together.

Dressing applied, Green seized the lapels of Aktar's lab coat. "Get on the Tank and watch where your mate goes!"

"Hassan?"

Green nodded weakly. Aktar trotted to the Abrams. The children returned, watching Green with scared, concerned eyes.

A dazed Cagney pulled away and blinked. Scorponi's foul, bloated face swam into view inches before his eyes. At the edge of his blurred vision Cagney saw the huge man's arm pull back and instinctively he dropped his own arm to protect his body from the blow which must surely come. The pain when it did arrive was unlike anything Cagney had ever experienced and blotted out all other thoughts. A white hot blinding sensation coursed through Cagney's brain and an unthinking unyielding rage seized him. Scorponi, in aiming for his body, had plunged the stiletto through his right arm between wrist and elbow up to the hilt – a killing blow; the narrow blade passing through had impacted into Cagney's rib, splintering one. Even now the huge man was trying to withdraw the blade but Cagney's arm muscles held it firm.

As if in a dream Cagney saw his blood wisping through the water. Scorponi's other hand came snaking through the water trying to wrest the regulator from Cagney's mouth; he gripped the wrist tightly. *God he was strong.* Scorponi's fat, evil face almost touched the Marine's. *He was smiling,* Cagney noted abstractedly – *he was smiling because he was winning.* Cagney knew he had not the strength to hold him off for much longer.

Abruptly Scorponi's expression changed as he realised he needed to breathe. Reluctantly, he released his grip on the stiletto and shook off Cagney's grip, turning his vast body around to swim to the surface. For a moment, a very brief moment, Cagney was tempted to go deep and lick his wounds but within him he knew that all he held dear and loved would be in mortal danger if Scorponi survived. He finned strongly upwards, ignoring the pain from his wounds. The pirate captain had almost reached the surface and the air he so badly needed when the long scarf trailing behind him was grabbed by Cagney's good hand. He wrapped the material round his wrist and, twisting his body around, dived deep. Scorponi's hands had just emerged into fresh air and were reaching for the boat's side when he felt the unrelenting pressure around his bulging neck and he was dragged struggling into the depths. Turning on to his back Cagney watched the monstrously bloated man as he towed him into the deeper darker cold.

Every time Scorponi attempted to grab him he spiralled gently away, evading the huge killing hands with ease. The pirate captain's hands went to his own neck, desperately trying to unravel the scarf but Cagney kept it tight, frustrating him. Bubbles began to issue from the fat lips and Cagney knew it was over; he pulled the body down and let it float up into the tangle of the Anastasia's rigging, releasing his hold on the scarf. Cagney studied the face, evil even in death. He noticed a small leather bag attempting to float to the surface but thwarted in its ambition by the cord around the dead man's neck. Snapping the cord, Cagney yanked it free and propelled his damaged body to the surface.

The Marine broke free of the water by William's hand trailing over the side; he squeezed it and spoke the lad's name. No response. Holding on to the gunwale with his good hand, Cagney pondered his next step. Shifting his grip, he grunted as the movement brought a fierce pain from his splintered rib. Time to get aboard and that was going to be a struggle with his injuries. He relinquished his hold, treading water and released his weight belt, letting it fall to the bottom. *Tanks next,* slipping his arm from the harness he tried unsuccessfully to ease his other out without catching the protruding blade. The harness snagged on the hilt of Scorponi's stiletto. Cagney choked off a cry and let the tanks drop, it would be difficult enough to get himself aboard, much less swing his tanks up. With a start he realised he had the little bag he had ripped from the dead pirate's neck still clamped in his good hand. He dropped it into the boat then finned hard to thrust his body up and lock an elbow over the side. Pausing, he took several deep breaths to compose himself for the huge effort he would need to make soon. Cagney could feel his strength ebbing and forced his other arm to swing round, with almost his last strength it was locked over the side with his upper body leant into the small craft. Cagney waited, trying to husband what little energy remained within his damaged body, then willed himself to make a second surge to lever his body aboard.

Now! It's got to be now! He finned furiously and focussed on transmitting power through his shoulders to lift him far enough. *Done it!* he crowed silently until the protruding blade caught on a plank and the searing pain caused him to start falling back.

Cagney's moan of despair was cut short by William's arm being thrust under his; the lad hauled steadily until Cagney lay in a heap in the bottom of the boat. Swaying unsteadily, William put his hand on the gunwale then sat down abruptly.

"You don't look so good," gasped Cagney, making an effort to smile.

William was beyond smiling; he touched his bruised and bleeding forehead. "S'not this, Sir, me arm's broken." Cagney grimaced, both with sympathy and pain. "You're not looking too sprightly yourself, Sir."

Cagney looked down at his bloodstained side and dagger through his forearm and nodded his agreement. "But we're alive, Will; which is more than you can say for him." Cagney struggled to a kneeling position and pointed down at Scorponi tangled in the rigging below, one arm waving as in greeting. William shuddered then threw his breakfast up over the side. "C'mon, I need a hand." Wiping his mouth, William helped Cagney haul the last chest aboard.

They sat exhausted by the effort; the Marine surveyed his swollen arm and fingers.

"Want me to pull it out, Sir?" Cagney's reply was interrupted by gunfire; a single shot followed by a burst of automatic fire. They both looked to the shore but were too low in the water to see anything. Wordlessly, but with pained, worried faces they sat at their oars, Cagney having to scramble to the far hull to reach his. They rowed slowly through necessity and had not made more than a few strokes before more shots were heard.

"Pistol shots," muttered Cagney, spinning in his seat but seeing nothing. "Row!" he ordered. The five hundred yards to shore took the sweating, injured pair forty minutes but in the minds of the two men it seemed like forever. They halted once when William informed Cagney that Dr Aktar was on top of the Abrams. Cagney called out but apart from a brief wave his attention seemed focussed inland.

After what seemed like a lifetime of effort and pain, the craft nosed into the shallows. Groaning as he raised his damaged body, Cagney stepped into the water and after retrieving the remaining M16 from the bottom of the boat, he padded barefoot up the beach. William watched him as he pulled the boat from the water with his good arm. He noticed in a distracted sort of way, the pain of his broken arm fuzzing his concentration, that the American's shoulders were burned by the fierce sun. He gathered up Cagney's clothing in an untidy lop-sided manner and followed him up the beach.

Cagney walked purposefully into camp, barely noticing as sharp stones cut into his feet. He halted, taking stock, swivelling his head seeking out potential threats. Aktar was perched on the Abrams looking inland and Philippa was kneeling, along with the children, by an obviously injured Green. He walked towards them, grimacing as he saw a pair of legs protruding from a blanket-covered body. The children saw him first; Rashid touched Philippa's arm and pointed. She rose to her feet and walked slowly to him, the AK over her shoulder, her mouth opening in horror as she saw his injuries.

"Scorponi," he said shortly, putting his good arm around her, his M16 clunking against the AK.

"Mikey has a musket ball in his thigh, not much bleeding, thank heaven."

"Hassan?" She nodded. "Where is he?"

Aktar's voice came from the Abrams. "Captain Hassan is behind that small mound, about a mile." His arm held out showed Cagney where.

Cagney nodded his thanks and walked over to Green, kneeling and peeling back his dressing. He ran his eye up and down the leg noting its unnatural angle. "Femur's gone, Mikey."

"Tell me something I don't know," croaked Green

"Salad tastes nice." A ghost of a smile. He rose and went to check Leila, placing two fingers on her neck; frowning he replaced the blanket over her head and prised himself upright.

William appeared at his side staring at the girl's legs. Tears rolled down his cheeks.

"Cry later," said Cagney roughly. "There's work to be done." He strode to the table, lifting Scorponi's telescope and handing it to William in exchange for his clothes. "Change places with the Doc and watch for Hassan."

"But . . ."

"Just do it!" The savagery in his voice surprised himself. "Doc; over here!" The scientist began to speak but Cagney brusquely overrode him. "Get down the dispensary; I need a dressing, local anaesthetic and a couple of steel rods . . . say about knitting needle size, sharp at one end . . .oh, and get a sling for Will's arm." Aktar hurried away. Cagney placed his rifle on the table and with Philippa's help started to dress. Impatiently he shoved his feet into his boots. "Will you do the laces, Honey, please?"

He stood and stamped his feet as Aktar returned, depositing Cagney's requirements on the table. Using Philippa's hands Cagney filled a syringe with a colourless liquid and wincing injected around the embedded blade. He watched as Philippa washed the rods with alcohol-soaked cotton wool.

"Has he moved?" he bellowed up to a morose William, who shook his head silently. Cagney gingerly prodded his damaged arm; *numb, good.* He looked up at Philippa and smiled; it was so unexpected it caused her to blush. "Need a hand to get this out; I'm tired of looking like a pincushion . . . in fact I'm just plain tired." He sat and rested his elbow on the table. "Slide these rods in down each side of the blade; I need air in there 'cause my muscle has gripped it and won't release.

Gritting her teeth Philippa did as asked; waggled the dagger free then removed the rods. Blood streamed from the re-opened wounds.

"I ain't got time for stitching so wrap a dressing round for me." He stood and flexed the bandaged limb. "Keep an eye on the shop and put a sling on Will's arm. I'm going for our favourite Republican Guard."   Picking up his rifle he strode determinedly to the Humvee, taking in at a glance the damage done by Green's bullets. The starter turned the big diesel but it obstinately refused to fire. Tight lipped, Cagney popped the hood then dropped it in disgust after seeing the injector pump smashed by a round from the Kalashnikov.

He walked back to the group. "Looks like I'm walking."

"Do you need to do this?" The question came from a concerned Philippa. "He no longer has a musket . . ." she pointed to the discarded weapon lying on the earth ". . . and can no longer harm us . . . please leave him."

"She has a point." Cagney's eyes dropped to Green's prone figure; he was pale beneath his tan and his voice weak.

"Doctor Aktar . . ." Cagney was curiously formal ". . . does Hassan have any talents that might conceivably blight our future?"

Aktar, invariably serious was sombre now. "He is an engineer; and an accomplished one at that."

"That settles it then!" There was finality in Cagney's tone and no-one argued.

"Hey, Boss." The words were barely audible. The American knelt by his wounded friend, his head close.

"Yeah, yeah, good." He stood. "If I were you folks, I'd keep my head well down!" Marching over to William on the Abrams he confirmed where Hassan had gone to ground. "You sure that's the right place?" William's reply was short.

Hassan sat with his back to a mound of earth; his shoulder was bleeding and he was tired; tired of running. This was where he had slept whilst he had watched events in the camp. There were a brace of pistols and a cutlass at his feet and he was determined to sell his life dearly when they came for him – as they surely would. A high pitched whine came to his ears and dread entered his heart when he identified it. The turbine engine of the American Tank. A few moments later the earth mound he was sheltering behind erupted as a high explosive round from the Abrams hit it and exploded. Hassan cowered down as dust earth and pebbles rained down on him. Another explosion, then another and again. The earth mound trembled as it was hit by another round, but no explosion this time though he noticed something had flown from his side of the mound at tremendous pace.

Cagney loaded a second armour-piercing round, adjusted half a degree left then fired. The heavy round barely noticed the soil it ploughed through from one side of the mound to the other its velocity diminishing only by a fraction. Cagney rotated the turret to its usual fore and aft position and climbed carefully out of the Commander's cupola. Carefully he lowered himself to the Low Loader and stepped deliberately to the ground. Stiffly he walked back to join his companions, taking William with him.

"How's the pain?" he asked, fishing in Green's tunic for morphine.

"Been better."

Cagney quickly injected Green's leg. "And you?"

"I'm fine, Sir," the lad replied dully.

Cagney addressed them all. Nobody moves 'til I get back, then we'll sort out the girl."

"Leila!" said William, hotly. "Her name's Leila!" Cagney apologised for his thoughtlessness and set off into the scrub to find and kill the Republican Guard. He walked mechanically, his tiredness and injuries robbing his limbs of their fluency. It was about a mile to where he expected to find Hassan; though he thought it likely the man was dead he took no chances and his path was designed to arrive a hundred yards or so from him. Cagney had never fired a muzzle loading weapon but imagined that distance to be beyond accurate fire. He tramped steadily, without haste, eyeing the terrain carefully to avoid stumbling or jarring his step which sent shooting pains through his damaged rib.

His forearm was competing pretty well with his ribs in the pain stakes as the local anaesthetic wore off and a dull throb pulsed up to his shoulder. Cagney tried to put his aches and pains in the background as he neared the danger area. He maintained his steady pace and kept his head turned, focussing on the rear of the earth mound. At first Cagney saw little, no body either alive or dead. Slowly he walked closer then stopped. There was a figure seated with his back to the disturbed earth, virtually indistinguishable from the background as he was covered in dirt from the shellfire. The Marine only noticed him because he had turned his head slightly as he watched him approach. *So, you're alive.* Lifting his rifle awkwardly in his left hand he walked slowly towards the seated man who did not move.

As he got close, Cagney saw a pistol near to the man's feet and kicked it away. He lifted his eyes to the man, noting that his posture seemed awkward in some way. With a shock he realised most of his right arm had gone; a belt was wrapped tightly round what remained of his bicep. Looking at the stain in the soil beneath him, Cagney knew it was too little and too late.

"Come to gloat, American?" The voice was surprisingly strong. Cagney shook his head and, placing his M16 on the

266

ground behind him, knelt by the injured man. He looked closely at the damaged arm.

"Do not waste your time, American."

Cagney fumbled in his pocket. "You want morphine?"

Hassan shook his head wearily. "The pain is almost gone . . . as am I." Cagney put the ampoules back in his pocket. "I am sorry about the girl; it was a mistake."

Cagney shrugged. "She's still dead!"

With a huge effort, the Iraqi used his good arm to remove his ID tags from around his neck. "Will you tell my family I died trying to kill my country's enemies?" Cagney took them. The dying man glanced at his blood soaking into the earth and gave a twisted smile. "My blood will enrich the soil, my soil, American . . ." his head lolled ". . . not yours," he whispered and died. Cagney checked his pulse then picking up his rifle, trudged back to camp.

The mood in camp was flat; Leila's death had hit everyone, particularly William. Cagney too was dispirited but unwilling to show it. Leila was buried a hundred yards away from camp; Aktar as the only fit man had dug the grave and despite his hands blistering due to the unaccustomed manual work he was uncomplaining. He read a passage from the Koran over the grave and was surprised when Cagney asked him to say a prayer for his one-time gaoler.

Back in camp the Marine set about tying up loose ends. "OK, everyone bar Will down to the beach to unload the boat." He slipped his M16 from his shoulder and gave it to him. "Look after the shop . . . and don't lose this one!" he tapped the rifle. William gave a half hearted smile in return.

The final chest was manoeuvred on to the sand by the adults. It was much too heavy to carry so Cagney opened it, distributing gold and silver plate to his helpers. He lifted out bags of silver coins as best he could with one arm then followed them up the beach. Two trips each and the chest was empty.

Cagney surveyed the camp going through a check list in his head.

Philippa joined him and held his hand. "Forgotten anything, James?"

He screwed his face up. "Don't think so, Honey; the camels and Spotty Dog are tied up and can't wander off. I need to get the Doc's device above ground and then we're good to go . . . hey I forgot." Philippa's face asked the question. "There's a sextant in the boat; I got it from the Scorpion."

"Stay," she said firmly before Cagney could take a step. "I will retrieve it." She turned after two steps. "Sit down; it is unlikely I shall be robbed." *True enough,* he thought, his mood lifting as it occurred to him that his wife was the most heavily armed person in the World with an assault rifle over her shoulder and a nine millimetre pistol in her pocket. *This is the last occasion I shall walk down this beach,* she reflected as she walked. Philippa looked forward to her new life. She ran her hand over the warm black stone that had dominated the skyline until recently. As Cagney had done before her she picked up a shard of basalt and slipped it into her pocket.

Smiling to herself she strolled to the small boat with the strange lifting gear amidships. She leaned in and grasped the shiny brass sextant and was about to return when she caught sight of a small leather bag under the thwart. She slid it out. Curiosity got the better of her as she tucked the brass instrument under her arm and untied the thong which held the bag shut and emptied the contents into her hand.

The sextant fell with a musical clunk. Awed beyond words, she sat hurriedly. There were three uncut diamonds, all half the size of a hen's egg, sitting in the palm of her hand. She stayed motionless, mesmerised. *This will not do!* Replacing the stones, she knotted the thong Cagney had snapped and slipped it over her head. Back in camp, Cagney was waiting for her by the Tank Carrier, her dress over his arm.

"Come with me, my darling." Philippa took him by the hand until they stood on the seaward side of the huge vehicle. They gazed out at the bay together looking at the scene for the last time remembering all the events, traumas, deaths and happiness each had seen. "Yours, I believe." Cagney stared curiously at the bag she had slipped into his hand whilst Philippa waited for his reaction

"Jeez; no wonder Scorponi kept them close!" He paused for thought. "Can you hide them?"

An impish smile crossed Philippa's face. "Oh yes, James I think I can keep them hidden; and when they are sold, ourselves and our fellow travellers will want for nothing." She held his hand as she looped the bag back over her head. "I need to shower and change – a girl must look her best when she is going on a journey – don't you think?"

By the time they had arrived at the trapdoor and Philippa negotiated the ladder, Aktar had carried his device to the surface and positioned it exactly where it was last fired. The umbilical as before trailed down through the aperture and into the laboratory.

The scientist stood motionless, deep in thought; he glanced up as Cagney approached. "Ah, Lieutenant, can we move everyone and the animals behind the device. If by some mischance there is a reduced perimeter of influence I have no wish to lose anyone."

"Sure, let's do it." Philippa emerged from the trapdoor, her dress brushing the machine's tether.

"Let me help." The four of them lifted Fairbrother easily and deposited him next to the children and a whining Spotty Dog.

"Take five, people; I'm gonna give Mikey some morphine. Lifting him will hurt." He administered a hefty dose to the grey faced Paratrooper who fell into an uneasy sleep, muttering incoherently. The heavy soldier was lifted without ceremony and placed alongside the Naval Captain.

Cagney turned to Aktar. "Happy? I think this is as good as it's gonna get."

Aktar gave a brief nod. "Yes Lieutenant, please seat yourself behind the weapon . . ." the scientist, without thinking, referred to the device as it was designed ". . . and aim at the vehicles. The trigger is wired in the ON position and I will initiate the program in the lab. It will operate for a predetermined period and then, Lieutenant . . . we are each in the hands of our own God."

Cagney settled himself behind the device holding the handles lightly as Aktar descended to the underground complex. Cagney looked over his shoulder and winked at Philippa.

Aktar's voice echoed from below. "Ten seconds." His mouth dry and stomach hollow, Cagney attempted to relax; he dropped his damaged arm to his side deeming it to be too clumsy. The device began its sibilant hiss and Cagney smoothly hosed the Humvee and Tank Carrier until the eerie blue light enveloped the vehicles then swirled menacingly towards them.

"All aboard the Skylark," came Green's sleepy voice.

Chapter 20

The young Paratrooper guarding the figure in the hospital bed was bored; he stared at what looked like scaffolding gleaming round the man's thigh and wondered just what the hell Sergeant Green had done wrong. The whole camp was on high alert with helicopters flying in and out all the while and Mikey here along with the people who arrived on the US Marine Chinook being confined to camp.

The figure stirred, opening one gummed eye. "Water."

The guard pressed a buzzer and a woman dressed in theatre blues came in and went to the head of the bed. "Hello, Mikey; woken up then?"

The young Paratrooper interrupted nervously. "Not allowed to talk to him, Ma'am."

Doctor Elizabeth Harding gave him a cool appraising stare. "Private Wilkinson, isn't it?"

He swallowed. "Yes, Ma'am."

She smiled without humour. "Tonight, Private Wilkinson, you are meeting one of my nurses; Nurse Hooper. You, I think, know her as Catherine?"

"Mm... err... yes, Ma'am." His eyes wide with surprise.

"Well, Private, Nurse Hooper has confided in me that she has a treat in store for you . . ." Wilkinson's face lit up, ". . . but unless you are the other side of that door, sharpish, I will make sure she is on duty tonight . . . and every other night . . . do we understand each other?"

The Para sidled towards the door. "Five minutes," he whispered urgently.

Elizabeth Harding turned her attention to Green who was smiling. She ran a finger along his scarred cheekbone. "You have been away two days, yet you have a healed scar that's at least twelve days old. Where have you been, Mikey?" Green's memories were jumbled and confused due to the morphine and possibly the journey. He recalled vaguely Sergeant Muller apologising for waiting out the sandstorm for an hour before returning and his astonishment at Cagney's yellowing bruised face. *Maybe they had only been gone for an hour . . . or seconds?*

"Seventeen sixty something, we were there two weeks or so." Green's voice was throaty.

"That's the rumour round camp too, but I saw you and the American two days ago." A queer smile hovered. "Got something of yours." She reached into her pocket and held Green's ID tag, swinging its chain weighted with a diamond ring. "This ring is beautiful and expensive – very, did you pinch it?"

Green shook his head vehemently and took a deep breath. "I want you to have it . . . to wear, I mean."

Elizabeth unhooked the chain and slipped the ring on to her wedding finger. "Like this?" Green nodded nervously. Her demeanour cooled. "Can't do it, Sergeant!" Green closed his eyes, unable to speak. "Quite simply, I can't do it . . . well . . ." Green opened his eyes "not until we've spent at least two weeks in bed." She leant over the bed and kissed his dry cracked lips. "You arse, Mikey Green, making me wait all this time. I've always fancied you!"

There was a low urgent knock at the door, the young Paratrooper entered. "The Major's coming."

Major Smythe entered the room, a preoccupied look on his face. "Off you go, Private." Wilkinson left after saluting. "You too, Captain."

"No, Sir . . ." Green's words caused Smythe's face to darken ". . . please." His eyes took in the entwined fingers of the pair and relented.

"You succeeded in your mission; two vintage Norton racing motorcycles are at the US Marine base as we speak. I, by way of contrast have in this camp a Sergeant with a musket ball freshly removed from his leg. . ." he tossed the lead ball into a nearby steel dish with a clang " . . . two more injured men, who definitely do not belong here, but whom you will be doubtless pleased to learn are well on the

272

mend. . ." Green smiled with relief. Smythe continued glumly, "I have in my care the beautiful Mrs Cagney who I have been instructed to keep in solitary confinement, but I'll be damned if I will, even if it costs me my pension!" Smythe recalled the previous two evenings when Philippa had been a guest in the officers' mess for dinner and had his officers almost drooling in their soup. The memory brought a brief smile to his face. "In addition there are two Iraqi children who claim they are yours, causing havoc in my base and a large Dalmatian which expressed its affection for me by urinating on my leg!"

Green made as if to speak, but Smythe held up a warning finger. "I have many thousands of pounds worth of gold and jewellery, a large bronze bell from a French ship named Egalité, a magnificent pair of duelling pistols, and last but far from least a large, malodorous and unhappy camel which answers to the name of . . ."

"Bastard," exclaimed Green.

"Quite, you will appreciate my dilem . . ."

The door opened and a middle aged man entered, immaculate in a tailored dove-grey suit and carrying a briefcase. "So you must be the infamous Sergeant Green?" The public school drawl and supercilious demeanour set the Para's teeth on edge. "My name is Carstairs – I am the deputy head of MI6 and you Sergeant . . ." his tone lent the rank a sneering contempt, ". . . owe us a great many answers." He pointed a soft, well-manicured finger at Elizabeth. "You, out!"

"No!" Green and Smythe spoke as one.

"No matter," he purred. "You are all bound by the official secrets act, and if anyone here breathes a word they will spend many long years somewhere cold, dark and very lonely. He looked around unperturbed by the contemptuous looks directed at him. Carstairs reached into his briefcase; his hand emerged clasping a dusty, cracked, old fashioned file sealed with wax. We obtained this file from the Admiralty; it gives a detailed account of your and

Lieutenant Cagney's sojourn in seventeen sixty one by an officer named . . ."

"Rotherhithe."

"Quite correct." The oily smile was devoid of humour. "Rather the little hero are we not Sergeant?" Green said nothing. "We want something, Green; we want the contraption which took you on your journey. Neither we nor our Colonial cousins can have it because Lieutenant Cagney smashed it with a hammer and then threw it from his vehicle in small segments as he drove along the highway, so it was lost to the scrap collectors of Iraq." He ran his fingers through his oily hair "We also want the name, the name of the scientist who so conveniently died." He paused; his eyes venomous then went on, his tone silky. "But I and my colleagues believe he is alive and well . . . and we will have him! Let me come to the point; we in the Her Majesty's security services wield much power and influence, if you do not supply us with what we want, life will become extremely difficult for you."

Green glared at him. "You don't scare me, you gutless, oily bastard!"

Carstairs wagged his finger gently. "Sticks and stones etcetera; those children . . ." Green was alert, now. Carstairs made a languid curiously effeminate gesture, twisting his wrist and fingers. "I am making arrangements for them to be deposited in one of the worst districts of Baghdad - after all, who cares about a pair of grubby wog urchins?"

Smythe cleared his throat. "You really are a prize shit, Carstairs!"

Carstairs continued, indifferent to the insults. "That, Sergeant, is just a start; your parents will mysteriously lose their pensions, be accused of shoplifting. The good Captain and her family will endure similar problems . . ." he linked his fingers and smiled easily, ". . . just give me a name and none of this need ever happen." His face creased with an ingratiating smile as an incoming helicopter drowned any speech.

There was a tentative knock on the door. "You're wanted, Sir." Smythe left, fuming. Elizabeth wrapped her fingers tightly around Green's as Carstairs continued in a similar vein. Green seethed with impotent anger.

The shimmering gems on Elizabeth's ring caught the MI6 man's attention; he leant across the bed and striking like a cobra seized her hand, squeezing it tightly. "I really don't think this bauble belongs to you, Captain . . ." he crushed her hand causing her to wince. " . . . I think you will find this is a gift from a looter!" He found and gripped the ring. "I will take this, it does after all belong to the Cro . . ." Carstairs head jerked back as Green's fist caught him in the mouth, mashing his lips. Breathing stertorously, Green slumped back; the sudden violent movement causing waves of pain to shoot up from his damaged leg.

Carstairs took a silk handkerchief from his breast pocket and delicately dabbed his mouth. "A court Martial offence, Sergeant; hitting a senior officer."

The door crashed open and Smythe stalked in. "Visitors, Sergeant."

"No visitors, Major!" The voice was hard and flat. "This man is under close arrest for striking a senior officer." Smythe's powerful form bundled Carstairs to one side allowing Cagney and Philippa to enter.

Cagney looked around the room, smiling at Harding. "Trouble, Mikey?"

Green gave a tired nod. "This tosser from Intelligence tried to pinch Dizzy's ring after threatening us and our families."

Cagney's face darkened. "We'll see about that!" He slipped his bandaged arm from its sling.

"I think not, Lieutenant. . ." Smythe interposed his bulk between the two men ". . . after all, you are injured." He turned to Carstairs and pulling his arm back threw a short right which impacted on his victim's jaw with an audible crack. Carstairs' legs folded and he collapsed with a dull thud. Smythe inspected his knuckles. "I do believe we may soon be sharing a Court Martial, Sergeant."

"It's not going to happen, people. Believe me!" Cagney's words caused everyone to stare and gave enough time for Philippa to introduce herself to Elizabeth. "In the four days since we've been back, things have taken off . . ."

"Four days?" echoed Green.

Elizabeth squeezed his hand. "You've been out to lunch dear, - two operations and a lot of anaesthetic."

Cagney continued, "Y'know the painting we salvaged?" Without waiting for a reply, he went on. "Well guys it's hanging in the Oval Office . . ." There was a stunned silence ". . . y'know number 1600 Pennsylvania Avenue." Nobody spoke. "When I got back to base with two "works" Nortons and a very tall story my Colonel threw me in the brig, where I'd still be cooling my ass if Sergeant Muller hadn't told one of our intelligence guys. He told his boss and it went on up the line until I was bundled into a plane, flown to Washington and hustled into the Whitehouse – still in 'cuffs." He gazed around at his spellbound audience.

"So I'm standing in the Oval Office, smelling like a Polecat, when the President and the Chief of Staff walk in. The Chief of Staff beckons me to a table and whisked off a sheet that was covering something." Cagney looked round; his eyes holding his listeners and grinned. Underneath there was an M16; not just any M16, but the one William dropped onto the wreck of the Anastasia. It was rusty as hell but the serial number identified it as mine. The President asked me if I recognised it, 'cause Marine engineers found it when they excavated the site of the ship on the orders of our intelligence guys to confirm my story."

"The President ordered my cuffs removed, sat me down and said, "Tell us the story, Lieutenant." So I did."

A groan from the floor interrupted him. "Bear with me for a moment, Lieutenant." Smythe went to the door, barked a few orders then stood to one side as two young Paratroopers entered. "Take that . . ." he pointed to the moaning figure ". . . put it on a helicopter and send it back wherever it came from." The soldiers hauled the semi-conscious man upright and frogmarched him out. The

Paratroop Major picked up Carstairs' briefcase and was about to throw it after him when he changed his mind and looked inside. "This might be interesting," he said, lifting out the Admiralty file and throwing the briefcase through the door. He closed it. "You were saying, Lieutenant."

"Thank you, Sir; I told 'em the whole goddam' story and then they left me there with the biggest breakfast a man could eat and a security guy for company. About an hour later . . . you got a glass of water, Mikey?" Green passed one over via Elizabeth "yeah about an hour later they came back. The Chief of Staff said "Son there's no doubt you're telling the truth but the whole thing just never happened." The President went on, "I just got off the phone to the British Prime Minister and we agreed that we would treat this time travel device like we treat germ warfare – we don't want it, ever."

Cagney gazed round with an air of quiet satisfaction. "So you see, Major, that spook, Carstairs was acting against the specific wishes of your own Prime Minister so your pension is safe and I'm led to believe we get to keep all the goodies we brought ho . . ."

"Apart from a fine pair of duelling pistols which will look rather splendid in the Parachute Regiment trophy cabinet. What say you Sergeant?" Green nodded grudgingly.

"Just had a thought." The sleepy voice belonged to Green. "How did Bastard get here?"

"Ah," said Cagney, smiling. "When we err . . . landed, Sergeant Muller got on the horn for a medevac chopper and every thing and everyone bar the camel and me was loaded aboard."

Philippa took up the story. "You had regained consciousness shortly after our arrival, you were dreadfully badly behaved and thoroughly disagreeable – in fact I really do not know what this lovely girl sees in you. You simply would not leave without . . . how did you describe it, James?"

"A mangy fleabag; I had to bribe the pilot with a bag of silver coins. We wrapped old two-humps in a cargo net then slung him under the Chinook – not before he bit Sergeant Muller."

"I am puzzled."

"What about, Sir?"

"Sergeant Green had been away from her for only two days or so but Captain Harding tells me his injuries are much older."

Cagney shrugged expressively. "I can't explain it, Sir, but I can tell you that we were away fifteen days, yet when we returned there was still sand in the air from the storm. I don't know for sure but I reckon we were away for micro-seconds – it seems the device returned us to the exact time we left!"

"I'm hungry." Green's voice was plaintive.

Smythe gave one of his rare smiles. "I believe that calls for a command decision." He strode to the door and called the sentry. "Five large breakfasts, and bring a table and chairs in here." The sentry hurried off. "Now, Mrs Cagney, gentlemen. In exchange for your breakfasts, Captain Harding and myself deserve to hear an account of your adventures . . . do we have a deal?"

One Year Later

"You sure you want to go through with this?" Cagney slowed the car over the bumps in the road so the baby in the back remained asleep.

Philippa gave him a small, nervous smile. "Yes, I must; we have come this far, I shall not turn back." They had planned this trip for some time and as soon as Cagney's medicine exams were over they had flown to England, hired a car and driven to Dorset. They intended to visit Mikey and the three months pregnant Elizabeth in the North of the country after they had concluded their business here. Cagney was looking forward to meeting Harry Fairbrother who was taking time off from his job at the Maritime Museum at Greenwich to travel to Mikey's. There were presents in the back for Rashid and Selima, and also for William if he could get leave from the Royal Marines - a branch of the Forces he had joined much to Green's chagrin.

Cagney was pleased at how things had worked out for his friends. The pirate booty had made all of them comfortably well off and the recent sale of just one of Scorponi's diamonds had enabled Cagney to open offshore accounts for them to the tune of several million dollars each. Despite the riches, Mikey and Harry had both elected to work, with Green in his first year of a teaching degree at university.

"Got any idea what you're gonna say to your descendants? . . . it's not gonna be easy to explain."

She sighed. "I know; but I must go . . . turn left here." She took her finger from the map and pointed.

"That's right, Honey," said Cagney, good naturedly.

Philippa glared at him. "Right again, that is the driveway."

He braked to a halt at the open gate and looked up the drive to a large manor cum farm house in the distance. "OK?"

"Yes." The determined expression he knew so well was in place. He drove over the cattle grid, the thrumming noise provoking a wail from the back seat. Cruising slowly, he parked by a small Fiat, the only vehicle there.

"Has it changed much?"

She licked her dry lips. "Extensions and windows I guess."

"Well, we're here; the phone book says Rotherhithe, let's say hello."

They left the car, Cagney picking up the carrycot and walked together to the front door. A chime sounded somewhere deep in the house in response to Philippa pressing the button; moments later feet clattered on wooden stairs then the door opened. A slim pretty blonde girl in jeans and tee shirt stood there.

"Francesca!" gasped Philippa, bringing her hand to her mouth.

"Well, it's my middle name," said the girl cheerfully. "Family tradition, Gemma's my first name." She wrinkled her nose. "I think the small person needs changing! . . . Come in." They walked down a corridor. "The kitchen's this way . . . are you friends of dad's?"

Philippa hesitated. "We are related . . . distantly . . . I'm Philippa."

"That's a coincidence," chuckled Gemma, yours and my names; my great, great . . .I don't know how many greats grandmother was named Philippa and her daughter was Francesca . . ." she waved a hand at a portrait of Francesca on the wall, *a little older than he remembered her,* thought Cagney. Gemma pointed to the other wall. "That's Francesca's mum . . . you look just like her!" Philippa smiled. "I read Francesca's diaries last year – all very romantic – an American rescued her and her mother from pirates, got her mother pregnant and she ran off with him." She laughed gaily.

"That about sums it up," grinned Cagney, his first words.

Gemma started at his accent, then her blood ran cold; backing up against a wall, she stifled a small scream. "It's you, isn't it . . . you're James!"

Cagney nodded. "Yes," he said gently. "You're on the money."

Gemma's eyes were wide open, her face white and panicked. "Are . . . are you ghosts?"

Her guests shared affectionate glances; Philippa rapped Cagney on the head with her knuckles. "That sounds solid to me and the smells from little Harry are most certainly not in your imagination!"

Gemma wrinkled her nose again and grasped Philippa's arm. "The . . . the, bathroom's this way, I'll help." She gave Cagney a frightened glance. "The kitchen's through there; put the kettle on.

Philippa lifted a capacious bag from her shoulder, giving it to Gemma. She lifted the baby from his carrycot then followed the girl into the bathroom. Cagney whiled away the time in the kitchen staring out of the window at the rural scene.

The two women returned, chatting cheerfully, Gemma holding the baby.

Philippa turned three sixty. "This was the parlour once." Gemma gave a nervous giggle and stayed well away from Cagney.

"Take me to the summer house, my dear; I have something to show you. Hold on to your bad tempered son, James." Gemma passed the infant over. The trio trooped out on to the lawn at the rear of the house, Gemma still keeping a discreet distance from the American. They halted at the summerhouse and Philippa walked around it until with a cry of satisfaction she found what she sought. She knelt and indicated a particular brick to Gemma. "Wiggle it free."

Biting her lip Gemma grasped the brick and with a little effort slid it from the wall of the summerhouse and placed it on the lawn. Philippa smiled encouragingly and gestured her to look inside the cavity.

Hesitantly Gemma put her hand in and withdrew it slowly holding a letter wrapped in oilskin. "There are lots more in here." She reached in further and pulled out many more letters, all wrapped similarly.

"Shall we return to the kitchen and see what my daughter and your great grandmother has to say to us?" Gemma nodded dumbly. They gathered up the letters and walked the short distance back.

Cagney sifted through the fifty or so letters strewn on the large oak table in the kitchen. He peered closely. "They're numbered." He concentrated on the faded writing. "Here's number one."

He handed it to Philippa who took it, her hands trembling. "Will you read it please, Gemma?"

"My hands are shaking as much as yours," she giggled, carefully peeling the oilskin away and unfolding the paper within. "Dearest Mama," she began "I promised I would write to you on the occasion of each of my birthdays and that is today, my eighteenth. Nicholas and I are married and sleeping close is our son of three months whom we have named Mikey James after our rescuers. I am so happy. . ."

Gemma stopped reading and gazed worriedly at Philippa's lovely face marred by tears. Philippa smiled through them. "And now I can be truly happy too."

Made in the USA
Charleston, SC
11 September 2012